Silverman found Ritchie's number on the legal pad containing his interview notes, and dialed. After a few rings, a woman answered.

"Hello, is James Ritchie at home, please?"

"Who is this?" she asked. Her voice sounded tired.

"My name is John Silverman. I'm calling from the U.S. attorney's office. Mr. Ritchie and I spoke the other day. Is this Mrs. Ritchie?"

"My husband is dead. It happened last night."

Silverman fell silent. He didn't believe what he had just heard. Maybe it was a cruel joke—Ritchie's way of keeping away from home? His thoughts were jumbled and coming too fast. Was it over before it had even begun?

GRAND JURY

RON LIEBMAN

BALLANTINE BOOKS • NEW YORK

For Simma, Shana,
and Margot.

Thank you, Aaron.

PROLOGUE

The grand jury is a creature of the law. It exists by order of the court, its members selected at random from voter registration lists.

> The court shall order one or more grand juries to be summoned at such time as the public interest requires. The grand jury shall consist of not less than 16 nor more than 23 members...
>
> *Rule 6(a), Federal Rules of Criminal Procedure*

It is a secret body, admittance strictly regulated, the public not permitted.

> Attorneys for the government, the witness under examination...a stenographer or operator of a recording device may be present while the grand jury is in session, but no person other than the jurors may be present while the grand jury is deliberating or voting.
>
> *Rule 6(d), Federal Rules of Criminal Procedure*

It has the power to charge a citizen with crime by returning an indictment.

> An indictment may be found only upon the concurrence of 12 or more jurors...
>
> *Rule 6(f), Federal Rules of Criminal Procedure*

The grand jury hears only the prosecution's case. The accused is not called before it to deny the charge or produce evidence. That happens later, in open court, when the accused is called to trial before twelve citizens.

The power of the grand jury lies in the hands of the prosecutor; it is he who determines who will be the accused and who will be not.

1

The son of a bitch. Three days since the storm had ended and the paths and sidewalks, once simply snow covered, thanks to the janitor's inattentiveness or drunken stupor—John Silverman didn't know or care which—were now a maze of lumpy ice hazards. Using his briefcase for balance, Silverman managed his way up the path to Wynnewood Road, his frosted breath enveloping his mumbled curses.

He'd fallen the day before and had to go back in to change to another suit. Another dark blue suit that looked more or less the same as the first one. Of course, he couldn't complain to Mary Ann. She hated living there. The "world's oldest living garden apartment," she called it. It had been his idea—a means of saving money for a while, a way to avoid buying a second car.

He pulled at the old wooden door and entered Wynnewood Commuter Station. Two years of this. Two winters of sitting in this cold station waiting for the next train to Center City, Philadelphia. The same pale green walls badly in need of paint, the same faces on those wooden benches lining the walls. The same cold, impersonal silence. He walked to the stationmaster's counter, bought the morning paper, and found an empty spot on one of the benches. Casually, he surveyed the morning's assemblage. Men outnumbered women ten to one, but they all seemed to wear the same clothes and the same deadened expressions, regardless of sex or age. He knew that by now he was part of the everyday sameness. But he was not yet one of them. Younger. Movements sharper. More agile. A near-noticeable sheen to his neatly groomed dark hair. Silverman was different, though. The difference went unnoticed by the flock.

His first week there, he'd noticed the churchlike directory box on the wall next to the plaque that announced: THIS STATION HAS BEEN PAINTED AND MAINTAINED BY THE WYNNEWOOD CIVIC ASSOCIATION THROUGH THE CONTRIBUTIONS OF ITS MEMBERS

3

AND FRIENDS. Tacked inside the directory box was a listing of the officers of the civic association, complete home addresses and even home telephone numbers. How bad a community can this be, he remembered thinking, if these people were bold enough to list their phone numbers on the station wall.

He hadn't noticed that the list was five years old. Once he tried calling one of the numbers and found it had been disconnected. And one morning about six months ago, he'd noticed that the list was gone; in its place, someone had etched into the board itself: "Rosemary Callara sucks." No home phone number. There had been a fourth word carved into the board, presumably describing what Rosemary sucked. But it had been obliterated. Silverman supposed that had been the stationmaster's work, but maybe he felt the message was all right now, suitable for the eyes of Wynnewood's daily commuters. Silverman hoped that for Rosemary Callara's sake, whoever she was, she never had need to enter this station.

It was 8:17 A.M. Almost sensing the train's arrival before its first audible rumblings, the commuters began to look up from their papers and glance at their watches, preparing to rise and board. Through the entrance door's dirty glass panel, Silverman saw the Paoli local crawling toward the platform. Briefcase and paper in place, like the others, he joined the line out to the platform.

Silverman found a seat next to the window and settled in for the ride. The train would be painfully slow for the next three stops; Narbeth, Marion, and Overbrook, all carbon copies of Wynnewood. After reading the news sections, he folded the sports page, which contained the previous day's race results, into as small a surface as possible, then removed his list of the previous day's selections from his breast pocket and made his comparison. Only two winners out of nine races. Damn. He was going to have a loss for the week unless he did better that day and the next. He copied the winning amounts onto his list.

Moving faster now, the train headed for Thirtieth Street Station and then Penn Center-Suburban Station. He removed some work he hadn't finished the previous night from his briefcase and read until the conductor entered the car and announced, "Suburban Station, last and final stop," the tone of his voice conveying his unalterable belief that there was a difference between the two. Silverman returned the papers to his briefcase and stood in line to get off.

It was called Suburban Station even though it was in the heart of the downtown district. Silverman mounted the stairs, and as he did each morning, walked to Mike's News Center where he bought the *Daily Racing Form*, spent a few minutes sharing remarks over the previous day's results with the man he assumed to be Mike, although he never knew for sure, then headed for the main concourse and the subway entrance.

His hands never faltered as PAC-MAN'S REVENGE, the newest of the series, glided smoothly and ominously across the screen. A young black boy of about fourteen, a regular, on his way from one game booth to another, stopped to watch Silverman play. Silverman was good, obviously in command of the game.

"Get that sucker," the boy said.

Silverman smiled and nodded but kept his attention fixed to the action on the screen. He liked this game. It gave him a sense of control and power that was too often missing in his daily life.

When the game was finally over, Silverman smiled with pleasure at his high score. He felt exhilarated and ready to face the day as he retrieved his briefcase and *Daily Racing Form* from between his feet and hurried from the station.

He had to make his connection. It was a short ride on the Market-Frankford line to Fifth and Market streets, but he could usually manage to handicap at least the first race. Most mornings he would accomplish this under the watchful eye of the woman he had nicknamed "the Subway Lady."

She was in her fifties, and looked like a government clerical worker; she got off at the same stop as he. She'd sit there in the subway car and watch him, in his dark suit and regimental striped tie, clean-cut, obviously a young lawyer, bent over the racing form, making notes in the paper's margins.

The Subway Lady would give him looks. Looks that ranged from pity for his obvious tendencies toward self-ruination all the way to unconcealed disgust.

Once, sensing that she was about to admonish him and wanting to finish his work on the first race before his stop, he told her that it was only a game. She didn't say anything, but her looks intensified. Now and then he would smile at her, knowing it would increase her silent rage.

He walked up from the station, through the shoveled pathways of Independence Mall, past the pavilion housing the Liberty Bell, and entered the U.S. Courthouse.

As Silverman walked the corridor of the U.S. attorney's offices, his body retained some of the chill from the early morning's commute. This was one of the country's newer federal courthouses, and was supposedly designed with both efficiency and comfort in mind. While there were plenty of thermostats in evidence, the temperature was actually regulated from some hidden source in the building's bowels. But there never seemed to be quite enough heat. What he needed was some hot coffee. So before stopping at his own office, he turned the corner and walked down the hall to Higdon's, whose secretary kept a pot going all day.

He heard an unfamiliar voice escaping into the corridor even before he passed the small wall plaque that announced in bold black print, "Raymond Higdon, Assistant United States Attorney." Once inside, he glanced quickly past the secretary's desk to Higdon's dark, unoccupied office. As usual, Ray was never in this early. Never.

Mrs. Ramondi was leaning forward in her chair, listening intently to the old man whose voice Silverman had followed into the room. He went past the two of them to the window behind Mrs. Ramondi's desk. On the little table beneath the window stood the tarnished electric coffeepot, its spout pointing at the glass, steaming part of the windowpane.

He put down his briefcase, unbuttoned his topcoat, and with his racing form tightly tucked under his arm, poured coffee into a styrofoam cup and turned. Mrs. Ramondi shifted briefly in her chair and smiled at him, then turned back to the old man. Silverman paid no attention to the man or his words; he drank his coffee and watched Pat Ramondi.

There was definitely something about her, something that made her quite attractive at times. He supposed it was a combination of things that intrigued him. While she was in her middle forties and just a bit overweight, somewhere in her dark hair and clear, pale skin there was beauty. He knew that it was partly the warmth and sincerity of her smile, partly the way she moved. And on the days she wore her gray sweater, like today, the contours of her large breasts pressed their way to visibility, and her whole body took on an added sensuousness.

Silverman turned and poured more coffee into his cup. He thought of the contrast between Higdon and his secretary. She was so industrious, so pleasant and cooperative. And he, well, he was something else. Yet, curiously, she had worked for him for nine years. He suspected that it wasn't so much that she genuinely liked Higdon as it was her pride in being secretary to someone in his position. And she was good at her job. The previous year, at her own expense, she had had a plaque made up that was displayed at the front of her desk: "Mrs. Ramondi— Secretary to Mr. Raymond Higdon." Silverman could picture

6

her on Sunday afternoons visiting with friends and relatives and receiving compliments on her responsible government position: secretary to the senior public prosecutor.

He turned from the window and for the first time looked at the old man who was talking to her. He noticed the frustration in the old man's face, but he had seen that look before. The "interested citizens" who came to the prosecutor's offices to complain about the world's injustices just didn't usually make their appearances this early in the morning.

Silverman thought of the previous Wednesday's visitor to his office. That old man had complained bitterly about the president's ordering the chairman of the FCC to send painful radio waves to the man's dentures to prevent him from relating his information incriminating the president in high crimes and misdemeanors. He had been an easy one to get rid of. Silverman had sent him to the Philadelphia Dental Clinic for Citizen's Band "removal surgery."

When he had first joined the office, he had felt some sympathy for these disturbed callers; but when his receptiveness caused them to become habitués, interfering with his work, he, like everyone else in the office, got rid of them as quickly as possible.

This one looked a little different, more conventional in appearance, a bit better dressed—not exactly prosperous, but not as disheveled looking as most of the others. Neatly dressed in a conservatively checked sport coat with matching solid-colored slacks, he wore a fresh white shirt, and his wide tie, while old-fashioned, was clean and neatly tied. His gray hair was parted down the middle; he had probably worn this hair style since boyhood, when it must have been quite fashionable. He was wearing a gold wrist watch, and Silverman noticed a wedding ring on the man's left hand.

Having no more than a passing interest in what made this person different from the others and not really caring, Silverman, cup in hand, rose to leave.

He hadn't taken more than a step when Mrs. Ramondi held up her hand, gesturing for him to stay a moment longer. Apparently, she was uncomfortable getting rid of the man herself.

Silverman complied. He stood by her desk, sipping his coffee, and began listening to what the old man was saying.

The man's eyes shifted momentarily to Silverman, then back to Mrs. Ramondi. But, Silverman's presence barely registered with him; he was completely absorbed in his own words. His voice contained a strange mixture of politeness and desperation.

7

"I'm sorry to be such a bother," he continued, "but I've been calling him for two weeks now. Of course, you know that. I've left a message every time, and he hasn't returned any of my calls. This is very important. I must see him without further delay. It's very—well, it's most important. I called yesterday. You told me he wouldn't be in for the day but that you expected him to call you in the afternoon. I asked that he be requested to call me from his home. I waited at home all day. So today I came downtown to see him. I'm prepared to wait until he can see me. And now you tell me you're not sure, but you don't think he will be in today, either. I don't understand this. What is going on? Why won't he talk to me?"

Behind her pleasant smile, Mrs. Ramondi tried to mask the discomfort she felt. Lately, she had to make excuses for Higdon's absences more and more often. Not only to citizen callers but defense lawyers and judges as well, and occasionally to the U.S. attorney herself. It was a good thing for Higdon that Miss Eccleston was so in awe of him.

"I'm terribly sorry, Mr. Ritchie. Mr. Higdon has been so tied up in court."

She flushed slightly, embarrassed by her lie. Higdon hadn't been in court for six weeks. She composed herself; Silverman's presence had given her an idea.

"Mr. Ritchie," she began, "this is John Silverman. He works with Mr. Higdon. Perhaps you would like to speak with him. He . . ."

Before Silverman could protest, Ritchie interjected, "I don't want to speak to his assistant. I must speak with him personally! How in the world does one manage to do that?"

Unwittingly, Ritchie had hit a nerve. Silverman felt it rising inside him again. Eighteen months. Eighteen months "working" with Higdon.

Silverman had first heard of Raymond Higdon, chief public corruption prosecutor, the year after he graduated from law school. With his high academic standing and having been an editor of the law review, Silverman had managed to be selected to the prestigious position of law clerk to a federal appellate judge. Whenever Higdon argued a case before the court, everyone made a fuss over him. He was the guy who put so many corrupt government officials in jail.

After his clerkship had ended, Silverman was selected as an assistant U.S. attorney, one of thirty in the office. That had been two years ago, and during the first six months—even though he was "junior man"—he had pushed himself close to

8

Higdon. He soon came to realize that the great prosecutor was vexatious, a strange and disagreeable person. But he was brilliant, his work sheer artistry. And Silverman was hungry to learn. So as early as his first month in the new job, he had suffered Higdon's annoyance and had gone to him rather than to the other prosecutors with questions and problems with his cases.

Then, after six months, an opening appeared in Higdon's public integrity section, and Silverman was offered the job. It was the U.S. attorney, Anne Eccleston, who actually made the offer, but he knew it had been Higdon who had done the selecting. And Silverman had been thrilled. They would work cases together; he would learn directly from the master.

But his expectations soon fell flat. Eighteen months had passed. Eighteen months of waiting. Higdon seemed to spend almost as much time out of the office as in. And when in, he kept to himself. He'd answer an occasional query, but that was pretty much it. No teaching, at least not enough.

Another thing he'd learned about Higdon: even though he was a loner, even a recluse, he had an absolute penchant for creating a strong public image of himself as the lion of public corruption prosecutors. No one else in the office, not even the U.S. attorney herself, received the public recognition that Higdon did.

Silverman felt he had been abandoned by Higdon. At first, he'd been hurt; then his feelings turned to disillusionment. Now he was annoyed. Annoyed at the time he was wasting. Annoyed because his job had come boring.

With effort, Silverman managed to suppress his thoughts. He forced his attention back to the room, but there was an uncomfortable tightness in his stomach. Well, he wasn't about to interject himself there. Not for Higdon. Let him handle his own paranoids. He smiled benignly at the old man and started for the door.

"Mr. Silverman and Mr. Higdon work very closely, Mr. Ritchie," Mrs. Ramondi insisted, looking at Silverman. "I'm sure he can help you."

Ritchie studied Silverman. Silverman could see in the old man's face that he was being considered. And then Ritchie spoke. "What I have to say, Mr. Silverman, is of a highly confidential nature, and it is absolutely imperative that Mr. Higdon learn of it as soon as possible. If I do meet with you, will you see to it that he gets my information promptly? Young man, do you report to him directly?"

Silverman's stomach started up again. How much longer would he have to cover up for the "great" Raymond Higdon? He was about to "suggest" that rather than his reporting anything to Higdon, it might be best for Ritchie to continue his attempts to speak directly to Higdon. But before speaking, he glanced at Mrs. Ramondi. Her eyes pleaded with him to be nice and spend a few moments with the old man. He paused, considering. Okay. For her, he'd do it.

With obvious resignation in his voice, Silverman assured the man that, yes, he would receive his information confidentially and report all of it promptly to Mr. Higdon.

Ritchie shrugged, disappointed at having to accept second best but equally resigned—this was his only option. Silverman gestured toward the door, inviting the old man out ahead of him. As they left, Silverman turned to Mrs. Ramondi, and with a smile, feigned annoyance at her for getting him into this.

Neither man spoke as they walked down the corridor to Silverman's office.

Inside, Silverman removed his topcoat and hung it on the rack by the door, placed his briefcase on the floor next to his desk, then tossed his racing form onto one of the yellowing stacks of old editions on his worktable at the side wall. Ritchie watched the prosecutor, then looked at the stacks of racing forms. His expression when he looked again at Silverman was unmistakable: a modified version of the Subway Lady.

Gesturing at one of the wooden chairs in front of his desk, Silverman said, "Please have a seat, Mr. Ritchie," then nodded at the piles of old racing forms and lied. "Investigation into corruption in the racing industry . . . Reference materials."

The old man seemed satisfied, and they both sat down. Silverman placed a yellow legal pad before him.

"Now what can I do for you?" he asked.

"Mr. Silverman," he began, "it has not been easy for me to come here. I've agonized over it. But I know I just cannot live with this. It is just so wrong—so terribly wrong."

He paused again, this time with a pained look on his face. As he continued, his eyes drifted from Silverman. "They know I've decided to do this; I've told *him*. They don't know I'm here today, but they know I cannot withhold what I've learned. They've been calling me. At first, they were quite pleasant . . . it was as if it was all insignificant . . . all so trivial somehow. They both wanted to meet with me and talk about it. But lately the calls have become rather unpleasant. Not threats exactly. Well, I suppose they are threats. You know they . . . they talk around things so. They never seem to say them directly. The calls don't bother me, but Mrs. Ritchie is quite upset. I'm sure you can understand that."

Silverman nodded politely, indicating that of course he understood. He smiled at the old man and silently calculated how much longer he would have to sit there with him before he could get rid of him. He figured five more minutes. Perhaps he'd end it with a few quick words about how law enforcement had benefited from this citizen's visit.

Ritchie, misunderstanding Silverman's smile, accepted it and smiled back, then frowned in thought, trying to find where he had left off. "They are clever men, quite clever. And very powerful . . . but what they are doing is *so wrong*." He smiled again at Silverman—that smile of an older man who has seen so much in life to a younger man who has seen less. "He's not at all like his father. His father was a fine, fine man. A gentleman in the truest sense of the word. A man above reproach. It's just as well he's no longer here to see this . . . to see what his son has become."

Silverman leaned farther back in his chair. This was going to take forever. He had to put some order into this. He had work to do this morning. Leaning forward, he took out his pen. "Let me interrupt you for a moment, if I may, Mr. Ritchie," he began. "I've got to get some preliminary information about you before we go any further. What is your full name, sir?"

"James P. Ritchie," he responded obediently.

"And your home address, sir?"

"1800 Twenty-second Street, Apartment 2301."

"Phone."

"877-1393."

As he wrote the information at the top right-hand corner of his legal pad, Silverman marveled at how this ploy always worked. People would stop anything, no matter how important, to respond to name, address, and place-of-employment questions. It was as if not doing so were unpatriotic. A few "vital statistic" questions to get a rhythm going, a pointed question or two about who was doing wrong things and to whom, the little speech of gratitude on behalf of law enforcement everywhere, then good-bye and back to work.

"How old are you, Mr. Ritchie? What is your date of birth?"

"I'm seventy-three. I'll be seventy-four the day after tomorrow," he said with unconcealed pride. "January fifteen, nineteen hundred and . . ."

11

"You're retired, then, are you, sir?"

"Well, no, not exactly. I've been with Ames International for quite some time. In fact, long before it was called 'International.' I still work there, although I don't have set hours any longer. I pretty much come and·go as I please. My responsibilities have, of course, been considerably reduced in recent years. But I still go in most days." Then, in a reminiscent daze, he added, "Joshua and I were good friends."

Silverman sat up a little. "Did you say Ames International?"

"Yes."

Silverman's first reaction was simply to leave it alone, let the old man finish. But Ames International . . . First of all, it wasn't Joshua. The chairman of the board was Donald Ames. He was one of the wealthiest and most influential men in Philadelphia. His close friendship with the mayor had been the subject of much speculation, and plenty of allegations had been raised by the press about his political associations—and influence. He was a controversial man—no question about that—and well enough known, Silverman supposed, for this poor old man to fit Ames International into his delusions.

"You said Joshua. You meant Donald, didn't you, sir?" Silverman teased irresistibly.

"No, Joshua. Donald's father. That's right," Ritchie explained, not catching Silverman's tone. "He was a fine man. It was an honor to be associated with him those many years. Donald is the chairman of the board now; he's Joshua's son. But I tell you, Mr. Silverman, if his father could see that boy now . . ."

Some boy, thought Silverman. Donald Ames was in his late fifties and quite worldly. There had been several pictures of him in the press; Silverman remembered one he'd seen in an article about campaign financing methods used in the last election. The photographer had caught Ames, outfitted in a well-tailored topcoat, as he was stepping into his chauffeur-driven limousine.

As Ritchie rambled on, Silverman leaned back in his chair and thought of Donald Ames—what a prize target for a prosecutor. He was a fat cat: a politically connected, rich businessman. He had all the earmarks, too—a "high roller," a reputation as a ladies' man, shrewd and careful. He had taken his father's successful business and expanded it into a conglomerate. And he had bought the majority interest in companies that built office buildings and housing developments,

12

owned prime downtown real estate, operated a large catering concern, and probably more.

Allegations of fraudulent business practices had been made over the years, but there had never been any proof. The press had watched him for years, but then the local papers scrutinized the conduct of most wealthy businessmen who had political ties.

Ritchie stopped speaking. The silence brought Silverman back. He looked across the desk and saw that the man's look of concern had returned. He must be thinking about Higdon again, Silverman thought. Sure, he still wanted Higdon.

Now Silverman felt annoyed. In less than an hour, he had to be before the grand jury to present a tax evasion indictment, and he had some last-minute reviewing to do. He'd come in early that morning to work on that case, not to be Higdon's surrogate again. "Look. If you want to wait for Higdon, I don't mind. Believe me, I don't. I won't be offended in the least. I've got to be in the grand jury in a few minutes, and I've got work to do." Silverman started to rise. "Maybe it would be best if you tried Mr. Higdon tomorrow, Mr. Ritchie."

Either because he was fearful of losing his one opportunity to make his disclosure or because he saw a spark of fire in the young prosecutor, the old man quickly spoke. "No, no. Let me continue. Please. I'm sorry." And without taking a breath, he went on. "I went to work for Mr. Ames—Joshua Ames— in 1928. After the Depression, he became very successful, mostly in downtown real estate. Mr. Ames had two children, a daughter, a lovely woman who's now married to a doctor and lives in Arizona. And Donald.

"After college, Donald joined his father in the business, and, of course, he has done quite well since his father's retirement. Donald has treated me well. Even though I'm up in years now, he has provided me with an office to go to and has allowed me to continue working for the firm. At my own schedule, of course. I know he's done that only out of respect to his father's memory . . . Oh, he's never said it. But I know.

"Mr. Silverman, I'm an accountant, a bookkeeper. I'm not a CPA. Never bothered to take the exam. In my day, it wasn't really necessary. I worked . . . work in the accounting department; it's now called the comptroller's office. It's sort of the nerve center of the company. All of the vital records are kept there; you know, the files—that sort of thing."

Ritchie sighed. The introduction was over. It was now time— the first time—to tell an outsider what had happened, what he

13

had found. He felt a tinge of nervousness. He waited a few seconds more to summon strength, then began.

"I first learned of it by accident. They didn't know I was there. You see, Mrs. Ritchie, my wife, had her monthly ladies' club meeting that night; it's held at the Barclay. I usually go with her because it ends late in the evening, and I don't like her coming home alone. So we go together. I don't stay. Sometimes I sit in the lobby and read or watch the people; sometimes I walk over to the office, since it's only a few blocks away.

"Well, that night I went to the office. You see, one of the young men in the comptroller's office had misplaced a file earlier that day. The file contained some important papers, and he couldn't locate it, so I told him I'd help him find it. So I thought I'd look for it that evening. I looked all around the office that night but couldn't find it. Then the thought occurred to me that perhaps one of the secretaries might have accidentally taken the file into the back room where the old, closed files are stored. So I went back there, and sure enough, I found it.

"Well, I stayed back there for a while, looking through the file to be sure I had found the correct one. Then I went back to my office. In fact, I believe I was still reading the file as I walked into my office. I sat down at my desk, put the file where I would remember it in the morning, and was about to pick up the evening paper when I heard their voices. The voices came from the office next to mine. Evidently, they had gone into the office while I was in the back room, so if they had looked around, they would have found all the offices empty. They didn't know I was there; of that I'm certain."

"Who is *they*, Mr. Ritchie?"

"Donald and . . . Mr. Stavaros, John Stavaros."

Johnny Stavaros. Another fat cat. And a well-known one, too. He was a wealthy entrepreneur, but of a different sort than Ames. In his youth, he was a longshoreman and was reputed to have been a thug, a strikebreaker for the mob. In fact, there were still rumors floating around linking him to organized crime. He had made his fortune on the docks, had gone into the import-export business, and then branched out into a lot of different areas. He had become quite a philanthropist and managed to gain considerable respect in some circles.

Stavaros was younger than Ames. He was not known to be a political animal, his name never having been linked with politicians, or with Ames, for that matter. Silverman seemed to recall that the U.S. attorney's office had tried to make a narcotics case against Stavaros. He was supposed to have bank-

14

rolled a big heroin shipment from the Far East that had been confiscated from a cargo ship on the docks. But they couldn't make it stick.

"Well, I don't know why Donald chose to meet with him in Rašcover's office—that's whose office is next to mine—but the two of them were there; the door was open, and I could hear everything they were saying. I recognized Donald's voice at once, but not the other one. Actually, I didn't know who Donald was speaking to until—well, I'll get to that. Let me try to tell you this in order."

The old man paused again. His recollections of that evening flooded to his mind faster than he could speak the words. His heart began beating faster; he felt short of breath. He inhaled deeply and began again. This was very real to the old man; Silverman could see that. He listened.

"Well—they were reviewing the profits earned by Regal Construction Company. Stavaros was asking questions about public contracts—when they had been awarded, how the work was going, and the amounts of payments the company had received from the state. Are you aware of Regal? What it is?"

Silverman nodded. Sure, he had heard of Regal. Regal Construction Company was one of the largest, most successful roadbuilding concerns in Philadelphia. In recent years, it had been a substantional contractor on a state-funded improvement program for the city of Philadelphia's streets and roads, which included the major long-term effort at renovating the dilapidated Schuylkill Expressway, the city's external artery. In the past, Philadelphia had taken care of its own streets and roads, but like most cities, its funds were long gone, so it continuously sought mercy at the feet of state government. The state was only too happy to help—after it received a contribution from the federal government. The city would get its money, the state would run the show, and private contractors would do the work.

The press had tried to uncover something about Regal. The company had been in existence for a relatively short period of time but had managed to become one of the most prominent and successful public contractors. But road-construction contracts in Pennsylvania, as in most states, were awarded on a sealed-bid basis. Besides, thought Silverman, Regal was a corporation doing public work. The stock ownership of the company had to be a matter of public record. There had never been any mention in the papers of Ames and Stavaros having stock ownership interests in Regal; if there had, it would have been big news, especially in light of Ames's well-known friendship with the mayor.

Silverman leaned back again. This story was beginning to pique his interest.

Suddenly, he had an idea. "Mr. Ritchie, would you please excuse me for a moment? I've got one pressing matter I've got to take care of." Silverman was at the door. "Just have a seat here in my secretary's office for a few minutes. We'll continue as soon as I make this call." Silverman smiled; the old man left the office obediently.

Before Ritchie was even seated, Silverman had closed the door. He picked up the phone book from the credenza behind his desk, found the number he wanted, and dialed. After a few rings, the switchboard answered.

"Ames International."

"James Ritchie, please."

"Hold on, sir." Another ring.

"Comptroller's office."

"I'd like to speak to James Ritchie, please. Tell him it's important."

"Hold on please." A click. Music played.

As he waited for the "real" James Ritchie to come on the line, Silverman tried to think of how he would explain this call. Then he realized that he didn't have to; that they were getting him right now confirmed his suspicions—the old man's tale was fabricated. He was about to hang up, but there was another click, the music stopped, and a woman came on.

"I'm sorry, sir. Mr. Ritchie isn't in today. May I take a message? If it's important, he left a number where he could be reached."

"Well, uh, I'm, uhm . . . I'm not sure I have the right gentleman. The, uh, person I'm looking for is, uh, an older man, in his seventies . . . ."

"Yes, sir."

"So then, I, uh, have the right person?"

"Well, Mr. Ritchie is in his seventies."

"Well, uhm, you see it isn't absolutely necessary that I speak with him directly; I, uh, have mail, some personal mail to direct to him. Perhaps I could just send it. Would you give me his home address, please?"

"I'm sorry, sir. We're not allowed to give out that information."

Silverman needed verification. "Actually, I believe I have his address. That is, I'm not sure that the address I have is the correct one." He glanced at his legal pad. "Does he live at 1800 Twenty-second Street?"

She paused, considering. "Yes, sir, that's correct."

Same address.

"Okay. Well, I guess there's no need for me to leave a message. I'll just send the mail to that address." He was about to thank her when he remembered her offer of a phone number where Ritchie could be reached in an emergency.

"Maybe I'd better get that number he left in case there is a problem." In the second or two before her response, he wondered if this woman would question his bumbling attempt at information gathering.

"The number is 729-1590, extension 209."

That was the U.S. attorney's office number and Higdon's extension. Silverman could feel his excitement growing. Maybe this Ritchie guy really had something. Silverman quickly thanked her, hung up, walked to his door, and opened it. Ritchie was right where he'd left him. Too absorbed even to smile, Silverman motioned to him to come back in. They resumed their places. Now Silverman fired his questions at Ritchie.

"Why were Ames and Stavaros talking about Regal? Why was Stavaros there at night with Ames? Did you know of any relationship between these two men prior to that evening?"

Ritchie sensed the change in Silverman's attitude. He opened up.

"I knew they were acquainted," he explained. "Mind you, I didn't know the other man in that office was Stavaros, not until later. You understand that?" he asked, seeking reassurance.

Silverman nodded, eager for Ritchie to continue.

"I had seen Mr. Stavaros in our offices on several occasions, and I had been introduced to him. Donald always introduces me to others as his father's long and trusted employee." He lingered momentarily in his recollection, then continued. "I was introduced to him. Donald and Mr. Stavaros had lunched together a few times." With undisguised displeasure at the extravagance, he explained how Ames had hired his own personal chef when he became chairman of the board. He had remodeled his father's office and put in a kitchen and the private dining room where he entertained clients. Ritchie also made reference to Ames's having eaten there with "certain young ladies."

"Mr. Stavaros seemed a pleasant enough man," he continued. "That is, he was pleasant to me when I saw him at the office. But there's something frightening about him. His pleasantness seems forced; there's a toughness that comes through." He became absorbed in Stavaros and frowned, losing himself in his memories.

Silverman remembered the phone calls the old man had mentioned earlier. "Please go on, Mr. Ritchie."

"Well, I just sat there in my office. I didn't move. I listened. They talked about Regal. I heard a lot of figures. And then they spoke about...." He was telling too much. He caught himself and paused. No, he would hold that back, save it for Higdon. "They, uh, spoke about other matters."

"What other matters?" Silverman asked. He thought he detected revulsion in Ritchie's face.

"Other matters. Please, let me continue, Mr. Silverman."

Silverman knew he was in no position to push.

"They stayed for about twenty minutes or so, and then they left. Actually, Mr. Stavaros left first. Instead of turning right as he walked out of Rascover's office—you know, toward the exit—he turned left. He was right in front of my open door when Donald called out to him that he had gone the wrong way, that the exit was to his right. He stopped, then quickly turned around—he never looked in my office. He had no reason to, I suppose. He didn't see me.

"Donald stayed in the other office for a few more minutes. He made a phone call before he left." Ritchie leaned forward and lowered his voice. "I think he was speaking to his mistress. Then he left; I heard the exit door slam shut."

He sat back and looked at Silverman. "Because of what I had heard, I did something I had no right to do. You see, there is a large wall safe in Donald's office; his father had it installed. Actually, it was built for Joshua's office when we were in the Packard Building, but when we moved to our Girard Plaza offices, it was ripped from the wall and reinstalled. It's a rather clever thing, with a bookcase that is half real and half façade. The right side is on hinges, sort of like a door, and behind it is the narrow steel door to the safe. The safe itself is a steel-lined closetlike room which contains file cabinet drawers."

Joshua Ames had entrusted him with the combination to the safe; only the two of them had known it. He hadn't been in that safe for years, not since they'd moved, and he was sure that Donald was unaware that he knew the combination.

That night, after hearing Ames leave, he had waited a few moments without moving. Then he went to Donald's office. It had been quiet, so unnaturally quiet, as he walked down the thickly carpeted hall. By the time he reached the office, his hands were trembling; he was terrified that Ames might have forgotten something, might return. He would see him at the safe and realize that he had overheard the conversation. Or what if Ames looked up just before stepping into his car and noticed a light on in his office. No, that was unlikely; the offices were on the thirty-fifth floor; too high to notice. Still, he had been frightened. He stopped his story to explain to Siverman how difficult it was for someone his age to absorb that kind of stress and anxiety.

Once in the office, he opened the bookcase façade and found the safe just as it had looked before. He tried the combination, but it didn't work. Donald must have had it changed. He had closed the bookcase and was about to leave, but for some reason, he decided to try it again. He knew he was taking too long in there. He felt the weight of his anxiety, but he had to try. When the last tumbler clicked over, he had reached down and pushed on the handle. It opened. He had opened the safe.

Inside, the file drawers were the same, but they had new labels on them. Donald's labels. He ran his finger down the front of the drawers, reading. The third one down read "Personal Business." He opened it. It was full of manila files; toward the back of the drawer, he saw them: three files marked "Regal Construction #1, 2, 3." He removed them and sat down at Donald's desk.

"I found it in the second file," he told Silverman.

"You found what?"

"The document. I knew there had to be some kind of document. It was a corporate paper, an agreement. It looked official; there were spaces at the bottom of the page for signatures, but there were none. It was a copy. The original must be with someone else.

"The agreement said that the stockholders of Regal, that is, some of them—I believe the holders of about eighty percent of the stock—were nominees. They held the stock in their names, but they didn't own it. They held it for the benefit of Donald and Stavaros. *They* are the real owners of that stock!"

He then told Silverman how he had looked through those three files and then all of the files in that drawer and had removed them a few at a time, placing them on Ames's desk. Absorbed in the files, he had lost track of the time.

He'd been sitting there, consuming the information in the files, and hadn't even heard him enter the room. He had jumped forward, knocking a few of the top files to the floor, when he had heard him say, "Good evening, Mr. Ritchie."

At first, in his fright, he hadn't recognized him. It was the night watchman. Trying hard to seem at ease, Ritchie had explained that his wife was at a meeting downtown and that he had taken the opportunity to do a favor for Mr. Ames. As he spoke, he saw the watchman's eyes move from him to the open safe to the files on the desk. When Ritchie had finished his explanation, the watchman had looked at him once again, then nodded and said good night.

Not sure if the watchman had bought the story, he had quickly gathered up some of the files, taken them down the hall to the copier, and made copies.

"I took those copies home with me that evening. The agreement and other papers. We have this lock box in the closet of our bedroom. Our personal financial papers are in there, so I..."

Ritchie was about to continue his story when Silverman reached for his phone. "Jan, please ask Bob Jacobs to come in here right away."

Silverman didn't notice the look of panic on the old man's face. What in the world was this young man doing?

"Mr. Jacobs is a special agent with the intelligence division of the Internal Revenue Service. He has been assigned to the public integrity section of the U.S. attorney's office. He's a very able man; I want him to hear this. I'm sure he can help us."

Ritchie sat speechless, staring at Silverman. Silverman was too absorbed in his thoughts to notice; his mind was going over what Ritchie had said. Ames and Stavaros owned Regal Construction Company. This had actually happened. It was true, he thought. He wanted to believe it. There was a case here, and Silverman wanted it.

There was silence between the two men as Silverman waited for Jacobs. After a few minutes, there was a knock at the door, and without waiting for a response, Bob Jacobs walked in.

Robert Jacobs was a black man in his late thirties. He was a Phi Beta Kappa graduate of the Wharton School of Finance. His appearance belied his education; large and athletically built, he looked more like a high school football coach than an expert accountant. He had been in the middle of another case when he received Silverman's message. He was jacketless, his sleeves rolled up and his tie loosened at the collar. Whatever he had been doing must have been important because he wore a look of impatience.

Silverman quickly went through the formalities of the introduction, still oblivious of the old man's discomfort. Even before Jacobs had time to sit, Silverman launched into Ritchie's story.

When he had finished, he looked at Jacobs for a reaction, but Jacobs remained cool. He then turned and saw for the first time the old man's dismay. He went on, trying to recapture the momentum of a few minutes earlier.

"Okay now, you said you had seen and copied other documents. What other documents, Mr. Ritchie? What were they about?"

Ritchie looked first to Jacobs, then to Silverman. Now he was certain that talking to him had been a terrible mistake. This man was too impulsive, too young, he thought. He had betrayed his confidence without so much as a second thought.

"I think it would be better if I continued this with Mr. Higdon. I would very much appreciate your seeing to it that he contact me as soon as possible. I really must be going." He stood.

Silverman felt his heart sink. He'd blown it. He realized that his hasty action had frightened the old man, spooked him. Damn it, he thought. Here he had assured the man up front of confidentiality, and without even asking, he had brought in another person. And a black man at that. Even these days, most seventy-three-year-old white men are not very trusting of a strange young black man. This old guy is positive he made a mistake by not waiting for Higdon, he thought. He's sure I'm irresponsible.

Silverman stood. He couldn't let this go so easily. "Please have a seat, Mr. Ritchie. This man is part of our office. He can be trusted. He's part of our team. Believe me, it's okay." He sat down, hoping Ritchie would also, but he didn't. "Now what else did you discover in those files? Did it have anything to do with the other things you overheard Ames and Stavaros talking about?"

But he was pushing too hard, and Ritchie wasn't going for it. The moment had been lost. "I've really got to be going. I would very much appreciate hearing from Mr. Higdon. Thank you for your time, Mr. Silverman."

As he started for the door, Silverman followed him. "One last thing, Mr. Ritchie. You said you told some people about your discovery and that they had been calling you. Whom did you tell?"

The old man turned and stared at Silverman, deciding whether to answer. "Why, Donald, of course. I told him what I had done, what I had seen, what I felt I had to do . . ." He caught himself, turned, and again started for the door.

"Well, who has been calling you? What exactly have they been saying?" He wanted to engage the old man again, get him talking, then lure him back to the desk.

Without turning around, Ritchie looked down. "I really have to leave."

The meeting was over. But Silverman couldn't give up. He had to know about those documents. "Mr. Ritchie, those documents could be quite important. I want to be able to assure Mr. Higdon they're in a safe place. Could you tell me exactly where they are so I can tell him?"

Ritchie turned around. He'd bought it. "They're safe. They're in that box I told you about in my closet. The file is marked 'Real Estate Account.' My wife inherited some property, and I keep her papers in there. Good day, gentlemen."

As the door closed behind him, relative calm returned to the room. Then the intercom sounded. Silverman picked up his phone; Jan reminded him that he was due in grand jury in three minutes. Taking a file out of his cabinet, he said to Jacobs, "Look, I can't talk now; I've got to be in grand jury. Can you see me later?"

"No. I don't have the time now. Not today."

"How about after five?" Silverman searched Jacobs's face for some of the excitement he felt.

"Can't. Let's talk about it tomorrow morning. It's not going anywhere." Jacobs showed no emotion. But then, he rarely did.

"Okay. Eight o'clock."

"Nine-thirty."

"Okay."

Silverman left the office first, his grand jury file under his arm, his mind on Donald Ames.

2

It was two days after Ritchie's visit. Hazy morning sun filtered through his office window as Silverman sat trying to concentrate on his Daily Racing Form. Yesterday had been an all-around bad day. Seven races. Silverman's speed handicapping calculations had found sure winners for three and solid bets for the rest. He had opened the paper with confident expectation.

Seven losers. Not one winner. That put him $197 in the hole, and it was only midmonth. He sighed, put his feet on his desk, and reread the past-performance charts of the horses listed in the previous day's *Daily Racing Form*. He redid his calculations—his figures maintained he'd made the right selections. Unfortunately, the horses had been unaware of the accuracy of his projections. Too bad, he mused; it might have given them an incentive. Well, it was only a game. He folded the racing form back to page one and picked up the phone.

"Anything from Jacobs?"

"No," Jan said. "Nothing yet."

He hung up and opened the racing form again. Part of the problem, he knew, was insufficient concentration. Shit. He closed the paper and tossed it on his desk. Where was he?

Jacobs hadn't come to work the day before; he had called in and told Jan he'd be on annual leave for the day and that he'd see Silverman at nine-thirty the next morning.

It was now ten o'clock and still no Jacobs.

Silverman had spent the last two days going over the old man's story. He had reread his interview notes several times, all the while cautioning himself not to get too excited. It could all be nothing.

But Jesus, it could really be something. It could be the case of a lifetime, the kind of case prosecutors dream about. Public contracts. The mayor's best friend and benefactor. If Ritchie's story were true, there was a significant prosecution lying somewhere in what the old man had overheard that night. This was the kind of corrupt activity Silverman had hoped he'd get a crack at investigating when he'd come to public integrity. Until then, he hadn't even come near what he was after.

Where the hell was Jacobs?

He didn't know Jacobs well. They'd worked together on a few minor cases, nothing of real importance. The Internal Revenue Service had assigned Jacobs full time to the U.S. attorney's office. It was part of the new "interagency cooperation in federal law enforcement" the president had announced the previous year. He was good; Silverman knew that. He was an experienced and well-respected criminal investigative agent. He was said to have good instincts and a nose for smelling out juicy cases. Despite his educational background and position, for some reason he still lived in a ghetto in North Philadelphia. Silverman had once heard about his having or supporting a large family.

But as good as Jacobs was, Silverman sized him up as a classic career government employee. Nine to five. Never missed one day's annual leave. Never got really excited about a case. For guys like Jacobs, it would never be more than a job, something to retire from with a pension after the prescribed number of years. He was not someone Silverman could count on for vigorous assistance.

With this matter he needed someone with experience and good judgment. One did not begin investigating allegations such as these unless there was something substantial to go on. He wanted the benefit of someone else's expert judgment. And there was no one else Silverman could rely on. Certainly not Higdon. Not yet, at least.

If there were a case here, Higdon eventually would have to know. And Silverman was fearful that Higdon might push him aside, fearful that the case would disappear inside Higdon's office, as Higdon himself had for most of the last eighteen months.

But if there was a case, two things would be true. One, he would eventually need Higdon. A case of this magnitude required Higdon's experience—and brilliance. Two, whether he wanted him or not, Higdon would be in. Even though he wasn't the U.S. attorney, Raymond Higdon was king here.

He thought of Miss Eccleston. He considered her proof of the theory that old families bred themselves out over generations. She had gone to all the right Philadelphia schools, knew all the right people, even had a grandfather who had been governor of Pennsylvania. She had old money, breeding, and charm—Silverman liked her. But as U.S. attorney she was in over her head. Soon after her appointment, she had tried a criminal case and had made such an ass out of herself that she hadn't stepped into a courtroom since.

Why had she been selected? And how? Silverman supposed it was because there was still pressure on the Justice Department—in fact, on the federal government generally—to put, and keep, women in important positions. And while there were many able women lawyers around, a few of them assistant U.S. attorneys right in this office, Miss Eccleston's family stature and money—and her safe mediocrity—made her a popular choice for sensitive appointed positions. She'd held a succession of public service jobs, this being the latest.

If anything came of Ritchie's accusations, she would have to be told. She'd be pleasant, probably wouldn't appreciate the implications of the information, and then she would turn to Higdon. And he would lead her by the nose.

Silverman watched the traffic. It was beginning to snow again. Mary Ann was going to be impossible. She still hadn't fully recovered from her last bout of "cabin fever," when she'd been cooped up in the apartment with their young daughter for three days.

She'd noticed the previous night that he had been pensive. When she'd asked if he was all right, he'd lied that he wasn't feeling well. He didn't want to tell her. Not yet. Not if it were nothing.

He watched the cars on the street below slowly line up for a red light, their windshield wipers slapping aside the falling snow. Where was Donald Ames at this moment? What was he thinking about? Had the old man told the truth? If he had, was Ames thinking about him?

His buzzer sounded.

"Mr. Jacobs is here," Jan announced.

Silverman looked at his watch. Ten-fifteen.

"Tell him to come in."

He sat down and leaned a foot against the edge of his desk. He didn't want Jacobs to see him ruffled. They might have to work together, and he wanted to be in command.

Without knocking, Jacobs walked in, waved, walked over to the chair that Ritchie had sat in, pushed it over to the side of Silverman's desk, and sat down. Clearly, he had just arrived at work. Though jacketless, his tie was still fastened at the neck; his shirt-sleeves, customarily rolled over his forearms, were still down. He leaned back, stretched his legs straight out in front of him, and smiled at Silverman. There would be no apology for missing the previous day's meeting.

"How you doing?" he said.

"Nice of you to show up today. You're sure it's no problem for you to spend a few minutes with me?" Silverman couldn't conceal his annoyance.

"Come on, man. Slow down. I'm here. Let's talk." Jacobs liked Silverman. John was a bright and aggressive prosecutor. He was as good in court as any young prosecutor he'd seen. But he was still green, too excitable, too impulsive.

"Well, what do you think?" Silverman wasn't going to bother with preliminaries.

Jacobs returned the question. "What do *you* think?"

"Come on. I waited for you two days. Tell me. Do you think the old guy's for real?"

Jacobs stared at Silverman. "Have you done anything to check the man out? Any attempts at verification of identity?"

Silverman explained how he had put the old man in his secretary's office and had called Ames International, verifying the old man's employment there.

"All that proves is that he works there. It sure ain't corroboration of his story. Lots of people have read or heard about Ames and his political influence. Maybe this guy sat there in the comptroller's office doing some little shit clerical job watching Ames, the boss's son, take over. Maybe he spends years hoping that all the stories in the papers about Ames are true. Then one day he just gets too old, and in his mind the stories become real. He wants to get Ames, so he becomes an actor in the drama. But the drama's in his mind." Jacobs sat back in his chair. "That isn't so unusual, you know."

"So what are you suggesting? Just drop it? Forget about it?"

"No, no. Not yet at least. There's a possibility, but you can't move yet. There's nothing to move on. No, I think all we can do now is talk to the old guy some more; then we'll see where we are." He noticed Silverman's smile. "Let's try to get him in here again, to talk to him some more. He's going to want Higdon here. You spoken to Ray yet?"

"No, he's been out," Silverman said quickly, hoping Jacobs wouldn't push. "I think you and I should try this first."

Jacobs shrugged. "Look, John. This guy wants Higdon; he wants to unload his tale of woe on the senior prosecutor. Talk to Ray. Then call Ritchie and set up an appointment for him with Higdon. We'll all be there. Otherwise, you're not going to get him in here."

Silverman resisted. "Let me just call him first. I'll tell him that I've discussed this with the great man himself but that we need another meeting, that Higdon wants more information. I'll keep it vague; I won't tell him that Higdon won't be there. I'm telling you, if we have to wait for Higdon to come and then schedule a meeting, this guy's going to die of old age." Silverman forced a laugh.

Before Jacobs could argue, Silverman had picked up the phone.

"Jan, get me Ames International. Just buzz when you have the switchboard operator." He paused. "No, wait a minute. Forget it." He turned to Jacobs. "Maybe we ought to try him at home. Maybe I should call him there tonight. He might be uncomfortable talking to me at the office. What do you think?"

"What I think is that you're making a mistake by not having Ray in on this. If you call him and he insists on Ray, will you please assure him that he will be at the meeting?"

"Yeah. Yeah. Okay, I'll assure him."

"Then call him at home. He said he is semiretired, doesn't keep set hours. Try him right now. Maybe he's home."

Silverman found Ritchie's number on the legal pad containing his interview notes, and dialed. After a few rings, a woman answered.

"Hello, is James Ritchie at home, please?"

"Who is this?" she asked. Her voice sounded tired.

"My name is John Silverman. I'm calling from the U.S. attorney's office. Mr. Ritchie and I spoke the other day. Is this Mrs. Ritchie?"

She didn't answer. Silverman repeated the question. "Is Mr. Ritchie at home? May I speak to him, please?"

"No. I'm sorry, you can't."

Silverman didn't have time for games. He was about to tell her how important this was, even use Higdon's name, if he had to, but she continued.

"My husband is dead. It happened last night."

Silverman fell silent. He didn't believe what he had just heard. Maybe it was a cruel joke—Ritchie's way of keeping away from him? He wanted to tell the woman to come off it, let him talk to Ritchie. He looked desperately to Jacobs for some kind of assurance that what the woman had said was not true. But he knew it was.

Silverman felt angry. This was Jacobs's fault, he thought.

If he hadn't stayed home yesterday . . . If he had shown some interest . . . His thoughts were jumbled and coming too fast. It was over before it had even begun. But there were questions to ask. Had the old man been murdered? Had Stavaros had him murdered? Mrs. Ritchie was waiting for a response, or at least a reaction. How could he ask questions of this grieving woman? He tried to swallow his discomfort.

"I'm sorry. I didn't know," was all he could say.

She said nothing. He heard a click as she placed the receiver on its cradle. He took the phone from his ear and held it, as if hanging it up would terminate whatever might be left of this case as well.

"He's dead. Died last night."

"How?"

"I don't know. Can you find out?" He hung up the phone.

"Yeah. I'll call you. Stay here. I'll call you in a little while." He left.

Silverman was staring out the window when his secretary buzzed him.

"It's Mr. Jacobs on line one."

As he pushed the blinking yellow button, he heard traffic in the background. "Yeah. Where are you?"

"A phone booth—Twenty-second and the Parkway," Jacobs answered. "Here it is: James Paul Ritchie. White male. Seventy-four years of age. Ambulance was called to 1800 Twenty-second Street at 2:15 A.M. Wednesday. Man in apartment 2301 complaining of chest pains. Ambulance took him to University Hospital. Arrived at 2:57 A.M. Patient dead on arrival. Cause of death: ACUTE MYOCARDIAL INFARCTION." He paused. "Died on his birthday."

"What now?" Silverman was despondent. It was just a dream, after all, he thought. But then he remembered the records. Of course! Ritchie said he had copied the Regal Construction nominee agreement and other records. If he had been telling the truth, there was a file in his bedroom closet. "The records. The Regal agreement. That's it, isn't it?"

"Right," Jacobs answered. "Snow's letting up. Get a cab and come on over here. Let's pay a condolence visit to the widow. We'll see if she'll let us look for those papers."

"Now? Shouldn't we wait?" Silverman remembered Mrs. Ritchie's voice on the phone. "Do you think that's a good idea? The guy just died yesterday. She may not be in any mood to cooperate with us." He wondered if Ritchie had told his wife how annoyed he had been with the prosecutor's impulsiveness.

"No, man, it's got to be now. You're the lawyer; you know that. Ritchie's estate's going to be probated. Some lawyer's going to ask the widow to collect his personal financial data. If those papers are there in that file—*if*, John—then we've got to try to get them now. Later, they may be in someone else's hands. And then things will get complicated."

"Yeah, you're right . . . Okay. But it's not going to be easy. Where can we meet?"

"You know where his apartment is?"

"Yeah. Near the art museum. It'll take me about twenty minutes to get there."

"I'll meet you in the lobby. Place is called, uh, the Franklin."

"Okay. Twenty minutes."

Silverman grabbed his raincoat from the coat rack and left.

Silverman and Jacobs stood before the elevators in the lobby, Silverman on one side and Jacobs on the other. As they entered the building, the doorman stopped Jacobs and asked if he could help him; Jacobs said he was waiting for a friend. For Silverman, the doorman merely held the door and smiled.

Noiselessly, the doors to the elevator slid open, and an elderly man walked out. Jacobs caught the door before it closed again. The man gave him a funny look. Jacobs just smiled and nodded; the man turned again and walked away.

"Come on," Jacobs said, holding the door for Silverman.

As they walked the carpeted hall, the sounds and smells of domestic life filtered through the stale inner air of the corridor. Someone's TV was on too loud.

Jacobs pushed the small square doorbell of apartment 2301 and took out the black leather case that contained his badge. The peephole darkened and a woman's voice, thick with caution, asked what he wanted.

He smiled at the darkened peephole and held his badge in front of him.

"Excuse me, ma'am. I'm with the Internal Revenue Service. I'm Special Agent Robert Jacobs. May my colleague and I speak with you for a moment, please?" He bent down. "Here, I'll push my credentials under the door so you can get a better look at them."

The two men waited for the door to open. After a few moments, they heard the clicking of locks being turned. She opened the door, but the chain was still across it. She looked first at one man, then the other, and closed the door again. They then heard the chain sliding from its bracket. The door opened, but no more than twelve inches. Mrs. Ritchie stood with her face in the opening and her body behind the door. She handed back Jacobs's credentials.

She was not what Silverman had pictured. She was thin and pale, with hardly a line on her face. It looked as though she had been crying. She seemed to be waiting for an introduction, so he told her his name and position. He was about to ask for permission to come in when she exploded. "For God's sake, why can't you people leave me alone! You killed him! You all did. He was obsessed with it. It was too much for his heart. He's dead now. Aren't you satisfied with that? You all should be satisfied." She was crying hysterically now. "Leave me alone. He can't tell you anything anymore. He can't tell anybody anything. Go away. Please go away." She slammed the door in their faces.

They looked at each other and said nothing. Silverman thought that she didn't understand who they were. Maybe in her grief she had confused them with Ames's people, the ones who had been calling her, *if* anyone had been calling her.

They left the building without speaking. The snow had stopped, but the sky was still gray, and it was turning colder.

Jacobs broke the silence. "Let's go somewhere where we can talk."

They walked into the drugstore and slid into an empty booth at the far end of the wall. The warm smell of people and food was comforting. They ordered coffee.

"This is not turning out to be one of my better days," Silverman said with a faint smile.

Jacobs shook his head. "You make any sense out of what she said?"

"Nope."

The waitress brought their coffee. There was no need to discuss alternatives; they both knew there was only one. With nothing but the old man's story, they couldn't justify issuing a subpoena to Donald Ames or Regal Construction or any of his companies.

"We've got to subpoena that file from her. She's going to think we're Nazis, but we've got to do it now," Silverman said.

"Yeah. Well, have Jan type something like 'Please call on receipt' on the subpoena. She's not going to disobey a grand jury subpoena, but if she thinks part of the order is to call you, maybe you can open up a line of communication with her. You know, try to persuade her to let us come and look through that file in her apartment. Tell her she can avoid going downtown before the grand jury if she'll let us see the file." He took a sip of his coffee. "You know, we'll get the file one way or another, but there may not be any copied Regal or Ames records in there. You'd better be prepared for that."

"Yeah, yeah. I know that." But Silverman wasn't prepared. "Look, I'll get the subpoena out today. I'll have a deputy U.S. marshal serve it. Our next grand jury session is in four days, so I'll make it returnable for then. I don't see any reason not to mention Ames or Regal, do you?"

"No, I guess not. But make it broad. And don't mention Stavaros. Just in case. Let's keep that name to ourselves for a while."

"Yeah, right. The subpoena will call for all records, financial or otherwise, that relate in any way to James Ritchie's employment with Donald Ames or any company in which Ames has a financial interest, including, but not limited to, all files or papers of Regal Construction Company. I'll also mention the real estate file in a separate paragraph. You know, in case she doesn't know the copied papers are in there."

Jacobs stared at him.

"*If* they're in there," Silverman added to please him.

Neither spoke in the cab on the way back to the U.S. Courthouse. Silverman thought of the subpoena he was about to have the grand jury issue. Technically, it was the grand jury that had the power to issue subpoenas, not the prosecutors; they were merely its agents. But in reality that was not how it worked.

The grand jury would not hear about Ritchie's story. Silverman wouldn't tell them. Not yet. He'd learned that much from Higdon. Higdon treated grand juries delicately, as though they were children. "Grand jury control," he called it. Prosecutors should tell the jurors what they needed to know, and no more, because they lacked the sophistication required to make the necessary fine distinctions, he said. No point in whetting their appetites. No, if Higdon were handling this, he wouldn't tell them yet either.

It was Tuesday of the following week. The subpoena had been issued to Mrs. Ritchie several days earlier, but Mrs. Ritchie hadn't called. Silverman had discussed with Jacobs whether he should call her, but they agreed it was best to do nothing, just wait. It was the day that she was supposed to appear before the grand jury with the records.

Her not having called troubled him. As each day passed, he became more convinced that she hadn't responded because there were no records and there never had been. The old man's fantasy had gotten the best of him. Silverman was going through his morning mail when the phone rang; he watched the yellow light blink with each ring, remain yellow as his secretary answered, and flicker on and off as the caller was placed on hold.

"It's Jonathan Webster. He says he's a lawyer and is calling in reference to a grand jury subpoena."

"Okay. I'll take it." He pushed the flickering yellow button. "Hello, can I help you?"

"Hello, Mr. Silverman. My name is Jonathan Webster. I'm calling in reference to a subpoena issued to Mrs. James Ritchie. I'm a lawyer, but I'm also Mrs. Ritchie's nephew. The subpoena is due today, but I'm afraid there's a problem."

Silverman heard a young, nervous voice. "What's the problem, Mr. Webster?"

"Well, you, uh, know that my uncle—Mr. Ritchie—passed away last week . . ." He waited, expecting words of condolence, but Silverman only asked him to continue.

"Well, uh, my aunt has been staying with her sister in Atlantic City. She left Friday and returned last night. When she arrived home, she discovered that her apartment had been burglarized." He stopped again. He'd told his aunt that a federal prosecutor was not going to believe this. "You see, they broke in, ransacked the entire apartment, and took some things—"

Silverman cut him off. "What things?"

"Well, uhm—that's the strange part about this. They didn't take the usual things, you know, like the TV or jewelry . . . They took papers: Mr. Ritchie's canceled checks and the like from a closet in the bedroom. . . . I guess they were looking for blank checks to forge and pass. She called the police. There's a police report. You can check it."

"Mr. Webster, the subpoena mentions records that relate to Donald Ames and certain of his companies. Where are those records?"

"Uhm, my aunt says that she has never seen any such records. But, uh, at any rate, all that stuff was apparently taken last night. The burglars had probably just scooped up all the papers, hoping that blank checks would be in there. They probably threw whatever else was in there away. And I'm afraid

Mrs. Ritchie doesn't know anything about those papers. My uncle kept all their financial records; he was an accountant, you know."

Silverman remained silent.

"Does, uhm, she have to appear today? I mean is it still necessary for her to come downtown?"

"No." Silverman's voice was cold. "No. But tell her that she should treat the subpoena as continuing in nature, and if she should find any of the documents called for by the subpoena, please contact me. If we need her to appear, I'll contact you. What's your number?"

The lawyer gave him the number. Silverman hung up without saying good-bye.

It was real. It was real, after all. The old man had told the truth. And Donald Ames knew it.

3

"Daddy, you be the doctor, and I'll be the nurse."

Silverman looked down from his newspaper to find his three-year-old daughter standing at his side, doll in one hand and toy doctor's kit in the other.

"Okay, until Mommy calls us for dinner," he said, "but it'll cost you two kisses."

Jamie leaned forward and kissed her father twice on the lips. Silverman smiled. His daughter was a source of never-ending pleasure to him. He got down on the floor with her, and they played until Mary Ann called from the kitchen that dinner was ready.

The sprawling red-brick garden apartment complex in which they lived had been built years before for that vast, amorphous class of Americans called "middle income." Its conveniences, or lack of them, reflected what its designers and builders felt, at the time, were sufficient for members of that class.

The kitchen was narrow, windowless, and hot. And crowded, now that Jamie no longer needed a high chair. At meal times, if the family was eating together, Mary Ann had to bring a chair for herself in from the dining room and squeeze it between the small rectangular table and the stove. She would sit there, her husband and daughter at either end.

He watched Mary Ann leaning over to help Jamie. She was so beautiful. He had been in his first year at Harvard Law School when they'd met—at one of those awful mixers, the ones he'd sworn never to go to again. His roommate had talked him into it. It had been at Smith College, where Mary Ann was a sophomore. They had spent the entire evening talking together on the corner sofa in the dormitory lounge. He'd taken her out the next night, already in love.

John Silverman had dated a non-Jewish girl only one other time in his life, in high school. His mother had not approved,

34

had given him the silent treatment, her way of showing displeasure toward members of her family.

Not that Silverman's parents were observant Jews. And, they considered themselves liberals. Which they were, up to a point. His father, a lawyer with a small general practice in Chevy Chase, Maryland, was as unbiased and fair as anybody. His mother was, too, except when it came to intermarriage. For that there was the silent treatment, and a subtle campaign to make John see the light.

For Mrs. Silverman, however, it was a hopeless cause; John had fallen quickly and deeply in love with Mary Ann. She eventually relented. They had been married during a semester break, and both sets of parents had supported them through school. John vowed that after graduation he would not be dependent on his parents, or hers, for support again.

Following graduation, Silverman had received a clerkship with a well-respected federal judge, and they moved to Philadelphia. Jamie was born that year. Any trace of resistance that may have lingered in his mother vanished with the birth of her first grandchild. And Mary Ann adored motherhood.

"Daddy, I hate broccoli," Jamie protested, tilting her head to see around Mary Ann, who was leaning toward Jamie's plate. "Please, Daddy, tell Mommy I don't have to eat it."

"Come on," Mary Ann insisted, hiding a smile as best she could, holding Jamie's fork in her own hand.

"Yuck! I hate it, Daddy!"

He smiled but didn't interfere.

"Come on; let's go," Mary Ann had scooped some of the cut broccoli and held the loaded fork at Jamie's mouth. "Come on . . . It's the only way to get dessert."

Jamie released one last "yuck," then opened her mouth to admit what she considered to be, without question, one of the vilest substances known to man.

Mary Ann coaxed Jamie through two more forkfuls, then rose to get dessert and coffee.

Silverman watched as his wife reached into the cupboard for cups and saucers. He had been attracted to her the moment he'd seen her. So delicately fair, her hair a subtle mixture of shades of light auburn, she was so very feminine. And as he later discovered, there was something luxuriously wonderful about the feel of her skin, as if those pale freckles that covered her body emitted a radiant, silky warmth.

He was pleased that she had kept her figure after Jamie had

35

been born. As soon as she could, she had exercised back the firmness temporarily lost during pregnancy.

Mary Ann finished preparing dessert and stood sponging off the small counter near the sink. She was wearing tight jeans, and even under her loosely hanging blouse, her lovely breasts were noticeable. Their first argument—it had been their first or second date, he couldn't remember which—had concerned his rather strong perseverance at trying to caress them. If he'd known then how really lovely they were, covered with a creamy, pale layer of freckles and with soft pink nipples, he wouldn't have lost that argument. He watched her breasts sway with her movements at the counter.

Mary Ann had grown up in McLean, Virginia, not far from the Silverman family's Silver Spring, Maryland, home. The distance, though, was much greater socially than geographically, and their paths had never crossed. Mary Ann's parents were listed in Washington's "Green Book," the city's social register. Her father was a nationally prominent Washington-based architect, and she had grown up with all of life's luxuries.

Mary Ann had not completely adjusted to living in the Wynnewood Apartments.

But she coped as best she could. The apartment was adequate, really. Except for the kitchen, the rooms were a decent size, and there was a nice view from the living-room window. Yet Mary Ann couldn't help feeling they were living an extended postgraduate school existence. She was tired of waiting for their real life to begin. She wanted a house, a home, not so much for the snob appeal to it but to have a social base from which to function as a full-fledged wife, entertaining appropriately for her husband, and as a mother, who could offer her child broader horizons. Enrolling Jamie in a private nursery school had helped a little. That was one expense that would not be spared. And Mary Ann had become friendly with some of the other mothers. That helped, too. And on the really bad days, the days when the walls seemed to close in, there was Bonwit Teller.

A few hundred yards away, on the same side of the road, was a shopping center, not surprisingly named Wynnewood Shopping Center. It contained the usual stores: supermarket, cleaners, drugstore. But it was also the home of the suburban branch of Bonwit Teller. While in the strictest sense the store may not have been the royal sister of Saks Fifth Avenue or Neiman Marcus, for Mary Ann, on those really bad days, temporary salvation lay within its four walls. Down its aisles, behind its counters, stood the symbols of the life-style she had once had and was waiting to have again. He teased her about her trips there, but he understood; he knew it wasn't as frivolous as it seemed. For Mary Ann, there was a kind of reassurance in that store, a reassurance that her world hadn't disappeared, that it was still there, close enough to see, to touch.

She hardly ever bought anything; that wasn't what she needed. But she'd walk through the various departments gazing at the finery, occasionally trying on a dress in the designers' section. The sales people, with their trained eyes, would sense that this woman belonged there and would treat her accordingly. It was her reassurance, and it helped.

Mary Ann's desires, her requirements, were really quite simple. Despite her education, her background—her intelligence—she wanted nothing more than the kind of life her mother led. A good life, a life of comparative luxury, a life of motherhood and family caring. And a social life, of which they had practically none.

Silverman drank his coffee and watched his daughter work her way through her chocolate pudding, a good amount of it winding up on her cheeks rather than in her mouth. She had her mother's looks; no question about that. Except for those big brown eyes, a gift from Silverman's genes, Jamie was as Scotch-Irish as her mother. Maybe their next child would favor him. His looks, in that narrow region between Jewish and Italian, were dark, his skin lighter than olive, his hair black and reasonably straight. He was slightly taller than average, well built, perhaps a bit on the slim side. And, of course, he had the bright brown eyes all Silvermans had.

"Good, huh?" he asked, smiling first at Jamie, then at Mary Ann.

"Yup," she answered, digging her spoon deep inside her dish.

As Mary Ann emerged from the bathroom, Silverman placed the book he had been reading to Jamie on their bedroom dresser.

"She's asleep," he said.

Mary Ann tossed her head to the side to free her hair, which, until a moment ago, had been confined in a shower cap. Her robe clung to her still-damp body, suggestively silhouetting her shape. Silverman looked at her. It was a look she knew. She walked over to him and slid her arms around his neck. "I love you," she said. They kissed. Gently, he opened her robe and

37

looked at the delicious curves of her body. They kissed again; then he gently slid the robe off her shoulders.

He closed the door. She pulled back the covers as he undressed. She lay down, and he knelt beside her. Although he hadn't touched her yet, their bodies were alive with anticipation.

She watched as he bent forward, running his hands through her pubic hair. Tenderly, he kissed the inside of her thighs. She squirmed as his lips moved upward toward her breasts. She held him, moving with the pleasure brought by his mouth, her low murmurs just barely audible. They made love.

Afterward, she lay curled on her side, close to him, her arm resting on his bare chest.

"Can we talk?" he asked.

She moved slightly. "Uhm hum."

He told her about the events of the last few days, about James Ritchie, the burglary, everything. She listened, saying nothing.

When he had finished, he looked at her for a reaction, but she waited for him and still said nothing.

"What do you think?" he asked when he had finished. "Think I should pursue it?" He sat up and leaned against the headboard. "It could keep me in the office for a while longer than we'd planned. This could be a major prosecution; it could take a while."

"Do you want to do it?" she asked, although she knew the answer.

"Yes, I do."

She let out a small sigh. "If that's what you want, then I guess you should do it." The thought of spending more time there made her heart sink. She tried not to show it.

"You know Ames and Stavaros are powerful people. There are no guarantees," he said.

"But you believe in this, don't you?"

"Yeah. I'm not sure it's quite that simple . . . but yeah."

"Honey, I really don't understand all the implications, but if you feel it's right, and you want to do it . . . then you should do it, I suppose." She sat up, exposing her breasts. She kissed him. "You do what you think is right."

Later, as Mary Ann lay on her side, her nightgown back on, John, still nude, asleep beside her, the warmth and comfort she had felt during their lovemaking slowly evaporated. Suddenly, she felt frightened, and curiously, betrayed.

* * *

The blue-green video haze emanated from the TV screen, reaching out toward the darkened living room. It was 4:15 A.M. The home cassette version of Pac-Man's Revenge had been on for the past hour. Slouched in his easy chair, bare legs dangling over the side, Silverman pushed at the buttons of the wired remote control in his lap as expertly and decisively as he had at the arcade in Suburban Station. The game was set on its highest level; Pac-Man moved with speed, rarely missing the tiny dashes that were its prey, only occasionally getting eaten itself.

He barely moved, the game an extension of his finger tips, his whole being engaged in the challenge. An hour before, he'd lain awake, staring at the ceiling, Mary Ann asleep beside him. Sleep had kept its distance. If he had been asked, Silverman would have said insomnia, just insomnia. First, he'd tried the *Daily Racing Form* in the bathroom, thinking it might keep the tension at bay. But that hadn't worked. Now his fingers guided the action on the screen, his dark hair mussed with sleeplessness, his four A.M. eyes still not fully adjusted to the unnatural light. He drew satisfaction from the game as though it were fresh air from an open window. Winning. Control. Unquestioned, instinctive control. The fear that had awakened him lay in hiding, held at bay by his absorption in the game.

Silverman's life had thus far been relatively uncomplicated. Hard work and ability. Drive and the right breaks. Control had been easily maintained; life's passage remained set on automatic pilot. Harvard Law. Mary Ann. Jamie. Assistant U.S. attorney. Up ahead, private practice in a big-city, prestigious law firm. Still ahead, the right clubs, and on and on. But he was edging toward a new course, plotted by the events he'd set in motion. The change in direction, if not reversed, would propel him toward totally unfamiliar terrain. And the only controls Silverman held on to were those of Pac-Man's Revenge.

He played at his game. The uneasiness he felt—insomnia, he would have said. But he had never had it before.

4

"Is she free?" Silverman asked Miss Eccleston's secretary.

"Let me check." She pressed the intercom button on the phone. "John Silverman's out here. He wants to see you." After a short pause, she said, "Yes, ma'am." She hung up and looked at him. "She says to go in."

He opened the door to Miss Eccleston's office. There she was. Sitting behind her desk in her customary pose, looking the same as always. Tall and angular, pushing fifty, she was, Silverman thought, unattractive. Her hair, straight and colorless, was habitually pulled back behind her head with a tight twist. Day in and day out, she wore one of three identical, custom-made, drab suits, and her blouses were all pale affairs with frail lace fronts. She looked up as she saw him, and smiled.

"Come in, John." At least she's pleasant, he thought.

Silverman took one of the chairs in front of her desk. The U.S. attorney's office was large and impressive, the showplace of the entire office: the furniture was of a higher government grade than the rest, the wood deeply polished, and there was a leather Chesterfield sofa and matching chair in the corner. To the right of her desk stood the American flag, complete with bronze eagle.

"How are you, Anne?" Silverman smiled. This was going to be a short meeting. He had planned exactly what he was going to say.

"I'm fine, thank you."

"Anne, something has come across our desk." He had decided to imply Higdon's participation from the very beginning; it would make this easier—and faster. "It may very well be nothing, but we thought you ought to at least be made aware of it. We've gotten some preliminary information—I won't dignify it yet by calling it evidence—that Donald Ames and some others may be holding secret interests in Regal Construction . . . you know, one of those large road-building outfits. It may very well be nothing, but we're checking into it now." Then he added with a reassuring smile, "We'll keep you advised, of course."

He thought he saw her frown. Maybe she knew Ames. Perhaps some analytical thought was trying to hatch itself up there behind that patrician forehead. He didn't intend to provide the silence needed for incubation. He quickly changed the subject.

"I also wanted to tell you that I finished the Wasserman brief that you so kindly allowed me to write instead of the guys in the appellate section. I want to send it down to you while it's still in draft form, and I'd very much appreciate your views on how I handled the subpoena for a lawyer's records issue." He smiled deferentially.

"Yes, certainly, John. Send it down. I'd like to review it."

It was time for his retreat. "Okay, great. Thanks, Anne. All right, we'll keep you advised on that other thing," he said. They exchanged smiles, and he left. He closed her door and hurried down the hall to Higdon's office.

Donald Ames leaned toward the phone perched at the edge of his massive desk and dialed the number himself on his private line. Mary was away from her desk, and besides, he was confident that Stavaros himself would answer. He always answered that private number.

"Yes," Stavaros said. Ames could sense that he was busy.

"It's me. Have you heard anything?"

"No. And I won't, and neither will you. Stop worrying. It's nothing. Nothing's going to happen."

"Yeah, I know . . . I was just curious. I know it's okay."

"Look, even if our friend did talk to someone, there's a . . . a credibility problem. And no one's going to pursue his . . . uh, beliefs without serious reservations."

They were both accustomed to guarded phone conversations.

"All right. I was just curious," Ames repeated. "I'll see you Thursday. Okay?"

"Yeah. Good-by." Stavaros hung up.

Ames put the phone down. He was worried. He knew Ritchie a lot better than Stavaros did. Ritchie was a peculiar man. But if he had gone to the newspapers before he died, Ames figured he would have heard from a reporter by now. Besides, reporters didn't trouble him. He had taken that kind of heat before. Without proof, there wasn't going to be any story that he couldn't handle. And there was no proof—at least no longer. He'd gotten those copied records back but hadn't told Stavaros about it. He wouldn't understand; he would see it as a mistake. And that idiot he had hired to make it look like a real burglary. Some professional, he thought. A neighbor had knocked on the door, and he had panicked, waited a few seconds, grabbed up the papers, and left without taking anything else. Ames was convinced that the fewer who knew about it, the better.

He absent-mindedly played with his ring. It was hard to imagine Ritchie doing anything that would hurt the company. He was too loyal for that. But what if Ritchie *had* spoken to the authorities before he died? Oh, how they would like to go after Donald Ames. If they knew about the records—and the burglary—they'd be suspicious. But so what? No, if something had happened, he would have heard of it by now. Somehow he would have heard. Well, he wasn't going to worry about it anymore. He relaxed his large frame deep into the high-backed executive chair. He'd think of more pleasant thoughts. Like tonight . . . that young blonde he had met the other night. He anticipated the feel of her pale skin under that silk dress she had worn . . . Ritchie was forgotten—at least for now.

Pat Ramondi was on the phone when Silverman charged through the door of Higdon's office. He waited for her to finish.

"Hi. How are you?"

"I'm fine, John."

He watched as she took a pink message pad and wrote the name and message of the caller on it. After she had torn off the sheet and placed it on the right tip of her desk, he turned his head to read it. "Mr. Higdon—Miss Eccleston wants to see you when you're free." Well, it certainly hadn't taken her long, he thought. He looked at Mrs. Ramondi and picked up the pink piece of paper. "Tell Ray to talk to me before he sees her. Tell him it's important." He replaced the paper on the desk.

"I'll make sure he calls you first, John."

Silverman picked up the interoffice line, expecting Jan.

"You want to see me?" Higdon said.

"Hi. How are ya?" Silverman asked with forced friendliness.

"Yeah. Hi." Higdon sounded customarily impatient. "Pat said you wanted to see me."

It was a command, not a request. Silverman told him he'd be right in.

42

Raymond Higdon's office was an extension of his personality, his loneliness, obsession with privacy. It contained only the government furniture allotted to each assistant U.S. attorney. There was a total lack of adornment. No pictures or diplomas hung on the walls; no knickknacks or other items sat on his desk. His desk and worktable were barren except for a green blotter, some half-used legal pads neatly stacked, and a government ball-point pen on each table.

Higdon had become a lawyer later in life than most others. He was a near genius, having earned his college degree at seventeen. During adolescence, his physical and emotional development always seemed to lag behind his intellectual growth, and he had become increasingly isolated from his peers. He was, in common parlance, a loner. After college, he worked in a clerical job for the government, then, after several years, enrolled in the evening division of a local law school. Although the program was designed for a four-year course of study, he completed all the requirements in three and graduated with the highest average the school had known. He was, however, ashamed of his night-school background. He had never married, had no real friends, and lived alone.

His appearance was as nondescript as his office. Of medium to slight build, he was pale, and his light-brown hair was showing the first signs of thinning. He wore neatly pressed, conservative, but cheaply made suits, mostly browns and grays. His one extravagance was his shirts; they were all white, French cuffed, and heavily starched. In spite of his sterile appearance, behind his thin horn-rimmed glasses, encased in dark rings of sleeplessness, were expressive, telling eyes.

The Raymond Higdon within, the one behind the veil of privacy, was a complex, difficult, and essentially unhappy person.

He insisted that no one be permitted in his office without first being announced by Mrs. Ramondi. The young lawyers in the office found this practice offensive; no one paid him a visit except on business.

Mrs. Ramondi buzzed to tell him that John had arrived. He told her to send him in.

Silverman wore his customary look of friendliness as he entered the office. He had learned early in their association that geniality, although rarely returned, made discussions with Higdon easier.

"Hi. How are you feeling?" Silverman sat in one of the chairs in front of Higdon's desk.

"Fine." Higdon sat and waited with apparent impatience. When he was in, he always acted busy, as if he had no time to waste. Silverman always suspected this was a defensive ploy.

"Uh, listen, something came up last week that may be interesting. You got some time to talk about it?"

Silverman was nervous; he was going to have to cover his decision to withhold Ritchie's story from Higdon until now. He smiled and shook his head.

"I'm really still kind of surprised that I'm in here talking to you about this. It really looked like nothing at first. Uhm . . . let's see, it started with this old guy who came to see you. In fact, you might remember getting some of his messages . . . James P. Ritchie? . . ." He could see that Higdon was impatient, waiting for the point. Silverman shifted in his chair.

"Pat talked me into seeing him. We both thought he was another 'interested citizen.'" He went on to tell Higdon all that had happened. He had originally intended to supply only the bare essentials. No point in giving Higdon everything on a silver platter. But as he spoke, he found himself telling all. He wanted Higdon's opinion; he needed assurance that he really had something here.

When he had finished, Higdon leaned back in his chair and raised his eyebrows slightly. "Well, isn't that interesting," he said. "Why is Miss Eccleston interested in seeing me? Have you spoken to her about this?"

Silverman told him about his visit. Higdon was not displeased.

"All right, I'll see her when we're finished. Don't worry about it," he said, tapping his fingers on his desk. "Now, what have you done so far? Have you planned your first move?"

Silverman caught Higdon's use of the singular pronoun. Had he done that intentionally?

"Jacobs and I have talked about what we ought to do." He wondered how Higdon would interpret his use of "we." "Of course we've got to begin by finding a copy of the Regal nominee document. I suppose there are two ways we could move. One way would be for us to subpoena the Regal Construction records in the hopes that a copy of the nominee document is in them. That way we would least get the name of their accountant, and then we could subpoena his records and look for it there . . . That's the conservative approach.

"The second way—and frankly I favor the second way—

is to make a broader sweep...You know, to work on the assumption that Ames and Stavaros are in Regal and that we'll find evidence of it. I'm convinced that we will...Well, the second way is this..."

He leaned forward, animated by Higdon's apparent interest, and outlined his scheme.

When he finished, he sat back and looked at Higdon, eager for his reaction.

Higdon took a legal pad from his worktable and tossed it over to Silverman. "You're close. Now listen to me." He picked up his phone and dialed Jacobs's number.

"Yeah. This is Ray. John is here with me. Can you get three or four younger agents from the IRS to spend some time working on this new project of yours without letting their superiors know what they're doing? At least not for now...not until there's more. Okay, good. John will have a few jobs for them. We'll need one who could pass for a college student, someone who'd look like he was writing a term paper. I'll want him to go to Harrisburg to the state offices and ask for the public files on the awarding of Philadelphia street- and road-construction contracts.

"Okay, next. John is going to send a teletype to the commissioner of Internal Revenue in Washington and to the disclosure guys at the Department of Justice, requesting expedited, immediate disclosure of income tax returns and all related information on Ames, Stavaros, and every company we know they're associated with." He looked at Silverman and put his hand over the mouthpiece. "We'll talk about how to get the names of those companies in a minute." He removed his hand. "John's going to call Washington this afternoon and then twice a day until he gets oral permission for disclosure. We'll worry about the formal letter later. But in the meantime, I want you to call your friends over at records; tell them to send the tax returns to you immediately, but have them give you, over the phone, the names of all the accountants who are listed as preparers on those returns. My guess is there will only be about three or four different names. You hold on to those names until John tells you that he has received official permission to get those names; then you give them to him. Put a memo to that effect in your file." Looking at Silverman, he added, "John will get oral permission within forty-eight hours."

Jacobs acknowledged his orders with only an okay, then hung up.

"All right, now listen, John. You send our college kid to Harrisburg . . ."

Higdon sat perfectly still, his arms on the sides of his chair, and rattled off his game plan as if he were a general at West Point delivering a lecture on a battle he'd already fought. Silverman, the student, took notes. Once again, he was in awe of Higdon. It was simply incredible. He had taken this complex puzzle and within seconds had arranged the pieces into a simple, clean fit. Not a thought or word out of place.

Step one: an agent would be sent to the lobby of the building in which the offices of Ames International were located. Unobtrusively, so no one would notice that he was collecting information, he would record the names of all the companies that were listed as occupying the same floor as Ames International. He'd repeat the procedure at Stavaros's offices in order to get the names of all the companies he was associated with.

Step two: subpoenas would be prepared in two groups. The first group, group A, would be for the accountants' records on Ames, Stavaros, Regal Construction, and all the companies from the directory boards. Group B would be subpoenas for the state construction files for the Philadelphia improvement program, and, finally, the business records themselves from all of the Ames and Stavaros companies.

Step three: Higdon leaned slightly forward. "Okay, now, tomorrow the grand jury will be in. They have to be spoken to. It's a bit tricky. It's time for their formal authorization, but *we* don't want to whet their appetites. We'll talk to them off the record . . . I'll handle that."

Silverman looked up from his note taking. So Higdon was going to become an active participant. He smiled; this job was finally coming alive. He and Higdon were going to do this together. They were going to turn over the rock and expose what lay underneath. The lecture stopped, Higdon's look conveying his impatience with Silverman's reverie. Note taking was resumed. But damn, they were going to do it together.

Step four: the group A subpoenas would be served. The accountants would complain—insufficient time, too many records. Silverman would handle them, get them in front of the grand jury, let them feel the heat. The accountants would go back to their clients, and tell them what it was like.

Finally, step five:

"Now on the day when the group A records come in," Higdon continued, "Jacobs and the other agents should make

46

an immediate search of those records. We're going to need to find something to prove that we weren't simply fishing for evidence, that there was a valid reason for the issuance of the subpoenas. My guess is they'll find it—whatever it is—right away. As soon as they do, we'll have the agents serve the group B subpoenas. It'll probably be the afternoon of the same day. In fact, you should send one of the agents to Harrisburg with the state subpoena that morning so he'll be ready to serve it. The subpoena on the state and the subpoenas on the companies should be served on the same afternoon; everyone subpoenaed will be in touch with everyone else—that'll shake the tree.

"Some of those subpoenas are going to be challenged, but we'll be able to tell the judge of our 'probable cause.' I'm sure we'll win any motions to quash the subpoenas.

"Now, we'll need a room, some space to store those records. I'll take that up with Miss Eccleston."

The lesson was over. Silverman realized that Higdon had mapped out his strategy for this blitz in total reliance on his young colleague's perception and judgment of Ritchie. Did he think that much of him, or was he so anxious to go after Ames that he had overlooked everything else? Or was he doing some kind of Machiavellian thing here? Investigate with Silverman's; head on the line; if there is a case, jump in and steal the glory; if not, watch Silverman's head roll. Silverman wanted to feel Higdon out, test his motives.

"Do you think . . . *we're* being too ambitious, trying for too many records all at once? There could be manpower problems."

Higdon tried to be patient. "There are a lot of things we don't know yet, but if we don't suck up all the records at once, we'll lose valuable mileage right at the beginning." Silverman knew he was right. "But what about the press? When that subpoena is served on the state, it's going to hit the papers; the press is going to be over this thing like flies over shit." He didn't need Higdon's reply to that one. "Well," he continued, "I guess if we are on solid legal ground, that's an unavoidable consequence of doing our job."

Higdon waited to see if there was something else. There was.

"There's one thing we haven't discussed, you know." Silverman coerced his amiable smile. "The mayor." He was about to articulate the risks and possibilities of investigating a close friend of the mayor's, but Higdon was ready for the question.

"What are you asking me? If you're asking me if the mayor's

47

dirty, the answer is yes, sure he's dirty. You can't be friends with a fat cat like Ames and not be dirty . . . If you're asking me if we're going to get him, my answer is probably not. He's too smart. Ames is too smart. People like that very rarely, if ever, leave a trail."

Other questions would have to wait. The meeting was over; Higdon once again signaled his impatience.

"Okay, I'll get that teletype out," Silverman said. "You'll, uh . . . see Miss Eccleston?"

Higdon nodded. There was nothing further to discuss. Silverman was on his way.

"Thank you, Frankie," John Stavaros said in his usual quiet manner as the young waiter placed the oversized bright-red lobsters in front of him and Ames.

Frankie stood for a moment, his black hair too long and too manicured, combed high over the top of his head, his waist jacket the same powder blue as the restaurant's tablecloths. When satisfied that his presence was no longer required, he retreated silently.

This restaurant had been a Philadelphia institution for years; its ownership had remained in the same family. A fine old restaurant. Then one day, about a year ago, Stavaros began eating there regularly. So far as the public knew, there had been no change in ownership. The same name as before remained on the liquor license. Although no one ever really told him, Frankie knew he was serving the new owner. And he knew who—and what—the new owner was.

Fastened around Ames's and Stavaros's necks, covering their chests, were plastic throwaway bibs, with a reproduction of a lobster on each. At first glance, the effect was almost comical—these two well-heeled, middleaged men, dressed in expensive suits, sitting at the table like children, holding silver lobster crackers, breaking away brittle red shells as if they were engaged in a school crafts project. But any notion of the innocence of childhood was quickly dispelled as one looked closer.

Ames, portly, the clear product of overindulgence, sat absorbed in his task of extracting every morsel of lobster from behind its shell. Stavaros, prematurely graying, trim from his afternoons at the athletic club, exuded an ominous quietness even in the early silence of their meal. His lined and pockmarked face was that of a man who had been through hard times. Yet his mannerisms, voice, everything else, spoke of a peaceful, deliberative nature. Save one feature. His eyes were cold. And hard.

Holding the delicate fork in his large hand, Ames dipped a fat chunk of lobster in his butter dish and brought it toward him, drops of melted butter trailing their way across the table.

"You feeling better now, Donald?" Stavaros asked.

Without looking up, Ames answered, "I'm fine."

"You see, there was no need for worry. I told you nothing would come of it."

Stavaros nodded in the waiter's direction. Within seconds, Frankie was at the table.

"Yes, Mr. Stavaros," he said, his voice just a touch too respectful.

"Frankie, bring us a bottle of wine."

"I'll bring you the wine list, sir."

"No. You select it, Frankie." Stavaros smiled. "You bring us a nice bottle, okay?"

Frankie nodded, trying to conceal his discomfort, and turned to go to the wine cellar.

"Donald, have you said anything to . . . the man?" Stavaros's fist tightened around the lobster cracker with more force than was necessary. The shell crunched, then splintered.

"No. Nothing."

"Good. No need to trouble him. He has enough on his mind."

Ames hadn't looked at Stavaros since the meal had been served. He continued eating now, trying to hide his nervousness. Then he felt Stavaros's stare and slowly raised his head. He was frightened of Stavaros; he, too, had heard the stories.

They'd known each other for several years, ever since the last election when Ames's friend, Phillip Lane, Brooke had become mayor. Stavaros had sought out Ames, had entertained him, flattered him, done him favors, offered him lucrative business opportunities. Then, almost before Ames realized it, he was returning favors, doing whatever Stavaros asked. Without admitting it to himself, he was afraid not to.

Stavaros may have been curt with him once or twice, but never really ungentlemanly, certainly never ruthless. He never lost his temper, was always in control. Yet he always seemed to be controlling a different inner self, a dangerous, hostile man who would stop at nothing to get what he wanted.

Stavaros's mouth turned into a smile; his eyes remained cold, unemotional. He sighed.

"Donald, your nerves are on edge. That's bad for your health. You ought to relax."

"John, I'm fine. I'm—" He stopped in midsentence. Stavaros had placed his hand on his arm. But for the eyes, it would have seemed a gentle act.

"No, you're very tense. My doctor says that's bad for your health. You need to calm down. You're worrying too much. It affects your decisions, Donald. People make mistakes when they're tense."

Ames slid his arm from under Stavaros's hand. He wanted out of this. Stavaros was making him squirm. He knew that there was no way Stavaros could know that he had ordered the burglary. Yet he couldn't be sure. The man he'd hired was supposed to be discreet, a professional. Yet he was well known in some circles.

"I'm fine. I'm okay."

Having waited for what he thought was the proper moment, Frankie approached on seeing Ames return to his lobster. As quickly as possible, he uncorked the bottle, poured a small amount of the chilled white wine into Stavaros's glass, and waited.

Stavaros ignored it. "Try it, Frankie," he said. "You tell us if you like it . . . if it's right."

Obediently, Frankie lifted the glass and sipped at the wine. He forced a smile, sensing he was on trial.

"Very nice, Mr. Stavaros."

"Good. Fill the glasses."

Frankie lingered, hoping Stavaros would pick up his glass. He didn't, merely indicating that Frankie could leave.

"You know, Donald," Stavaros continued, "you're acting like we've done something wrong. We haven't, you know. It's politics, that's all."

Grateful that Stavaros didn't know—or had chosen not to pursue—anything about the botched burglary, Ames shook his head, relaxed a little, and smiled back.

"Politics," Stavaros repeated softly. "No one's getting screwed. Certainly not the taxpayers. It's simply the way the machinery of government works in this country."

Stavros lifted his glass and carefully examined its contents. He took the smallest of sips.

"Frankie."

The waited quickly appeared. "Yes, Mr. Stavaros."

"Bring me a beer, Frankie."

As if he'd known all along this was how the game would end, Frankie began his rehearsed apology.

"Is the wine wrong, Mr. Stavaros? I'll bring another..."

"A beer, Frankie," Stavaros said, this time looking at him.

"Yes, sir," he whispered, and disappeared.

"Anne Eccleston. You know her, Donald?"

"We've met."

"She's of the same political party as... your friend?"

"That's right."

Stavaros resumed eating. "It's okay, Donald. Just politics. Nothing to worry about."

Delicately, Frankie placed the beer bottle and frosted glass before Stavaros, his eyes conveying more than sufficient apology. But Stavaros didn't notice.

"Thank you, Frankie," Stavaros said quietly.

5

The grand jurors were filing into the room in groups of two and three. Some chatted in early-morning tones; others were quiet, carrying white styrofoam cups filled with steaming coffee. As they passed John Silverman, standing by the entrance, they nodded or said their good mornings in a friendly, trusting way. This grand jury had been empaneled over nine months ago. During that time, they had met in session about once a week. They had become comfortable in one another's presence; some had even made friends. By now they felt like a group, a team. And they liked Silverman.

Higdon had once delivered a lecture to the office on the grand jury. He had emphasized that acquiring the grand jury's trust was of vital importance to the overall success of any investigation.

"You must convince them that you're a nice young man or woman, doing your job—and no more—with appropriate zeal. They must trust you. If you make a representation, they want to, and *must*, believe you. You accomplish that, and when it comes time for them to vote on an indictment, you won't have any trouble."

As he stood there making eye contact with each grand juror entering the room, Silverman felt sure he'd been successful with all but one or two of them. Mrs. Franklin, for one, was an odd duck and had all the signs of being a potential source of trouble. In a group of twenty-three jurors, it was not uncommon to have one, maybe two, who would habitually swim against the tide and take whatever position was opposite to the majority's. Higdon said people like her simply had to be carefully controlled in a way designed not to offend the others.

Paradoxically, though, the real source of trouble was Higdon himself.

While he was, without question, a superb interrogator—Higdon had no equal when it came to drawing testimony from even the most recalcitrant witness; he was also in total contradiction to his teachings, as impatient and condescending with grand jurors as he was with everyone else. It hadn't caused him a serious problem; not yet at least. He had always had more than enough evidence to indict. Besides, he could intimidate many of these ordinary people, who were not as bright and articulate as he, so that they would perform their duties as he directed.

The grand jury room was simple. The windows were small. This was one of several internal rooms, its entrance hall cut off from the public corridor in order to secure secrecy for those compelled to appear and testify. The walls were blue, the carpeting a dull orange, the lighting a soft flourescent white.

The furnishings consisted of rows of long blond wood tables behind which were plastic seats the color of the carpet. One such table, separated by a space of about three feet, stood facing the others; this was for the prosecutors and, for formality's sake only, the grand jury foreman. Against the wall, occupying part of the space separating the tables, stood the slightly elevated witness box. It, too, was made of blond wood. The box was positioned so that the witness faced the door. The witness would have to turn to hear the question. Below the box, to the side, was a small stool where the stenographer sat.

They waited for the grand jurors to settle down.

"Ladies and Gentlemen, quiet please," Higdon demanded. He rose to address them.

"Some information has come to our attention which indicates that a man named Donald Ames and certain other people here in Philadelphia may have been involved in improprieties involving the awarding of state contracts for the construction and improvement of our city's streets and roads." He then went on, describing in vague language how it was the duty of the grand jury and its agents—the prosecutors—to pursue these leads by subpoenaing records and compelling the appearance of witnesses. He explained how the investigation might very early prove fruitless and quickly be abandoned or could result in a long, protracted inquiry lasting many months, with most of the work being done for them by the prosecutors and IRS agents.

"We will bring witnesses in here when appropriate, and we will, of course, keep you advised of what records we have subpoenaed in your name. So, in a moment, I'll take questions, if there are any," he concluded with an air of questions being out of order, "and then we'll put on the record our request for

53

your authorization to pursue this matter on your behalf and, of course, your permission for us to issue subpoenas for you."

"Mr. Higdon." Mrs. Franklin had her hand up. "Mr. Higdon, I think we have a right to know exactly how you all came across this information. I mean, from whom did you get it? And also, sir, I would like to know the identities of *all* of the people you think may be involved in these improprieties."

Higdon struck with deadly force. He began a long discourse, his words, his expression, even his stance, conveying to the others in the room that this woman was somehow, with malicious intent, attempting to destroy everything that America stood for. He wanted to make it difficult for any of the other grand jurors to take her side; and he succeeded. The other jurors seemed completely intimidated by his tirade.

When Silverman saw that Higdon was winding down, he waited for the bone he knew Higdon would throw—some concession to her question so that no one could accuse him of being unresponsive.

"Mrs. Franklin," he said, sitting down, "the sources that provide information such as we have here are not a part of the grand jury process; we have assured them of confidentiality. Not even the U.S. attorney herself is demanding to know *their* identities, although she has a right to know. Now if you insist on knowing more names at this early stage"—he paused and sighed, pretending annoyance at having to provide her with this information—"Okay, we have also received information that a man named John Stavaros may be a possible target of this probe." He glared at Mrs. Franklin and turned to the other jurors.

"Ladies and gentlemen, any other questions?" He waited about three seconds. "All right, then..." But Mrs. Franklin wasn't finished.

"Just a minute, please, Mr. Higdon. I would just like to state that unless we are provided with more information about this case, I will not be able to vote in favor of providing you with permission for subpoenas. For all we know, you may be proceeding on the vaguest...uhm, I mean the most general of evidence, information. What I'm trying to say is, you could be launching a fishing expedition, and we have a duty to uphold everyone's rights, particularly from government harassment."

Higdon was on his feet again. "Okay, let's take a vote on it. How many people here want to continue this discussion?"

To Silverman's surprise, three other people quietly raised their hands, but four out of twenty-three did not pose a problem, at least not for now. A two-thirds vote would get them the authorization they needed. And the prosecutors were sure the other nineteen jurors would vote yes. The battle was over.

"I'm sorry, Mrs. Franklin. The majority here do not wish to continue this. You vote how your conscience tells you to vote."

Higdon quickly nodded toward Silverman, then went for the door. Silverman and the stenographer rose and followed him out.

As they stood in the hall waiting while the jurors cast their votes, Silverman leaned against the wall and watched Higdon, whose mind seemed to be elsewhere. Was he thinking of Ames? Was he thinking about . . . The door opened; they went back in.

The foreman was standing, but Silverman indicated to him not to speak until the stenographer was ready.

"Mr. Foreman, has the grand jury voted?" Silverman asked.

The foreman glanced at the stenographer before speaking. Silverman had noticed before that people seemed afraid to have their words taken down on that machine. The foreman nodded. "Uh-huh."

"You are indicating," Silverman interjected, "that authorization as requested has been given by an affirmative two-thirds vote of the grand jurors present."

"Yes, that's right . . . correct." He sat down.

"Okay. Thank you, ladies and gentlemen. That's all we have for today. We will meet one week from today at ten A.M. Subpoenas will be issued today, so next time you can anticipate some witnesses in here."

Before they left, Silverman wanted to mend any faltering good relations. He was conscious of Higdon as he spoke, apprehensive that he would think him too soft with these people or trying somehow to erode his authority.

"Folks, Ray and I assure you that we will proceed with this thing cautiously." Then, looking directly at Mrs. Franklin, he said, "You can be assured we will keep you fully advised of all relevant happenings." He smiled broadly at them and told them they could adjourn.

At Sixth and Chestnut streets, one block from the U.S. Courthouse stood the small cluster of historic buildings that had once housed the first American government. Bob Jacobs had lived in Philadelphia all of his life but never had set foot inside any of these buildings. Jan had told him that he would find Silverman inside Congress Hall.

He went from the small anteroom into the large chamber and almost immediately sensed the secluded, still atmosphere within. An industrialized city had grown up around this area. There was a busy city street outside, seldom without traffic, but the presence of modern, urban Philadelphia was muted to the point of near nonexistence inside here.

Jacobs surveyed the large room.

"Welcome," said the woman who had been seated near the door in the last row of semicircular desks and chairs. She smiled. "This is Congress Hall," she said, as if he had asked. "You can see this chamber was once a courtroom, but the Congress met here when this was the seat of our nation's government. The furniture is a replica of the original desks and chairs. You can sit in one if you like."

Jacobs nodded absently, searching the room. He saw Silverman seated at the far end, behind one of the desks, absorbed in the *Daily Racing Form*.

"George Washington was inaugurated here. For his second term, of course. And John Adams—"

Jacobs interrupted and said loudly, "I've come to see the senator from Maryland." He pointed in the direction of the racing form.

The woman giggled. "The Senate met upstairs, sir. This was the House of Representatives. You mean the congressman from Maryland."

Silverman closed his paper and rose. He was annoyed with Jacobs. They were to have spent the morning together, working. Jacobs hadn't shown.

"Good-by, Frances," Silverman said as he followed Jacobs out.

"Bye, John. See you tomorrow." She sat down and returned to her book.

Jacobs stopped him as soon as they were on the street.

"You mean they let you do that," he said, pointing to the paper tightly folded under Silverman's arm, "in there?"

During the winter months, tourism in Philadelphia was, at best, sporadic. With the exception of an occasional straggler— and now and then a civics class—Independence Hall, Congress Hall, and the other buildings in the cluster remained empty except for the posted tour guides, most of whom were pleasant elderly women retired from careers of teaching. They would spend the days alone reading and so welcomed the young prosecutor's noonday company.

Silverman would grab a quick sandwich, then spend the remainder of the hour in the solitude of the old House of Representatives, playing at his "game." In the warm weather, he'd sit in the small park behind the buildings.

But he was in no mood to explain all of that to Jacobs right now.

"Hey listen. You know I sat on my ass all morning waiting for you."

"Sorry. Something personal. Couldn't be helped."

Silverman stared in disbelief at his casual attitude. "What do you mean, couldn't be helped? Where were you?"

Jacobs tried to control his mounting anger. "I took a few hours of my annual leave. Something personal . . . okay?" It was clear he wanted this conversation to end—now.

The career-bureaucrat syndrome again, thought Silverman. But damn it, there was work to be done. He'd have to put an end to this before it became a problem.

"Look, we may be working closely together in the months to come. I think we ought to have an understanding," he said. "You do your personal business on your own time, and not . . . the government's." He had almost said *mine*. "I expect you to be here during business hours and . . ."

Jacobs flared. "Don't lecture me, man. You're not my teacher . . . or my boss. You think you've got a complaint about my work, fine. You tell me. But stay out of my personal life. This is leave time. I've got it coming. I'll take it when I please. You got that, Silverman? You understand that?" He stood, defensive, poised for battle.

"Come on," Silverman said, turning, his body shaking imperceptibly with the fear and anger he felt from Jacobs's defiance. "Let's get to the office. We've got work to do." Fucking insubordinate asshole, he thought.

They walked on in silence, Silverman a few inches ahead of Jacobs.

As they crossed Sixth Street, Jacobs finally spoke.

"The accountants call?"

"Yeah."

"Go okay?"

Jacobs was coaxing him back into conversation, but the bitterness lingered; Silverman was still angered by Jacobs's insolence. That's just what I need, he thought, another prima donna.

"Yeah. Went okay."

And it had, with the possible exception of Gerald Stoffman, Ames's accountant. He'd been arrogant, demanding an explanation for the subpoena. He accused the government of harassing innocent people.

Silverman reminded him that if he didn't produce the records, he'd be jailed for contempt. Stoffman said he'd do it, but warned the prosecutor that his attorneys would look into the matter. Just before the conversation had ended, Stoffman had referred to the catchall language in the subpoena, had said there was an additional company, not specifically listed. Was he legally obligated to produce those records as well, he asked, the mixture of boredom and sarcasm in his voice blatantly audible. Silverman told him that the answer was yes. Stoffman had hung up without another word.

By now, Silverman and Jacobs had reached the entrance doors to the courthouse. Silverman opened one of the doors, but Jacobs grabbed his arm.

"Look, man, you're right. We've got to work together. Let's try and get along. Okay?"

"Yeah, sure," Silverman said as he abruptly turned and walked into the building.

Grand jury day.

Accountants were producing records. Higdon had acquired a room for document storage and review. He had notified Silverman and Jacobs of its location by memo. It was the only thing available, he had written. When they saw the room, they realized he had been apologizing.

Special Agent Robert Jacobs and his men would be spending the next several months in a prison cell. Two prison cells, to be precise.

This courthouse, like all the others in the country, had a U.S. marshal's office; in it was a cell block, a holding zone for prisoners awaiting trail. No prisoner ever spent the night there. They were transported to the cell block from their jails in the mornings and taken back in the evenings when court had ended.

On a lower floor, there was a second cell block that had never been used, was still freshly painted, and contained none of the prisoner smells associated with the other. Designed for overflow, only two cells and a narrow corridor, it was really quite well suited for the task that lay ahead.

The records would be stored there, in the cells. Three rectangular tables had been placed in the corridor. The working space was comfortable, although the bars were a grim reminder of what the job was all about.

The agents had begun sifting through the records as soon as they had been produced, looking for evidence of secret ownership or anything else that would provide corroboration.

The grand jury was in session. John Stavaros's accountant had just finished testifying. He had asked no questions, smiled throughout his appearance, and seemed not at all concerned about having his records subpoenaed. Stavaros had instructed him to be compliant.

All during the morning's session, Higdon sat in his usual seat, quiet, unobtrusive. It was not time yet.

Gerald Stoffman was the next witness. Silverman watched him take the stand, his right hand raised, as the stenographer delivered the oath. Stoffman's youthful appearance surprised him; he had sounded older on the phone.

In his late thirties, certainly no older than forty, Stoffman was tall and thin, with light brown hair that always looked perfectly coiffed.

This was a man who had begun to make money very quickly. His elaborate clothing, visibly expensive, telegraphed it. The same was true of his jewelry: gold cuff links too large, too ornamental, wrist watch nothing less than extravagant. Strong cologne permeated his presence.

Stoffman was not the first such person impressed with his position and himself that Silverman had come across in there. What surprised him, though, was their consistent failure to appreciate the need for dressing more sensibly for the grand jury. Those twenty-three ordinary people out there—probably without consciously knowing why—would dislike Stoffman from the moment they laid eyes on him.

The oath completed, Stoffman entered the witness box.

Silverman began his questioning with routine matters—full name, business address, date of birth, social security number. The witness shifted in his chair impatiently, his answers loaded with scorn.

Silverman's next task, the routine advice of rights, began with a little lecture about the need for truthfulness. He then reminded the witness of the penalties for perjury and false declaration. Stoffman's eyes widened slightly in disbelief that he was expected to endure this, to be spoken to as if he were a common criminal. He pressed back into his chair, his annoyance impeding his concentration. Silverman informed him of his right to have an attorney, who could remain outside in the hall and be available for consultation.

"Look," he snapped, "are you trying to tell me I need a lawyer? Because if you are, I'll go get one." He leaned menacingly forward in the witness box. "If you'll cut through this legal mumbo jumbo and tell me what you're after, maybe we can get somewhere. You're wasting my time and my client's money . . ."

Before Silverman could respond, Higdon came to life. He put his hand on Silverman's arm, indicating to his young colleague that he would handle it. He leaned forward slowly and placed his arms deliberately on the table, poised for battle. There was a storm brewing within Higdon, and Stoffman could see it.

When Higdon finally spoke, his words were soft and deliberate.

"Mr. Stoffman, is it?" Higdon asked. The accountant nodded. "Well . . . Mr. Stoffman," Higdon repeated, the faint smile on his lips conveying anything but friendliness. "I think we have to come to some understanding here. You see these people?" Higdon's eyes slowly scanned the room.

"Well, you see, these people are the grand jury. And you . . . Mr. Stoffman . . . are here because *they* have compelled your appearance. You took an oath just now. Remember that?" he asked, his voice rising. "You swore to tell the truth. In a moment, Mr. Silverman is going to tell you about your right to invoke the Fifth Amendment and refuse to answer questions because a truthful answer may tend to incriminate you. But for now, I want you to understand way down in your gut . . . Mr. Stoffman . . . that you don't have a choice. You are here to testify . . . to answer questions. That's your job today, Mr. Stoffman. Asking questions is Mr. Silverman's.

"You do not run this proceeding here, Mr. Stoffman. This is not your accounting firm. This is a grand jury, and you are a witness and nothing more. And with respect to this mumbo jumbo you referred to, let me put it to you in plain English.

"You see these people here? They have the power to indict you and send you to prison if you fail to cooperate and testify truthfully. Is that plain enough for you, Mr. Stoffman?"

Higdon had accomplished his purpose. Stoffman was completely cowed. He didn't respond, merely watched Higdon, waiting to see if the prosecutor had finished.

"Speak up, Mr. Stoffman," Higdon demanded. "Answer my question."

"Yes," he whispered.

Satisfied, Higdon sat back and turned to Silverman. Silverman could now continue questioning.

He was asking Stoffman if he had produced everything in his firm's possession described by the subpoena when someone outside rapped on the door. A grand juror opened the door slightly, then motioned for Silverman to come over.

It was Jacobs. He looked excited.

"I've got to see you and Higdon, right now," he said.

A short recess was called. The grand jurors would remain in their seats, and Stoffman, in the witness box. As the prosecutors stepped from the room, Silverman noticed how Stoffman, seated stiffly, was suffering the jurors' curious stares.

Jacobs was animated. "We're on our way," he told them, handing each a small packet of Xeroxed papers. "Here, I've made copies for each of you so you can follow along.

"Look at the top page; that's a copy of the no-longer-elusive Regal nominee agreement."

Silverman smiled victoriously at Higdon.

Jacobs studied his copy. "We found an unsigned copy in Stoffman's Regal Construction tax file. Strangely, though," he said with obvious sarcasm, "the Regal Company records did not contain this agreement. I guess somebody just forgot to give it to us."

Silverman was about to speak; Higdon had already turned to page two.

"Ah, but there's more," said Jacobs. "Understand now, we've made only a cursory examination of the records we've gotten so far. God knows what else there may be in there. Page two..." Silverman flipped the top page of his packet. "Page two is a Xerox of a page I've taken from a corporate charter which legally created and organized a company we never heard of. It's an Ames company; that is, he owns stock in it. The company is called Resort Time, Inc., and as near as I can tell from a quick look at the file, Resort Time owns a resort complex in the Bahamas... It's called the Club something or other; I can't remember right now. Plus it also owns some stock of other companies that own resorts in the Virgin Islands, and I think Vegas. But Resort Times's main asset is the Club whatever it is that it owns outright.

"Resort Time was not listed on the directory. Stoffman's firm does the accounting work for it, and he probably produced the records because of the catchall language in the subpoena... 'including, but not limited to' and so forth..."

Silverman thought of the additional company Stoffman had mentioned on the phone.

"Now listen carefully," Jacobs continued. "Page two, in front of you, is a page I've selected from the corporate charter. The corporate charter document in Stoffman's file was an onion-skin copy; the original must be in the lawyer's file. As you can see, because of the thin paper, it was hard to Xerox. Now the page I selected is the one which lists how the stock of Resort Time, Inc. is to be distributed. There are three names, the first of which is Donald Ames. Forget the other two for now."

Jacobs grinned at the prosecutors. "I know you're both thinking, well, this is interesting, but why is he telling us this now, when the grand jury's in session." He turned to the last page of the packet. "This is why.

"If you turn to the last page, page three, you will see what at first looks like an identical version of page two, only the print is much paler. Page three was not found in the Resort Time file. We found it just a few moments ago when we were reviewing the records in another file Stoffman produced. The name of the file is unimportant. The document we found is apparently a Xeroxed copy of the one we found in the Resort Time, Inc. file. Somebody must have made himself a copy of that one page. We found this page folded over twice and stuck between two pages of a loose-leaf ledger, obviously misplaced.

"And now for the interesting part. It didn't Xerox well because it's in pencil. But if you'll look next to Ames's name and the amount of stock he was issued, you'll see that someone has written in the margin in pencil: 'D.E.A., 66.5 percent,'— that's Donald Edward Ames—and then directly below that 'P.B.L., 33.5 percent.' Apparently, somebody wanted to remind himself of something, and it looks like that something may be that Ames only owns two-thirds of the stock issued in his name and is holding the other one-third for someone else . . . Mr. P.B.L."

They knew without asking whose initials those were. Phillip Brooke Lane, mayor of Philadelphia.

Silverman experienced a strange chilling sensation.

"Do you think—" he began.

"Wait a minute. Hold it." Higdon handed his papers back to Jacobs. Now was not the time to attempt to consider all the possibilities, but there was an opportunity to be taken advantage of.

"Listen closely," he said. "This is what we're going to do.

Bob, go downstairs and get me the folded paper that you found in the other file—the actual piece of paper; that's the one with the original penciling on it, right?"

"Right. It's a Xerox of the onion-skin page with the penciled notations written in the margin."

"Okay. I understand," Higdon continued. "I want that and about, oh, let's see . . . five or six other papers. Take them out of the Resort Time tax file."

Higdon outlined his plan. He was going to enjoy watching Stoffman squirm.

The two prosecutors re-entered the grand jury room. Holding the packet of papers he had gotten from Jacobs, Silverman walked to his seat. He finished questioning Stoffman about the subpoenaed documents. Then, as Higdon had suggested, he rose, picked up the new papers, and placed them on the ledge of the witness box.

"Some recent matters have come to our attention," he said to Stoffman, standing in front of him. "I want to ask you some questions."

He lifted the first sheet.

"I hand you grand jury exhibit one for today. Exhibit one, you will see, is a copy of an agreement which states, in part, that Donald Ames and John Stavaros—" He turned to the stenographer. "That's S-T-A-V-A-R-O-S," he said, then turned back to the witness. "That Ames and Stavaros hold an undisclosed interest, financial interest, in Regal Construction Company. Their interest is held in the names of nominees . . . front men, if you will. Now I represent to you, sir, that grand jury exhibit one came from your firm's tax file on Regal. How long has your firm done the accounting and tax return preparation work for Regal?"

"I don't know exactly. I would say about five years, ever since Mr. Ames acquired an interest."

"I see. Who did the accounting work before then?"

"Brown and Struthers."

"What information do you have as to why Mr. Ames and the other gentleman have a secret interest in Regal, a company whose business is to build and improve public roads?"

"Information? What information do I have?"

"Yes, right, that's the question."

"I don't know what you mean." Stoffman looked nervously at Higdon, bracing himself for a further attack. But Higdon seemed inattentive. Nevertheless, Stoffman kept his eyes on Higdon while Silverman repeated the question.

"What information do you have as to why?"

"Why? Well, I don't, uh, uhm, have any direct information."

"Mr. Stoffman, if you have any information, direct or indirect, please tell us what it is."

Out of the corner of his eye, he thought he saw Higdon shift in his seat. "All I have is hearsay information."

"Hearsay information is admissible in this grand jury room; this is not a courtroom," Silverman instructed him. "Did you speak to someone about this? If so, tell us to whom you spoke and what was said."

Stoffman looked down at the stenographer; this was going to be on the record. His face betrayed his discomfort. "I, uh, had a conversation with Mr. Ames about it. It was a while ago, and I cannot tell you word for word what was said."

"Of course you can't; I'm not asking you to. Just tell us, as best you can, what you can remember. But tell us *all* that you can remember."

"Well, Mr. Ames called me several years ago and told me that he and the other gentleman had purchased controlling interest in a construction company. He said that they would be holding their stock through nominees . . . Mr. Silverman, may I make a statement?"

"Yes, so long as it is relevant."

"Well, I just want to say that you used the word 'front men' before when speaking of this agreement." Self-consciously, he held the exhibit toward the prosecutor. "There's nothing wrong with someone holding a financial interest in anything through a nominee so long as all the tax consequences are taken care of—you know, if income is reported properly and so forth."

"Mr. Stoffman, do you know what kind of work Regal does and for whom?"

"Yes. Regal builds and improves streets and roads. They have been, and are, doing that for the city of Philadelphia. Their work is awarded on the basis of competitive bidding; the lowest bidder gets the job. Nobody gives Regal anything unless their bid is the lowest."

"Let's get back to your conversation with Donald Ames. What else did he tell you?"

"Well, he said that the lawyers had drafted an agreement, that everything was going to be done by the letter of the law." He stopped, leaned back slightly, Higdon in his sight. "And he told me that he unfortunately had to have a nominee hold his interest, because if the press"—he decided not to mention the government—"and certain others learned that he owned an interest in the company, they wouldn't leave him alone and would make a lot of nasty, unfounded innuendoes. He said he didn't care for himself, but that, uhm, he would not do anything to unjustly embarrass"—Stoffman was not going to be the first one to volunteer the mayor's name in the grand jury—"certain individuals. That's all I can remember of the conversation."

The witness was ready for Silverman's inevitable question asking for the identity of "certain individuals." But the prosecutor surprised him. He asked Stoffman to excuse him for a moment and turned away to whisper something to Higdon.

Stoffman tried to overhear their conversation but couldn't. He looked at the jurors, but feeling their hostility, remained fixed in his position, looking, instead, at the exhibit still in his hand. After a few seconds of skimming, he put it down in front of him, then noticed the small pile of documents lying on the ledge. The top paper was facing up. He looked over at the prosecutors; they were still talking. He quickly looked to his right; the stenographer had turned from his machine and was smoking a cigarette. Stoffman glanced at the top sheet, tilting his head a bit in order to read it.

In his nervousness, he hardly saw the document at first. Then it came into focus. As he began to read the paper, he instantaneously forgot his surroundings. My God, that's impossible, he thought; that paper was in the private Ames file, the file in my locked cabinet where I keep the private papers. They must have burglarized my cabinet; they must have the whole file. He panicked. No, it couldn't be. How did they get it? It's folded; that's the paper. How much do they know? My God, what are they going to ask me about that? Should I ask for a lawyer?

Silverman could not see the accountant, but he could see Higdon, watching and reacting. Higdon waited while Stoffman stared at the Resort Time paper, and Silverman saw his mouth curl just slightly upward—not a smile, merely interest. His fish was nibbling at the bait. When Higdon was satisfied that the trick had worked, he leaned toward Silverman.

"Okay, get him out of here," he whispered.

Silverman turned around. His movement caused the startled Stoffman to jump away too quickly; he was a child caught in the act. He stared at Silverman and saw him turn the papers over, but he couldn't tell if Silverman knew he had read the page.

"Mr. Stoffman," Silverman said, smiling, "that's all we

65

have for you for today. We are going to go through your records in the next several weeks, and you may very well be back here, sir, to answer more questions. Is there anything you would like to say before you are excused?"

Stoffman had not yet caught up to Silverman. He sat and waited for his brain to compute what he had just heard, then absent-mindedly shook his head. Silverman pointed to the stenographer, so Stoffman began speaking. "Oh . . . uhm, no. No. I have, uhm, nothing. Uhm . . . no."

Silverman told him he could leave. Stoffman's eyes shot involuntarily to the overturned packet as he quickly rose. As he walked into the hall, he barely noticed the black man leaning against the wall, watching him.

The door to the grand jury room closed. The jurors began mumbling; most of what had just happened had been lost on them. Mrs. Franklin raised her hand. Silverman left, leaving Higdon to handle the question.

He smiled at Jacobs. "Let's get the group B subpoenas out. Don't forget to add Resort Time, Inc. to the list."

Silverman headed down the hall ahead of Jacobs. Before he knew it, he was almost running. Consciously, he slowed his pace, tried to keep the adrenalin shooting through him in check. He didn't want Jacobs to see him uncontrolled. Damn, he thought. This is really happening. There's a case. And he and Higdon were on to it.

Donald Ames was finishing dinner. He had spoken to his wife only when necessary; it had been a marriage of appearance for some time now. He put down his fork, asked the servant to bring him a brandy in his study, excused himself, and went upstairs. After closing the door to his study, he walked to the window, pulled the drapes back, and stared outside. He then went to his desk and dialed the phone.

"Hello . . ." Mrs. Nelson answered.

"Yes, hello, Mrs. Nelson. This is Donald Ames. I'm terribly sorry to bother you at home."

"Oh, it's no bother at all, Mr. Ames," the mayor's secretary assured him with deference.

"Mrs. Nelson, I would like to see him tomorrow night. I know this is short notice, but perhaps he and I could have dinner together, say, around eight, eight-thirty."

"Oh, I'm sorry, Mr. Ames. He already has a dinner engagement, but I'm sure if you'd like to dine with him, he would . . ."

"No, no, that's not necessary," he interrupted. "Tell him that I'll be at his home at eleven P.M."

"I'm sure that will be satisfactory, Mr. Ames."

There was no need for Ames to instruct Mrs. Nelson to keep this confidential. She had been with the mayor for years and was well aware of the close relationship between the two men. He thanked her and said good-bye.

"Can I get you something?" Mary Ann asked as she walked through the living room, her third trip since Jamie fell asleep.

"Uhm?" Silverman said, his video game allowing no competition for his attention.

Mary Ann looked down at him. It's no use, she thought. She didn't bother to repeat the question. If Silverman had looked up, he would have seen the hurt in her eyes, but his eyes remained glued to the screen. He didn't notice as she turned and left the room.

Mary Ann sat on his side of the bed, her best nightgown on, her hair freshly brushed. It was best to leave him alone, she thought. For now.

6

    Silverman lowered the racing form and grinned at the Subway Lady. Things were looking up. A couple of days left in the month and his system was finally working.

He was picking winners, might even end up with a small profit this month—at least less of a loss. The lights flickered as they approached the next station.

The case was moving all right too. Stoffman had fallen for the bait. No question but that the accountant had run to Ames.

And the group B subpoenas had been served. Soon those records would be coming in as well, so there would be plenty of work for the agents who were still digging their way through the group A records.

And there was a new dimension. Well, a possible new dimension, he thought, trying not to be overly optimistic. In a way, he didn't want to think about it. "P.B.L." The mayor. Higdon had said that men like the mayor were too smart, too clever; they wouldn't leave a trail. But he hadn't even for a moment considered the possibility of noninvolvement or innocence. It was guilt by association. If Ames was your friend and you were a public official, in Higdon's book, you belonged in prison.

Silverman thought about the paper Jacobs had found. Was it evidence of some crime or merely part of a logical explanation of innocent conduct?

He hungered to speculate. Mary Ann had listened, but he couldn't expect a professional analysis from her. He wanted to share his projections with someone involved in the case, but he and Jacobs were barely speaking. Their relationship was strictly business, and he was at a loss to characterize his relationship with Higdon.

They were working together now. That pleased him. But communication with Higdon was permitted only when necessary for the performance of a given task. He wasn't complaining, though. Things were a lot better now than they had been.

Silverman rose as the train entered the Fifth Street Station.

"Please call down to the records room and get Jacobs on the line," Silverman said to Jan as he entered his office.

As he was hanging his coat on the rack, she buzzed.

"Yeah, Bob?"

"No, it's Jan. The agents say he's over at IRS, at a meeting."

"Oh, okay. Call over there for me, will you?"

"Miss Eccleston's on the other line, holding."

"Okay. I'll take it. Get Jacobs when I hang up."

"Hello, Anne. This is John."

"Yes, John. I called Ray, but he isn't in."

What else is new, thought Silverman as he waited patiently for her to tell him what she wanted.

"I had a call this morning from the state attorney general . . . Bill Grasmick. I was out, but he left a message that his call was in reference to the subpoena served on the State Roads Commission."

Silverman hoped that Higdon had informed her of the latest grand jury happenings so that he wouldn't have to explain. "Ray's spoken to you, hasn't he?"

"Oh, yes . . . I thought it might be appropriate for Ray to return his call. He . . . and you are up on all the details of the case . . ." Ann Eccleston was not one to engage voluntarily in the adversary process. "Since Ray's out, perhaps you would want to call him."

"Sure, did he leave any other message—you know, anything about his reaction or the state's reaction to the subpoena?"

"No, nothing."

"Okay, Anne, I'll call him."

"John, I know Bill Grasmick. He's a very decent man."

What did she mean, Silverman thought? Another blue blood? He knew the man only by reputation. It was a good one. That was good enough for him.

"Hello, sir. This is Assistant U.S. Attorney John Silverman. I'm returning your call to Miss Eccleston."

The voice that Silverman heard was unmistakably that of a politician; the deep, resonant, friendly tone belonged to a man who had spent considerable time winning votes.

"Yes, John, appreciate your calling. I frankly wasn't sure whom to call; I decided that protocol required my initial contact be with the U.S. attorney herself. I figured she should at least be given the option to involve herself in this matter personally."

Her reputation must be known far and wide, Silverman thought. "Yes, sir. Well, you're speaking with the right person now."

"Frankly, I thought I'd be speaking with Raymond Higdon. Isn't he in charge of this case?"

Silverman stiffened but told himself to remain cordial. He explained, almost too politely, that he had been assigned to the case and if the state attorney general wanted to speak with someone, it would be he.

Bill Grasmick told Silverman that the commissioner of the State Roads Commission had complained bitterly about the subpoena and had asked him to go to court and fight it. There was no animosity in Grasmick's voice as he told Silverman the Commissioner felt the subpoena was unreasonably broad and oppressive.

Silverman prepared himself for yet another "subpoena conversation" and was about to respond when Grasmick assured him he would not stand in the grand jury's way and that the records would be produced. He wanted to know if the federal agents would come up to Harrisburg to look at the records. Silverman said no.

Without any loss of friendliness in his voice, Grasmick once again assured Silverman that the records would be produced without a fight. But since there were a lot of records, could he have a one-week postponement? He told Silverman that if he'd like to think it over and call back, that would be all right.

Silverman caught Grasmick's tactfulness. If Silverman were unable to make the decision without Higdon's approval, he was being given a graceful way out. That was decent of him, Silverman thought.

There weren't going to be any bombshells in those records; the files merely contained necessary data for proof at trial later on. Silverman said he didn't need any time to think it over. He granted the extension.

"Thank you, John. I appreciate your courtesy. I'll write you a letter confirming this conversation and our agreement."

Silverman waited for his good-bye. There was a pause.

"John . . ."

"Sir . . ."

He'd changed his mind. "Good luck" was all he said.

Silverman had a strange sense that Grasmick knew something. Did he have information that they were on the right track? Did he know about Ames or Stavaros? Whatever it was, Silverman knew it would stay with Bill Grasmick, politician.

He walked out to Jan's desk.

"You can get Jacobs now."

"I called over there, John," she said, obviously puzzled. "They said he told them he was over here with you."

"Do we have his home number?"

She reached for her employees' roster. "Yes, I have it. I'll try him there."

This poolroom was like the others in North Philadelphia. Even those accustomed to "hanging out" there had no difficulty sensing the hostility that crept through the smoky, darkened room. The wrong movement, word, even the wrong look, could trigger the eruption of violence, sometimes death.

Today, like most days, the poolroom was busy. Loud music pounded from an old distorted speaker, cue balls clicked, and the men played or watched others play. This was the graveyard for the neighborhood's young, futureless wastes.

Overcoat unbuttoned, tie loosened at the neck, Robert Jacobs stood inside the doorway, waiting for his eyes to adjust to the darkness. A few of the customers recognized him. They stopped playing. He was not welcome here, no longer one of them.

He walked a few feet into the room. A tall man with a beard and an earring dangling menacingly from his left ear stepped in his way, slapping his cue stick against his open palm. Jacobs looked at him, then stepped away. He saw whom he'd come for, a young man, a shade darker than he was, thin, his clothes slept in, sitting on the rotting bench against the wall.

"Get up, Jimmy," he ordered his brother.

Jimmy peered over his sunglasses. "Fuck off, man. Leave me alone," he growled.

Jacobs grabbed his brother's collar and swooped him to his feet. He removed his sunglasses and looked at his eyes.

"You're on that shit again. Jesus fucking Christ!"

The man with the earring came over and pressed his cue stick against Jacobs's arm. "Leave the brother alone," he warned.

All activity in the room had stopped; everyone stood silently, watching, anticipating.

71

Jacobs pushed the stick from his arm. "You lookin' to die?" he asked, his voice betraying his own youth in the streets. The man retreated.

Without another word, Jacobs pushed his brother toward the door. They walked home, Jacobs nudging his brother each time he slowed down.

"As if I don't have enough trouble already," he said, shoving Jimmy onto the living-room couch. "I'm not going to let you kill Momma . . . Look at you!"

Jimmy rose, swaying, too high for coherence.

"Fuck you, man. I don't got to listen to you. You ain't nothin'."

The phone rang. Jacobs ignored it. He pushed his brother back on the sofa, his muscular arm remaining extended as though Jimmy would bounce up again like a rubber ball.

"You're going to go to that shrink. Now I pay for those appointments whether you go or not. You miss one more like today, man, you're not going to be able to walk to that pool-room."

The phone hadn't stopped. Annoyed, Jacobs turned and grabbed the receiver.

"Yeah. Who is it?"

"It's the guy you told everyone you're with." Silverman had him now.

"You know, Bob, this can't go on. There's a lot of work to do. Now I don't want to have to go to your superiors . . ."

"Look, Silverman." Jacobs was steaming. "I'm coming in later. And I'm coming to see you." He hung up, stared at his brother slumped on the couch, and shook his head. How difficult was life going to be?

Jan stood in the doorway. Silverman, still angry from the call to Jacobs, hadn't noticed her at first.

"There's a call for you."

He didn't feel like talking to anyone. "Take a message."

"It's Richard Franklin White calling from Washington."

Richard White? Why is Richard White calling me, thought Silverman. White was a nationally famous criminal defense lawyer, his clients the rich and powerful. He reached for the phone.

"Hello."

"Yes. Hi. This is Dick White. How are you?"

"*The* Richard White?" He heard laughter.

"You're too kind, too kind," he said. "My recognition factor only serves to make me a bigger target for you young Turks. It makes you all work harder at night so you can beat my ass in court the next day."

Silverman laughed. "I haven't heard of too many who've succeeded. What can I do for you, sir."

"I've been retained to look into some grand jury subpoenas that were served on the custodian of records of about twenty or so of Donald Ames's companies."

"Seventeen."

"Seventeen."

"Do you represent the companies and Mr. Ames or only the companies, Mr. White?" Silverman was searching for some clue as to how concerned Ames might be. Had Ames already gotten himself a defense lawyer? A lawyer like Richard Franklin White?

"That's unclear at the moment. It all depends on what you fellas up there want. Let's say, for purposes of this discussion, I'm authorized to speak for Mr. Ames as majority stockholder of the subpoenaed companies."

Silverman knew the term *majority stockholder* was ambiguous; it could mean that White's clients were the businesses, with Ames as a client only insofar as he owned majority financial interests, or it meant that Donald Ames had retained him as his personal criminal defense lawyer. The chess game had begun.

"Needless to say," White continued, "my representation is in connection with your grand jury investigation only."

"Needless to say." Silverman was on his guard. He chose his words carefully. This was, after all, Richard Franklin White.

"But tell me, John, since you brought it up, are you guys looking to indict Ames?" White's casualness was disarming. He was testing the young prosecutor, making mental calculations about experience and ability.

Silverman had learned that the answer to a question that assumed that a client had been targeted for indictment so soon after the grand jury had begun subpoenaing records and before they had collected evidence would return to haunt the government at a later date in court. He laughed.

"Now you know I can't answer an awful question like that. Why, it assumes all sorts of terrible things. If you've called about some subpoenas, though, I'd be happy to discuss them with you."

Knight to Bishop Three.

White sighed. "Your subpoenas are extremely broad and

vague. They call for too many records. But we are more than willing to cooperate with your inquiry. So, if you will send me a letter describing the particular documents you want, we'd be happy to send them to you . . . originals or copies, it doesn't matter. Of course, we would want you to rewrite the subpoenas to make them call for the specific records; otherwise, I'm afraid we're going to have to file a motion to quash those subpoenas as unreasonably broad and oppressive."

"Sorry, I can't agree." Silverman knew that White did not expect affirmative answers to these questions. He was offering to "cooperate" only for the record; he wanted to be able to tell the judge that *his* client had tried to be reasonable with the government. He was also trying to trick him into giving something away.

"Well, if we produce all of these records, it will disrupt the business operations of many of these companies." White sounded sincerely concerned. "We'd be happy to make the records available to you in our offices; your agents could go over there and have full access to them."

Sure, Silverman thought. That way Ames could keep tabs on what we're finding out.

"I can't agree to that, either. But most of the records are noncurrent, from the last six years. Tell your clients that they can have access to them while they're in the grand jury's custody. And you have my word that we will review and return the current records promptly." Silverman, too, had to appear cooperative—for the record.

"John, I'd sure like to be able to come to some agreement with you on these damn subpoenas . . . Look, in return for some concessions from you, we might even answer some questions now. If you'll agree to help us out on these subpoenas, well . . . you can submit written questions to us and we'll consider answering them."

Silverman caught the nearly muted "*consider* answering." He asked if White would give his word that Donald Ames personally would answer all questions in writing and under oath. White laughed. Game one was over.

"John, I guess I'm going to have to file a motion to quash these subpoenas." There was never any doubt in either lawyer's mind that this is how it would end. "Who's the grand jury judge in this case?"

"Montarelli, Dominic Montarelli."

"Hmm. Good judge. Okay. Would you mind if I called him to tell him that we are about to file a motion to quash the subpoenas and to ask for a hearing in chambers? I'll tell him the government would like the hearing as soon as possible."

Technically, it was improper for a lawyer to communicate with a judge ex parte, without the other side present. Silverman knew he could trust a lawyer like White to speak to the judge alone, on an introductory basis, and not make unfair representations. But he didn't want White to have the opportunity to charm the judge—and with White, probably to impress the hell out of the judge, as well.

"Why don't you call the judge's law clerk and explain the situation to him; he'll tell the judge." He expected White to insist.

"Okay. What's the law clerk's name?"

"George Bryant."

"I'll have my assistant drop a copy of the motion off to you at your office."

"Okay, thanks."

"I hear Ray Higdon is also working this case. Is that true?" A lawyer of White's caliber was much too experienced to label any prosecutor junior or senior. In due time, he would see for himself who was in control.

"Ray and I are working this case together. Do you know him?"

"I know him," White said. Silverman could sense that White had something against Higdon and did not want to discuss it. His friendliness returned.

"Listen, John. Save some time after the hearing. We'll shmooze, get to know each other a little. I have a feeling we're going to be seeing each other more and more as the days go by."

"Sure, love to."

"Mr. Silverman?"

"Yes?"

He had just entered the waiting room, on his way out. She had been sitting in one of the seats. She rose, extended her hand.

"Hi. Denise Owens. *Philadelphia Inquirer*."

They shook hands.

"I asked for Mr. Higdon," she explained, "but I understand he's not in today."

"Uh uh."

"I was told you're working with him?"

He looked her over. She looked like a reporter. A bit unkempt, her clothing a near miss at stylishness—the result of living too long on a reporter's salary. Part midwestern American prettiness, part unmistakable intelligence, her features emitted, if not beauty, a certain engaging quality.

"What can I do for you?" he asked.

"Can we, uhm, talk someplace?"

"About what?"

"You're working on the grand jury probe, aren't you?"

"How are we talking?"

"On the record."

There were rules for this game, too. Silverman had learned them. "On the record" meant that whatever he said could be printed verbatim and attributed directly to him.

"On the record," he repeated. "That's easy. We don't need time, Miss . . ."

"Owens."

"Miss Owens. On the record, no comment. Bye."

He walked out into the hallway, leaving her in the waiting room. Recovering quickly, she followed, catching up to him at the elevator.

"How do you want to speak?" she asked, her tone revealing her effort to engage him in conversation.

"I don't."

He pressed the down button.

"How about deep background?" she asked.

Deep background meant that the reporter could use the speaker's words but not in direct quotations. And she was not permitted to identify the speaker in the article. She could only credit "a source" or "a source close to the investigation."

The elevator's frosted white down light blinked on; there was a quick, dull metallic chime as the doors opened.

"You're wasting your time, Miss Owens," he said, stepping into the already-filled noontime elevator. "There's nothing for us to talk about."

She pushed her way in beside him. They rode the crowded elevator in silence. She tilted her head to see which newspaper he carried folded under his arm. She saw it was the *Daily Racing Form*, thought it was an odd choice for a prosecutor but decided it would be best not to ask about it. It might prove counterproductive to her efforts.

When they were both out of the elevator, she asked, "Going to lunch?"

"Yeah." He continued walking, quickening his pace a bit.

"Mind if I join you?"

He stopped and turned.

"Miss Owens, I said there was nothing to talk about. I'm only going to the federal cafeteria for a quick sandwich, and then I've got some personal business to take care of." Delicately, he pushed the racing form farther into the tight space between his arm and ribs. He nodded what he hoped was his final good-by and continued walking.

"Mr. Silverman," she called, moving behind him.

At first, he continued walking, hopeful that she would finally give up. Then, abruptly, he stopped and turned, his stance displaying clear annoyance.

When she had caught up to him, she stopped, pushed back some loose strands of brown hair from her forehead, and adjusted her shoulder bag as if to show him that she, too, was becoming weary of the chase. She sighed softly and smiled. She was prettier than she first appeared, her green eyes both gentle and sharp.

"Okay, we don't have to talk about your case. My editor has assigned me to the federal court. It's my new beat. I don't know anyone here yet—except you, I guess." She smiled again. "Can't we at least be friends?"

He stared at her. As he turned, he spoke.

"Come on," he said with gentle resignation. "But no questions about investigations."

She quickened her pace to keep up with his, deciding she'd wait until they were eating before trying again.

The cafeteria's serving area, a large space separated from the dining area by the cashiers' counters, was designed with a marketplacelike motif. The food was served from behind several stalls, one each for hot dishes, cold prepared sandwiches, and the like. Denise selected a paper dish filled with cottage cheese from the "Farmer's Market Salad Bar." She held it up, examining the maraschino cherry pressed under the tight plastic wrapping, a few drops of its crimson juice having been absorbed by the chalk-white cheese. She searched for a more appetizing one; this seemed the best of the lot. She shrugged and took it with her to the coffee line.

Silverman paid the cashier for his sandwich; tray in hand, he headed for the tables at the floor-length windows. He noticed the four IRS agents who had been working with Jacobs seated in the center of the room and walked over to them.

"Hi, John," one of them said as he approached. The others turned and said hello.

"Hey, guys. How's it going?"

They said they were fine. He smiled and was about to leave when one of them rose.

"Uhm, John, can I speak with you for a minute?" he asked, circling the table and approaching him.

Just then, Denise approached, carrying her tray. He motioned to the tables along the glass wall and told her he'd be there in a minute.

"What's up?" he asked the agent.

Obviously uncomfortable at what he had decided to say, the agent shuffled slightly and looked away.

"Uhm, you may think this is none of our business," he began, "but we heard about uhm . . . what happened this morning . . . you know, with Jacobs." He shrugged, deciding not to tell him that Jan had overheard him on the phone with Jacobs, and had told some of the other secretaries. "Things like that travel fast around here, I guess."

Silverman was about to tell him that it *was*, in fact, none of his business, but the agent continued.

Jacobs was a widower; his wife had died several years ago. Accidentally shot during a supermarket holdup, she had died in the arms of one of her children. Since then, he'd been trying to hold his family together. His mother, old and in ill health, lived with them.

There were three children. The oldest was twelve now and was a constant source of trouble. It had been in his arms that his mother had died, and he hadn't been the same since.

Jacobs had also resumed responsibility for one of his brothers. The agent wasn't quite sure what his problem was; Jacobs very rarely spoke about him.

He told him that Jacobs had already been in trouble for taking more leave time than was due him to tend to his never-ending family emergencies. He'd received an administrative warning; one more such incident and he might be in danger of losing his job.

The agent and the others at the table waited for a reaction. But Silverman could say nothing. Hearing the story of Jacobs's life made him feel chastened, ashamed of his treatment of him. He thanked the agent for the information and headed toward the table where Denise was waiting.

He had really misjudged Jacobs. He had never really given him a chance to explain, had jumped to conclusions, had been accusatory from the first incident. Just like a rookie prosecutor. And Jacobs would storm in for a showdown this afternoon. Wonderful.

Denise was removing the plastic wrapping from her dish as he placed his tray on the table. She noticed he looked a bit sullen.

"Cherry?" she asked, holding up the sticky red maraschino.

He shook his head and unwrapped his sandwich. She placed the cherry in the ash tray, realizing it was up to her to begin the conversation.

"So, how long have you been in the office?"

"Couple of years."

"Where'd you go to law school?"

"Harvard."

"Oh!"

She stabbed at her cottage cheese.

Now seemed like as good a time as any to try again. She looked at him.

"I've already got the story. All I want is a comment from your office."

He put down his sandwich and stared at her.

Nervous, she quickly continued.

"Several days ago, your grand jury subpoenaed State Road Commission records, and you also subpoenaed the records of some private companies . . ."

"I thought we agreed that we wouldn't talk about investigations."

"Look, what I need is names." She leaned forward with an air of confidentiality, ignoring his protest. "I don't have the names yet, but I think I've got enough to write that you've already involved several public officials in this thing."

She sat back, trying to sound as authoritative as possible. "Now unless you tell me right here and now that I'm wrong, my editors are probably going to let me write it. You can tell me on deep background."

Silverman smiled, shaking his head.

"Miss Owens," he said quietly, "don't try and bullshit me. If you've got something, write it. But don't try to con me into discrediting one of your theories. I will neither confirm nor deny that there is an investigation underway or that subpoenas have been issued. If you want to write about public officials, go ahead. It's your ass. If you're right, you've got a scoop. If you're wrong—well, a bright, attractive woman like you can always do something else for a living."

She could see that she was getting nowhere. Silverman wasn't going to be easy.

She reached for her handbag and took out her cigarettes.

"You mind?"

"No. Not at all."

She blew out the match, gray wisps of smoke filtering their way to the ceiling.

"All right. I've got the part about the subpoenas," she said, pointing her cigarette at him accusingly. "And I'm going to write it. Whether you comment or not."

He shrugged.

"Listen, Silverman," she said, smiling. "You'd better get used to me because I'm going to be bugging you."

Her lips were a bit on the thin side, but her smile was warm and pretty. He watched as she pushed back a lock of hair from her forehead.

"Owens," he said, mimicking her, "you are very pushy."

"Well, I like you, too," she said, rising, her shoulder bag already on her arm. "See you, Silverman." She smiled and walked away.

Robert Jacobs stood before him, glaring.

Seated behind his desk, Silverman raised his hands, palms outward, as if he were a policeman stopping traffic. He smiled faintly.

"Before you get started," he said, clearing his throat, "I'd like to say something."

7

On the side of the building, below the restaurant's name was a small, inconspicuous sign: STORYVILLE—LOWER LEVEL. Inside was an empty Italian restaurant, the tables set for the next day's business. Jacobs pointed to the stairway. They could hear the music below.

As they walked down the narrow carpeted stairs, the music grew louder. At the bottom was a large dark room. The band was off to the right, and there were small square formica tables radiating out toward the ends of the room. For a week night, there was a decent crowd.

Jacobs was chatting with the maître d'. "John, come over here; I want you to meet someone."

The maître d'. was a tall black man sporting a well-trimmed Vandyke beard. His wrists were filled with silver bracelets, and he wore a purple and blue tuxedo jacket that reminded Silverman of a tapestry. The music had become louder. They had to shout to make themselves heard.

"John, this is Charles." They shook hands.

While still holding his hand, Charles smiled at Jacobs. "Is this the man, too?"

Jacobs laughed. "Now does he look like the Man?"

"From his Ivy League head down to his Ivy League toe." Charles smiled warmly at Silverman. "Welcome, friend."

Silverman returned the smile, but he felt ill at ease.

This is not what he had expected. He had never really been to a place like it and had declined when Jacobs first suggested it, after Silverman's apology, after they had sat in his office for the better part of two hours, just talking. Silverman and Jacobs were heading toward friendship. He reluctantly had agreed to go because his friend wanted to go. So he had called Mary Ann and told her he'd be home late, ignoring the disappointment in her voice when she'd said fine.

Jacobs was quite a remarkable guy, he had realized as they

81

had talked in his office. One daughter in prep school, full scholarship. "Just as pretty as Betty was," Jacobs had said, momentarily avoiding Silverman's gaze, the memory of his slain wife still painful. A brother, his ward, addicted to heroin. A son who idolized his brother and loathed his father. "The Man," he called him scornfully. Accused him of being a "Tom." Jacobs had smacked him, hard, right across the face. It only made matters worse.

And Jacobs had been full of questions about Silverman. But Silverman hadn't been able to open up. He talked instead at length about his racing game, filling his portion of their conversation with explanations of how he never bet real money, simply handicapped the races with imaginary bets and followed the results in the *Daily Racing Form*, keeping a running tally. He seemed embarrassed, ill at ease, when Jacobs's questions came too close. Jacob hadn't pushed, suggesting a night out instead.

"Where would you like to sit?" Charles asked Jacobs.

"Doesn't matter. Anywhere. How's the group tonight?"

"Well, they're kids—a little rough yet, but not bad. Follow me, gents."

He led them to a table on the far side of the room, about midway from the bandstand. Once they were seated, a waitress came over and took their orders.

Silverman watched the band. Charles was right; they did look young. There were six musicians, some black, some white; all were dressed in jeans. Their instruments looked and sounded electrified. The tempo of the music was quick but seemed a bit louder than it should have been. Silverman wasn't sure, though; he looked around to see if the others were enjoying it.

The room was not shabby, just dark and bare, with a slightly stale smell. As he surveyed the room, he noticed several groups of young people—probably students—with green and brown bottles of beer in front of them. There were some middle-aged black couples, some young women alone. He began instinctively to understand that this was one of those few places where anyone could come and be comfortable alone with the music.

The waitress brought their drinks. Jacobs held his glass high, nodded at Silverman, then turned in his chair toward the band.

Slowly, Silverman began to pay less attention to his surroundings, becoming absorbed in the intricacies of the music. After a while, comfortable and relaxed, he leaned back in his chair and closed his eyes, his mind filled with nothing but music.

Jacobs looked over at Silverman. He ordered another round of drinks and turned back toward the stage.

The morning couldn't have been more dreary. The darkened sky was swollen with moisture, and the dawn had crawled from the night like some ponderous, lumbering child that had been slowly expelled from the womb of its lethargic mother.

It was cold. But the schoolyard was filled, the neighborhood's younger children, behind the high chain-link fence, playing on the blacktop, some in groups, some alone, all waiting for the bell.

Raymond Higdon stood on the sidewalk, as he had on other mornings, and watched the children through the links of the fence. He stood motionless, his shoulders hunched, his hands in the pockets of his old black raincoat. And he watched.

It was a curious sight. This pale, thin, almost frail little man, watching the children. Certainly not the image of a powerful lawyer and federal prosecutor. It must have seemed perverse. But that was not it.

The neighborhood was mostly white, decidedly working-class. The school had been there a long time. It reminded Higdon of another school.

Higdon's apartment was less than a block away, at Lombard and Twenty-fifth. It really wasn't an apartment although years ago, when it was up for rent, that's what the sign had called it. The landlady, in plastic hair curlers and cotton print dress, its faded patterned flowers covering her heavy rear, had led him up the two musty staircases of the narrow row house to the third floor, to a small room with bath. The landlady, ignoring the fire laws, had added a small kitchenette and advertised the room as an apartment. Its size, or name, made no difference to Higdon. It was the neighborhood that drew him. It was like another he had known. And even now. though he could afford to move, he stayed.

Strange how his recollections of that very early period were a mixture of vividness and dreamlike fantasy. He was a child, content, with his mother, in the old neighborhood, the one like this one. He could still remember the schoolyard, playing, his mother there at the bell, smiling, waiting to walk him home. There was no father; never had been. But that neighborhood, the schoolyard, his mother there waiting for him were memories he cherished.

He could still hear the sound of the bell, could still remember that one day, years ago, when it seemed to the child that it would never stop its clamor: shrill, like a scream, persisting. He could still see through the child's eyes, searching at the schoolyard entrance in the group of waiting mothers. But that day she hadn't come.

And he could still see the other woman, unexpectedly crouching before him, her dress hiked up over her bony knees. She didn't have to tell him she was Auntie Flo, didn't have to keep repeating her name. He recognized her. He must have been crying. She held onto each of his arms too tightly and kept asking if he remembered her. She said things to him about Mommy, things he couldn't understand. Not until later, much later actually, when he was taken to see her and he stood before her and watched as she sat, so still, her gaze wide and blank, directed nowhere, catatonic, hospitalized, kept in a public institution she would later die in; not until then did he understand that for him, Mommy was gone.

A ball slammed into the fence, rattling the chain links, then bounced off, and pattered slowly to its death, just inside the yard, but on a line with Higdon's feet.

It brought him back. He watched the little boy run up for the ball, stop, and smile. Higdon simply watched. The boy froze, uncertain. Higdon noticed the teacher, the same woman as before, keeping her distance but pulling the boy away. She knew, he supposed, that he was not a parent. He could see her suspicion, how she watched him whenever he was there, cautiously, always from a safe distance. He didn't care, paid her little attention.

The boy receded into the playground, rejoining his group and becoming once again an indistinguishable component of the mass of children. Higdon's thoughts drifted once more to the past, to the playground of his school, to that day with Auntie Flo.

She had held him so tightly, leading him away. He had struggled, crying, searching frantically through the small group of women for his mother. Then he stood before the big car, dusty brown, its hood so beveled, the tarnished chrome at his eye level a putrid greenish gray. When she opened the door, he could see the suitcase perched on the rear seat. And then he knew.

At first, it was okay living with Auntie Flo. The house was

a real house, with a garden. But there were no other children, no real neighborhood. She'd made a fuss over him at first, though later that changed. Later, it all changed. She spoke of the new school. A proper school; a church school. It had a funny name: All Saints Parochial. The child kept repeating it silently in his mind, afraid that he would have to pronounce it and couldn't. Only a few days alone with Auntie Flo had preceded his first day at the new school.

That first day, the sun's cold fall glare was intense. It seemed to shine too brightly, casting an unnatural brilliance over the playground of All Saints. He had had to squint when the young nun with whom Auntie Flo had left him in the darkened school corridor led him outside, where the other children were.

It had happened that very first day. An incident he had never forgotten, a recurring recollection that retained for him the acute sensations of terror and humiliation that had accompanied the actual experience. And although he had thought about it so often, so many times that he no longer needed to replay the scene in sequence, it never lost its original poignancy.

The little girl had come right up to him almost as soon as he had been left alone in the playground. Her hair was thick and dark, her cheeks part of her rosy smile. She asked him where his tie was. He then noticed the other children had uniforms: the boys wore white shirts and short blue ties with an emblem embroidered on each, and the girls, white blouses with blue skirts. He must have said he didn't know, but she didn't seem to care, and they played. She said she had a secret place; if he would be her friend, he could see it. She led him to the little row of hedges near the gray stone wall where the playground ended and the nuns' residence began.

They sat, as children do, enjoying their hiding place, cozy in their concealed solitude. They were quiet at first, listening to the sounds of the children playing on the adjacent playground.

It was her suggestion. He didn't understand it, and she really didn't, either. It seemed all right, and it was his new friend's suggestion, made to him with her sweet rosy smile.

His pants were down and her skirt up; her underpants, which he noticed were almost the same as those around his ankles, were on the ground near the base of one of the hedges. She was giggling, delighted somehow at what they were doing; and he, well, he didn't know what to feel, as they continued sitting side by side, except a sort of pleasure at having a friend and doing something that seemed to please her. He smiled, and she continued giggling, her little hands curled in front of her mouth.

At first, he simply seemed to be losing his balance, didn't know what was happening until he felt the hand that had grabbed at his shoulder and was pulling him from behind the hedge. The hand yanked him, his pants still around his ankles, back the short distance to the edge of the playground. The other children quickly noticed and began to gather.

He stood before the old nun, her black habit worn shiny in parts. He could hear the snickering of the other children and wanted to bend to retrieve his trousers, but sensed the need for stillness before Mother Theresa.

She said nothing for a moment; then her thin wrinkled mouth curved upward. He mistook her expression, the one he later learned always accompanied punishment, for a smile. Somehow he knew that he should now refasten his pants, so he reached for them. Sister Theresa slowly placed her hand on the boy's head, stroking his hair and speaking softly to him. He smiled up at her. He couldn't understand what she was saying, had no idea what "sin" meant, had never heard the word before.

He continued watching the old nun, towering before him in flowing thick black cloth, then saw the fire slowly begin to blaze in her eyes. He could still see it, as vividly as he had that day, years ago. He was acutely aware of the other children; they had become absolutely silent.

For the first time, he saw the old nun's pale, dry hand as it moved away from his head, noticed the immaculate, crisp fingernails, the blue veins protruding through near-transparent skin. He watched helplessly as the hand slowly lowered and grabbed at his crotch, held the little boy's balls and squeezed until he screamed.

He had never felt such pain, such humiliation; crying, he repeated what she told him to say. He repeated what to him were sounds, not words; he had no idea what he was saying, although instinctively he understood. He was atoning.

When apparently satisfied, she released her grip, turned, and walked slowly away. Whimpering, he stood as the small semicircle of children remained before him, silently staring, then slowly dispersed.

He never went near the little girl again, never played with

the other children. Strangely, it was Mother Theresa that he had carried from that horrible experience. On other days, alone, distant from the other children on the playground, he would watch her. Unknowingly, she became his study; he observed her unobtrusively as she controlled the other children. He watched her inflict punishment, her quiet manner, her exercise of absolute authority. It fascinated him and seemed to fill a void created by recent events. It became for him a substitute for what he no longer would receive from a mother, no longer would seek from others.

By now, most of the children from the playground before which Higdon stood, blindly staring, had entered the school. The teacher, remaining outside near the last few still in line at the entrance, kept a protective watch, her gaze on Higdon, even though the fence separated them.

His hands still in his pockets, Higdon turned and walked back up Lombard Street. He'd be back there again tomorrow. Or maybe the morning after. Back to watch the children on the playground, to let his mind travel back to the old neighborhood and its euphoria, to the old playground and its terror. And to Mother Theresa.

It was already past ten, and Silverman was still in the apartment. He'd gotten home after two the previous night and had been unable to get out of bed when his alarm sounded. He dressed quickly and went into the kitchen to kiss Mary Ann and Jamie good-bye. Mary Ann seemed a bit quieter than usual, but he was late, so he barely noticed. Jamie had toast crumbs and jam over her face and hands. He leaned over gingerly and kissed her quickly before she could do too much damage. The butter and jam tasted good.

He bought a newspaper and caught the train just as it was leaving. The car was half-empty. He scanned the paper—nothing on the front page. He turned to the top page of the local section and searched the headlines; it was in the top right-hand column: "U.S. Subpoenas State Roads Records for City Highway Projects." He quickly read the first paragraph, then skimmed the article, turned to the jump page inside, and read the last paragraph:

Sources close to the case say that veteran prosecutor Raymond Higdon is in charge of the investigation. The sources have indicated that Mr. Higdon's participation is some indication that the Department of Justice considers the probe an important one. Mr. Higdon was unavailable for comment yesterday. Assistant U.S. Attorney John Silverman, who is also assigned to the investigation, refused all comment.

He returned to the first page and read the rest of the article. It was accurate. All it really said was that records had been subpoenaed, and it quoted unnamed sources in the State Roads Commission complaining about the volume of records sought by the subpoena. Another unidentified someone had called the probe a fishing expedition. Ames and Stavaros were not mentioned. Silverman flipped back to the top page again and looked at the by-line. "Denise Owens."

As soon as he arrived at his office, Jan told him that Miss Eccleston wanted to see him or Higdon right away. Higdon wasn't in. He walked down to her office.

Her secretary told him to go right in. He knocked and opened the door. The man with prematurely graying hair seated in the chair in front of Miss Eccleston's desk did not turn around. Silverman walked around to the side, and their eyes met.

They stared at each other in silent recognition. Silverman knew who this man was without ever having seen him before. The man rose.

"This is Mr. Stavaros . . . Assistant U.S. Attorney Silverman," Miss Eccleston said.

They shook hands without speaking; neither looked at Miss Eccleston. Stavaros sat down again; Silverman stood there longer, then took the empty chair next to Stavaros, instinctively moving it away before he sat down. Their eyes never parted. What in hell was he doing here? Silverman thought. And what in hell was she doing meeting with him? Alone. There should be a witness in case there was some later dispute over what was said. What an idiot she was. He looked over at her, waiting for her to fill him in on what had happened so far. She looked nervous.

"Mr. Stavaros and I have been speaking about the subpoenas that were issued to some of his companies." While she continued, he again looked at Stavaros, who hadn't taken his eyes off him. "He seems to think we have been a bit heavy-handed with him. He's, uhm, asked for an explanation of the subpoenas . . ." She stopped, hoping Silverman would speak. He didn't. After the silence became conspicuous, he looked back at her, and she spoke again.

"I've explained to Mr. Stavaros that you and Mr. Higdon are handling this matter and that any explanation should most properly come from you." She seemed satisfied, having feebly managed to throw the ball to him.

He knew he had to exercise extreme caution before he spoke; his words—and whatever Miss Eccleston had said before he got there—would most probably be repeated someday in a court of law. He also had to keep *her* in mind. He couldn't say anything to Stavaros that would embarrass her; that would show him a chink in the government's armor. And if she were stung by his words in front of an important man like Stavaros, she might take it out on him later.

"Thank you, Anne. I appreciate the courtesy." He turned to Stavaros. "I'm sure that I merely echo the sentiments of the U.S. attorney and am about to tell you what she would be saying if she hadn't been kind enough to permit one of the line prosecutors to respond to your inquiry." Stavaros had the coldest stare he had ever seen.

Silverman nodded to Miss Eccleston for her to speak in support. "Yes, of course. That's right, John."

"I'm afraid, sir, that your visit here today is most inappropriate. I can't tell you anything about the grand jury's work. All I can say, sir, is that if you feel the grand jury is not treating your companies fairly, then retain counsel and seek relief from the courts. With all due respect, your being here, sir, demanding a reason for the grand jury's secret inquiry, is improper. I don't think that we should communicate with you directly. I'm thinking of your rights, sir. In fact, I don't think you should say anything in here. I really think that if you want to communicate with us, you should get yourself a lawyer and have him speak with us."

Stavaros was not used to being spoken to this way. "I've done nothing wrong, Mr. Silverman. I don't need a lawyer. If I hire a lawyer for this and it gets into the papers, everyone will think I've done something wrong." He paused, staring at Silverman again. "And I haven't. I want an explanation why my business records are being subpoenaed."

Silverman had expected a rough, guttural voice to come out of that hard-looking face. Instead, he found Stavaros unusually soft-spoken; he pronounced each word precisely. The effect was eerie.

Silverman felt himself becoming angry. "Mr. Stavaros, I said it would be improper for us to speak with you directly. We cannot control what appears in the newspapers except to

89

the extent of our continued refusal to give information to the press." He nodded in Miss Eccleston's direction. "I'm really afraid, sir, that we must ask you to leave."

Silverman sat motionlessly as Stavaros's eyes widened slightly in disbelief. The man then rose and walked out of the room. He opened the door with apparent calmness, but slammed it shut.

Silverman turned to Miss Eccleston. She was shaken and mumbled something about a prosecutor's job sometimes being unpleasant.

As soon as he could, he left and walked directly to Higdon's office. He opened the door to the suite. Pat Ramondi looked up.

"Is Ray in yet?"

"No, John. I think he'll be calling me soon, though."

"Get him on the phone." He walked into Higdon's spotless office, turned on the light, and waited.

"He's on."

He picked up the phone. "Yeah, Ray, how are you?"

There was a long pause; Higdon's signal that he didn't like being disturbed at home. "Okay," he said coldly.

"You plan on coming in today, Ray?" He didn't even try to sound friendly.

"Why?"

"I just came from Miss Eccleston's office. And do you know who I had a nice little chat with? John Stavaros. Neither of us was here this morning, and our U.S. attorney met with him alone, before I got there."

"Did she say anything she shouldn't have?"

"I don't know."

"Did you handle it once you got there?"

"Of course." This was counterproductive; it wasn't going to accomplish anything. He changed the subject. "Richard Franklin White represents Ames. He's filing a motion to quash."

"Well, you're going to speak in opposition, aren't you?"

"Yeah, but I'd at least like a chance to talk to you about it."

"Well, we can talk about it on the morning before the hearing. Is there anything else?"

"No. Nothing else."

"So long."

Silverman sat alone in Higdon's office, the image of John Stavaros still with him. One boss who's always around, but useless. One who's a genius, but rarely around.

This office must need more heat, he thought. He felt a chill.

8

The oversized pale-green accounting sheets lay spread over Silverman's desk like maps in a war room. Jacobs had discovered them in one of Gerald Stoffman's files, and together the two men had spent the last hour poring through them. The sheets had generated questions, questions that needed answering.

The documents were check receipt and disbursement ledgers—in the vernacular, "check spreads." Recorded in the various vertical columns was every check received by Donald Ames personally and every check written by him on his personal checking account. The amounts, dates, even the reasons for each check, were listed.

Check spreads were accountants' tools, a means of tracing all incoming and outgoing money. Strangely, though, Jacobs had only found check spreads in the first year's records. None had been produced for the other years.

Once each month during that year, Ames had received a $12,000 check from Resort Time, Inc. In black ink, in the column labeled "Investments," someone had printed the words "cash-capital" each time such a check had been entered. But next to those words, in light pencil, once again appeared "D.E.A., 66.5 percent—P.B.L., 33.5 percent." However, the handwriting was not the same as that found on the paper Jacobs had discovered the day Stoffman had been in grand jury.

They had scanned the outgoing checks to see if they could trace the money. Nothing. Ames used the account to pay his personal expenses: gasoline, clothing, etc. It all seemed routine. Once a month, he'd written a check to someone represented only by the initials "E. R."—no name, his mistress, no doubt. To be safe, they had compared the Resort Time checks coming in to the "E. R." checks going out. The amounts didn't match; there seemed to be no pattern.

Silverman stared at the check spreads. Why were there none for the other years? Was it simply that the record-keeping system had been discontinued? What about the penciled "P. B. L." and the percentages? Why would someone write that in in pencil and then turn it over to a grand jury? Especially a guy like Stoffman, who was clearly the enemy, a guy who almost shit himself when he saw that folded paper in grand jury.

No, Silverman was convinced that Stoffman didn't know those check spreads had been turned over to the grand jury. Had he taken the others out of the other years' files? But how could he have missed these? That didn't make sense. Unless there was no reason for him to look through the tax files on Ames's personal returns in the first place. Maybe he thought there was no reason because the check spreads weren't supposed to be in there. But if that were so, how did they get in there?

Silverman leaned back in his chair. "I think we ought to get Stoffman back in here, invite him in for an informal interview."

"Think he'll come?"

"Yeah, I think so. He's got to be keeping one eye on the accounting disciplinary board; he'll want to tell them someday that he tendered full cooperation to the government."

"Okay. Let's bring him in."

The lawyers were seated in front of Judge Montarelli's massive oak desk, waiting for the grand jury hearing to begin. As was the custom, prosecutors occupied the chairs to the left, defense lawyers to the right. The preliminaries were still underway: a stenographer was inserting paper into his machine; a law clerk leaned ceremoniously over the judge's desk, arranging the briefs.

This hearing, of course, would not be held in open court; this was a grand jury matter, by law secret. Unlike grand jury, there would be no testimony. This was a hearing on law motions, called by the judge at Richard Franklin White's request.

Silverman reviewed his notes. He would have liked more time with Higdon, but all Higdon had allowed him earlier that morning had been ten minutes. He had listened, nodded what Silverman took to be approval of his argument. And that was it.

Silverman glanced at White and his two assistants. White

looked better than his photographs. Of medium height and build, unquestionably athletic looking, he seemed to be in his late fifties. Accompanying his well-fitted clothing was the perfect trial lawyer's face, one that a jury would instinctively like and, more importantly, trust. His features were more or less ordinary, but he had a certain presence. He was the kind of man people noticed—and admired. He had the gift of being able to make anyone feel at ease in his presence.

His assistants were about Silverman's age. They were unfriendly and, Silverman thought, arrogant. They seemed very impressed with themselves, and obviously enjoyed basking in White's reflected glory. Silverman had recognized one of them; he had been an upperclassman at Harvard during Silverman's first year there; but Silverman hadn't mentioned it, had merely shaken hands.

The judge called the hearing to order. Since it was his motion, White was invited to speak first. He smiled confidently at the judge and began.

His legal argument, without question articulate and well organized, was delivered with an air of respect for the court, but at the same time with a touch of subliminal condescension, as if the points really were so simple, his position obviously so correct, that the judge would somehow prove himself inferior to White were he not to agree. Silverman's furious note taking stopped momentarily; he allowed his concentration to subside long enough to absorb, and enjoy, the sophisticated quality of White's style.

From time to time, White would quote language from other cases used as precedent. Having memorized these quotations, he would deliver them directly to Judge Montarelli as if he himself were another judge telling his colleague what obviously should be done in this case.

Silverman glanced at Higdon, who sat quietly, seemingly unimpressed by White's performance. When entering chambers that morning, they had shaken hands and exchanged cold hellos. Their mutual animosity was apparent, dating, Silverman assumed, from some earlier case.

White finished. There was a silence in the room that was felt more by Silverman than the others. Now it was his turn. He waited anxiously for the judge's recognition, then proceeded.

His beginning he thought disjointed. Nervous speaking in front of White, he stumbled through his first point. But into his second point he noticed White slumped over, taking notes just as furiously as he himself had done during White's argument. More relaxed now, he continued.

He must have done a good job, he thought, because even before he had finished, he noticed White, erect, leaning forward a bit, poised for quick response. And sure enough, no sooner had he ended than White began.

White cleverly chose not to respond directly to Silverman's argument. Instead, he changed directions, his goal to move the judge's attention to another area. An area White had reserved as insurance in case things hadn't gone to his liking. His movement quick, he launched into his new attack before anyone had time to object.

"Your Honor," White said, his confident smile once again in place, "there is a most serious problem here. We..." He used the pronoun as if it were a foregone conclusion that he and the judge were on the same side. "We have had absolutely no showing—not one factual assertion—as to why all of these companies' business records have been subpoenaed. Now in order for this court to appreciate fully the legal issues in this case, Mr. Silverman must come forward...if he can, with facts."

With self-assurance, he crossed his legs and leaned slightly to the side. "Your honor, the grand jury may have far-reaching powers, but before Mr. Silverman can force businessmen to surrender all of their records for scrutiny, he must disclose to us *why* the records are wanted. He simply cannot launch such a massive investigation using some frail innuendo or speck of hearsay evidence as a foundation. We *must* be told the facts in order for a judgment to be made about the legality of the subpoenas."

He'd caught Silverman off guard, switching away from the legal issues and shifting the burden of proof to the government. Should he dare mention James Ritchie? Or the check spreads? Maybe White knew and had been saving this all along, he thought. How would the judge react to their having decided to go on the old man's story alone? Or maybe it was a trick. Maybe White didn't know; maybe he was merely fishing for facts. One thing was clear: with a few sentences, White had shifted the focus away from himself and onto Silverman. And he knew the judge was looking at him, waiting for a reply. He was about to offer what he hoped was the correct response.

"Your Honor," Higdon interjected before Silverman had a chance, "Mr. White is correct."

Silverman looked at Higdon's expressionless face.

"Correct in part, that is," Higdon continued.

Silverman self-consciously tore his gaze from Higdon as the senior prosecutor quickly and smoothly repelled White's new attack. He told the judge that the government would gladly disclose its facts—but to the judge, not White. With a little speech about the rules and policy behind grand jury secrecy, he managed to convey, without really saying it, that if White and his client were to learn of the grand jury's evidence, they would leak it to the newspapers, or worse, try to obstruct the investigation. Silverman noticed White squirm, angered by Higdon's innuendo.

The judge bought it. Once again, Higdon had saved them. As the law clerk escorted White and his men back to the anteroom, White thanked the judge and smiled graciously, but his eyes were on fire.

Higdon's factual presentation was over almost before it began. He spoke in broad generalities. Nothing he said was untrue; he knew that White would indeed someday read this record and challenge anything he could. But Higdon said very little of substance. If the judge pressed him for more, Higdon responded with a bit more detail, but only as much as the judge insisted on. He mentioned Regal Construction by name and Ames's and Stavaros's secret ownership and the allegation of their having illegally gotten road-improvement contracts. To explain the investigation of the other companies, he spoke of illegal financial benefits to "certain individuals." He made it clear that the search could not be completed without all the records.

When White and his assistants were back in the room, the judge told him that he found the facts sufficient and the subpoenas properly issued. He told White he would write an opinion explaining in detail his resolution of the legal issues. Motion denied.

His assistants glared at the judge, but White smiled politely and thanked him.

Silverman began placing his notes in his briefcase; however, White had not yet finished.

"Your Honor, there is one other matter," he said. "An awful lot of records have been subpoenaed. We'd like a postponement."

Judge Montarelli looked to the prosecutors, uncertain now which one would respond. Higdon spoke with blatant condescension.

"Your Honor, even Richard Franklin White should be treated as everyone else. No one subpoenaed has failed to produce. Those records are due tomorrow, and that's when they should be produced." He sat back, smugly confident.

White smiled directly at Higdon. "Mr. Higdon has neglected to disclose to Your Honor that the government has allowed the Pennsylvania State Roads Commission a one-week postponement. If they can have an extra week, then so should we. We should not be penalized because we've challenged the subpoenas when the state hasn't."

Smiling directly back at him, Higdon was about to deny the allegation, and more. Silverman quickly spoke.

"Mr. White is correct. The state did get a postponement." He could feel Higdon's eyes burning into his neck.

Higdon was silent.

"Postponement granted."

The hearing was over; the lawyers returned to the anteroom, and everyone shook hands.

"You did a nice job, John," White said.

"Thank you."

White and Higdon exchanged distant smiles; then Higdon turned to Silverman.

"I want to see you outside."

They stood near the wall in the corridor directly opposite the door to the judge's chambers. Higdon was furious.

"When did you give the state a postponement?" He didn't wait for an answer. "You may have forgotten," he added with dripping sarcasm, "but I work here, too. If it isn't too inconvenient for you, I would appreciate your involving me in your decisions."

He was right to be angry. Silverman knew he had made a mistake. But, damn it, Higdon hadn't been in that day. Silverman wondered if he should remind him of that.

"Ray . . ."

But Higdon wasn't finished.

"You know what you've done now, John? You're created a precedent, that's what.

"Haven't I told you that we've got to get records fast, before *they* have a chance to think. You've taken the pressure off. From now on, even if we want records quickly, we're going to have to grant anyone who asks a week's postponement. Because if we don't, the judge will. Even if we smell something fishy, unless we have evidence that something is going to happen to those records, we're going to grant a postponement.

97

And then we're going to sit on our asses and pray we'll get all the records."

Just then, the door to the judge's chambers opened, and White and his assistants walked out, laughing. Higdon turned instinctively toward the noise. Silverman could tell from White's reaction that he realized Higdon was scolding him. He wondered what White would think. They walked by without a word.

"And you did it, John," Higdon continued when the others were far enough away. "Congratulations, you did a nice job," he added, mimicking White.

Higdon turned and stormed off, leaving Silverman alone in the hall. He stood there for a while before walking upstairs to his office.

Silverman was reeling from the prosecutor's reprimand. He'd made a mistake, fucked up. He tried to rationalize his way out of it: Higdon's absence, his own inexperience. It didn't work. He felt embarrassed. Worse, stupid. Still, he'd have to put it behind him, forget it. There was a case to be made. That was the important thing. And with Higdon's help, goddam it, he would make it.

The view was spectacular. Donald Ames, his tailored suit successfully camouflaging the girth of the good life, stood at the floor-length window of his thirty-fifth-floor Girard Plaza office. The day was crystal clear. Below was the city in perfect relief—miles of buildings, streets, and people. Famed City Hall was across the way, other high-rise superstructures were within view, and just below the horizon, one could even see the faraway slums of North Philadelphia.

Here at the top, for Ames, there was a kind of intoxication, a dizziness caused not by the height but by the knowledge that so much of what lay below was his for the asking.

He'd been fortunate. By the time he had been old enough to realize it, his father was a millionaire. The money had been made mostly in real estate and construction. His father had always been protective of his employees—in their eyes, he was a benefactor—but most others with whom he dealt considered his business practices ruthless and often "questionable." Donald Ames had taken his father's success further than anyone could have imagined. He had enlarged the scope and reach of the business. And when it came to business ethics, he was his father's son.

Donald Ames was more than just a name in this city and

state; his was a name people associated with power, a name to be respected and feared.

Donald Ames understood how the world worked; not the way it was explained in college textbooks but the real way, the way rich and successful people knew it worked. And he understood that it would never change. Never. Not so long as people sought wealth. All the politicians' rhetoric, all the newspaper editorials, all the propaganda, was window dressing, camouflage. Those really in power knew.

Sure, there would always be some people who professed an uncommon sense of morality. The causes would vary over the years, but the people were always the same. Society's self-proclaimed guardians. And the Donald Ameses of the world were their targets.

Ames understood them, too. They were after power, just like everyone else. But their power came from destroying the enemy. They would ruin for others what they themselves had been unable to achieve.

And there were the younger ones. They were the easiest to understand. Not yet fully matured, they were temporarily infected by idealistic notions of what the world should be. Ames had seen them, years later, become absorbed in the very power structure they had attacked. Willingly, even eagerly, they would assume their rightful position, even if it meant usurping the positions of those they had displaced.

Donald Ames was not a petty briber. There was no one who could ever testify he'd received an envelope stuffed with cash directly from Donald Ames. He thought of James Ritchie. There was no way Ames was going to be the victim of some perverse notion of morality. He had worked hard for all this, had played life's game and had won. No one was going to take it from him.

He turned at the sound of his intercom.

"Yes, Mary?"

"He's here, sir," his secretary said.

"Show him in, please."

Ames stood by his chair as Gerald Stoffman entered. Stoffman smiled respectfully.

"Sit down, Gerry. We've something to talk over."

9

While much of Society Hill's eighteenth- and early nineteenth-century townhouses had been renovated into fashionable, and sometimes luxurious, dwellings, the "society" in Society Hill was not as the name implied.

In 1682, William Penn granted a charter for the area to a development company—destined, unfortunately, for little more than sporadic success—known as the Free Society of Traders. The area was nicknamed Society Hill, and for some reason the name continued.

Another development company, a consistently successful one, owned by a present-day Philadelphia consortium—Donald Ames inconspicuously among its members—had built a beautifully designed multitiered shopping arcade on the fringes of Society Hill. Growing geometrically from an inner courtyard, the structure, built of glass and steel, contained connecting outdoor and indoor corridors arranged among staggered levels of exquisite speciality shops and small boutiques.

The Silverman family enjoyed an occasional Saturday afternoon there. John, Mary Ann and Jamie would stroll leisurely through the arcade's overlapping levels, window shopping. The biggest treat of all, though, was Jamie's: a visit to her favorite spot in all of Philadelphia.

On the second level of the arcade was a small indoor playground. There was a sliding board and some swings; they, however, were not the main attraction. On the center floor space were four brightly colored, geometrically shaped animals. They were for climbing, of course, their many angles and curves holding countless adventures for a child's imagination. Of the four, there was only one for Jamie: the large yellow lion.

This Saturday, Jamie was growing impatient. She began tugging at Mary Ann's hand, trying to get her parents to move a little faster toward the playground. But Daddy kept talking to Mommy, and that was causing the unacceptable delay.

For the last several days, all Mary Ann had heard had been his constant chatter about the case. It seemed the only topic in which John had any interest. He was so excited, so pleased by its early progress, he couldn't restrain himself from talking about it. Mary Ann continued listening, though it seemed clearer to her every day that "their life" had been largely overtaken by "his life."

John's description of Stavaros and his visit to Miss Eccleston's office bothered Mary Ann. John sensed her concern and told her not to worry about it, that it didn't mean anything. Still, she didn't like his having anything to do with a man like that.

As they reached the playground, Jamie ran in ahead of them. John was in the middle of telling Mary Ann about his misunderstanding with Bob Jacobs and how it had been resolved. She was grateful to hear something that didn't deal exclusively with technical legal points or questions of strategy. She found Jacobs's family situation something she could really understand, something with which she could empathize.

Inside the playground, they spotted Jamie. The lion had another occupant, an older boy who sat atop its head staring down at her as she waited patiently for her turn. They sat on one of the benches surrounding the animals.

"Do you think he'll marry again?" Mary Ann asked; to her, marriage was the obvious solution to Jacobs's problem.

Silverman said he didn't know, his attention momentarily focused on Jamie, who was still waiting her turn. The boy, older than Jamie, firmly ensconced on the lion, sat peering down at her, obviously enjoying the deprivation he was causing.

"Does he date?" Mary Ann asked, also watching Jamie but not as tuned in to the situation as John was.

"I don't know," he said. "I guess so. We've never discussed it."

Jamie ran over to her parents.

"That boy won't let me on the lion," she lamented.

"You'll have to wait your turn, honey," Mary Ann said.

"Look! He's off now!" Silverman told her, noticing that the boy was now on his way to the blue hippopotamus.

Jamie turned and ran for the lion. The boy, seeing she still had an interest in the animal, quickly ran for it and was back astride it by the time she arrived. She stood there again, waiting.

Silverman rose to straighten out the problem. Mary Ann held his arm.

"Let her handle it."

He returned to the bench, but kept his eye on the situation.

"I think we should have a dinner party next Saturday and invite Bob Jacobs and a date," Mary Ann said. She might just as well have added, "Those children of his need a mother."

John said it was fine with him. He watched Jamie run back to them, her eyes loaded with tears, ready to flow. No sooner had she arrived than the earlier scene repeated itself. She returned once again to stand below the lion—and the boy. There was no mistaking the delight in his eyes as he sat glowering over her.

Mary Ann sensed John's concern. "Let her handle it," she said again. "It's not time to interfere yet." He continued watching.

"So it's settled," she said. "We'll invite your friend. I'll ask another couple."

"Okay. Fine."

"What about Ray Higdon?"

Even with Jamie's plight, he turned to look at his wife. "What about him?" he asked, knowing full well what she meant.

"I think we should invite him."

"Are you crazy? First of all, he'll never come . . . to a dinner party?" he added, as much to himself as to her, as if the notion were beyond human possibility. "And second of all, I wouldn't know how to ask him. He'd stare at me as if I'd lost my mind."

"Well, it's the right thing to do," she said, offended by his overreaction. "You work with him, too. Both men are your colleagues. It's not right to invite one and not the other."

Jamie had finally figured it out. Slowly, she walked around the lion, eying the boy at every turn. Then, furtively, she glanced at the hippo. She stood quite still, then broke into a run for the other animal.

The boy lunged from the lion and raced to the hippo. Halfway there, Jamie abruptly stopped. The boy dashed by her, totally oblivious of her plan. He leaped for the animal, settled himself, and peered below, a victorious gleam firmly in place, ready to savor every morsel of the little girl's sunken heart. His face drained as he searched, finally finding her astride the lion, totally ignoring him. He dismounted and returned to the lion; he stood at its feet, bewildered.

Silverman laughed proudly. "Okay, you think we should invite him. We will. Only you do it . . . He'll never come," he repeated, still laughing at Jamie's cleverness.

"Now it's time to interfere," Mary Ann said, dashing for the lion. The boy had his hands over his head, about to tear Jamie from her favorite spot in all of Philadelphia.

"Fine. Thank you, Donald."

Stavaros put down the receiver. Ames had reported in. Stavaros hadn't told him to, but Ames knew to do it, anyway.

The accountant had been made ready. It was done, just as Stavaros had "suggested."

There was no satisfaction in Stavaros's face, nothing to show relief. It was simply business. A job done.

The two men seated across from him had been reporting to their boss about a proposed business venture Stavaros was considering when the phone rang. Now they waited obediently for the signal to continue. Instead, with the simple nod of his head, Stavaros dismissed them. They quickly rose and left, quietly closing the door behind them.

Stavaros ran his fingers across the layer of pockmarks lining his cheeks. He never touched his face except when alone. Now he permitted his fingers gently to circle each of the misshapen little holes, left many years ago by a childhood disease. They were once the subject of ridicule and scorn. But no more. No one acknowledged their existence. No one dared.

Stavaros silently reviewed the plan. Ames had done what was required. It would work.

His attention was caught by the parakeet he kept in an elevated cage in the corner of his office. The bird was jumping from one perch to another, chirping. Stavaros rose and walked to the cage, opened the door, and put in his hand. Immediately, the bird jumped to his forefinger, and Stavaros removed it from its home.

It waited obediently, hardly stirred at all. It had learned what would happen next. And how to survive it.

Stavaros stared at the parakeet for a while, and then, with his other hand, he covered its body. It remained frozen. Slowly, he began to squeeze, steadily applying pressure until the bird was one pulse throbbing in the vice of Stavaros's grasp. He held the pressure until he reached the crumbling wall of the parakeet's tolerance, then released his hand.

103

Even when freed, the bird still didn't budge. It waited, perched on Stavaros's finger. Immobile. But alive.

Stavaros continued to hold the parakeet. He smiled down at it. Satisfied.

Silverman was unsure whether Mary Ann was asleep or merely brooding. He was awake, watching her as she lay on her side, her back to him. The dinner party had been an absolute disaster.

She had called Higdon as she said she would. She couldn't get him, so after her third try, she'd relayed the invitation through Pat Ramondi. He never called.

Silverman had been in the kitchen mixing drinks for their guests when he had arrived, business suit, starched white shirt and all—even brought a bottle of wine. Silverman smiled to himself, recalling the sight: fearless Raymond Higdon, standing in their doorway, nervously adjusting his eyeglasses, thrusting a wine bottle at Mary Ann.

In addition to Bob Jacobs and his date, an attractive light-skinned black woman with the most unusual green eyes, Mary Ann had invited the Tuckers.

The Silvermans had never been together with the Tuckers before. Betty Tucker was the mother of one of Jamie's schoolmates. And she was a pleasant-enough woman, a bit too vivacious for Silverman, perhaps, but she had not been the problem. It had been her husband, Dr. Harold Tucker, D.D.S.

Older than Silverman—Higdon's age, come to think of it—Harold Tucker was nothing less than a pretentious bore. His clothing and jewelry were definitely from the Gerald Stoffman school, his cordiality toward the black couple seated near him excessive.

He seemed to need nothing more than a few leading questions from Betty—"Why don't you tell them about the new house?"—and a few lukewarm expressions of interest from the others. The cocktail and cheese-dip hour was consumed with stories of Harold's extravagance. His video-cassette recorders, stereo systems, and not to forget, of course, every inch of their goddam new house.

Silverman leaned forward to check Mary Ann. He shook the bed gently; she wouldn't move.

Always the perfect hostess, she'd delivered her expressions of interest at Tucker's boring stories. Silverman could tell that her enthusiasm was forced, but she would never admit that now, not after what had happened.

And poor Bob Jacobs, busting his ass trying to keep things together at home, forced to sit there and endure those awful spendthrift stories.

Higdon hadn't said a word, merely sat quietly sipping his Coke. It wasn't until later, just before dessert, in fact, that Tucker had seemed to notice, and unfortunately been bothered by, Higdon's pensive silence. He had decided to take on Higdon, and that had been the beginning of the end.

His broad, perfectly capped smile plastered over his face, he had gazed at Higdon as if he were a new patient about to get the drill. Higdon adjusted his glasses.

"Been a *government* prosecutor long?" Tucker had asked, as if there were some other kind. Higdon had merely nodded his yes, his eyebrows slightly raised. He was way ahead of him, could see what he was up to, and knew how it would end.

Why Tucker had decided to commit conversational suicide, Silverman didn't know. Higdon's silence apparently conveyed to Tucker a disapproval of him, his life-style, an abhorrence of everything he valued. Tucker simply couldn't let that go, not from some career government lawyer who didn't make a third in annual income of what he made. But he should have let it go.

Tucker treated everyone, his eyes unswervingly on Higdon, to his views on "the waste of taxpayers' money" caused by "the political witch hunts of *government* prosecutors ever since Watergate." No one could have thrown a more appropriate gauntlet at Higdon's feet.

With little effort, Higdon destroyed him.

Not only did he mutilate Tucker's theories, but he analyzed what it was in Tucker's character that made him say what he had said. The finale had been a short but incisive cross-examination about all the tax deductions Tucker had taken for the trips, restaurants, gadgets, claiming them as business expenses when, in fact, they were all for personal use.

In less than fifteen minutes, the Tuckers had gone home, Betty mumbling something about their baby sitter's curfew as she raced for their coats.

Silverman, Jacobs, and Higdon spent the remainder of the evening huddled in a corner of the living room discussing the case. Mary Ann and Jacob's date had cleared the table, then chatted in the kitchen. At one point, Silverman went into the kitchen for more coffee. She looked up at him. Daggers.

"You asleep, honey?" he whispered, leaning over again.

She didn't move.

He turned off the light and lay down. He felt guilty for denying her the kind of social life she wanted. He also realized he wasn't coming any closer to wanting it himself.

Donald Ames insisted that she turn off all the lights and open the window shades so that the blue-tinted, shadowy moonlight could filter through the room. He had rushed her through dinner, hadn't wanted to talk. Now a natural, dark iridescence lay over the bed sheets. Muffled cocktail music played on the stereo in the living room.

He was forceful with her, had kissed her a few times, then sat on the edge of the bed and made her take him into her mouth. When she had finished, he pushed her onto the bed.

And he was hurting her now, not only with his weight but with every thrust. He forced himself deeper inside her. Her pale arms held onto his big back. He began groaning.

Why did she do this for him? He had been generous with her, but she was still just someone to fuck; she knew that. And sometimes he'd made her do things against her will. But he was important and rich. And she liked being seen with him, liked having people treat her as important and special.

She began to breathe more rapidly, excited in knowing that this important man wanted her.

She knew every inch of his body. Her excitement was mounting. He wasn't hurting her as much now, and he began moving faster, pleading for her. She forced her groin into him. Then could no longer hear him, could only hear a woman's voice in the distance, her voice, moaning, "Oh, God, Oh, God." He climaxed, and she begged him not to stop. Then she exploded; she held him, trying to prolong the ecstasy. He stayed on top of her for a few more seconds, then rolled over onto his back, still panting.

She felt hot and sweaty, the skin of her breasts and abdomen still reddish from his weight.

She watched him as she lay silently next to him, her arm resting on her forehead. His eyes were open, his breathing close to normal. What was he thinking about? He seemed troubled, even worried.

Silverman's hand crashed onto the alarm clock. The room was dark, too dark for early morning. The damn thing kept ringing. In his confusion, he brought it up to his face, as if demanding an explanation for its refusal to shut up. Three-thirty?

Mary Ann stirred. "Answer it," she murmured.

The phone. Of course, the phone. Back to the night table for the phone. A book tumbled over, its pages fanning the table's edge on the way down.

"Yeah," Silverman answered, his voice thick. "Who is it?"

"Silverman?"

He knew the voice. A woman's. He'd been asleep over an hour now; he was still climbing toward full consciousness. The identity of the voice was too far away.

"Who is this?" He tried clearing the hoarseness from his throat.

"I'm sorry to wake you . . . You awake?"

"Who?"

"Denise Owens. I said I'm sorry to wake you."

Mary Ann wanted to know what was wrong. He told her nothing and to try to go back to sleep. She groaned and rolled over, taking too much blanket with her.

He was too tired to scold the reporter for her call. He lay on his side, the receiver resting between his ear and shoulder. He was drifting back to sleep.

"Silverman?"

"Uh?"

"Look, I'm sorry," she said, shouting a little to keep him awake. "My editor just called me. There's a story in tomorrow's Sunday *Times*. They've written that Donald Ames is a secret owner of Regal Construction Company." She stopped shouting. "Can you comment? Can you tell me anything? I've got to get something." Her voice barely concealed the sting she still felt from her editor's annoyance with her for allowing the *New York Times* to scoop the *Philadelphia Inquirer* on a Philadelphia story.

Silverman leaned up on his elbow, pulling some cover from Mary Ann.

"What else did the story say?" He checked the clock again and rubbed his eyes.

"That your office is investigating Ames, close friend and confidant of the mayor, for undisclosed crimes . . . something like that. Will you confirm the story? Can you give me anything? Some other names?"

He was sitting up now, leaning against the headboard.

"Sorry. No comment."

107

She didn't push. She hadn't expected him to. Her editor had awakened her and demanded that she call the prosecutors. Now at least she could report back that she had done so.

"Okay. Thanks, anyway."

Silverman sensed that she was being compelled to go through the motions. He felt sorry for her.

"Try Higdon?"

"Yeah."

"What'd he say?"

"Nothing. Just hung up." She sighed. "It's late. Look, I'm sorry."

"Forget it," he said gently.

In the darkness, he guided the receiver toward the phone, trying not to knock anything else over.

Mary Ann rolled over.

"Who was that?" she asked.

"A reporter who's been covering the case. She wanted me to confirm some information for her."

"John, it's three-thirty. Couldn't she have waited until tomorrow?" Mary Ann sounded incredulous and vaguely accusatory, as if this latest intrusion into their life was somehow his fault.

"Look, I'm sorry. Please try to go back to sleep."

But she knew she wouldn't sleep, not now. She felt too angry. The memory of the dinner party came flooding back to her. And now this phone call. When would it all end? But she didn't want to argue, to push it. It seemed as if all they did lately was argue. She turned away from him and pulled the covers over her. "I'll try" was all she said.

But Silverman couldn't sleep, either.

His feet slid into his slippers as he positioned himself onto the edge of the bed. He felt his way through the dark and into the kitchen, took a Coke from the refrigerator, and sat in the darkness. His stomach churned. It was cold in the apartment. He should have put his robe on.

"The *New York Times*." Strange how they had gotten Ames but missed linking Stavaros with Regal Construction. He wondered who their source was. It could have been anyone who knew about the investigation. He sometimes even wondered about Higdon.

Was one of his untaught tactics to leak certain information to the press, information that might "shake the tree"? Or did he seek favorable publicity for himself by giving them a little so that they could return the favor? But good reporters probably wouldn't go for that.

Strange how the *Times* had written about Ames and not Stavaros. Suddenly, Mary Ann appeared in the doorway, holding his robe. "I couldn't sleep," she said as she handed it to him.

"Thanks . . ." He didn't want to tell her that the only thing on his mind was the case.

She took a sip of his Coke, then sat in the other chair.

Neither spoke for a while. She rose to fill the kettle.

"Want some tea?" she asked.

"No."

The gas jet hissed, the tips of its sharp blue flames frantically licking the kettle's base. It cast a dim campfirelike light toward the table, the glow softly illuminating their faces.

"I'm sorry about tonight," he said.

She didn't answer. About what, she thought. The phone call? The party?

"Oil and water."

She looked at him for an explanation.

He smiled. "Tucker and Higdon. They're oil and water."

"He was really rude."

"Which *he*?"

"*Your* he."

"That's right. Ray Higdon doesn't have a social grace in his body." He decided not to remind her who had invited him. "But he didn't start it. He was minding his own business when *your* he took him on."

Of course he was right. But she was annoyed, frustrated that her one try at entertaining had bombed. And she was embarrassed at the thought of having to face Betty again. When she spoke, it was with obvious defensiveness.

"Ray was a guest in your house. Even if provoked, he should have known better."

"Honey," he protested, "Harold Tucker, I regret to say, is a flaming, fucking bore. For him to come here and rub his new-found wealth under the noses of our guests is—well, he deserved what he got."

In the silence, he studied the teakettle. Let's not fight about this, Mary Ann thought. She knew she had to say something, try to tell him what was really bothering her. She reached across the table and squeezed his hand. "John, I want to get out of here soon. I want our life to start."

109

He looked away as if trying to escape, but then turned back to her. "I know."

The water in the kettle was awakening. The first traces of steam began escaping from the kettle's lip.

"You know, honey," he said, "when Ray and Bob and I were talking about the case earlier, we went over it all: the initials on the resort deal, the secret ownership of Regal, all of it." He turned in his chair, animated. "It looks good. Bob and I think so. But Ray kept telling us not to get too excited." He shook his head. "He's a strange guy. I asked him what he meant, but he didn't say anything, just raised his eyebrows the way he does. Then he repeated it. Said it didn't mean anything yet, said not to get too optimistic."

Thick steam shot from the kettle. But neither got up to turn it off. John sat absorbed in his thoughts of the case, apparently reassuring himself that all was going smoothly.

Mary Ann watched him, hoping he was right, hoping once again that her husband would win his stupid little war and then take his family home. But something inside, something indefinable, was telling her it wouldn't be that simple. Somewhere deep inside, recessed well below conscious thought, it was there again, churning, bubbling, forcing its way to the surface. A sensation, intuitive, propelled upward like steam from the kettle.

Something was terribly wrong.

10

Gerald Stoffman stood before Jan's desk.

"Yes, sir," she whispered into the phone, then looked up at him. "Mr. Silverman will be with you soon. Please have a seat."

Stoffman removed his overcoat, sat in the chair across from Jan, who had resumed typing, and subconsciously appraised her. Not really attractive. Not cheap looking. What was she? Mousy. That's it, she was mousy. Thin, small features, light brown hair. Mousy. His eyes drifted to the hint of her tiny breasts hiding below the carriage of her typewriter. She sensed his stare and looked up. Their eyes briefly met. Was she interested? He looked away.

He fumbled in his coat pocket. "Mind if I smoke?" he asked, locating the nearest ash tray.

She kept typing.

His chest heaved as he sucked smoke deep inside his lungs. He'd been up most of the night, restless, worried. Finally, with too much booze, he'd put himself to sleep. That had been a mistake; he had awakened from what little rest he'd had feeling absolutely wretched.

He'd postponed the meeting last week. Couldn't handle it. It had been rescheduled for today. He peered at Silverman's closed door. Any minute it would open; any minute it would all begin. Or end.

How quickly life could sour.

The Ames International account had been a blessing to him. He had demanded and received full partnership, with his name in the title. Rosen, Emerson, and Stoffman. From low-level night-school junior accountant, someone the firm silently considered inferior, to senior partner, an equal among equals. And his life-style had changed almost overnight. Now he could afford the finer things, could be seen with the right people. Mr. Ames liked him. Why shouldn't he? Stoffman had assigned

111

a team of junior accountants full-time to Ames's affairs. And he didn't ask too many questions.

But if he wound up testifying against Ames, he could kiss all that good-bye.

God, how he had run from that grand jury room, like some common criminal. He'd charged to the nearest pay phone and had called Ames. Panicky, he had babbled endless apologies for allowing the folded paper to slip into the subpoenaed records.

Then Stoffman remembered. Ames didn't know about the folded paper. There was no way he could. With every fiber of his body, he'd summoned strength, slowed himself down, and with forced calmness had explained.

It had happened during the audit. A question had arisen. Stoffman's assistant had wanted another look at the previous year's check spreads. But they'd been returned to Ames as they always were. The assistant got them back from Ames's secretary and noticed the penciled initials and percentages that had been added in the interim. He had shown them to Stoffman. The assistant was told to forget what he'd seen and to return the spreads, not to leave them in the file.

It was then that Stoffman had put the notations on the other paper, the corporate charter document, the one he'd seen in grand jury. He had wanted his own record of the transaction. But he thought he'd put the paper in the safe; somehow it had gotten mixed in with the records.

There was silence on the other end of the line. Stoffman died in that silence, waiting. Then he realized. Jesus! He shouldn't have said all of that on the phone. He listened more closely. Ames wasn't there; he'd hung up. Slowly, Stoffman replaced the receiver on its hook.

Later, Ames contacted him. An appointment had been made, the two of them, alone, the previous week in Ames's office. Ames had delivered instructions. Stoffman had agreed. But would he be able to do it?

He was frightened. Frightened of the consequences of lying, frightened of the consequences of telling the truth.

"Mr. Stoffman?"

Silverman's voice shook him from his reverie. He'd been so lost in his thoughts that he hadn't noticed that Silverman was standing at his open doorway, beckoning him. He rose.

Inside, he was directed to the vacant chair in front of the desk. There was a black man seated next to him. He looked familiar; he'd seen his face somewhere before. Hadn't he been the one standing in the hall the other day, outside the grand jury room? Silverman introduced them. Stoffman smiled. He was going to try to get through this by being friendly, and stupid. Maybe that would dissuade them from putting him on the stand.

As Silverman sat down, Stoffman recognized some of his firm's files on top of the prosecutor's desk.

Silverman picked up a pencil and examined the point, slowly turning it between his fingers as though he were appraising a rare gem. Then he stared at the accountant as if Stoffman's mere presence sickened him. He wanted to make him squirm, to feel as uncomfortable as possible. Yet when he spoke, his words were unemotional, businesslike.

"We appreciate your accepting our invitation, Mr. Stoffman. Please understand, though, that you're here voluntarily. If you want to leave at any time, you may. I'm not going to advise you of your rights, and you won't be under oath."

Stoffman's smile returned, but it was not yet his turn.

"Of course, I hope you will be cooperative and answer our questions," Silverman said, once again examining the pencil's fine point. "But I want you to understand something. This is an informal question-and-answer session. If you want to, you can probably lie to us today and get away with it..."

Stoffman stiffened. "Why I wouldn't..."

"Please let me finish." Carefully, he returned the pencil to his desk. His words, still businesslike, now contained a touch of hostility. "Keep in mind that it is possible for you someday soon to find yourself back before the grand jury, and I'll be asking you the same questions you'll answer today—but you'll be under oath and subject to the penalties for perjury. So if you lie to us today, you might get away with it—today—but someday soon it'll catch up with you."

Stoffman smiled and nodded, assuring Silverman, then Jacobs, that he was more than pleased to answer their questions, although he feared they would be disappointed by his lack of information. He called them both by their first names; their displeasure was apparent. Saved for last was the apology he'd rehearsed.

"Listen, fellas, I'm sorry about our having gotten off on the wrong foot. I really do want to cooperate with you. In any way I can. It's just that this is all so new." He waved his arms around the room, indicating his first "brush" with the law. He stared innocently into the prosecutor's face, awaiting the first question.

Silverman remained silent, studying the situation, evaluating the new Stoffman as if he now were the rare stone that needed appraising. In the silence, the faint sound of Jan's typing drifted into the room, its steady staccato rhythm punctuating the tension in the room. Silverman sat back and tilted his head slightly to the side, searching Stoffman's blank eyes.

"How many conversations about this investigation have you had with Donald Ames since your appearance before the grand jury?"

The question surprised him. It didn't seem fair; he had expected to be asked about the subpoenaed documents.

"John, uhm. Oh. I really do want to help, but, uh, should, should I answer that? You know, I mean isn't there an accountant-client privilege?"

"No."

"What?"

"No. No, there's no such privilege."

"Really! I thought there was," he said with pretended interest, as if he couldn't wait to tell the boys at the firm what he'd just learned. The faint sounds of typing returned. Stoffman shifted nervously in his seat. They were waiting.

"Oh, I don't know . . . we spoke a couple of times, maybe. But not really about the investigation in particular." He looked from Silverman to Jacobs, smiling.

"What does that mean . . . 'not really about the investigation in particular'? Did you or didn't you talk about the investigation?"

Stoffman smiled blithely. He didn't know what to say, how to avoid answering the question. He had not yet fully committed himself to the fact that he was going to lie today.

"Well, uh, we spoke, but just in general terms. You know, I told him I was here—"

"Anything else?"

"Really, I can't, uh, think of anything specific. You know, we just spoke."

"Can you remember anything general?"

"Uhm . . . no, not really."

"Tell us what you know about Donald Ames's passing financial benefits to public officials."

"Financial benefits?"

"Yeah."

Stoffman feigned total ignorance of the meaning of the phrase. He smiled blankly, first at Silverman, then at Jacobs. Then, as if he had just remembered something delightfully important, he beamed and nodded his head.

"Oh, well, I do know that Mr. Ames has made campaign contributions to candidates in many elections. He's been very active politically in—"

"Forget about campaign contributions. We're not interested in those. Tell us about other things of value going to public officials."

"Other things of value?"

Silverman sighed. "Yes, other things of value."

"Well, I really don't understand. Could you be more specific, John?"

Silverman looked at Jacobs and sighed again. Jacobs returned the smile and shook his head slowly. He made a note on his legal pad. Silverman often felt like an actor in some grade B movie when he went through charades like this in front of witnesses. To him, his hostility seemed so transparent. Yet, for some reason, the routine had rarely failed to interject some discomfort in a reluctant witness. It was a trick, but it almost always worked.

Stoffman watched them, felt nervous with their silence. He leaned forward. What were they going to do next?

"Really, I don't understand. I, I do want to help. If you'd just be more specific..." What the hell did they want him to say?

Silverman spoke with obvious sarcasm. "Sure, we tell you what it is we already know. And then when you find out that we already know it, you'll tell it to us, too." He smiled as he spoke, then let the smile slowly evaporate. "Come on, Mr. Stoffman. It doesn't work that way, and you know it."

Stoffman smiled unrelentingly. "I'm sorry. I simply don't know what you want."

"What we want is the truth. Okay, we'll do it your way. Tell us about Resort Time, Inc."

Stoffman began a long, detailed, and irrelevant accounting history of the company. They let him ramble on for a few minutes; then, at a point when Stoffman was speaking directly to the prosecutor, Silverman turned to Jacobs, smiled, and said, "Do you believe this?"

Things were moving too quickly for Stoffman. He looked at Silverman and smiled nervously. "I don't understand. What's the matter? What do you want?"

Silverman leaned forward and took the folded paper from a file. He slowly unfolded it and placed it before Stoffman.

115

Stoffman glanced quickly at the paper and then away, as if a prolonged view might cause blindness. He removed his hands from the desk.

"Ever see that before?" Silverman asked.

"Yes." He looked at Jacobs, who had stopped taking notes.

"Where?"

He kept his eyes on Jacobs. "It was in our files, I guess."

"What does it mean?"

"What does it mean?" Stoffman repeated.

Silverman said nothing, waited for the silence to bring Stoffman's eyes back to his own. He stared angrily at him.

"It's a copy of a page of the Resort Time corporate charter. It shows who got stock in the company." He never looked at the paper.

"How about the penciled notation? Whose handwriting is it?"

Now Stoffman picked it up and studied it as if he had never before seen it. Then, hesitantly, he answered. "It looks like mine. It may be mine."

Silverman leaned back. "It *may be* yours? Are you telling me you don't recognize your own handwriting?"

He smiled again. "I'm fairly sure it's mine."

"Fairly sure . . . What does it mean? Why did you write it?"

"Well, it says D.E.A. owns 66.5 percent . . ."

"I can read it, Mr. Stoffman. We can all read it. I'm asking you to tell me what it means."

"Well, it says that D.E.A. owns 66.5 percent and P.B.L. . . ."

Silverman rose, walked out of the room and closed the door. Stoffman looked puzzled. Jacobs told him to wait for Silverman.

After a few moments, Silverman re-entered the room and handed a document to Jacobs. "Serve it on him," he demanded.

As Jacobs placed the subpoena in Stoffman's hands, Silverman returned to his seat.

"Okay, Mr. Stoffman, we're going to do this the hard way. Mr. Jacobs has just served a grand jury subpoena on you. You are to appear next week. This time, I *am* telling you to get yourself a lawyer, a criminal lawyer. Because you need one. You're in deep-shit trouble. You're about to become a defendant in a perjury prosecution. I told you that you could bullshit me in here for free but not in the grand jury. This meeting is over. Good-bye."

Stoffman didn't move, stared frozenly at Silverman. "Wait a minute. Hold it. Please, John . . . Mr. Silverman. I'm not . . . bullshitting you. Please, ask me what you want to know. Please." All of a sudden, he felt hot and very uncomfortable about what he was about to do, but his mind seemed to decide automatically. He clutched the subpoena; he was ready to do it.

"I'm only going to ask you this one more time, Mr. Stoffman. What do those penciled notations mean?"

Stoffman looked directly at the prosecutor.

"Mr. Ames called me sometime ago and told me that he was going to give—sell some of his interest in the Resort venture to a friend. He said he wanted me to know because he wanted everything to be reported properly."

He had stepped over the line. Nothing like that had really happened, and when he had rehearsed it the previous night, just in case, he thought it would be harder to say. He finished and braced himself for a challenge from Silverman, but there was none. No one accused him of lying.

"When did that conversation take place?"

"I don't remember exactly. About four or five years ago." He felt some of his control come back and didn't want to lose the moment, so he continued. He was afraid he was speaking too quickly, but he couldn't slow himself down.

"Mr. Ames said that his friend would acquire a future interest in the company. The friend did not want to have a financial association with the company for several years. He said that if the friend should exercise his option to join Resort, he would be expected to pay all of his share of the costs and expenses. He wanted me to know all that. And that's pretty much what he said."

No one had yet mentioned the name of the friend—P.B.L. Even Silverman was hesitant to ask, to have the name finally spoken aloud, officially associated with the investigation.

"Who's the friend, Mr. Stoffman?"

"Is it necessary for me to say it?"

"Yes."

Stoffman lowered his eyes to the desk and spoke as if he were ashamed. "Mayor Lane."

"What were you told as to why the mayor's interest wouldn't be acquired until the future? When in the future?"

"As I remember it, Mr. Ames told me that neither he nor the mayor wanted to do anything that could run the risk of embarrassing the mayor. And so they agreed that the mayor wouldn't exercise his right to buy into the company until after he left public office."

117

"Has the mayor exercised his option yet?"

"No, not that I've been told." He quickly added, "And I'm certain I would have been told."

"Has he ever received any money from the company?"

"Not that I'm aware of. You've got the company's books; you can verify that for yourself." The smile returned; he didn't want to sound as if he were challenging them.

It wasn't a bribe, just a careful business deal. The entire transaction was crumbling before Silverman's eyes. He felt a hollowness in the pit of his stomach. They hadn't even discussed the check spreads yet. A vision of Higdon's telling him not to be too optimistic crept into his mind. He tried to expel it, knowing now was not the time, but it was locked in, wouldn't leave. Is this what Higdon had meant? No, he couldn't possibly have anticipated this.

The accountant was watching him, clearly curious as to why the momentum had stopped. Silverman ignored him, turned to Jacobs as if they were the only two in the room. They exchanged glances.

Jacobs read his look, understood Silverman was still digesting what he had just heard, and saw that he needed time.

"Mind if I ask some questions?" Jacobs asked him.

Silverman shook his head distractedly.

"Do you personally prepare Donald Ames's tax returns?" Jacobs asked, turning to face the accountant.

Do you prepare the returns? That was an IRS agent's routine question, asked during nearly every audit Stoffman had been involved in. He began to feel at ease. The worst was over. He allowed himself to relax a bit.

He explained he had the ultimate authority, but his assistants would do the work. He would review the completed tax return with Mr. Ames.

Jacobs nodded. "I see. Tell me, Mr. Stoffman, how does your client get his tax information to your firm?"

Another routine question; Jacobs seemed to be following established procedures. Stoffman was convinced that this was the tail end of the interview. His answers became less friendly and more businesslike.

"Well, his secretary prepares check receipt and disbursement spreads for each year. She sends those and interest earnings' statements and other materials to us each year at tax time. We review the papers and prepare the returns."

"Uh hum, I see. Do _you_ ever review the papers she sends?"

"On occasion, if something comes up which requires my looking at them."

"Those check receipt and disbursement spreads . . . We didn't find anything like that in your files," Jacobs lied. "Why not?"

"We send them back to Mr. Ames as soon as we've finished with them."

Jacobs appeared satisfied, took his pad and made some more notes. Then he looked over at the accountant once again as if he'd forgotten something.

"Is there any other writing that you're aware of that contains any reference to Mayor Lane's future interest in the Resort Time venture?" He was testing him, of course, looking blankly at Stoffman to see if he would tell them about the check spreads. Stoffman's answer surprised him.

"Well, I seem to recall . . ." Stoffman appeared to be re-collecting some old, fragmented conversation. "Uhm, let's see . . . Mr. Ames told me something about . . . he and the mayor had put their agreement in writing . . . a letter of some kind. Yeah. I'm pretty sure he said it was a letter. You know, I'm not positive. This took place about five years ago, but I'm pretty sure he mentioned a letter. I've never seen it."

"Any other writing?"

"Not that I know of."

Jacobs studied Stoffman, then glanced quickly at Silverman, who was doing the same. One more question.

"Mr. Ames doesn't report any income from Resort Time on his tax returns. Is it literally true that no money has come in to him?"

Stoffman smiled at the agent's ignorance. "Oh, no. Money comes in. He receives about five thousand dollars a month, but, you see, it's not income.

"The company borrowed twenty million dollars to build the resort, and the final cost of construction was only"—he cleared his throat—"eighteen million. So, you see, they overborrowed by two million dollars. That two million has been distributed to the stockholders on a monthly basis at five thousand a month. But it's not profit; it's sort of a cash flow, so it's tax free, at least for now."

"I see. Thank you." He turned to Silverman. "That's all I have, John."

Silverman stood; he wanted to be alone with Jacobs, wanted Stoffman out of there as quickly as possible. He nodded. "Thanks for coming in, Mr. Stoffman."

"What about the subpoena?" Stoffman asked, clutching it in his right hand.

"If we need you again, we'll call you."

Stoffman rose, quickly shook hands, and escaped.

11

The session was over. Like students, at the three o'clock bell, the grand jurors noisily filled the hall on their way home.

Inside the empty grand jury room Silverman and Higdon sat quietly behind their table as though there were still more to be done. But there wasn't. The day had been a total bust: four witnesses, four identical stories.

J. Willard Bellski, Anthony Travota, John Herman Dykes, and Francis Newman. The four original owners of Regal Construction Company, the men who had sold eighty percent of their nearly bankrupt road construction business to Ames and Stavaros, had been unshakable. Owning now a mere twenty percent of Regal among them, they were wealthier than ever before in their lives, and they were not about to throw it away.

Silverman had hammered at them for hours. Each one steadfastly insisted that he had done nothing more than sell a percentage interest in Regal Construction to two knowledgeable investors. Quite readily, each admitted that he had relinquished control, that he had become a passive figure in a company the four had owned together for years.

Purely a business decision, each had insisted. And in a way, of course, they were being truthful. Before the takeover, Regal Construction was rarely a successful low bidder on public projects; after, however, it had been awarded so many municipal contracts that the company was now among the largest and most successful in Philadelphia; in fact, in the entire state. Their explanation? The new owners were experienced businessmen and knew where to pump new blood into their floundering company. With expert cost accountants and other such people, the new investors had made the business run more efficiently and more profitably. Naturally, low bids followed.

Each had insisted that his present job was to see that the contracts were performed, the city's streets and highways built or improved, and that was all. The business decisions were no longer theirs.

Higdon had not intervened. He quickly understood that these four men were not easily intimidated by lawyers or grand juries. They had worked their way up in the construction business, probably beginning as laborers. Lawyers didn't frighten them; the prospect of jail—if necessary—was tolerable.

But the official records still listed these four men as the only owners of Regal Construction. Why? each had been asked, when, in fact, they were holding eighty percent of the company in their names as nominees for the two new "investors." Their words had varied slightly, but their answers were the same.

The corporate lawyers for the new owners had advised them that it was all proper, all legal. Only "owners of record," the lawyers had said, needed to be supplied to the state road authorities. But why handle it that way, Silverman had insisted. Because Ames and Stavaros believed the use of their names would create unfavorable publicity, and with it, unfounded accusations and innuendoes. The State Roads Commission would be pressured into pursuing a witch hunt; Regal Construction would be suspended, or worse, unfairly disqualified from bidding on city and state projects.

That much is true, thought Silverman. If the takeover had indeed been only a business deal, then there was something to what Ames and Stavaros believed. He felt the tentative presence of uncertainty, like some third person in the room, prying into his consciousness. He resisted. His job was to try to uncover whether this "deal" was an illegal device, part of a scheme. Righting all of the world's wrongs was not in his job description. Yet some small part of that uncertainty had managed to imbed itself within him.

It would have helped if he could have shared some of this anxiety with Higdon. But that was impossible. Even when he and Jacobs had told Hidgon of the Stoffman interview, there had been no reaction. Higdon had asked to be shown the letter if it were produced. Nothing more.

The grand jury room, with its pastel blush of colors, was now as quiet and still as the outside hall. Business for the day had been suspended, and these two men were seated side by side, each alone, each deep inside the recesses of his own thoughts. To Silverman, at that moment, it was painfully clear that he and Higdon were not partners, not a team. There was, and would be, no sharing. He remained a few seconds longer, then gathered his papers and left.

Raymond Higdon slowly rose, walked to the witness box and stood before it. Pensively, he touched the narrow ledge; with a strange tenderness, he ran his fingers over its smooth surface. He turned and glanced at the empty rows of tables. Alone, he permitted the soft sigh of disappointment to escape, adjusted his glasses, and left.

Jacobs stood before Silverman's desk, unnoticed. Silverman was well into the fourth race, his *Daily Racing Form* folded open in his lap. It was too late in the afternoon to get any work done, especially after his day in grand jury.

"John?"

Silverman didn't look up. He was busy computing the vital statistics needed for handicapping race number four.

"It was in the records White produced," Jacobs said. He raised his head and looked at Jacobs for the first time since he had entered the room. Jacobs was holding a single white sheet of paper. Silverman placed his racing form on the credenza behind him and held out his hand to receive the letter Gerald Stoffman had told them about.

It was a photocopy from the subpoenaed files of Resort Time, Inc., dated June, five years ago. Ames to the mayor, it set forth the agreement between the two men. The letter spoke of how the mayor, then in his first term, had been thinking about retiring from public life sometime in the future, of his fondness for travel and his interest in becoming financially involved in some travel-related business. In the letter, Ames offered the mayor an option to purchase a part of Resort Time, Inc. after Lane left public office.

It described the understanding reached between them that Lane would be obligated to pay full expenses at exercise of the option and association with the company. He wasn't getting anything for free.

Silverman handed the letter back to Jacobs.

"Show it to Higdon yet?" he asked.

"I'm about to."

There was something about this Jacobs didn't like. It simply didn't feel right to him. Why a letter? Why not an agreement, prepared by a lawyer, like the Regal nominee agreement? And why didn't Stoffman, the company's accountant, receive a copy, something for *his* file?

"What do you think?" Jacobs asked, noticing the same expression on Silverman's face as he'd seen after the Stoffman interview.

Silverman couldn't react. All he could see was the case falling apart before his eyes. He reached for his racing form. "I don't know," he said. "I don't know what to think." Ignoring Jacobs, he lowered his head and turned his attention back to the fourth race.

Jacobs understood. Silverman was not being rude; he just needed time.

The next time Silverman looked up, Jacobs was gone.

He stood and went to his window. It was pouring outside, the rain hitting the streets in broad, violent strokes.

If Stoffman had told the truth, if the letter was genuine, then what exactly had they uncovered so far? One document showing Ames and Stavaros as silent partners in Regal Construction. So what? Without more, all they had succeeded in doing since Ritchie's death was to fill two empty jail cells with records and terrorize one accountant. Maybe there wasn't any more; maybe that's all there was.

His phone rang. He returned to his desk and waited as Jan answered, then buzzed.

"Yeah."

"It's Denise Owens calling you."

Not now. He wasn't up to fencing with her now. "Tell her I'm in conference."

"She says it's urgent, that she's got to speak to you right away."

"Tell her I'm not here. Tell her I've left for the day."

He turned back to his racing form and lost himself in the fifth race.

Rush hour was in full swing. Those hurrying home, escaping from the tedium of their weekday lives, did so this evening with even greater than usual urgency. The swollen nighttime sky was dumping its storm all over the streets of downtown Philadelphia.

His package firmly under his arm, Raymond Higdon pushed open the framed glass shop door and left the shop. His umbrella up, his raincoat rebuttoned, he leaned against the wind and quickly joined the moving crowd.

The salesgirl stood by the counter watching as her customer left. She had waited on Higdon once or twice a month for the last three years. Even though he hardly ever spoke to her, never asked her for advice about selections, she was the one he always waited for. If she were busy with another customer, he'd wait patiently by the side of the counter until she was finished. He would not permit any of the other salespeople to assist him.

There was a time when she thought he was interested in her. Not that she was attractive, but then neither was he. Her life seemed to begin and end in the record and book shop she'd been working in for the last five years.

But he never really spoke to her. Shy as she was, she'd tried to make conversation. She'd even read up on his two apparent interests. Asked him about his purchases. But he never really would answer her. And so, after a while, she simply accepted her role and waited on him when he appeared in the shop.

She stood at the counter a moment longer, watching as Higdon disappeared into the crowd. She was not attractive, but her hair was thick and dark, her cheeks rosy like a child's.

Like a child Higdon once knew on a playground in a church school on a very sunny day many years ago.

The last few inches of the elevator's descent were an infinitesimal crawl as it leveled itself with the lobby floor. Silverman fastened the top button of his raincoat, preparing himself for the downpour that still raged outside. How appropriate, he thought. A perfect ending for a shitty day.

The doors opened smoothly, presenting Denise Owens, thirty feet away, waiting. She'd been waiting for the last hour, watching each elevator's descent, searching for one specific passenger, the one now being discharged.

She stood defiantly, clutching her shoulder bag, awaiting Silverman's approach. As he neared, he wondered if she were going to confront him with his lie. But as he came closer, he perceived that she had more pressing business on her mind. Indeed, he was no sooner within range than she began.

"I've got to talk to you," she demanded.

The tone of her voice only reinforced his desire to avoid her. "Talk to Higdon," he replied, and kept walking, bypassing her completely.

She moved in front of him. "He won't talk to me. But you will." She stood firm. "I've got a story that—"

This time he successfully sidestepped her and headed for the doors. Moving faster than normal, he skipped down the marble steps and pushed open one of the large doors leading out onto Market Street. It was pouring. Ordinarily, he would have waited a few moments to see if the rain would let up, but with her in the lobby, he raised his collar and dashed out.

Sharp gusts of bitter wind seized the torrent and whipped it through the streets, causing rain to lash his face and hands, the droplets stinging like tiny pinpricks. He leaned his head down into the wind and dodged past the rush-hour traffic creeping through Sixth Street. He crossed again at Fifth, then quickly went for the steps to the Westbound Station, Market-Frankford Line.

In the underground passageway leading to the next set of steps, which, in turn, led to the platform, he stopped momentarily to recover from the storm.

Rain beat on the wide steps behind him; an eastbound train had just arrived, its cars noisily grinding to a halt; westbound passengers were walking by.

Someone violently grabbed the sleeve of his coat. He turned. Denise was holding on to him. They were both drenched; her hair was matted to her forehead as if she'd just stepped from the shower. Conversation had to be shouted.

"Look, Silverman. I've got a story. I've got to talk to you about it." She kept her fist tightly clenched onto his sleeve.

The noise, the rain, his day—it all came together. Anger swelled inside him like a balloon blown to bursting proportions. He tore his arm from her grasp.

"What the hell's the matter with you?" he shouted, instinctively taking a small step toward her. She shrank, stood motionlessly, wet and helpless. "Can't you understand what no means? No! I don't want to talk to you. Can't you understand that?"

Some commuters loitered nearby, seemingly disinterested but taking in every word of this public dispute. One man looked as though he were trying to decide if he should interfere.

Prosecutor and reporter faced each other, frozen in confrontation as the activity around them slowly resumed. Then, abruptly, he turned and walked for the second stairway. As he reached it, not knowing why, he turned and looked at her. She hadn't moved, was watching him. He was too far away to see the tears swelling in her eyes.

He felt an urge to go back to her. A westbound train approached the platform below; he stayed there, watching her until after the train had completely stopped; he heard the doors open, stayed a few seconds longer, then turned and fled down the stairway.

* * *

The storm had all but ended by the time Silverman walked from Wynnewood Station to his apartment. Blackness now fully covered what had been an iron-gray evening sky.

The lights in the apartment seemed warm and comforting, but tonight he needed more. He removed his soaked raincoat, hung it over the shower rail in the bathroom, and went to the kitchen to get himself a drink. He found a nearly full bottle of J & B in the cabinet above the sink.

The ice was already in his glass, and he was pouring the Scotch when Jamie came in.

"Daddy's home," she called out to no one in particular. "Hi, Daddy. Play with me?"

He took his first hard swallow. "Not now, honey. Maybe later," he said, his back to her.

But she was so happy to see him that she didn't notice his mood. She tugged playfully at his hand.

"Come on, Daddy. Let's play doctor," she persisted.

He jerked his hand away, much as he had done to someone else less than an hour ago. His voice was harsh. "I told you, Jamie, not now."

Her eyes widened in astonishment. As if in slow motion, her mouth went from a slight pout all the way down to a deep cry. Her eyes instantly filled with tears, her mouth open wide, but no sound came out. Her momentary muteness frightened him; he watched helplessly as she began to sob.

She ran from the narrow kitchen into the arms of her mother, who had been standing in the doorway, watching. She pressed Jamie's head gently against her shoulder and stroked her hair to comfort her. But she kept her eyes on John, waiting for an explanation.

Ashamed, he couldn't look at them. He studied the contents of his glass as if something alive were swimming around inside it.

"Let's go out tonight. See if you can get a babysitter," he said, trying to avoid responsibility for what had just occurred. Jamie's cry was now a whimper.

"It's too late," was all Mary Ann said.

He looked at his glass again, then drained it.

Storyville was accustomed to seeing people alone. Yet Silverman felt uncomfortable as he descended the steps to the club. It was quiet; the band was on a break. His timing seemed bad. He didn't even have the comforting skirt of blaring music to hide behind.

Charles, wearing the same blue-purple tapestried tuxedo jacket, remembered him, smiled and asked for Jacobs, then showed him to a table on the side, against the wall. The maître d's casualness and total disinterest in Silverman's solitary presence helped put him at ease.

He needed to get out tonight. Mary Ann had remained sullen, her silence an unbearable rebuke. She said she didn't mind his going alone. He didn't search for sincerity, simply left.

He had decided to go to a movie but almost instinctively came to the club instead.

The waitress placed his drink in front of him as he watched the musicians slowly return to the small stage. The group, all black men, was older than the one he'd seen before. They were better dressed, still casual, no coats or ties, somehow, though, more middle class looking.

The saxophonist, Silverman supposed—he was wearing the thin elastic neck strap used to hook a saxophone onto—sat at the baby grand piano and fiddled with its keys. Silverman guessed he was trying to work out a melody or refrain, something in his head, perhaps something he wanted to use during the next set. Another musician, probably the pianist, stepped onto the stage and stood by the piano, tranquilly attentive.

The audience seemed only partially interested, not at all disturbed that the performers were on the stage, yet not performing for them.

It wasn't amateurism; Silverman could see that. With this kind of music, this kind of night club, *performing* was not what one usually expected. There was no showmanship, no smiles or glitter—only music. Jazz. America's only true art form, Jacobs had called it. While the visual dimension was interesting—the surroundings did seem to add a certain quality to the music—it was the music, and the music alone, that was performed. The audience seemed comfortably prepared to wait until the musicians were ready.

The standing pianist said something to the man at the piano. Silverman couldn't hear his words, but it looked as though he'd made a suggestion. The man at the piano tried it. He shook his head; no, that wasn't right, either. Then he tried another passage; it was similar but shorter than the one he'd just played. That was it. He looked up at his colleague and smiled serenely. Gave him the thumbs-up sign for victory. He tried it again to make certain he had it, then rose and walked to his saxophone, which stood, reclining like a torch singer against a piano, on its portable metal support in the center of the stage.

By now, the other musicians were all in place. All at once, the room was quiet. Without anyone's taking the lead, all six began playing, exploding in absolute unison. The music was quick, syncopated, and abstract. Yet there was total precision; these men were polished, in control of their music. The room came alive.

Silverman sat on the darkened sidelines, well out of reach of the excess spotlighting that spilled over the stage onto those seated nearest the band. The saxophonist was playing the refrain he'd mastered at the piano, working it over and over, furiously improvising on its foundation. As Silverman watched and listened, the music slowly began to fade into the back of his consciousness, like the droning of an air conditioner on a hot summer's day.

His mind was filled with random thoughts. He examined them as though they were the disarranged pieces of a puzzle spread out before him on a shaky formica table, like the ones his mother was always doing on the bridge table at home.

He could still remember one of them from his childhood; the puzzle was hardly put together, but lying beside the pieces was the box top with a picture of the finished product: a French impressionist painting, a lazy Sunday afternoon on the grass by a lake, turn-of-the-century Parisians, strolling ladies with parasols, lounging gentlemen. Georges Seurat. "Sunday Afternoon at . . . something or other Island"; the complete title had long since escaped him.

But there was no finished picture for *his* puzzle; he couldn't tell what the outcome would be. He examined each of his thoughts, looking for patterns. The investigation and Higdon— two pieces. Was there a fit?

What did he want from Higdon? A father figure? Someone to pat him on the head, tell him it would all be all right, that the case would finally be made? Higdon was Higdon. Silverman knew he couldn't expect anything more than the opportunity to learn from him, to become a better lawyer by the association.

But how would he learn if there were no case, no crime. Higdon would withdraw again, out of reach. There would be no more investigation. And, ironically, that would be worse than if an investigation had never begun.

He would have to keep doing his job: investigate and then shut down after a proper determination of noncriminal involvement. He would have to keep to himself the belief that these men were innocent. Who believed that targets of grand juries were innocent? If indictments didn't ensue, innocence was not presumed; it merely meant that the criminals were too clever—or the prosecutors not clever enough. That sort of "defeat" was not going to help him land a job in some prestigious law firm, the kind Mary Ann wanted for him.

Mary Ann. Another piece of the puzzle. How long could she hold out? How difficult was he making it for her? And Jamie, standing in the kitchen, injured by his thoughtlessness. He knew it was wrong of him to bring the case home at night.

But if Ames and Stavaros were guilty, it was his job, his duty, to go after the evidence. What the hell did he want, anyway? His life to be always serene, like the painting on the box?

One had merely to fit the tiny jagged pieces into the right sequence and the game was over, the picture complete; the result, a beautiful scene, a mathematically precise composition.

That was the problem, of course.

This was no puzzle, no Pac-Man, no *Daily Racing Form*. For Silverman, this was a new game, with real stakes, and he wasn't sure what the outcome would be. This case, which at first seemed to be a change in direction, an interesting diversion from his everyday routine, had taken hold of him completely. Now it seemed to Silverman that he played at *its* whim. He was no longer in control. For the first time in his life, he couldn't see where he was headed, and he didn't like the feeling. Not at all. But one thing was sure. If this was a new game for Silverman, it was one he needed to win.

The music began drifting closer, growing in volume and intensity, its seemingly random rhythms and complicated melodies much like the impressionist painting on the puzzle, containing mathematical form, motif, movement—a beginning and an end.

He ran his fingers through his hair, then signaled the waitress for another Scotch.

Higdon had never been to a bullfight in his entire life. Yet he knew as much about the spectacle as did most devotees.

The wrapping from the oversized book he had purchased on his way home lay crumpled on the floor beside his chair. With a strange hunger, he read the details below each of the glossy photos of matadors engaged in the kill.

Outside his apartment, the fullness of evening had replaced the storm, now spent, all but gone, except perhaps for a few final remnants of the cloudburst that lingered, embraced by the cold night air.

Higdon studied the photos, examined with near-professional care the position and stance of each torero. Of course, the odds were overwhelmingly against the bull. Yet there was a strange thrill Higdon always experienced at that moment, frozen in each picture, when the sword, inches from the beast's head, was fixed, ready to plunge its way through flesh and bone.

When he'd finished, Higdon rose from his chair and added the book to the rest of his collection. He'd never been to a bullfight, never really thought about going. He was perfectly satisfied with his books and their photographs. He didn't desire—or need—more.

It was the same with the music. He'd never been to the opera. Never heard Wagner—the only music that interested him—performed in public. Only on his records.

Again, he had read vast amounts both about the composer and his works. He knew most of what there was to know.

Slowly, carefully, he placed the phonograph's arm on the outer edge of the record, adjusted the volume, then returned to his chair.

To most, the music would have seemed bombastic, shrill, discordant. Not to Higdon. He loosened his tie, leaned farther into his chair, his eyes closed, his head almost imperceptibly weaving in rhythm with the repetitive strains of the soprano's screeching.

He wouldn't move. Not until the record was over.

Frankie stood at a safe distance while Mr. Stavaros ate. When he was in the restaurant, by instruction, Frankie served no other customer.

The tip he received more than made up for the loss of his other tables. Still, he was always relieved when Stavaros had finished his dinner and left.

Standing away from the other waiters, Frankie discreetly watched as his solitary customer finished his main course. Frankie stood ready, awaiting the nod for coffee.

Just outside, at the curb, stood Stavaros's limousine, awaiting its owner's return, droplets from the recent storm glimmering over its shiny black hood like some iridescent metallic rash.

Frankie caught his signal for coffee. Quickly, he brought it over, and as he did so, he all but counted the minutes until the cup would be drained and Stavaros would be outside again, in his limousine.

And away from him. At least until tomorrow night.

At about the same time as Stavaros took his last sip of coffee, two other men sat at a table, in the official residence of the mayor, dining. In private. Their table's rich mahogany surface shone from its twice-daily buffings. The china and crystal service, elegantly appointed, lay before them, each set a mirror of the other. All as befits a mayor.

Donald Ames had just finished briefing him. Lane had asked no questions, made no comments. But now, his food cooling beyond appeal, he slowly rose, walked to the low brown cabinet at the dining room's edge, and poured himself a whiskey. His tall frame as erect as ever, his back still to Ames, he took a hard swallow, held the glass before him, then took another.

Ames had been with the mayor many times and was very familiar with Lane's self-controlled, confident, public image. But tonight he had seen fear in his eyes. The same fear he himself felt.

The plan had been devised, set in motion, locked in. There was no turning back. Stavaros said it would be all right.

But would it?

12

two other...

Silverman's late-night out had taken its toll. It was 8:20. He had overslept and was shaving when he thought he heard Mary Ann calling him. Tightly twisting the faucet so he could hear, he watched as the basin swallowed the small puddle of gray milky water, the last ounce disappearing with an indelicate slurp. He listened for her calling him but heard nothing except the slow patter of reluctant droplets from pantyhose drying over the tub. Just as he again turned on the hot water tap, he heard his name.

He moved to the living room; Jamie was playing on the floor, and Mary Ann was on the sofa watching TV.

A nondescript, yet bright little morning tune lay just audibly under the announcer's resonant voice as he soothingly informed his audience that it was now twenty-five past the hour and the network would temporarily suspend its morning news and information program for five minutes for local stations "across the country" to broadcast local news, weather, and traffic conditions. The picture quickly flipped to the first of too many commercials, a celebrity and his TV family joyously singing the virtues of a frozen, synthetic, orange-colored juice drink.

The string of commercials finally, mercifully, ended.

It was time for the first story.

As the newsman read from his script, large, grainy black and white photos of both Ames and Stavaros flashed onto the screen behind him. In an exclusive *Philadelphia Inquirer* story, he told them, it had been learned that the federal grand jury investigating allegations of corruption in the city highway program had discovered that two influential local businessmen, who together secretly owned one of the largest highway construction companies in the state, were also involved in a lucrative Bahamian land deal with Mayor Phillip Brooke Lane.

Obviously unaware that the *Inquirer*'s story contained one important inaccuracy—Stavaros was not involved with Lane in Resort Time, Inc.—the newsman's voice contained all the urgency and allure of audience-ratings broadcast journalism. Almost breathlessly, he continued, identifying Ames and Stavaros. Their pictures were then instantly replaced with a large color photo of the mayor.

With Lane's frozen gaze peering over his shoulder, the newsman told how the *Inquirer* had disclosed that the grand jury had recently discovered the link. He described Stavaros as "a man with reputed underworld connections."

He shook his head as he rose to change the channel to the other local news program. It was essentially the same story, done in a similar manner. He returned to the bathroom and hurriedly wiped the drying shaving cream from his face.

That morning, for the first time since moving to Philadelphia, Silverman stood out from the other commuters at Wynnewood Station. The final rush-hour train had just arrived, and a small group of office workers were leaving the comfort of the heated room as he entered, half-shaven, wearing only jeans and a T-shirt under his parka. He opened his coat and reached into his tight pants pocket for change. Newspaper in hand, he went home.

Despite the bitter morning chill, he read the entire article as he walked. His ungloved hands stung from the cold, but he barely noticed. What was more important was what he was reading. According to the last paragraph of the story, the mayor had scheduled a press conference that day at three P.M.

He could hear the phone ringing before he had his key in the door. He stood outside and waited until he heard Mary Ann hang up. While he was out, she had gotten dressed as though someone had suddenly died and she wanted to be decent for any unexpected callers.

Several reporters had called; she'd told each that he'd already left for the office. The phone rang again. This time he picked it up.

"Silverman," the woman's voice announced with blatant confidence, "would you care to comment on today's story?"

He recognized Denise Owens's voice. Clearly, she was reveling in the triumph of her scoop.

There would be no friendly, cute introductory conversation—not after yesterday.

She expected a flustered "no comment," would hang up and use it in the next day's follow-up story.

134

"Owens?" he asked, making absolutely certain of her identity.

"Yeah," she answered, her expectant inflection every bit as effective as if she'd said, "Are you sorry now?"

"Want to go off the record for a few minutes?" he asked, his voice composed—she thought submissive.

Why not? She had her story. "Sure."

"It's wrong. I'm sorry to have to tell you this, but your story's wrong."

She'd tried all day yesterday, even after that episode in the subway, and had then convinced herself that her story was accurate, that she didn't need more confirmation. So she had assured her editor that she had checked it out with *everyone*.

Stunned, she didn't say anything, wished she hadn't called. Then she burst with questions.

"Wrong? What do you mean? Where? Where is it wrong? What are you talking about?"

"I'm sorry. I can't tell you. You know that. If I tell you what's wrong with your story, I'll be confirming the rest of it."

She was angry, demanded to be told what part wasn't true.

He repeated his refusal; she argued. It was he who hung up. A few seconds later, the phone rang again. He told Mary Ann to let it ring.

In no hurry to get to the office, he took a late train, rode with matronly shoppers on their way to Center City for the afternoon. He stopped in the video arcade, stayed much longer than usual, then went for breakfast: pancakes and sausage, two cups of coffee.

Jan was engrossed in the "Home Entertainment" section of the morning paper as he walked in. "Hi," he said, seeing that any excitement caused by the *Inquirer* story was completely lost on her. "Higdon in?" he asked.

"Nope."

No surprise there, he thought.

"A lot of calls for you this morning," she said as she handed him a small packet of pink message slips.

He smiled, momentarily envying her for having nothing but this year's new fashions on her mind. He took them from her and entered his office.

Looking through them, he saw that the top two were from Denise Owens; he crumbled them and let each fall into the wastebasket. The third was from Jacobs, reporting that he

135

and the other agents would be at IRS that day for a "briefing." Silverman understood the message: bureaucratese for removing the investigators from the immediate line of fire. The rest of the messages were from reporters; they followed Owens's into the trash.

"Miss Eccleston in?" Silverman asked into the phone.

"Yes, but she has some people with her. Can she call you back?" her secretary asked.

He said it wasn't necessary, that he'd get back to her later.

By tonight, it would be in all the newspapers, on all the stations. As if to punish himself, he visualized the worst headline he could think of. "Mayor Linked to Mobster."

He slumped into his chair and stared across the room at the yellowing stacks of paper resting like two decaying tombstones on his worktable.

The *Daily Racing Form*. He'd completely forgotten to buy that day's edition.

Silverman stood in the doorway, allowing his eyes to adjust to the premature afternoon darkness. The tavern, within walking distance of the courthouse, was definitely a workingman's retreat. Even though squeezed into a small, shabby retail district, it was a neighborhood place, simple and familiar.

Three P.M. was minutes away.

Silverman mounted one of the stools nearest the door, away from the other two or three inhabitants perched at the far end of the bar. He didn't sense any danger in there, but it was best not to intrude.

The bartender was a paunchy, Slavic-looking man in a short-sleeved shirt with a fighting marlin tattooed over his hairy right forearm. Silverman ordered a beer and asked him to turn on the TV that hung suspended high above the rows of whiskey bottles like the glistening eye of a giant cyclops.

The barman reached up and flicked the button. When Silverman asked if he'd switch from the soap opera to Channel 12, he looked at his new customer, frowned at the imposition, but again reached over his head, changed stations, and walked back to the far end of the bar.

A voice announced that the following special program would pre-empt the regularly scheduled show. The camera slowly panned the roomful of reporters, then focused on the unoccupied rostrum bearing the official seal of the city of Philadelphia. Another voice, as though reporting a golf tournament, whispered into a microphone that the mayor had entered the room.

Phillip Brooke Lane was every inch a statesman, tall, with a closely cropped crown of hair surrounding a bald scalp, but aristocratically handsome. He was rumored to have gubernatorial aspirations. Smiling, he ascended the few steps to the small stage and walked quickly to the rostrum. He put on the reading glasses he had been carrying in his left hand, reached into his breast pocket, and removed his statement.

Silverman took a sip of beer.

With the same self-assured but unobtrusive manner that had won him a lifetime of elections, the mayor wasted no time in getting to the point. In less than ten seconds, he managed to set the right mood with a subdued, martyred lament over his having to spend time "and the taxpayer's money" publicly refuting "will-o'-the-wisp accusations from so-called *informed* anonymous sources." He belonged elsewhere, he said, tending to the pressing business of the city, his "clear mandate from the people at the last election." However, silence would be taken for acquiescence, and so he was here.

With the slight flair of a conjurer, Lane produced an edition of the morning *Inquirer* seemingly from out of nowhere, and held it aloft, waiting patiently for the TV cameras to get a well-focused shot. The paper had been stored on the shelf under the rostrum for easy access, a necessary stage prop for that day's performance.

His smile had now completely evaporated; this was serious business. The mayor told how the article made reference to a John Stavaros. He mispronounced the name, deliberately, Silverman figured, alleging that Stavaros and Donald Ames were majority owners of Regal Construction Company. (The newspaper vanished as quickly as it appeared; no point in generating too much interest in the headline.) If that part of the story were true, he said, neither he nor anyone on his executive staff knew about it. Anyway, he reminded everyone, city-street and highway construction contracts were awarded *only* by competitive sealed bidding, the mayor's office having nothing whatsoever to do with the bid submission and selection process, all of which was done in the state capital in Harrisburg.

Silverman's attention was momentarily diverted to the other end of the bar. An argument was underway; a few words had been shouted, something to do with a union. He returned to the mayor, suspended high above the bar.

137

Lane removed his glasses, for sincerity's sake no doubt; the highlight of the speech was nearing.

"I am a citizen of this great city and state," he protested. "And as such I am entitled to the freedom to pursue the same dreams and goals as all of you are. The fact that I am mayor does not mean . . . should not mean . . . and *must* not mean that my rights as a citizen are denied." Regarding Resort Time, Inc., it was time to "set the record straight."

Silverman watched and listened as Lane repeated essentially what was in the letter Jacobs had discovered the day before: a fondness for travel, a desire to retire someday from public life, the right to *purchase* an interest in Resorts, nothing for free, all in the future.

"I am not now, nor have I ever been, associated with Resort Time, Inc. or any other so-called Bahamian land deal with Donald Ames or anyone else. I have never received any money from any such company. And furthermore, this Mr. John Stavaros has never been a party to any interest in Mr. Ames's resort venture."

The bartender had moved closer, his meaty arms folded across his chest; a dishcloth hung limply at his side. He stared suspiciously up at Phillip Brooke Lane.

It was time for the final salvo. There was a long pause, Lane clearly savoring the anticipated reaction.

"I wish to inform the residents of this great city that your mayor is not a subject of the federal grand jury's investigation. My people have spoken with the United States attorney herself, and we have received her personal assurance that I am not now, nor have I ever been, the subject of any grand jury action.

"Now I will take questions," he said, and pointed to one of the outstretched hands pleading for recognition.

The bartender shook his head. "What a crock of shit," he said.

Silverman studied him, deciding if a response were advisable. "What is?" he asked.

"Him." He flicked his dishcloth at the TV. "They're all alike." He mimicked the mayor. "The residents of this great city—my asshole. They'll get him."

Silverman suppressed a slight smile. This was clearly a man who knew everything about everything. In Philadelphia, as elsewhere, such men usually worked behind bars; sometimes they drove taxis.

Silverman played along. "What makes you say that?"

138

"Because they're all guilty as shit, that's why. Listen, those boys in the—what do you call it?"

"United States attorney's office?"

"Uh—" The bartender paused, unsatisfied with Silverman's contribution, then discovering the phrase he liked, added, "D.A.'s office," momentarily staring at Silverman to show him he was still in control and knew damn well what he wanted to say. "Those boys in the D.A.'s office," he repeated. "Shit. They wouldn't go after big shots like that if they didn't have the goods on 'em. They're smarter than that. Hell, they wouldn't touch them unless they had their asses in a sling already."

Yup, those boys in the D.A.'s office sure are smart, Silverman thought. Especially the one who stayed home this morning.

Silverman, despite his predicament, was now slightly amused by the lecture he was receiving. He wanted to hear the rest. "But the mayor said the D.A. told his people he wasn't under investigation," Silverman said, suppressing a slight smile.

The bartender smiled broadly at his customer's naïveté. "That's all bullshit," he instructed. "Hey, she's gotta say that. It don't mean nothin'. Shit." He leaned toward Silverman. "Look. It wouldn't be in the papers. You know, where there's smoke there's fire."

From force of habit, the bartender took out his cloth and wiped the counter around Silverman's beer bottle and glass, took out a package of cigarettes, offered one to Silverman, shrugged when he declined, and lit one for himself. He leaned back against the cash register. Their attention returned to the TV.

A reporter had just asked Mayor Lane to describe the written agreement to which he'd referred. He said it was a letter. The reporter asked if he'd release it to the press. No, he wasn't going to release it, he said. It would only lead to additional baseless speculation and far-fetched stories, and he wanted to spend his time administering the business of the city, not answering unfounded accusations.

The bartender snorted. "Shit," he said again. "But you know what it means?" he asked. Without waiting for Silverman to respond, he took a deep drag on his cigarette and continued speaking, the escaping smoke muffling the sound of his voice. "They'll all get convicted and go to some country-club prison for rich people and sit, real polite like, on their asses for six months." Flicking cigarette ash to the floor behind the bar with practiced precision, he continued. "Take a guy like you," he said, pointing at Silverman; then, perhaps because his new customer was wearing a suit and tie or simply to show he could be generous with his examples, he added, "or somebody like me. Little people. Nobodies. We get caught stealing, it's the slammer. Hard time. None of that minimum-security shit."

The bartender began what was to be a full recitation of all his customers who've done time but was interrupted by one of the men at the far end of the bar, calling for another beer.

The press conference had ended. Silverman looked up to see the mayor carefully step from the stage to shake hands with the reporters. The announcer said that Channel 12 Eyewitness News would present an exclusive filmed interview with U.S. Attorney Anne Eccleston at six P.M.

Silverman left enough money on the bar to pay for the beer plus a generous tip and walked out into the afternoon's sharp sunlight.

He paused briefly on the sidewalk until his eyes readjusted to daylight, located the pay phone on the corner, and walked over to call Jan. He told her he wasn't feeling well, wouldn't be back to the office today, was going home instead.

During the ride home, he wondered what the bartender would think when he read about the investigation's ending without indictments. It would only confirm his theories. He'd tell his customers that some big shot had obviously put the fix in.

He got home and headed straight for the bedroom for a nap. Mary Ann woke him just as the six P.M. news began.

Together, they watched a filmed report of the mayor's afternoon press conference. At the end, the mayor was shown invoking Miss Eccleston's name; the film changed to a shot of the U.S. attorney seated behind her desk. Her name and title appeared in superimposed white letters across her chest. A man's hand held a microphone with the number 12 attached to it. She was asked if the mayor had spoken accurately.

The camera slowly drew into a close-up shot of her head; it seemed as if each hair in her tight bun had been separately placed. "Well, as you know," she said with a nervous smile, her fingers, out of camera range, gently fidgeting, "matters occurring before the grand jury are strictly confidential. But yes, I did today advise members of the mayor's staff that *he* was not under investigation by us, that no allegations have been made against him in any way whatsoever."

What a fool, thought Silverman. He wondered if Higdon was watching. By stating that one of the three men was not a target, she had just confirmed to the world that Ames and Stavaros were, in fact, targets of the grand jury. And what was she going to do if next week or next year the mayor did come under investigation and she was asked the same question? She would be forced to say no comment, and then the world would know that he, too, was under investigation. Well, she was lucky there, he thought bitterly. That wasn't going to happen.

The reporter asked about Stavaros. "There's been a rumor for some time, Miss Eccleston, that your office received some evidence linking Johnny Stavaros to narcotics traffic but because of the disappearance of a key witness, no case was ever made. Is there any truth to that story?"

She smiled nervously into the waiting camera. Silverman could see that she hadn't expected the question and was trying to dodge it. Her silence was lasting too long. Silverman sat forward.

"Well," she began, now smiling inanely, "any investigation of Mr. Stavaros took place before my administration, so I'm unaware of details—"

"My God, what the fuck is she doing?" Silverman stood and stared at the TV.

She must have realized she had said the wrong thing because she quickly added, "Mind you, I cannot confirm for you the existence of investigations . . . that is . . . whether or not Mr. Stavaros or anyone else was ever the subject of an investigation in this office. As you know, grand jury matters are secret."

By now the smile was frozen. She sat helplessly at the mercy of the microphone.

Silverman turned off the set in disgust.

Raymond Higdon lay on his bed. He wore one of his white shirts, cuff links included, and a pair of suit pants. His feet were bare.

He aimed the remote control at the small black and white TV that stood on a tarnished gold stand at the foot of his bed. A picture of Anne Eccleston reflected off each lens of his glasses. He watched the interview, then clicked the remote control. The picture disappeared instantly.

He stared at the dark green-gray empty screen.

* * *

At first, John had remained in the living room, sulking, digesting the day's events. Then he walked to the kitchen and stood in the doorway, watching Mary Ann. He began to enjoy the warmth of the kitchen, laced with the aroma of dinner cooking. It brought him around, eased his frustration. He wouldn't have to think about all this for at least a few hours. He walked over to Mary Ann and gently touched her shoulder. She looked up at him, her eyes expectant. He could see it had affected her, too.

He took her wrists and tenderly lifted her arms to his shoulders.

She remained that way, searching his eyes, then took her arms away, but carefully, so as to show him it was not a rebuke. She had something to say, something important to her. "John. Leave the government. Give it up." She waited to see if he were going to protest. He said nothing, so she continued.

"There's no point in staying now, anyway, is there? I don't care if we stay in Philadelphia or go back to Washington. I'm just tired of treading water; I want our life to start. Let's get settled. Please, honey. It's time."

Silverman turned away. Maybe she was right. Maybe there was no point in staying any longer. But he didn't want to think about it now, not until he was sure this case was really over.

Silverman rose from the dinner table, and with exaggerated excitement, he told Jamie that the two of them were going to play doctor "all the way to bath time!"

Mary Ann was in Jamie's room; he had put Bach's Brandenburg Concerto on the stereo, turned the volume up high, and was lying on the sofa, his shirt on the floor. He was the patient, and Jamie had insisted that he remove his shirt just as she was required to do at Dr. Eddy's. She stood at the sofa, administering invisible medicine; he laughed when she insisted he needed an injection in his "tussy."

He felt relaxed, relieved to be enjoying the pleasures of home. The case had receded to what seemed its proper perspective. It was, after all, only a job; and jobs ended.

Mary Ann came into the living room to watch them play. She stood there for a while and then returned to get things ready for Jamie's bath. Someone knocked at the door.

"That's going to be Mrs. Berman from next door," she said, "to complain about the stereo. Turn it down, John, and go tell her you're sorry."

He turned the stereo off and ran for the door. His smile disappeared, and the first few words of apology fell from his lips. John Stavaros was standing in the doorway.

Silverman stood there, his hand cemented to the door. Stavaros didn't speak. He took a step forward; Silverman instinctively stepped aside, allowing him to enter. He closed the door. Stavaros's back was to him now. He watched him look around, then followed him into the living room.

Still smiling, Mary Ann came around the corner, a pair of pajamas in her hand.

"Did you tell her..."

She stood face to face with him. He looked at her, then turned to Silverman. He stood there for a few seconds, sighed as if he had unpleasant news to deliver, then spoke.

"I'm unhappy about what happened today." His voice was too soft; his words came too slowly, and his cold eyes added untold meaning. "I don't want it to happen again. Not ever again. I can't let that happen..."

Silverman tried to put a sentence together, to tell him—ask him—to leave. He couldn't. He was afraid to look at Mary Ann, afraid to look anywhere but at him.

He hadn't finished. "You're not going to let it happen again. You're going to stop this, Silverman."

Stavaros was staring at him. Had he finished? Was he waiting for a response? Silverman had no answer. He waited. Afraid.

Jamie broke the silence. "My daddy's a lawyer."

Silverman watched Stavaros look down at her. She was standing between the two men, looking up at him. The indirect lighting formed grotesque shadows on his pockmarks. Stavaros smiled distantly at her and held his hand out to touch her face. She shrunk behind her father's leg.

Stavaros looked at Silverman.

"Nice little girl."

Silverman's mind filled with the implication. Stavaros looked at Mary Ann, then left.

They stood there paralyzed until they heard the hollow echo of the outside entrance door slamming shut. She was the first to react, nearly hysterical, both angry and frightened.

"My God," she cried. "Are you satisfied now, John?" She scooped Jamie into her arms and held her tight. She cried, clutching her daughter, and walked into the bedroom. Jamie started to cry.

Silverman walked to the window and looked down at the street. He watched as a man in a dark topcoat opened the rear door to a limousine for Stavaros. He watched until the car was completely out of sight.

Silverman stayed in the living room, sitting on the sofa, staring at Jamie's Dolly Hobby doll house. Its doorway contained a little cardboard plaque: "Happy Is the Home that Welcomes a Friend."

My God, he thought, this was no game. This was real.

13

Silverman stood braced against the numbing cold as the coffin made its precarious descent into the open grave. Now and then it would skim the side of the hole, chipping away small chunks of dirt that fell with sullen hollowness onto the simple wooden lid. Those at the ropes would stop, wait respectfully for stability, then slowly lower it farther. The wind punched at the canvas tarpaulin, a symbolic shelter for the grieving family, its grass-green color out of place in the desolate, frozen winter cemetery. Mary Ann stood shivering next to her husband.

A mother's sobbing hung over the air like the black limb of a barren, leafless tree. Robert Jacobs comforted his mother as best he could. But she had lost a son.

Watching them, huddled together at the foot of the grave, Silverman couldn't help thinking of an earlier scene played several years ago at a grave site a few feet from where they now stood. He'd noticed Betty Jacobs's tombstone on the way in. The same family, the same children standing beside their father and grandmother.

Jacob's brother had died a predictable, violent death. A need for drug money. A holdup attempt. The two bandits were nervous—and careless. They hadn't seen the store owner grab the revolver that lay hidden beneath the counter until it was too late. The merchant fired at point-blank range; the coffin remained closed during the mourning period.

Mary Ann hadn't taken her eyes from Bob's mother. Since Stavaros's visit, the loss of a child had added meaning for her.

Not that Silverman hadn't had his moments as well. The night of the visit he'd lain awake; every night noise, every creak in the old apartment, had brought his attention to the front door. For about an hour, he had sat in the living room halfheartedly playing at a video game, then went back to bed. Mary Ann slept. He had dozed fitfully.

By dawn, he had realized that Stavaros's purpose was to scare him and nothing more. There was no question about his having succeeded, but Stavaros wasn't going to do anything, not after a personal appearance like that.

If anything happened to Silverman or his family, he would now be the prime suspect. No, if a man like that wanted a murder, there would be no announcement beforehand. Stavaros wanted to scare Silverman into closing the case down. If he wanted to kill someone, he'd go for the witnesses; not that they had any. But there'd always be another prosecutor.

The coffin lay at its final berth; the minister, his head bowed, his hands clutching a worn goldedged Bible, delivered the final benediction in a rich baritone voice reminiscent of sweeter times.

Jacobs's mother was on her knees, wailing, her arms extended toward the open grave, frantically reaching, pleading for her dead son. Silverman looked away and for the first time saw Ray Higdon standing alone off to the side, away from the crowd surrounding the grave. Their eyes met; they nodded respectfully at each other. Higdon looked away as though embarrassed to have been spotted at so human an event, then walked off.

Silverman drove through the run-down neighborhoods of North Philadelphia quickly, cautiously aware that sudden stopping, for any reason, could bring danger.

From the cemetery, he and Mary Ann had gone to Jacobs's house, carefully selecting their parking space before entering, and sat in the uncomfortable presence of aunts and uncles and other relatives, drank strong, hot coffee to warm themselves from the cold, and left as soon as they could. They drove away in silence, Mary Ann pensively watching the rows of slums and near slums appearing and disappearing on their way out.

"You all right?" he asked.

"Um hum."

He tried to think of something to say, to make conversation. They continued driving in silence.

She had been like this: unresponsive, mutely compliant, numb, since Stavaros's visit. When Silverman had realized what the man's real purpose was, he had talked to her, had explained. She listened but hardly reacted, as though she were in some sort of shock, defenselessly awaiting her fate. The previous night, he had wanted to make love. She complied, but mechanically. He had sensed it, had fleetingly decided to discontinue, but was strangely embarrassed, as if those closed pale-green eyes of hers were secretly watching, recording silent assessments of him. And so he'd finished, uncomfortably conscious throughout of her emotional detachment. It hadn't been good for either of them.

"Want to stop for lunch?" he asked, quickly glancing at her, then back at the road.

"Up to you."

Mary Ann continued staring out her side window. The heat had become stifling. John turned the lever to low and cracked open his window; immediately, cold air filtered in to diffuse the heat. She paid no attention.

He'd have to leave her alone, he supposed, let her work it out for herself. He'd do that. But he needed the comfort of conversation, needed to recoup his self-assurance by sharing his thoughts—and his anxieties. Because maybe his analysis of Stavaros was wrong.

With whom, though? Who would listen, who could advise? Not Higdon. He considered, then rejected, Jacobs. Bob would listen as a friend, but he'd also hear as a government official. To swear him to secrecy, to forbid him to file an official report that would begin a separate inquiry of Stavaros for his visit, would put Jacobs in a terribly unfair position. And to allow an official investigation to be begun might be a self-fulfilling prophesy, might result in the very violence he had discounted. No, Jacobs was out.

It had to be someone outside government. Someone with experience. But who?

Of course. He had it. He'd—

"John!" Mary Ann instinctively grabbed for him.

The car screeched to a halt; the red traffic light glared down at them from high atop the center of the street. Some men, huddled at the corner, passing around a bottle, watched as he slowly backed out of the intersection.

Uncomfortably, he waited for the light to change, kept an unobtrusive watch on the corner, then pulled away.

"I'm sorry," he said, but he ignored her silence. He knew. He knew whom to see. He should have thought of him earlier. He'd call Stanton Turner the next day.

Stanton Turner's secretary said he was in Washington but was expected back the following day. He told her he wanted to make an appointment to see Mr. Turner. Fine. She'd tell him when he returned.

She called the next day to tell him that Mr. Turner would meet him for lunch Thursday at the Philadelphia League. Did he know where it was, she asked. Yes, he knew where Philadelphia's fanciest private men's club was.

After politely interrogating Silverman for daring to have crossed over the Philadelphia League's very private threshold, the gentleman's gentleman coldly directed him to "the salon." It was there that he would be permitted to wait for Stanton Turner.

Almost immediately after seating himself in one of the high-backed maroon leather chairs, several newspapers were placed on the glossy wooden table at his knees. Would he care for a cocktail? No, he was meeting someone, thank you. He would wait.

The newspapers remained untouched as Silverman studied his new surroundings with a mixture of amusement and disdain. Predictably, the room—"the salon," he reminded himself—contained the look and feel of ancestral opulence. Rich oak-panelled walls were filled with large, ornately framed portrait paintings of grim, aged men, long since dead.

Several small groups of men were seated in chairs not unlike the one containing Silverman, enjoying preluncheon cocktails. Absorbed in their own discussions, they paid him no attention.

Silverman noticed that the furniture was strategically arranged so that several groups could enjoy simultaneous conversation with privacy. And the conversation there was lofty; he had no doubt of that. These men, these Brooks Brothers pin-striped, silver-haired, fungible-looking men, comprised a significant proportion of this city's old moneyed power. For Silverman, the "League," as its members called it, stood not only for old money but bigotry, a narrow, out-of-date, exclusive world. A world in which Stanton Turner, his membership and his family tree notwithstanding, did not seem to belong.

It was at Harvard, during Silverman's final year, that he had first met Turner. A senior partner in one of Philadelphia's most prestigious law firms, following a yearly tradition, Turner and one of his younger partners had come to the law school to recruit senior students for the firm. There could be no finer drawing card; Turner was an active member of the board of trustees of the law school, a national officer in the respected American Bar Association, and during the term of an earlier president, had served as deputy attorney general in Washington. Silverman later learned that years before, after graduating cum

148

laude from Harvard law school, Turner himself had served as an assistant U. S. attorney in Philadelphia.

Despite their obvious ancestral dissimilarities, the senior lawyer had taken an immediate liking to this bright, aggressive law student. And while Silverman had not accepted his job offer, coming to Philadelphia for other opportunities, they had remained in touch ever since. Once or twice a year, always at Turner's invitation, they would lunch together. But never before here.

Silverman's quandary over Turner's choice of eating places—maybe his secretary had made the reservation—was interrupted by Turner's "Hello, John. Good to see you."

Silverman rose to shake hands. Turner certainly looked like one of them, Silverman thought as they sat down. He fit in this room as easily and as comfortably as anyone in here. Even seated, his legs crossed, Turner was erect, stately, his rich gray hair just a bit floppy but well above his ears, his incisive eyes gleaming, missing nothing.

A waiter in red waistcoat and black bow tie approached and stood obediently.

"Drink, John?" Turner asked, rubbing his hands as if in pleased preparation.

Silverman would have liked a beer, but embarrassed by his rich surroundings, ordered a sherry.

"Two," Turner said.

They spoke for a while. Nothing of substance, just polite conversation. Silverman studied Turner. Button-down white shirt, highly polished English cordovan shoes. Every bit a lawyer. The drinks were served. Turner told him about his recent trip to Washington and how pleasant he felt the nation's capital had become over the past decade. He had been summoned to the White House; there were some inquiries about new tax proposals. He and other lawyers "with some knowledge in that field," Turner had said with modest but unconcealed pride, had met with the president.

Turner had been to the White House before, had given advice to other presidents. He spoke of this president and the questions he had asked as he probably would have of any new executive client. The president's questions, he said, didn't show the kind of grasp of the proposed legislation he thought the man should have. Was it the president, or did the fault lie with his staff advisers?

He asked for Silverman's family. How was he doing? But this conversation was merely preface. Both knew that. According to the ways of America's upper class, it would not be appropriate for Silverman immediately to begin an explanation of his problem. Silverman knew that at places such as the League one engaged in polite introductory conversation. It was a social requirement. Business matters would await their turn. To blurt out a problem was to exhibit lack of control. And control, of one's self and all situations, was the quintessence of capability. The president did not summon to the White House someone who lacked the control to put problems in their proper perspective and place in life. So Silverman waited.

Nothing was to be gained by offending Turner. He knew Silverman had a problem; the mere fact that they were sitting there at the young prosecutor's initiative was sufficient evidence of that. The discussion would wait its correct place in the luncheon meeting. It was up to Silverman to choose the time, and it was important to Turner's perception of him—and his problem—that he do it properly.

The gentleman's gentleman walked to them, bowed almost imperceptibly, and informed Turner that his table was ready. Would he like to dine now or wait? Turner turned to Silverman.

"Hungry?"

The discussion would be at the luncheon table.

"Yes, sir."

They were respectfully led into one of the several small dining rooms. Silverman wondered if the other rooms were as heavy and overbearing as this one. Everything was decorated in brown again. The walls bore the same old, deeply polished paneling. The ceiling was high, the room too brightly lit. No questions about this being a "men's" club. Their table was against the wall, with one of those silly little lamps in the middle of the immaculately white tablecloth.

They studied the menus. Turner described the Dover sole, said it was flown in fresh each morning from England and grilled in butter, "quite tasty." They ordered it.

The waiter left. Now it was time.

"Care for another drink, John?" Turner asked.

He politely declined, waited a few seconds to make certain his timing wasn't off, then spoke.

"Mr. Turner, I'm faced with something of a dilemma," he began, looking as relaxed and "controlled" as he thought appropriate. "I would very much like to share it with you and seek your counsel. That is, *if* you feel it's not improper for me to discuss the matter with you."

Turner nodded but said nothing, waiting for Silverman to continue.

"It has to do with the grand jury investigation, sir. I would try to speak in such a way so as to avoid disclosing grand jury information. But I do need to speak to someone. Someone in whom I can confide—and trust."

The older lawyer looked at him, considering. "What seems to be your problem?"

The green light. Silverman smiled in appreciation.

The remainder of the luncheon was consumed with Silverman's story. Turner listened intently as his young acquaintance, with suitable discretion—no names except Higdon's were mentioned, no precise facts disclosed—unfolded the history of the case, its frustrating lack of progress, and the hopes and disappointments that revolved around Raymond Higdon.

The dishes had been removed; coffee had been served. With the exception of an occasional question or two to clarify some point Silverman had made, Turner hadn't spoken, assessing the situation, Silverman supposed.

Silverman was recounting the evening visit made to his apartment by "one of those under investigation," Mary Ann's reaction, and his analysis of Stavaros's motives when he noticed a flash of excitement in Turner's eyes.

At first, he didn't understand, continued talking, but then he too saw what Turner had immediately seen. He stopped talking virtually in midsentence. It filled his mind like the intense brightness of afternoon sunshine flooding a room after a passing cloud. The case wasn't going well; no real evidence had been uncovered. Surely any insider—like John Stavaros—would have known that. Yet he wanted Silverman to stop investigating, to shut down. There could only be one reason: Stavaros was worried, perhaps even frightened that a continuation of the probe would uncover something. There was something there. An innocent man wouldn't have reacted as he had.

Like a teacher watching his student unravel some complicated equation, Turner waited for the realization to sink in, then spoke.

"John. You can't give up now. You must pursue this case." Turner took his last sip of coffee, then delicately patted his mouth with the starched white napkin that had lain over his lap. "Prosecutors are impatient." He didn't say the young ones; he didn't have to. "You've simply got to continue digging. If you've exhausted one avenue, try another, and another if you must." He placed the napkin on the table beside his cup, a signal that there really wasn't much left to say, that the luncheon would soon be over.

"You must pursue this case, John. You see that, don't you?"

"Yes, sir. I do."

"If Higdon works with you, fine. That'll make it easier. If not, you'll simply have to do it without him."

Silverman tried not to let his excitement show. This was just what he had needed to hear. But how would he sell this to Mary Ann? She was counting on the case being over. As if reading his mind, Turner smiled.

"May I intrude into your personal life?"

Silverman smiled his yes.

"Your wife needs a change of scenery. She's had quite a shock. A short vacation—if you can manage it," he added delicately, "might do the trick."

Turner quickly changed the subject. "When this case is over, John, and you're ready for private practice, do you think you'll be staying in Philadelphia or going back home?"

Silverman said he wasn't really sure. But it wasn't until later, on his way home from the office, that he'd realized Turner's remark was not idle curiosity; it was intentionally made, for Mary Ann's benefit. He was hinting that Silverman could have the very sort of position in private practice Mary Ann wanted for him. A position with Turner's prestigious law firm. He had given Silverman something special with which to appease his wife.

Turner looked at his watch and smiled at Silverman. "I've got another appointment, John," he said with an air of its being no less important than this one was. "Got to be going."

"Mr. Turner, I really do thank you for listening to me. And helping me, sir."

Turner received his appreciation with open warmth. "If you find it helpful, call me again. If you'd like, we could meet periodically to discuss your progress. It's an important case. I'll help you in any way I can."

Silverman placed his napkin alongside his cup, his side of the table now a mirror image of Turner's. He knew he had to be careful about talking to Turner, an outsider. Silverman was, after all, a public official, bound by grand jury secrecy. Yet his resolve was fortified. He couldn't wait to get going again. He wanted to make the case, get Stavaros and the others, now more than ever.

* * *

Silverman finished recounting his lunch with Turner.

"I love you John. You know that, don't you?"

Mary Ann said nothing more, looked up into her husband's eyes, her expression conveying everything she wanted to say. She was trying—God how she was trying—coercing herself to withstand the intolerable. Trying to hold on while John pursued what he wanted. She would wait because she had to, because there still seemed no other choice. She would try with every bit of strength she possessed to hold on, to endure. To survive.

They had taken Stanton Turner's advice. The Carribean holiday had nearly depleted their meager savings, but so far it seemed well worth the temporary loss of a bank balance.

The evening was delightfully warm; a delicate, subtle breeze brushed past the couples on the patio dance floor. The hotel was perhaps second class, but even in its simplicity, it seemed beautiful to Mary Ann. She felt more relaxed and happy than she had in months. But she was worried, even here, about John. He seemed so preoccupied, so inaccessible. As if part of him wasn't here at all.

Dinner had been served on the veranda, and from there John and Mary Ann walked the few steps to join the outdoor dancing.

He held her, the soft Latin rhythms swirling slowly by, the unnatural electric multicolored incandescence flooding the surrounding palm trees, all creating the festive atmosphere paid for by the hotel's guests. She snuggled closer, the warm, fresh comfort of her body pressed to his, her yearning green eyes sadly searching his face. He smiled down at her, then looked away, trying to let himself drift with the music. But he couldn't.

No matter how hard he tried, this place for him was a prelude, a chore, an obligation to Mary Ann, something to be done so he could get on with something else. He could feel his body tense, it seemed as if he were holding Mary Ann up. He wanted to sit down, waited impatiently for the music to end. Grand jury talk, by silent mutual consent, had been forbidden. Yet it rarely left his mind. Three more days and they'd be back in Philadelphia. Three more days and he could finish what he had started.

It was their last full day. Silverman had insisted; just curious, he told her, and it was so close, twenty minutes by plane. They'd make a day of it, fly over for the afternoon, walk through Donald Ames's Hotel Caribe, have lunch in the nearby town, and then fly back.

153

Mary Ann had not been pleased. But she agreed.

They walked through the ornate lobby.

"I feel uncomfortable here, John. Let's go. Let's have lunch and fly back." But Silverman was determined.

"Come on. Just one quick look around, and then we'll leave, okay?" Mary Ann sighed. She wanted to remind him that they were here to get away from all this, but she realized that it was useless to protest.

They approached the sign indicating that the pool area was ahead.

Donald Ames sat on the shaded balcony of his permanent penthouse suite, his abdomen hanging over his expensive bathing suit, the matching cabana jacket lying on the table beside him. He hated the sun.

He was looking down at the pool area, watching her sunning, wondering why she did it, her pale skin always burned. He was growing tired of her; she was getting on his nerves. This trip she had been so quiet, so submissive. She did whatever he wanted without complaint, but lately she seemed merely to endure him. She'd always been terrific in bed, but this submissiveness made him uncomfortable, bored him.

He stretched and took a sip of his drink. He felt better now. Everything was going to be all right, after all. Stavaros was right. Nothing was going to come of it. He rose and went inside.

Silverman and Mary Ann walked into the pool area, strolled through the aisle between the lounge chairs. He noticed the young woman in the black bikini lying on the lounge to his left. She was beginning to burn.

14

Mixed in with his other office mail, the envelope seemed curiously out of place—pale-pink, note-sized stationery, the address and the word "personal" written in a rounded, feminine script. Silverman opened it first. It was a handwritten apology from Denise Owens.

Everything Silverman had seen in Denise Owens was contradicted by her handwriting. Perhaps behind her hardened reporter's façade lived some other very different, very feminine woman. But most likely her script was merely the last remaining trace of a schoolgirl childhood long since left behind.

Silverman's speculation turned to suspicion. Why had she written to apologize for her conduct? He reread the letter before satisfying himself the gesture was sincere. Denise closed with a reaffirmation of her embarrassment and an offer to apologize in person "over coffee."

Silverman left the remainder of his mail untouched; it was time to leave for the meeting.

Jacobs was already seated in Higdon's office when Silverman entered. He took the empty chair.

"How's your mom holding up?" he asked Jacobs.

"As well as can be expected, I guess."

"How about you?"

Jacobs merely shrugged.

Bob looked older to Silverman; he noticed the beginnings of gray in his short, wiry hair. Maybe not older, just tired, he decided, conscious now of Higdon, waiting impatiently behind his desk for Silverman's attention.

"Hi, Ray," Silverman said, turning to provide the obedience Higdon required.

"How was your trip?" Higdon asked with sufficient disinterest for Silverman merely to respond in kind.

"Fine."

To business. Higdon looked first at Jacobs, then Silverman.

155

Silverman had requested the meeting by memo, suggesting they consult on the investigation's progress. But Higdon would begin.

"Well, we're here, I suppose," he said, "to decide what to do next. John, any ideas?"

Okay, Silverman thought, I've got some ideas. "Well," he began, leaning toward Higdon's immaculate desk, "I'd begin with a re-examination of the subpoenaed records." He turned to face Jacobs. "No offense, Bob, but maybe your agents missed some things. I'd have them go through that stuff again."

Jacobs looked over at Higdon. Silverman was confused by his reaction. He waited for an explanation.

"We lost the agents while you were away," Higdon explained. "IRS decided the investigation no longer justified that kind of support."

Silverman was about to ask why Higdon hadn't done something, why he hadn't tried to stop the removal of the agents. He decided against it.

"Can we do it ourselves?" he asked instead, turning and directing his question at Jacobs, quickly adding, "You and me?"

"We can try."

Higdon nodded his approval. It was clear he would not search through records. "What else?" he asked.

It was Jacobs's turn. "The letter," he said. "Is there anything we can do to check it out?"

"Nothing, I suppose," Silverman said. "All we have is a copy."

"Wrong," Higdon said.

Higdon picked up the copy of the letter, which had lain on his desk since Jacobs had brought it in a week or so ago.

"We should have a documents expert look at this. Even though it's a copy, he might be able to check the age of the typewriter that typed it, and there might be something else significant about it we simply don't know."

Higdon studied the letter clinically, like a surgeon examining a wound. "We may want to question the person who typed it. Miss M.B.," he said, reading the lower-case initials at the bottom-left corner. "That's probably Ames's private secretary. Before we get her in here, we should discover anything at all the lab can determine from the letter. I'll take care of this."

They discussed other tasks, some of which were rejected, some decided upon. Silverman mentioned that the grand jury hadn't had a session for a long while. The jurors were probably a bit bewildered, perhaps angered by all that they had read and seen about the mayor and a Bahamian land deal, none of which, of course, they'd heard about in the last grand jury session. Shouldn't they be brought in, even if it was just for a talking to, an update? he asked.

Higdon said no; it wasn't time yet.

"Anything else?" Higdon asked, leaning back in his chair, his arms resting on each side, striking the commander pose again. There was something else on his mind. Something the others hadn't thought of yet.

"Yeah," Silverman said. "The bidding process. I suppose we've got to tackle that, learn how it works and who handles it."

"Very good," Higdon said. And although he remained firmly seated in his stiff position, he nodded recognition toward the young prosecutor and smiled just slightly.

Silverman was pleased. He didn't return the smile, though, waiting in concentration, for Higdon's next question.

"What about the people in the State Roads Commission office in Harrisburg?" Higdon asked him. "What would you do about them? How would you determine which ones are the likely candidates for our attention?"

"Subpoena them to grand jury and question them?"

"Eventually, but not at first," Higdon said. There was a first step, one that interested him. He waited to see if Silverman knew. He didn't. Higdon looked at Jacobs. He, too, was silent.

"The press," Higdon said, leaning back into his chair again.

"What do you mean?" Silverman asked, clearly puzzled.

Higdon explained. The State Roads Commission was filled with political appointees. There were bound to be old news articles about them. The library retained the old editions of the local papers on microfilm. They should be reviewed. They might provide the leads they needed.

"That'll take forever," Jacobs said. "There's no indexing; we'd have to run the film on every old newspaper. That could take weeks, maybe months."

Silverman thought of Denise and her offer to meet for coffee. "I might be able to help," he said.

Silverman looked across the table at Denise Owens. "Thanks for the note."

Denise tapped the dangling ash of her cigarette onto the crumpled aluminum ash tray and took a sip of her coffee.

"Anytime," she said, smiling at him, but her tone was more subdued than it had been at their earlier meetings.

157

"I see you've survived your ordeal," he said, studying her, then quickly looking out the federal cafeteria's large window to the street below.

"Yeah." She sighed. "Guess so. My editor nearly killed me. Stavaros threatened to sue for libel. Hasn't yet. But I'm still here."

She smiled at Silverman until he returned his gaze to her; then, flicking more ash into the tray, her eyes still on him, she added, "Still on the story."

Silverman shook his head. "I consider that a mixed blessing."

There was clearly some sort of interest in her eyes. No sooner had Silverman noticed it than she let it fade.

"How you doing?" she asked.

"Okay. I guess."

"You got some sun somewhere."

"Yeah. Went away for a couple of days."

Strange. He had started to say that he and Mary Ann had gone away but didn't. He felt slightly unsettled. It passed quickly.

"Bahamian resort with Mayor Lane?" she asked, smiling, pushing loose strands of hair away from her forehead.

He laughed, more comfortable now. "We're off the record, right?"

"Sure."

"You know. I was there. Didn't stay there. But I saw it."

"Well?"

"Pretty nice place."

"Didn't happen to run into any of—your friends?"

"Uh, no. Fortunately."

Denise took a final drag on her cigarette, then stubbed it out, steadying the little ash tray with her free hand.

He spoke again. "Listen. I need a favor. Can't offer you anything in return, but you can help me."

She didn't say anything, lit another cigarette and waited.

"Your paper keeps—what do you call them, morgue files. Indexes and copies of newsworthy articles?"

"Of course."

"Would you be willing to get me copies of some old news clippings about certain people from your paper's morgue files without anyone knowing?"

Denise understood immediately. She held up her hand, her thumb and forefinger separated by about two inches to show the headline she'd concocted. "Federal Prosecutor Searches *Inquirer's* Files in Last-ditch Attempt to Save Investigation."

"Something like that. Will you do it for me?"

"Nothing in return? Not one little story? One tiny leak?"

"Nothing."

Denise considered it.

"Sure. Why not."

Mary Ann strolled through the aisles of Bonwit Teller's "better dresses" department for the second time in two days. Jamie was in nursery school, and alone, time passed a little easier for her in the store. Dresses on hangers obediently slid across aluminum racks as she searched for the right size and color in a dress she knew she wouldn't buy.

Mary Ann knew the store provided her with only the illusion of sanctuary, but it didn't matter. Time passed less painfully there; the sheer height of the rooms somehow helped. In the apartment, counting each hour, each day, only decreased the speed with which her life moved forward. John's case was still her ordeal. It wouldn't let go; she couldn't put it aside. At first, she thought the trip to the islands had helped, but as soon as they were home, it was as if they'd never left. The pressure began building again almost instantly.

Her emotions, contradictory, kept attacking her. She loved John. She hated their life. Her patience was at an end. He was selfish, unconcerned about her feelings. She felt confused. And frightened. Helplessly, she groped for a solution, her thoughts random, sometimes bizarre. What if suddenly she became deathly ill? John would have to take her home, back to her parents. Suppose she got a job there? What if they had another baby? What if she left John? That she would even think about that frightened her most of all. She was actually trembling. She'd have to get a grip on herself, hold on a while longer.

Just as she had the day before, she walked toward the designer section. Spring outfits were coming in each day; maybe there was something new to examine.

As she turned the corner, she immediately noticed the man with graying hair standing at the counter, his back to her. He began to turn; Mary Ann saw what looked like pockmarks on his face. It couldn't be. Her heart stopped beating. She froze, ready to scream. He turned toward her.

Of course, it wasn't Stavaros, merely someone waiting for his wife.

Mary Ann probably would have stood there a few more seconds recovering if she hadn't heard her name being called. As it was, she didn't respond at first, but after the second or perhaps third "Mary Ann," she turned to find Betty Tucker. She forced a smile; Betty hadn't called or spoken to her since the night of her and her husband's escape from the Silvermans' dinner party.

"So nice to see you, Mary Ann," she said with enough insincerity to fill a ladies' tea party.

"Hi, Betty."

"We've really been meaning to call you and John. But we've been so busy. The new house and all."

"That's okay."

"How is John?"

"He's fine. And Harold?"

"Fine." She held up the dress she'd selected. "Like it? We're going away next week, and I desperately need some new things. Looks like you've been away, too."

"Yes, we . . ."

"I really must be going," Betty interrupted maliciously. "So nice to see you again. We really must get together soon. Call us, will you?"

Mary Ann watched her walk down the aisle. It wasn't that she was really fond of Betty, but at least the Tuckers had provided some social life in Philadelphia. Now that too, seemed to be lost to her. She turned to leave. It was all getting to be more than she could stand.

"Miss Owens left these for you," Jan said.

Silverman took the two large manila envelopes from Jan's desk. He opened the first one; it was crammed full of copies of news clippings. On the top of the pile was a sheet of pale-pink personal stationery.

"Good hunting" was all it said.

The stacks of *Daily Racing Forms* that had lain on Silverman's office worktable had been placed on the floor. Now spread out on the table, in neat little piles, were the news clippings, arranged in various categories. Higdon hadn't come in today. Silverman and Jacobs spent the entire day reading the articles.

The *Inquirer* must have had a separate file on Albert Lacona, the state roads commissioner. There were at least fifteen articles about him, none of them really derogatory, mostly news stories about one of the state's senior bureaucrats. Generally, Lacona was depicted as a career civil servant who had received several important appointed positions, partly as a result of his political activities.

While federal employees, under the Hatch Act, were prohibited from engaging in partisan political activities, there was no such prohibition in Pennsylvania for city or state government employees. Lacona had been active in the campaigns of several state and city politicians, including Mayor Phillip Brooke Lane's. One of the articles described him as a long-time friend of the mayor's and one of those original party workers during Lane's earliest political career.

"He might be a good place to start," Jacobs said, returning the final Lacona article to the pile.

Silverman agreed.

"John?" Pat Ramondi said, rapping quietly on the open door frame.

She'd apparently been standing there for a few seconds, waiting for the right time to interrupt. Silverman noticed she was wearing the gray sweater again today.

"Hi, Pat," he said, looking quickly from the lovely curve of her large breasts to her face.

"Miss Eccleston sent this down for Ray," she said, handing him the letter. "I thought you'd want to look at it in Ray's absence."

Silverman read the letter, then handed it to Jacobs.

It was from Richard Franklin White, addressed, for formality's sake, to the U.S. attorney herself. White's opening salvo: in suitably polite legal language, it reminded Miss Eccleston that the grand jury investigation of Donald Ames had been pending "without resolution by indictment or otherwise" for some months now. Knowing full well that no action would be taken in response to his letter, White requested that either indictments be returned "forthwith" or the investigation be terminated. In the latter event, he requested a formal, written exoneration of his client.

White for the defense. He was now watching the clock. Naturally, the government would ignore his request except, perhaps, for a short response thanking him for his concern and reminding him that grand jury matters were secret, so that, unfortunately, he was not entitled to a progress report on his client's criminal status.

White wouldn't write again, but when he felt the time was right, he would file a formal motion to terminate the investigation.

Silverman guessed they had about a month, six weeks at

the longest, before Judge Montarelli, faced with having to rule on the motion, would require a representation from the government that enough evidence had been discovered to continue the probe. Silverman did not care to speculate on the consequences of the prosecutors' failure to satisfy the judge.

Jacobs handed the letter back to Silverman. "Guess we'd better get moving," he said.

Silverman's re-examination of the subpoenaed records had begun. The last three days were spent in the antiseptically tiled, hollow, narrow corridor of the unused cell block. At night, his briefcase packed with more subpoenaed papers, he took enough home to keep him busy until bedtime. Tonight, as he had the other two evenings before, he sat on the sofa, reading, but the item that interested him most was the one that Jacobs had given him—the Pennsylvania bid submission and selection manual.

Designed to be tamper-proof, the procedure for competitive bid submissions required that several steps be followed. No one person had exclusive control over any one step.

Step one: in order to submit the bid for city highway work, the contractor had to appear personally in Harrisburg at the State Roads Office. The bid was to be typewritten on the eight by ten form the commission had mailed to him. He would hand it, folded down, to a clerk, who would place it in a pale-green commission envelope. The envelope would be sealed in front of the contractor, the back of it stamped so no one could open it without detection. According to the rules, a second clerk had to be present at all times.

Step two: the clerk would then place the envelope through the slit of a locked ballot box that was to be kept in the safe when not in use. Two keys were needed to open the box. One key was held by the deputy commissioner and one by the commissioner himself.

Step three: the box and the sealed bids could be opened only in the presence of three state employees on the day of bid selection. All bids were to be kept in a folder after the conclusion of bid selection for inspection by the public.

How in the world could anyone penetrate and tamper with that process? he thought.

Silverman rested his head on the back of the sofa the manual lying across his knees like a sleeping lap dog. He yawned, his mind groggy from the exposure to so much detailed information, most of which, he realized as he went through the records, was completely irrelevant. He yawned again and stretched. It had to be done; no point in agonizing over it. Mr. Turner was right; every possible approach had to be tried.

He started reading again. It wasn't sinking in; he'd reached his limit for that night. He turned off the lights and went to the bedroom.

Mary Ann was in bed already, reading. He looked at the digital clock radio on the night table beside his bed: 10:05 P.M. She looked up from her book, "Are you coming to bed?"

"Yeah, I've had it for tonight. I'm tired."

Silverman undressed and slid in beside her. He lay quietly on his back and closed his eyes. The room was absolutely silent. He waited for the sound of a turning page. It never came. When he looked over at her, he saw that she was staring at the pages, only pretending to read. He turned on his side, facing her. She still didn't look at him.

He moved closer; their bodies touched. Gently, he removed the book from her hands. Finally, she looked at him, her eyes full of unspoken emotion.

Silverman let the book slip to the carpeted floor, its muffled thud the sound of a single heartbeat.

He kissed her, at first gently, then harder. All the tension they had been feeling these past few weeks seemed to melt away. Her mouth opened to receive his tongue; she pressed closer.

Silverman kicked away the covers. Mary Ann sat up and pulled off her nightgown, her breasts rising with the arching of her back.

He moved her on top of him and began kissing and licking her breasts, enjoying her soft groans as much as the sensation of his tongue on the soft pink flesh.

She moved down his body, and as she did, strands of her auburn hair gently cascaded over his chest. He watched as she touched his erection; then she bent over him, her hair folding over his groin.

He lay back on the pillow, closed his eyes, shut his mind to all but the pleasure. He groaned as his entire body felt the early tingling of his sperm, hot and beginning to force its way to climax. He touched her shoulders; she lifted her head. Gently, he eased her onto her back beside him. She lay there waiting for him, staring deeply into his eyes. He moved toward her.

They both started with the telephone's first intrusive ring. He hesitated.

"Let it go," she whispered.

It flashed through his mind that Jacobs was due back in

town from Harrisburg. He looked at Mary Ann apologetically. "I've got to get this. It might be Jacobs," he said as he reached for the receiver.

"Hello," he said, his voice hoarse.

"Hi. John?" Jacobs asked. "You all right?"

Silverman slid over to his side of the bed, turned his head from the receiver, and cleared his throat.

"Yeah. Fine."

Mary Ann stared up at the ceiling. The moment was lost. She turned on her side, away from her husband.

"Find anything?"

"I'm not sure John. Think so, though. Wanna hear?"

"Yeah."

"Albert Lacona's a heavy-set, middle-aged man. Wife and two teenaged kids. Lives in a home that's within his means. Modest, you white folks call it. Drives a Chevy to work. Doesn't seem to entertain lavishly—"

"Listen," Silverman interrupted, glancing over his shoulder as Mary Ann, her back still toward him, reached for the covers. She lay perfectly still. Silverman was about to suggest to Jacobs that information like this could have waited until tomorrow morning.

"Wait a minute, man," Jacobs said, as if anticipating Silverman's words. "Hear me out. What I've got isn't great, but there may be something here."

Silverman continued looking for a moment at Mary Ann's still body.

"Okay. Go ahead," he finally said.

"Like I said, the guy lives in an ordinary house. But the checking I did indicates he's purchased a lot of expensive items to go in there. A couple of big color TVs, stereo, fancy furniture—that kind of stuff."

"How'd he pay for it?"

"Best I could find out, most of it was bought on time. Some—a few, I guess—were cash sales. He pays his bills regularly, never misses a payment."

Jacobs read Silverman's silence. "Yeah, I know," he added. "Anyone can buy stuff like that on time. My neighborhood's filled with shit like that. But there's more."

Silverman sat up on the side of the bed. His back was now to Mary Ann. He didn't notice her slight trembling.

"Like what?" he asked.

"Like he's a boozer," Jacobs said. "Goes to this same lounge in this fancy restaurant every day, both at lunch time and after work.

"I sat on him nights. Actually, didn't think of it until the second night. Picked him up after work, watched him go to the lounge. Pirate's Den, its called. Then home to dinner. Both nights I tailed him, he went out again. Alone."

Silverman didn't notice when Mary Ann got out of bed, pulled on her nightgown, and walked out of the bedroom.

"Where'd Lacona go?" Silverman asked.

"First night to a porno flick. Stayed there for about three hours."

"You go in? How was the movie?"

"No, man. Stayed in the car. Hate musicals."

Silverman laughed. "So the man likes dirty movies. So what? What about the other night?"

"Well, he spent that night in an apartment until about two in the morning. I thought it might be a girl, so I checked. Apartment's registered to an Anthony Toscatta. Barber. I saw several other men go into the building; don't know for sure if they went to the same apartment. Lacona left alone. I think it was a poker game, so he's got some dough to spend on cards."

"How'd the others look?"

"Average working guys. They didn't look like high rollers. I don't think our man's playing for high stakes."

"Uhm."

There was silence in the apartment; the air was quite still.

"There's more," Jacobs said. He'd saved the best for last.

"The guy buys a lot of clothes. Nice stuff. He sure wasn't wearing great threads when I watched him. Dresses like a government employee. Like you and me."

"Like you," Silverman teased. "Maybe he wears the good stuff on weekends. How'd he pay for it?"

"All cash. Far as I can tell."

"Anything else?"

"Yeah. One other thing. Curious, too. Man goes to Philadelphia three or four times a month. Doesn't take his car. Greyhound bus every time. Stays overnight, then back the next day. Always alone. Doesn't take his family."

"Official business?" Silverman asked.

"Could be. But I don't think so. Pays for the bus tickets himself. Cash. Don't know where he goes or where he stays. It would take forever to run that down. It's peculiar, man. Why the trips? He doesn't look like a culture buff—"

Silverman missed the rest of Jacobs's sentence. He heard

the thud of an object being flung against the floor in the other room. He saw the empty bed, looked at the open doorway. Holy shit! he thought.

"Hey, Bob," he interrupted. "Gotta go. Thanks for the information. Let's talk tomorrow," he added, obviously in a rush.

"Can't, man. Been away three days. Gotta stay home. You know how it is."

Silverman hadn't heard him. "Right, I'll call you," he said, searching for his shorts. He found them and hung up.

Mary Ann was on the sofa, her legs curled under her like some hapless beggar. The bidding manual and the other papers Silverman had brought home lay strewn on the floor, the obvious aftereffect of her rage.

He sat down beside her, touched her shoulder.

"I'm sorry, babe," he said. "But Bob Jacobs just returned from—"

She sprang to her feet, turned to face him, her eyes reddened, furious.

"I don't want to hear about it, John. Not anymore."

"Quiet, honey, you'll wake Jamie."

"I don't care who I wake," she screamed. She grabbed a handful of the strewn papers and flung them at him. "I don't want to hear about your damned investigation again. I don't want it mentioned in this apartment ever again."

From her bedroom, Jamie awoke and started to cry. She called for her mommy. Mary Ann didn't move.

"I don't want this here," she screamed, pointing at the papers. "Work in the office. Don't bring it home. You keep it in the office, John. All of it."

Her anger held her tears back; she stood before him, no longer pointing, motionless.

He didn't answer her. There was no point. Jamie called out again.

"All of it, damn you. Do you understand?" she asked, clearly not about to move until he'd provided a response.

"Okay," he finally said.

The teacher had resolved to do it that day. She would walk right over to the fence and tell that strange little man not to come there anymore, not to stand there peering at the children.

But when Higdon arrived and took his usual place behind the fence, she did nothing but what she had done on all the other mornings. She stood on the sidelines of the asphalt playground and watched out for the children. And kept her eyes on Higdon.

There was something childishly lonely, almost pathetic, in his frail stance, his forlorn gaze. His skin was so pale, his cheeks so drawn, as he stood with his shoulders hunched, his hands in the pockets of his raincoat.

Even from a distance, she thought she could see a faraway look in his eyes, as though his mind were focused on some distant thought.

The young policeman passed the limousine at the curb, pretending not to notice it or the driver leaning beside its glossy black body. It embarrassed him that it could remain there despite the no parking sign, that he had to pretend it wasn't there. But he knew he couldn't touch it, so he walked slowly by, looking the other way.

The driver quietly watched the policeman as he passed. He saw the young cop's discomfort, and he enjoyed it.

They both looked about the same age; both were in uniform, the cop in blue, the driver in dark gray suit and matching topcoat. His gray cap lay inside the limousine, on the front seat.

A closer look at the driver would have disclosed something behind his boyish appearance, something the cop didn't have. He wasn't only a driver. He had another expertise, one that his boss would call on from time to time.

The driver leaned from the car and stood as he saw his boss leave the building. He reached to open the back door for Johnny Stavaros.

Silverman consciously slowed his pace, wanting to savor the afterglow he felt from his second luncheon meeting with Stanton Turner.

The first hint of spring could be sensed; felt, he thought, though not yet actually seen. It was, officially, still winter. No blossoms. No greening, even in the suburb of Wynnewood. Yet the air was a bit lighter, the sky less gray; and an almost imperceptible hint of gentle fragrance penetrated the still-present chill that hung on the city's streets.

The farther from the League's Gothic structure he went, the more optimistic he became. He unfastened the top button of his overcoat as he crossed through the traffic on his way to Chestnut Street and the courthouse.

The investigation was moving forward, he'd reported to Mr.

Turner; new leads were being followed, just as he'd suggested to John at their first luncheon. Once again, their conversation had been devoid of details, no identifying facts provided. Turner had seemed genuinely pleased. Silverman had felt proud, encouraged that his senior friend had taken an interest in the case.

Turner had noticed the last remnants of John's sun tan and so had asked about his trip and, in his delicate way, Mary Ann's condition. Embarrassed, Silverman had lied.

The trip had been a splendid suggestion, he'd told Mr. Turner, had apparently done the trick. Turner had smiled, quickly blotting from his lips with the starched white napkin the remaining fragments from his last swallow of Dover sole, and had said something about Mary Ann's soon enjoying more of the same, more of what she obviously deserved.

Strange, Silverman couldn't actually reconstruct the words Turner had used. Probably he hadn't really said what Silverman had heard him say. Yet he was sure the message of a future place for him in Mr. Turner's law firm was once again being transmitted.

It was an interesting prospect for the future; flattering, too, and one with which Mary Ann would, no doubt, be delighted. Curiously, though, lately, even the thought of big-firm life made him uncomfortable. But, wasn't that the very sort of position he was, after all, being groomed for? What had he been doing with his life if not preparing for that very moment. The moment of respected adulthood, of real responsibility: John Silverman, attorney at law, prestigious big-firm lawyer. Husband, father. Community leader. A Harvard man.

But was that what he really wanted for himself when this case was over?

He thought of Mary Ann. Since the other night, it was hard to deny that their spats were becoming more serious. Silverman thought that Mary Ann would come around eventually. She'd be all right. *They'd* be all right. They still loved each other, didn't they? Besides, he didn't have time to dwell on all this. It would work out. Things always worked out. Now he had the case to think of and more important things to deal with.

Silverman entered the courthouse and took the elevator to his office. The afterglow of lunch was gone.

Lunch the next day was to be a much simpler affair. A quick sandwich alone and then a half hour with the morning's *Daily Racing Form* in the back row of Congress Hall. But as Silverman approached the entrance of the building, Denise Owens appeared, on her way out.

"Hi," she said, smiling, standing before him.

"Didn't know you were into early American history," he said, curious as to why she had been in there.

"They told me you sometimes go in there at lunch time," she explained, pointing her thumb behind her at the building with what Silverman considered, although he didn't know why, irreverence for the old structure.

"Who said?" he asked.

She smiled again.

"My sources, of course," she answered, skipping down the steps, quickly looping her arm in his and pulling him away. "Come on, I want to talk to you."

He felt ill at ease, her arm in his, walking together down the street. Her touch was gentle. He stiffened slightly, but she paid him no mind; she was searching for a good spot for them to talk. Thinking that the act seemed innocent enough, he reconsidered, relaxed, and took the lead.

"This way," he said, guiding her to the little park behind the cluster of historical buildings. The late winter's chill had returned; all the benches were deserted.

She found the bench she preferred and led him toward it.

"So?" he asked, once they were seated. "What's so important?"

It was cold enough for his breath to crystallize. She watched the smoky rising of his words. Her eyes wandered from his mouth to his eyes. She was studying his face. He saw it, noticing how her eyes had taken on a sharper, more intense focus. She had done that once before. It made him uneasy.

She may have seen that. Her expression changed, her gaze now more distant, though still alert.

"What do you do in there?" she asked, her smile returning.

"In Congress Hall?"

"Yeah." She lit a cigarette, her breath heavy with the mixture of exhaled smoke and crystallized air.

"Pick winning horses."

"Right!" she said sarcastically. Obviously, he was lying. She had embarrassed him by prying into something too personal. Then she remembered the *Daily Racing Form* she'd noticed under his arm that day in the elevator. "You do, don't you?" she said, sort of pleased with the image of him, sitting alone in Congress Hall, poring over his newspaper.

"Would I lie to a reporter?"

He leaned back and placed his left arm over the back of the bench but immediately felt as though he were putting his arm around her, so, self-consciously, he let it slip back to his side.

"That's not why you wanted to see me, is it?" he said, trying to move beyond his last clumsy maneuver.

She seemed not to have noticed the arm at all. "No," she said. "Albert Lacona."

"What about him?"

"I made myself a copy of those news clippings I gave you."

"Figured you might."

"Yeah. There were a lot of articles about him."

"Are you on the record with me, Denise?"

"You mean, are you on the record with me?"

"Yeah. I guess I do." She'd caught him off guard.

She stamped out her cigarette, pushed the loose strands of hair from her forehead, and looked at him intently. "John. Let's have an understanding. You and I will always be off the record unless one of us says otherwise. Fair enough?"

"Fair enough."

"Anyway," she continued. "I didn't bring you here—"

"I brought you here."

"You didn't bring me here," she added with a touch of a smile, "for me to *ask* you anything. I wanted to tell you something. I hope you realize we're often on the same side. That is, if you do your job right—and fairly."

"Tell me what?"

"That was a good idea of yours, getting those old articles. Albert Lacona's an interesting guy." She waited a few seconds to see if he would react. He didn't, so she continued. "Called him a couple of times. He wouldn't speak to me. Tried to make an appointment to interview him at his office. Nothing. So I drove to Harrisburg last night. Was at his office at eight-thirty this morning. Wouldn't be interviewed. Told me I was a muck-raker and threatened to call the state police if I didn't leave him alone. Call the cops on me, a servant of the people?" She reached in her purse for another cigarette and lit it. "The cops on me! Can you imagine that," she added, smiling.

"The nerve of some people." He wondered if she had found anything.

"You guys been looking at Lacona, too?"

"You said no questions."

"One question. Big deal."

"No comment."

"Prick."

170

He laughed. "You reporters sure are a crass lot. Where are your ladylike manners?"

She stamped out her cigarette. Silverman noticed it was still long, mostly unsmoked.

"John, I don't expect you to respond to this. Let's just say I'm doing my civic duty. If you haven't looked at Lacona yet, do. If I only had subpoena power. I can't get enough to write, but I'm picking up rumblings about this guy." She instinctively fumbled in her purse for another cigarette and didn't speak again until it was lit. "If I get it first, I'm going to write it. But you ought to look at him, John. That is, if you haven't already." She searched his eyes for a reaction.

"Thanks" was all he said.

Lacona's overreaction to Denise's visit was interesting. Subpoena power. She was right. He'd tell Jacobs about this.

15

Silverman did tell Jacobs. Both men sat among the records in the otherwise-empty auxiliary cell block. Both agreed on Owens's instinct on Lacona. It fit with what little Jacobs had learned of him in Harrisburg. And both agreed on what to do next.

Getting someone's attention is what prosecutors call it.

The method of this exercise varies in detail from case to case, but the object is always the same. The person whose activities have come under suspicion—the target—is placed in a pressure cooker, his life slowly made miserable by government intrusion into his affairs. This intrusion usually takes the form of a tax-evasion investigation, a so-called "third-party net-worth case." IRS agents contact virtually every person who has had financial dealings with the target in order to learn how much money the target spent during the year. They then compare that amount with how much income he reported on his tax returns. If he spent more than he earned, then he had "income"—often from an illegal source such as bribe money—that he didn't report on his tax returns (for obvious reasons) and on which he didn't pay taxes. He would then be subject to prosecution for the serious federal crime of tax evasion.

When the government's main aim is to get the target's "attention," the probe is conducted with considerably more visibility than normal.

There are months of the target having to endure hearing regularly from his banker, accountant, stockbroker, that government agents have been snooping around, summonsing records, probing his expenditures. Then, when embarrassment turns to apprehension, the target receives his first direct contact from the prosecutor.

The phone call usually comes in the evening, to the target's home, after he has dropped his guard a bit after a harrowing day, maybe after a martini or two and dinner.

The target is asked if he has retained a "criminal lawyer." If the answer is yes, he is then told to have his lawyer call the prosecutor first thing the next morning. If the answer is no, he is told to get one immediately and have him call as soon as possible. And then, abruptly, the conversation would be terminated.

When the defense lawyer calls the prosecutor, a meeting is arranged. The target might be invited to the meeting only on the condition that he won't say anything, just listen. If he attends, the prosecutor does his best to intimidate him, addressing his speech to the lawyer but keeping his eyes riveted on the target's. Wise defense lawyers never bring their clients to these meetings.

The main point of the meeting is to offer the target his choices.

Choice number one: the target can do nothing in the vain hope that all of this will go away and nothing will happen. But he is made to understand that since it isn't going to go away, choice number one means indictment, public trial, conviction, and jail. In other words, choice number one is no choice at all.

Choice number two: the target can "seek a less than totally adversary relationship with the government": a plea bargain, lenient treatment in return for cooperation and testimony. It is explained that the witness can "cut a deal," end this nightmare right here and now. His part of the bargain requires his turning into a witness for the prosecution against his friends, business associates, and colleagues. This means taking the witness stand, admitting his own guilt, and pointing an accusing finger at others. In return, the government agrees to charge him with a less severe crime, or if he is really lucky, give him immunity from prosecution.

But before all of this can happen, before any target can even consider plea bargaining, the prosecution first has to place him in its vise, "get his attention." And in the case of Albert Lacona, there was a peculiar problem facing Silverman and Jacobs—time.

A standard net-worth investigation of Lacona could take as long as a year. And there was no telling when, or if, during the course of that investigation, he might be ready to crack, to try and cut a deal. Clearly, they didn't have that kind of time.

It was well past midnight when Silverman and Jacobs finished formulating their plan. The styrofoam coffee cups were empty; the Burger King wrappers had been pushed aside. It was a gamble. Both men knew that they'd have one shot at this and only one. Silverman had even endured the discomfort of having telephoned Higdon at his home that night to run the plan by him. He'd agreed. It was their only choice.

Their plan was a bluff. No one had apparently ever done it this way before. But despite the risk, there seemed no other way.

The IRS Intelligence Division would open a third-party net-worth investigation of Lacona. All the bureaucratic wheels would be set in motion. And then stopped. The IRS would not do a net worth on Lacona, but it wouldn't know that.

Jacobs would get the authorization to open a case file on Lacona, and he would have a junior agent assigned to the case. The junior agent would be told to put the file on the "back burner" and leave it there. No summonses would be issued. No agents would go out and question businessmen.

But with a case file officially opened, Jacobs could acquire Lacona's tax returns and from them learn the amount of income he had reported as having earned and paid taxes on.

The plan was to make Lacona believe that he was under investigation and at the same time to get enough financial data on his expenditures so that Jacobs could make a rough comparison with his reported income to see if Lacona in fact spent more than he earned. For that, they would use the grand jury.

Lacona would be "investigated" as part of the Ames-Stavaros road-construction case. Financial records of those with whom Lacona dealt would be subpoenaed by the grand jury and then given to Jacobs. Lacona, they hoped, would get nervous.

They figured all of this would take about two months. Maybe less, but probably not. They would then be in a position to call Lacona and give him the speech. By then, enough would have been done to tell him, truthfully, that he was in deep-shit trouble, that he was "facing" indictment for income tax evasion.

But it would be a bluff.

If Lacona wasn't receptive, if he didn't turn but chose to remain a target instead, they would not be able to indict him. The pressure would end right there. At least for some time.

One thing was certain. As much pressure as possible would have to be exerted on Lacona. There was an additional way to accomplish that.

Silverman would subpoena to grand jury all the employees at the State Roads office. That is, all but Lacona. He'd be the only one left out. The newspapers would probably find out: all the clerks would be subpoenaed to grand jury as witnesses but not their boss. Therefore, the press would conclude, the boss was going to be a defendant; the feds must have something on him. It would shake up Lacona. What could he do? He couldn't lie to the press when they asked—and they would ask—and say he'd been subpoenaed, too. He couldn't come down to the courthouse from Harrisburg with the others and hang around the halls as they appeared one by one before the grand jury. It could only help to intensify the pressure.

Silverman and Jacobs were tired. Each could feel the strain of all this in himself and in each other. Their fatigue was not discussed. But before they left the cell block, they sat in a sort of contemplative silence. This had long since ceased being just a job. Without really thinking about it, without consciously realizing it, Silverman and Jacobs knew that they were preparing themselves for the hunt. There were no thoughts of right or wrong. The effects of their "method" on a citizen, perhaps an innocent one, were not considered. That would come later. Silverman and Jacobs were after prey. This was civilized and socially acceptable, perhaps, but really no different from other hunts engaged in by men throughout the ages.

It caused a strange kind of fatigue. More than intellectual weariness; a bone-tired feeling. The kind that accompanied the risk—or was it fear—of losing. But the hunt would begin, no matter what.

Mary Ann's mother didn't just call a waiter to the table; she commandeered him.

This was not the first time Silverman had seen her in action. And, as usual, he felt like crawling under the table as he sat in the main dining room of McLean, Virginia's Rolling Wood Country Club while Mrs. Sutcliffe—"Mom" to him ever since his marraige—explained to the waiter with tired condescension everything that was wrong with her steak.

High on the list of the Washington area's finest country clubs, Rolling Wood was set among the lush green northern Virginia landscape. Its membership, while not exclusively Christian—there was a Jewish name or two on the roster, although Silverman had never noticed anything near a Jewish face in the place—was decidedly white. The clubhouse main dining room, just off the eighteenth hole, was a high-ceilinged, magnificently appointed room where Silverman endured Sunday dinner with his father-in-law and "Mom" Sutcliffe on those occasions when he and his family were in town for a weekend visit.

In the past, the event was something he managed to tolerate as one of those relatively minor burdens accompanying marriage. This Sunday, he found the experience unusually grating.

Back in Philadelphia, subpoenas had been issued for Lacona's financial dealings. Things looked promising; Lacona did seem to spend high. The next day, subpoenas for the State Roads Commission employees would go out. A little over a month had passed since the plan had been put into operation. As usual, Silverman and Jacobs had handled the day-to-day activities. Higdon, when he was in, stayed pretty much to himself.

The situation between John and Mary Ann had worsened. There had been no more arguments, certainly no discussions about the case. They both provided their usual loving attention to Jamie. But with each other there was nothing but perfunctory communication, with long silent periods, each harboring grudges, each becoming more remote in the other's presence. John worked late a lot of nights, coming home after she was in bed, asleep.

This had been the weekend to come to Washington to visit parents. Friday night and Saturday with John's folks. Saturday night and Sunday with Mary Ann's. And, of course, the ritual of Sunday dinner at Rolling Wood.

Spending the weekend in Washington was among the last things Silverman wanted to do. But he'd gone with little visible outward resistance. The ride down in the car had been a strain. When Jamie, who rode in the back seat, slept, he and Mary Ann hadn't spoken. It was like the ride after Jacobs's brother's funeral. Only this time Silverman's mind couldn't drift, ever conscious of her silence, feeling the discomfort of her resistance like a hostile stranger seated between them.

"And don't bring me the same steak back. I want a new one. Do you understand?" Mrs. Sutcliffe demanded of the waiter.

"Yes, ma'am," he said, with all but the deepest recesses of his dark eyes completely obedient.

As the waiter retrieved what appeared to Silverman to be a perfectly acceptable steak, he watched his mother-in-law aim her last warning glance at him.

She was something, all right. Her silver hair immaculately coiffed, the cosmetic surgery she'd undergone several years before providing her face with an illusory younger appearance.

176

An appearance substantially at odds with her hands. Nicely manicured and expensively jeweled but a grandmother's hands none the less. Just like his mother's.

Oh, she's a beauty, Silverman thought as Mrs. Sutcliffe told everyone at the table to go ahead and eat.

"Did your mother tell you I ran into her last week at Saks?" Mrs. Sutcliffe asked John as she helped Jamie get a hold of her oversized hamburger. Jamie always sat next to Grandma at the club.

"Yeah," Silverman answered. He couldn't remember if his mother had told him or not.

"She's looking so well," she said, as though his mother had been sick, which she hadn't.

Silverman continued eating.

"Everything all right these days in the U.S. attorney's office," Silverman's father-in-law asked, probably just to make conversation.

"Yeah. Um hum."

John felt Mary Ann's hard gaze on him. He caught Jamie's attention as Mrs. Sutcliffe delicately dabbed with her napkin at ketchup smeared over the child's chin and winked at her. Jamie submitted to the cleanup and smiled at her father.

Silverman's father-in-law was a nationally prominent architect. He was a nice guy, but very quiet, especially around his wife. Silverman liked him, although they weren't close.

John suspected that Mary Ann's parents had sensed from his uncharacteristically sullen behavior this weekend that there was a problem somewhere.

Mrs. Sutcliffe had studied her daughter ever since they had come over the night before. And face lift or not, she was still a mother. She could tell.

"When are you going to bring my daughter home? Get out of that job and join one of those nice law firms here?" his mother-in-law asked Silverman, going right for the jugular.

He glanced at her quickly, then over at Mary Ann, who was looking very intently at the food on her plate.

"Perry, you could help John," Mrs. Sutcliffe suggested to her husband with what Silverman thought was just a hint of the same tone she usually reserved for waiters. "You know many of the partners in the better firms. Why don't you help him?"

Perry softly said he'd be glad to, then went back to his food, seeing that trouble was brewing and hopeful that with a little additional silence, its fumes would blow away.

John could feel his mother-in-law's waiting smile. He looked up from his plate. She was poised for a response. What was more, she was ignoring the fact that Silverman's father was a lawyer. But he had only a small suburban practice in Chevy Chase. Clearly not the thing for her daughter's husband.

Silverman was pissed. He managed to maintain control, but just barely. He returned to his meal, ignoring her waiting glance.

Mrs. Sutcliffe was deep in contemplation, deciding what to say next, when the waiter returned and placed another steak in front of her. She'd been engrossed in thought, and so he'd caught her by surprise, but she rose to the occasion.

"Waiter, this is the same steak, isn't it?" she demanded with more than enough antagonism to challenge his denial in advance of its utterance.

"No, ma'am. It isn't," the waiter said, his tone mostly respectful but betraying his hurt.

"Yes, it is. And I distinctly told you not to bring back the same steak."

The waiter shrugged and reached once again for her plate.

Mrs. Sutcliffe was ordering him to send over Jean Claude, the maître d', when Silverman lost control.

"Leave it there," he instructed the waiter, who looked at him with the same astonishment as his dinner companions. He turned to his mother-in-law. "Eat the goddam steak and shut up." The waiter quickly disappeared.

Before his mother-in-law could recover from her shock, Silverman stood, slammed his napkin onto the table, and stormed out. All the eyes of the neighboring diners were on him, but Silverman could neither see them, nor did he care. He just knew he wanted out. Mary Ann stayed at the table.

That evening, when Silverman returned to Philadelphia, Mary Ann and Jamie remained behind.

In the car, on the way home, he thought about how they hadn't really discussed it. Mary Ann had said only that she would stay over with her parents a while longer. He'd said okay.

Now he was going home alone. Although he felt a certain amount of sadness and guilt, more than anything else, he felt relief.

Mayor Lane sat at the dais. He was, by tradition, the guest of honor at Philadelphia's annual Chamber of Commerce luncheon.

Donald Ames, under other circumstances, would also have been seated at the dais. But given the times, he had chosen to remain in the audience at one of the tables reserved for the city's business leaders. He had shaken hands with the mayor, much as the others had just prior to the luncheon's commencement. But everyone was watching, including the ever-present press. So the two men hadn't so much as glanced at each other during the remainder of the affair. Ames didn't like it, but he didn't show it.

John Stavaros didn't attend. But that was not unusual.

Silverman looked at his watch at least three times in as many minutes. He didn't like what he was hearing. Jacobs was explaining the results of his rough analysis of Lacona's expenditures. The grand jury had been called into session, their first time together in too long. There was likely to be hostility. Their meeting was scheduled to begin in just a few moments, and Silverman was anxious to get there, to speak to them just before the session formally began.

Jacobs's news was not all bad. But it wasn't good. Lacona did spend more than he earned. He was dirty. Jacobs was convinced. But there was a problem. A big one. If they conducted the net-worth investigation the right way, Jacobs guessed that the discrepancy would only amount to maybe two to four thousand dollars. He did spend more than he earned, but not enough to make Jacobs comfortable. There was a definite proof problem.

"In other words, a weak tax evasion case," Higdon said, seated firmly in his chair and adjusting his glasses with his right forefinger as he spoke.

"Yeah. I'm afraid so. That's right."

Silverman could hear the apology in Jacobs's answer. He shifted in his chair. He was afraid that Jacobs might be giving up on the case.

"I don't think the IRS or Criminal Tax Division at Justice would even authorize prosecution," Jacobs continued, averting his eyes from Silverman. "The discrepancy is that small."

"What else have you done?" Higdon asked, ignoring Jacobs and looking directly at Silverman.

"What?"

Higdon's question caught him by surprise. "What do you mean?" Silverman asked, glancing quickly at Jacobs.

"What else have you done? It's a simple question."

"You mean what other leads have we followed?" Jacobs

179

asked, trying to diffuse the confrontation that seemed on its way.

Higdon continued to ignore Jacobs, waiting for Silverman to speak.

Silverman's first reaction was to bridle his seething anger. But of all the fucking nerve, he thought. For openers, the son of a bitch is hardly ever here. He and Jacobs were spending all of their time on the case, busting their asses, pushing the case. And when something doesn't work out, Higdon has the gall to chastise them for not doing more. Why was he doing that? Was he simply being the great teacher again? Or was he disappointed, too? Could Higdon be as frustrated with their lack of success as he was? Was this his way of showing it?

Clearly, there was no time for Silverman to ponder this. An answer was overdue. When he finally spoke, it was soft— softer than usual.

"Nothing else."

Higdon's look of reproach was unmistakable.

For the few seconds they remained locked in each other's orbit, Silverman considered Higdon and his strange ways. He knew not to underestimate him. Higdon wasn't what he seemed. He was more. And less. But goddam it. Why shouldn't he work the case, too? Anger swelled again within Silverman, as it had the previous weekend during Sunday dinner at Rolling Wood. His body stiffened, but before he could speak, Jacobs interjected.

"Listen, Ray," he said. "Whether we can prove it or not, the guy's dirty. I know it, man. I know what I saw in Harrisburg. The TVs, the fancy clothes. I'm telling you. Somebody's paying him off. He's either got most of it hidden in a safe deposit box or he's spending it in a way we can't trace."

Slowly, Higdon turned, Silverman still easily in his range, but he wanted to show Jacobs he was listening.

"He's smart," Jacobs quickly added. "He doesn't blow the money on things we can pick up." Jacobs looked over at Silverman. "I'm telling you guys. We've got to keep leaning on him. Press him hard. Make him fold."

For a few seconds, no one spoke. The only sound in the room was the drumming of Higdon's fingers on the top of his desk.

"Did you see any connection between him and Ames or Stavaros?" Higdon finally asked.

"No," Jacobs admitted.

"So even if he's being bribed, it could be from some totally unrelated source. It could be a totally separate case. Right?"

Higdon leaned firmly back in his chair; he glanced first at Silverman, then Jacobs, his expression again containing that look of reproach for their not having accomplished more with the pursuit of other leads besides Lacona.

Jacobs was reluctant to take on Higdon, but he didn't want to give in. As he responded, defending his belief that despite the results so far, Lacona was still a viable target, Silverman realized that if they wanted to speak to the grand jurors, they would have to do it now. He interrupted Jacobs.

"Look. Let's finish this later. The grand jury's about ready to start. I think we should talk to them before we start with the witnesses."

"They'll wait. We'll finish this first," Higdon said, dismissing Silverman's request without even a moment's consideration.

Silverman rose.

"No. We'll finish it later, not now."

This was the first open disobedience he'd ever shown Higdon. He didn't move.

Higdon studied his colleague.

"Sit down, John."

Silverman stood before the desk just long enough for Higdon's eyes to repeat the command, then turned for the door.

"See you in grand jury, Ray," he said as he left.

Silverman was seated at the prosecutors' table, facing the grand jurors, his legs dangling, his smile, his whole body poised to display a relaxation that neither he nor the others in the room felt. The jurors were angry. They had been neglected, kept uninformed about the investigation. They were hurt, felt slighted, still believing that they really were a crucial part of the government "team."

Silverman knew that he had to soothe them, reassure them that they hadn't been ignored, that they were still crucial to the investigation. In fact, without their compliance there was no investigation. However, other than the power their legal existence placed in the hands of the prosecutors, they were mostly superfluous. He spoke soothingly, summarizing in only sketchy detail what had occurred since their last session.

When he finished, Silverman moved off the table and stood before them. So things were moving, he repeated. Now he and Higdon would prefer that they not place their "grievances on

181

the record;" that might cause legal problems someday for a case they might indict. It might enable some defendant to get off on a "legal technicality."

The grand jurors were caught somewhat at a disadvantage. Silverman stayed in the room, standing before them. He knew that there wouldn't be much discussion among them as long as he was present. He waited out the short period of murmuring. Finally, one of the older gentlemen from the rear of the room rose to speak.

He wanted to know if from now on the prosecutors would keep the grand jury advised of "all important developments."

Silverman had won. The juror's remark was a question, not a command. Silverman was still in control. He nodded reassuringly.

Mrs. Franklin, the one juror whom Silverman would have selected to bitch the loudest about the neglect the grand jurors had suffered, had remained strangely quiet. Silverman now noticed her, in her seat, immobile, curiously unresponsive. But his survey was too quick. Nothing really registered.

It seemed as though the problem was over. Silverman walked around the table to his seat. He arranged the papers he'd brought with him, then sat down.

"Okay, let's bring in the first witness," he said.

She was one of the State Roads Commission clerks whose job it was to accept the bids from the contractors. Silverman went through the opening formalities with her. She was young, probably just a year or two out of high school, and obviously not involved in any wrongdoing. She smiled nervously and kept smoothing the flip of her bleached blonde shoulder-length hair.

He took her through the bidding process, had her explain for the grand jurors what he had learned from the manual Jacobs had given him. Whenever her explanation had become too wordy or disjointed, he helped with additonal questions. "So what you're saying is—"

Her postadolescent pleasantness and obvious innocence seemed to filter through the room, dissipating what little remained of the earlier tension and hostility.

Midway through her testimony, Higdon quietly entered the room, taking his usual seat. Neither prosecutor seemed to take notice of the other.

After the bidding-procedure explanation, Silverman asked the young woman routine questions designed to discover if she had been a witness to anything that appeared improper. Naturally, much of this was intended for Lacona's ears, when today's witnesses, later, back at the office, would compare notes of their grand jury appearances.

Was she close to Lacona? No. Had she ever seen him with any contractors? No. Did she ever go to the Pirate's Den? She giggled her no to this question, embarrassed, but flattered that she had been asked if she had been to this apparently well known hangout. What about contractors? Silverman asked. Had any ever approached her or her coworkers, asked questions about their finances or private lives? No, she'd seen nothing like that. Did she know John Stavaros or Donald Ames? No.

Having finished with the witness, Silverman turned to Higdon, waiting to see if he wanted to ask any questions. He slowly shook his head. No interest. Silverman turned to the grand jurors. Did any of them have questions? he asked the group. A few did. They wanted more explanation about the bidding procedure.

When they had finished, Silverman thanked the young woman for coming and excused her.

The next witness was shown into the room. Dressed in a cheaply made suit and the standard J.C. Penney tie, the man was obviously a civil servant. He looked to be in his early forties. Silverman could not remember ever having seen anyone more nervous.

As the witness stepped slowly and cautiously toward the chair, Silverman wondered if he had some kind of medical condition that caused such nervousness. He noticed the man's hair was grayer than his apparent age and features indicated it should be.

After the oath was administered, the man stepped into the witness box, then perched, ramrod straight, on the edge of the chair, seemingly ready to explode with anxiety. Too quickly to really notice anything, he surveyed the room and his captors. Silverman was certain that if this man's tie were too tight, even if it were choking him, he would not raise his hand to loosen the knot. He sat stiffly, awaiting God knows what fate. Silverman quickly concluded he was far too nervous to be hiding anything.

He kept his questions about the bidding process short, then went straight into his Lacona questions. No, no real personal contact. He was merely a clerk. Had a contractor ever approached him directly? No . . . Well, maybe . . . he wasn't sure. He did speak to contractors when he took their bids. Is that what the prosecutor meant? Or did he want something else?

He sat there in agony, strapped in by his own words, not knowing what to say.

"Look, just listen to the question. It's quite simple. I'll ask it again . . . Do you want a drink of water?"

"Water? No . . . no."

"Has any contractor ever approached you personally and asked you any questions about your job, your personal life, your finances, anything like that? Now, take your time."

"I wish I could think of something, but I can't. I just simply can't. I'm sorry."

"That's okay. Next question . . ." He had to get this guy out of here before he had a coronary. "Have you ever witnessed any fellow employee or superior engage in conduct, during bid receipts or selections, which you considered to be in any way unusual? Do you understand the question?"

"Yes, I think so," he answered too quickly. Before continuing, he shot a glance from Silverman to Higdon to the grand jurors. "No, well, I don't know. I'm confused. I can't remember. No, that is . . . I can't remember anything."

That this was a classic case of stage fright seemed clear enough to Silverman, but for some reason, Higdon came to life. He erupted without warning.

"Sir, I simply don't understand your answer. You 'don't remember,'" he repeated with considerable sarcasm. "Let me advise you of something. You are here under oath, sir. If you have a recollection of something and you're asked about it, you *must* testify about it. Do you understand that?"

He stared at Higdon, frozen, terrified. He didn't say a word.

"I'm waiting for an answer . . . sir," Higdon said, projecting too much antagonism.

What the hell is he doing, Silverman thought. He had completely misread the witness. This was going to cause trouble with the jurors. He wondered if he should try to calm Higdon down—not that he had any idea how—but Mrs. Franklin was already in motion.

"Mr. Higdon, I wish to say something."

Higdon looked from the witness to her, then back to the witness. "We'll take questions at the end, ma'am."

"No, that's not satisfactory."

"I'm afraid it'll have to be." His gaze remained on the witness. "We'll take questions when I'm through."

She rose. "I wish to say something for the record. I am certain that the other grand jurors are quite displeased with the way this investigation has been handled. People's rights are being violated. We seem to be embarked upon a senseless fishing expedition..."

Holy shit! Silverman thought. What's she doing? That's all on the record. He looked at the stenographer punching away at his keys. Right in the middle of this witness's testimony. And when the witness leaves here, he'll tell his coworkers; then it'll spread to God knows where—Ames, the newspapers. But there was no stopping her now. To try would only make matters worse.

"This grand jury objects to the way this case is being handled. Our feelings must be on the record."

She finished and sat down. The room was deadly silent. Silverman looked at Higdon.

"Finish with the witness," Higdon whispered.

Silverman quickly went through the remainder of his questions and excused the man.

He questioned the remaining witnesses, all of them, and Higdon didn't say another word. The grand jurors hardly participated; they, too, seemed stunned by Mrs. Franklin's outburst, seemed to realize that what she had done might ultimately be harmful to the case. Everyone wanted the session to end.

After the last witness had been excused, Silverman told them they would not meet next week but would be called into session again soon. He reminded them of their oaths of secrecy and excused them.

The grand jurors began to leave. Higdon remained seated, but as Mrs. Franklin walked by, he spoke.

"I'd like to see you for a moment, Mrs. Franklin. Would you please stay in the room?" It was not a request.

Silverman stayed also, curious—and worried—about what Higdon had in mind.

The last grand juror left.

"John, please step outside."

"Ray, I..."

"Please step outside, John. I'll meet you downstairs."

Silverman didn't want to argue with Higdon in front of Mrs. Franklin. He walked outside but stayed in the corridor across from the room.

After a few agonizing moments, he walked closer to the door. Higdon's voice grew louder. He was scolding her; his words were bitter. Silverman heard him threaten to take her before the grand jury judge "for punishment" if she ever did that again.

Silverman retreated from the door. He paced the hall, trying

185

to think of something to do. What the hell was the matter with Higdon? He was only making matters worse, much worse. What if she went to the papers, violated her oath, and made public accusations about the integrity of the investigation—and them.

He turned, and without knocking, opened the door and went in.

Higdon turned and glared at the intruder. Mrs. Franklin looked like a prisoner of war under interrogation.

"Go home, Mrs. Franklin," Silverman said, his gaze fixed upon Higdon. She didn't move. "I said go home."

She walked toward the door. Higdon stared at him in disbelief.

When he heard the door open, he added, still looking at Higdon, "Mrs. Franklin, do you completely understand your obligation to keep what goes on in here secret?"

"Yes." She sounded strangely submissive.

"I want you to continue to remember that. For you to do otherwise would mean that you've violated the law. Understand?"

"Yes."

"Now go home."

She quietly closed the door behind her. Higdon didn't say a word, just stared at him. Silverman wondered if he should say anything, try to explain what he was doing. No, why waste his breath? He turned and walked out of the room.

He told his secretary he would be back from lunch a little later than usual. He needed extra time today with Mr. Turner.

16

Jan handed him the message slip. "I was instructed to give this to you as soon as you returned from lunch."

He glanced at it. No surprises. "See me *immediately*—Ray." He crumpled the paper into a small ball and tossed it onto Jan's desk.

"Throw it in your wastepaper basket, will you?"

"Mr. Lacona's on the line," Jan called into his office.

Before reaching for the phone, Silverman gave Jacobs, who was seated in one of the chairs in front of the desk, a "here goes" shrug, then picked up the phone.

"Hello. Albert Lacona?"

"Yes."

"My name is John Silverman. I'm an assistant U.S. attorney here in Philadelphia—" He waited a moment before continuing to see if there was any reaction. There wasn't. "I'm calling, sir, to advise you that as a result of certain information that has come to our attention, it would be advisable for you to retain a criminal lawyer—" Still nothing. "I would request that you retain such counsel and have him contact us as soon as possible."

To Silverman, the silence at the end of his speech seemed to last longer than it should have.

When Lacona finally responded, he sounded businesslike, unconcerned. "Can you tell me what this is about, Mr. Silverman?"

"No, sir. I believe I should discuss that with your attorney."

"All right," Lacona said, his voice still calm. "Is there anything else you wanted to say to me?" he asked.

"No. Nothing else," Silverman said.

"I'll have my lawyer call you then. Good-bye, Mr. Silverman."

"Good-bye."

Silverman slowly replaced the receiver on its cradle. He was surprised by Lacona's seeming composure. This was going to be a hard nut to crack. He didn't say anything to Jacobs. He didn't have to. Jacobs could see from the expression on Silverman's face that Lacona had kept his cool.

Besides, there was something else on Jacobs's mind. During the morning, he had spent the hours that the grand jury was in session in the cell block with some of the records that had been subpoenaed from Stavaros. What he found seemed interesting.

John Stavaros owned all of the stock of a large holding company, Eagle Real Estate, Inc. That company, in turn, owned all of the stock of other real estate companies, each one of which had built, and owned, an office building in Philadelphia, both in Center City as well as in most of the suburbs. Almost every one of these buildings rented space to the city for an off-track betting parlor. Several years before, the state legislature had passed a law legalizing off-track betting, as had been done in New York, New Jersey, and other places. In an effort to aid the financially troubled city of Philadelphia, the state made the city a sort of partner in its off-track betting business. Philadelphia ran its own off-track betting, took in its own revenues, and paid its own expenses, such as rent for betting parlors. At the end of each year, despite the popularity of the program, neither the state nor the city would show a profit.

Jacobs had pored over the records. On his second or third time through, he'd made the connection. He added up the total yearly rent paid by the city: five hundred thousand dollars. He then computed the total yearly salary Eagle Real Estate paid Stavaros. The amount, the same to the penny: five hundred thousand dollars.

Of course, Jacobs couldn't tell what Stavaros had done with the money, couldn't see how he had spent it. His canceled checks were his personal records, and by virtue of the Fifth Amendment, couldn't be reached by subpoena. But where did the money go? Did some of it wind up in the pocket of some public official, someone who had the power to see that the city rented the space for its betting parlors from Stavaros's companies? Did mayors have that kind of power?

Jacobs was midway through explaining his discovery to Silverman when there was a single sharp knock on Silverman's door.

Jacobs turned to see Higdon's defiant figure standing in the open doorway, glaring at Silverman.

"Bob, go get yourself a cup of coffee," he said to Jacobs, never taking his eyes off Silverman.

Jacobs turned to check on Silverman.

Silverman nodded in the direction of the doorway, indicating it was all right to leave, that he was okay.

Jacobs stood and passed by Higdon, who seemed to take no notice of him. After he'd left, Higdon closed the door, then advanced a step or two toward Silverman's desk. His rage was as evident as the obvious annoyance he felt at having to come to *Silverman's* office for this.

"I sent you a message," he finally said.

"When?" Silverman asked innocently. He already knew how he was going to play this.

Higdon didn't answer, stood erect, poised for battle. When he spoke, it was with the same sort of surliness he'd used earlier that morning in grand jury.

"I think you and I better have a talk."

"Sure," Silverman said, pointing to one of the chairs in front of his desk. "Sit down. What's up?" He looked directly into Higdon's glare. He had anticipated this scene, had gone over it at lunch with Stanton Turner. He felt prepared.

Higdon didn't move. Before he spoke, his darkened eyes focused even more acutely on Silverman.

"You are not in charge of the public integrity section. I am. You do not run the investigations around here. I do. I am not your assistant. You are mine. You do not tell *me* what to do. Is that clear?"

"Sure. What's the problem, Ray?" he said with feigned innocence. "Oh—it's that thing this morning with Mrs. Franklin. Listen, I'm really sorry about that, Ray. I just thought you were being a little too hard on the lady. I'm sorry if I . . . stepped on your toes. Really, I'm sorry."

Higdon's eyes flashed in astonishment. He hadn't expected this immediate concession. Silverman had taken the wind out of his sails, and his confusion showed. He wanted to persist, but he'd won—by appearance, at least. But Higdon was too good not to push a bit further.

"John, you're not going to run this case by yourself. I'm not going to be your second man. Not in this case, not in any case." He paused, to give full effect to what he would say next. "You're not good enough."

If Higdon had ever taken the time or trouble to know Silverman better, he would have recognized the flash of anger in his eyes. *I'm* not good enough, thought Silverman. I'm not the one who put the whole case in jeopardy this morning by badgering that witness. Silverman was seething inside, but he turned to Higdon with the most respectful smile he could manage.

"Ray, unless there's something else, I have a lot of work to do."

There was nothing Higdon could say. He turned and stalked out, slamming the door behind him.

Not yet, Ray, Silverman thought. Mr. Turner was right. There'd be no confrontation yet. Pursuing the case was pre-eminent. If there was to be a confrontation, he'd pick the time and place.

Mrs. Franklin took the money from her purse to pay the cashier. No, she didn't need a bag, she told her. The little spiral notebook she'd purchased would fit right in her pocketbook.

As she left the drugstore, she decided to go directly home and begin. No point in wasting time. She'd prepare her own detailed account; nothing would be left out. She'd put it all in the notebook. And then, someday soon, she would expose the grand jury abuse. The injustices to which she had unwillingly been a party.

By the time Jacobs returned, Silverman was back at work reading some of the Stavaros documents Jacobs had brought with him earlier.

"Got you some coffee," he said, poking his head into the room.

"Thanks."

"Everything all right?" Jacobs asked, placing the styrofoam cup before Silverman, its wisps of steam gently lifting themselves. Silverman didn't feel like talking about it.

"Yeah. Okay."

Taking care not to burn his mouth, Silverman slowly lifted the hot cup for a few quick sips. He could see that Jacobs was concerned, and he was grateful.

"Forget it, Bob. Everything's okay. No problem."

Jacobs sighed. There was a problem, but he knew there wasn't a damn thing he could do about it. So there was no point in dwelling on it. He, too, was a professional. Back to business.

"You ever heard of First Merchant's Bank and Trust of

Philadelphia," he asked Silverman, all the while trying to see if John really was okay.

"Sure, why?"

"Donald Ames has a personal checking account there."

"So?"

"Well. Just between us, we've got this file on them at IRS. Seems they may be microfilming and storing canceled checks. You know, they might have continued doing it even after the repeal of the Bank Secrecy Act."

The Bank Secrecy Act had been passed years before, around the time of the Watergate scandal. It required all federally insured banks to retain microfilm copies of every check they processed. It was thought that the law would aid criminal investigators in tracing fraudulent financial transactions. No longer could the canceled-check holder's right to invoke the Fifth Amendment and refuse production preclude the grand jury from subpoenaing the checks; they could get the bank's copies. But after intense lobbying from certain segments of the banking industry and other "special interest" groups, Congress had repealed the act.

"Who told the IRS the bank might still be microfilming?" Silverman asked, clearly interested.

"Insiders. Apparently, they do it for their own protection . . . *if* our information's correct."

"Wouldn't it be great if the bank had microfilm copies of all Ames's canceled checks sitting in their vault? Did the IRS ever check out the rumor?"

"Yeah. We asked. They denied. But we still keep hearing that they have. My guess is it's nothing sinister; the act's been repealed. They do it for their own record keeping, and they don't want to be put to the considerable time and expense to print the filmed checks for every subpoena that comes in. But they've never been asked formally about microfilming—by a federal prosecutor."

Silverman laughed at the uncharacteristic inflection of Jacobs's voice and the raised eyebrow that accompanied his last phrase, as though he were suggesting something really wicked.

"I'll call them," he finally said.

Jacobs smiled for the first time in days.

It was late, and he was tired. As Silverman stepped from the elevator into the courthouse lobby, he looked it.

Lugging his briefcase filled with more records to read at

home, he began his way through the high-ceilinged corridor to the main doors.

"Hi ya, Silverman," she said, standing in front of him before he had actually noticed her presence. He couldn't tell if she had been waiting for him or, coincidentally, just happened to be there. He hadn't seen her for a while; she looked good, and for some reason—he didn't quite know why, or didn't want to know—he was glad to see Denise Owens.

"Hey, how you doin?" he asked, shifting his briefcase so as to stand a bit straighter. He wondered if she would think his grin too friendly. He noticed then that she had her reporter's notebook out.

"Can we go on the record, Silverman?" she asked with all the formality of a seasoned courthouse reporter.

"Okay. On the record," he said, wondering if the disappointment he could hear in his voice was as evident to her as it was to him. There was no reaction he could see other than her obvious concentration on the question she was silently composing.

Her pen and notebook poised, she began her interrogation.

"Will you comment on the fact that today your grand jury heard testimony from certain employees of the State Roads Commission?"

"No," he said.

"Okay, 'no comment,'" she said softly to herself as she busily transferred his response into her notebook.

"Next question," she announced.

Her eyes seemed prettier to him than they ever had before.

"Will you comment on the fact that according to courthouse observers, Commissioner Lacona did not appear before the grand jury today?"

"No. No comment," he said. He realized that the article she was about to write might help add to the pressure on Lacona, but curiously, at that moment, he didn't really care.

He watched her as she carefully wrote in her notebook, and then, as though she had just become conscious of his stares, she looked up at him. With the top of her pen, she removed the wisp of short dark hair that had fallen over her forehead. His eyes continued to search her face, but whatever Silverman was looking for in her eyes, he couldn't find, so he resigned himself to the fact of her next question.

"Will you comment on what I intend to describe in my story as the pattern or tradition of the U.S. attorney's office of subpoenaing grand jury witnesses only? Never the actual targets of investigations? And that the vast majority of those who in the past have been targeted for prosecution have, in fact, been indicted?"

"No. No comment to that, either," he said. The weight of his briefcase once more made itself felt; he was weary, again wanting to go home. "Is that all?" he asked. But she had one more question.

"Will you comment on the fact that you look like shit today?" she said, her seriousness still firmly in place. "Off the record, of course," she added, now smiling.

Silverman quickly brushed his fingers through his hair, as though that would somehow improve his appearance.

"Yeah, I know," he admitted. "I'm really beat."

She closed her notebook and slid it and her pen into her shoulder bag. Denise took a step closer to Silverman, then reached for his tie and unceremoniously straightened it a bit. She remained close to him.

He could smell her perfume. Shalimar. The only scent he could recognize. His high school girl friend had always worn it, and since then, its aroma had always reminded him of his senior year and the evenings he'd spent necking with her, parked in front of her house in his dad's car.

He was surprised that Denise was wearing perfume; it didn't seem like her. Yet, all the same, he liked it.

"Shalimar," he said.

For a second, she looked bewildered, then understood.

"My, my," she said. "You are a man of many talents."

"Too few at the moment," he said, shaking his head to show his exhaustion.

"Tough day, Silverman?" she asked, half mockingly placing her hand on his shoulder, then slowly removing it.

"Okay," he said, getting ready to leave. "I'm not looking for sympathy."

She didn't budge.

"Looking perhaps for a friend to share a drink with and unwind?" she asked.

Those eyes again; they had the same look as that day on the bench in the park. It was unmistakable.

He started to decline. He had work to do. And besides, he felt queasy at the notion of going with her. He didn't consciously think of Mary Ann, but that was its source. Then, fuck it, he thought, why not.

"Sure. Come on," he said, leading the way out.

* * *

She stood by the bed and submitted to Ames, first as he roughly undressed her, then as he ran his meaty hands over her pale flesh, and finally as he alternately caressed and slapped her breasts. His breathing had quickened; an occasional hoarse groan escaped from his throat.

She stood and watched as he quickly undressed, throwing his clothes haphazardly to the floor. Then he waited as she loosened her barrette and allowed her beautiful blonde hair to fall to her shoulders.

He grabbed her again; his girth at first repelled her. She shuddered. But then, as before, she began to submit. He forced her onto the bed. She lay on her back as Ames mounted her. Following his whispered instructions, she reached down for his erection and guided him in.

And then, moving with his rhythm, her arms pressed hard around his corpulent back, as before, she satisfied herself. And him.

"Another round, folks?" the waitress asked.

Even in the nicest of hotel cocktail lounges, the waitresses, in their artificially darkened surroundings, were always dressed in such silly, yet interestingly skimpy costumes. This waitress, just slightly overweight, enough to provide a moderately heavy cleavage and legs, stuffed into black mesh stockings, a touch too thick, stood pleasantly awaiting orders.

The aged smile pasted under her platinum locks, however, was Howard Johnson plastic. It was easy enough to see that there was little indeed that any customer could say to her that could affect that smile. Silverman gave no thought to trying.

"Just the check, please," he said, not looking at Denise or asking if she wanted a second drink.

This place had been Silverman's choice. As they left the courthouse, he'd realized that it probably was a bad idea for him to be seen in a nearby bar with a reporter covering the investigation. Why risk people thinking he was leaking information? At least he thought that was the reason why he'd hailed a cab and gone to one of the cocktail lounges in the nicer hotels near Rittenhouse Square.

It was an attractive room. A thick, long oak bar faced the entrance, and at each end of the room was a half-hidden arrangement of love seats and low cocktail tables. They had been seated at one of those love seats. That meant sitting side by side with Denise instead of across a table from her. It meant that from time to time their legs touched.

He felt awkward, though she didn't seem to notice or mind. If he turned in the love seat to look at her while speaking, he felt uncomfortably close. When he spoke facing straight ahead, he felt a little foolish—as though he were addressing some invisible third party seated in the empty space across the low table.

Even worse was his conversation. It wasn't conversation. It was a monologue. He spoke of Jamie, his parents, everything he could think of but the two most important subjects: the investigation and his wife. He never said he was married. Did she know, he thought? Did she think he was divorced?

He somehow managed to stretch what should have been a few moments of opening small talk into more than a half hour's space, smothering any chance of real communication like a wet blanket over burning embers.

He wanted to go. He didn't often act this way. John Silverman was normally in control. Yet he wanted to stay, wanted to remain seated close to her.

He stopped speaking almost in midsentence. He stared into his drink. From the corner of his eye, he could see her move her arm up onto the back of the love seat. He could feel her looking at him.

Just then the waitress returned with the check.

"Thanks, folks," she said, leaning across the table to put it in front of Silverman.

Silverman raised his head as her cleavage, much larger than it was when she'd stood erect, started to shift toward him. Instinctively, he moved back an inch to get it in focus, to see it all.

To Denise, it seemed as though he were afraid the waitress's fleshy breasts were actually going to pop out of her costume and roll right into his face. She barely suppressed a laugh.

Oblivious to the source of Denise's mirth, the waitress straightened up.

Silverman realized why Denise was laughing. And he had to laugh too. Somehow this scene helped release some of his tension. But as he turned toward Denise with the first relaxed smile he'd felt since they'd gotten there, she reached forward, grabbed the check, and held it out to the waitress with a ten-dollar bill.

"Hey," he said, trying to grab for the check.

"It's on me," she said, smiling.

Silverman didn't persist. But he wasn't used to having women pay his bar bills. He sat back, not sure now how to react.

195

After the waitress had left for the cashier at the bar, Denise turned to him. Their thighs touched again as he shifted just slightly away. She didn't seem to notice.

"Next one's on you," she said, her smile strangely patient.

Her body was now shifted directly toward him. It was hard not to look into her face. He could feel her eyes reaching for and holding his. It was as though she were saying, "Relax, just relax." But it was he who spoke. When he thought about it later, he was sure it had surprised him more than her.

"Will you have dinner with me tomorrow night?" he asked.

Jamie sat on the green indoor-outdoor carpet of Mom Mom's porch and busily played with her dolls.

Mary Ann sat above her on one of two identical flowered chaise loungues, watching the child's absorption in her game.

The dolls were spread out on the carpet. One was Mommy, and one was Jamie. The third doll was Daddy, and he had just come back to take his family home.

Jamie was engrossed in her game. Much too busy to notice Mary Ann. Or the tears welling in her eyes.

17

Silverman turned to the jump page inside and finished rereading Denise's story in the morning edition of the *Inquirer*. Then he folded the newspaper and let it slip into the wastebasket under his desk.

He had just retrieved the day's *Daily Racing Form* for a few moments of handicapping when Jan buzzed. His door was open, so he called out to her.

"Yeah?"

"For you," she said.

He noticed the hold light of his phone blinking.

"Who is it?" he asked, putting the *Racing Form* aside.

"Don't know," she said.

He considered reminding her that asking who was calling was part of her job, but decided it was pointless. She would never learn. He reached for the phone.

"Hello—"

"John?"

"Yes?"

"This is Russ Haile. How you doin', buddy?"

Russell Haile had been a senior assistant U.S. attorney when Silverman first joined the office. He was one of Higdon's contemporaries, but a month or two after Silverman had come on board, Haile had left for a good offer in private practice with Wilkenson, Sherman & Peabody, one of Philadelphia's largest, most prestigious law firms. Silverman didn't know him well but remembered him as a big jovial Irishman with curly brown hair. While a prosecutor, Haile had acquired a reputation as being smart and tough but fair. He was well liked and rumored to be succeeding in private practice.

"I'm fine, Russ. How are you?"

"I'm fine, buddy. Been reading the papers about you guys this morning."

Silverman could picture Haile on the other end of the line,

his relaxed huge frame folded in his chair, his size fifteen feet encased in shiny cordovan loafers resting over the corner of his desk.

"You did?" Silverman asked.

Haile chuckled. "How's Raymond the Great treating you these days?"

There seemed no point in protesting to someone who'd been there and who obviously knew. Before answering, Silverman balanced his right foot against the edge of his desk. His sigh was purely internal.

"You know. It's had its bad moments. But then it's had its *bad* moments."

Afraid that his laughter sounded forced and not wanting to dwell on Higdon, he asked, "That fancy place you work at make you a partner yet?"

"Don't spread it around, buddy, but unless they're out to fuck me, I'm pretty sure December twenty-fourth is gonna be my big day."

"Hey, that's great," Silverman said. He admired Haile's forthrightness. Then Haile's voice became serious. The time for pleasantries was over. This was business.

"John, my firm's assigned me the representation of a new client. Name's Albert Lacona."

Silverman was suddenly alert.

"I spent five hours with him last night. Met with him again early this morning—before I called you."

"We'd like to meet with you and him." Silverman tried to suppress his eagerness. "How about later this afternoon." He was sure Haile would not bring his new client along.

He heard Haile's sigh.

"I won't bring him in, John. And I'm not coming, either."

Silverman hadn't expected a complete rebuff. Haile had been a prosecutor, knew the rules. He must have figured out what the government wanted. Why was he stonewalling? Before Silverman could figure out what to say, Haile spoke again.

"You got enough to indict him?" he asked.

Bluffing with a former federal prosecutor wasn't going to be easy. That much Silverman knew.

"We're making a case on him, Russ. When we have enough, and that'll be soon, we're gonna go with it."

Why had Haile flatly refused coming in alone just to hear the government's pitch? Silverman didn't know the answer, but he knew he had to take another shot at it.

"Listen, Russ," he added, trying to sound as though Haile

had simply not understood his earlier offer, "we know your guy's involved in a lot of stuff. But what we've got—what we're putting together—is tax evasion. Looks like about three counts. . . . But listen, I think we should talk. Your guy's in a position to help himself . . . and us. He's . . ."

"John," Haile interrupted with a finality in his voice that caused Silverman to stop speaking and listen. "Believe me. I wish I could help you. I see where you're going. I've been reading the papers. Please don't repeat this. My heart's with you. I'd like to see you get those fuckers. But my guy's something else; he's a strange man. I've never seen anyone as adamant as he is. Says he'll go to jail forever before he becomes a fink. Keeps telling me he doesn't know anything, anyway."

"You believe him?"

Silverman was sorry as soon as he'd uttered that stupid, bush-league question. Haile simple ignored it.

"I've never seen a guy as determined as Lacona. The entire U.S. government can light a big fire under his ass, and he ain't gonna move. Not even after he's toasted like a marshmallow. . . . I'm sorry, John. There's no point in our meeting." Another sigh. "Do I still get the usual courtesy of twenty-four hours' advance notice before the grand jury indicts?"

"Yeah. Sure."

"Guess I'll see you in court, then."

Silverman wondered whether he should ask Haile to call if his client changed his mind. He decided one stupid question was enough for this phone conversation.

"Sorry, buddy," Haile said.

"Yeah."

"See you."

"Bye, Russ."

Silverman slowly cradled the phone. He felt completely thwarted. One fucking break. All he wanted was one fucking break. Was that too much to ask?

He picked up his racing form. He tried to read it, but he couldn't even see the words on the page.

All Jan could hear from her desk was the sound of a newspaper crashing to the floor. Then silence. She looked perplexed for a moment, then went back to her *TV Guide* crossword puzzle, unconcerned.

Inside his office, Silverman was still seated behind his desk. The *Daily Racing Form* lay flung against the floor, on the other side of the room.

He wasn't going to give up on Lacona. If the flame wasn't

hot enough yet, he'd add more fuel. He'd keep adding fuel until the little fucker's ass burned, if that's what was needed to get Lacona.

He reached for the phone to tell Jacobs how it was going to be done.

18

It was their third dinner together. Each time they'd met at the restaurant. With each meeting he grew more relaxed, able to enjoy himself. But he planned to go home alone after dinner.

Sometimes they spoke; there were only two subjects off limits—by silent mutual consent: the investigation and his wife. Sometimes they sat comfortably across from each other without any need for conversation. That was how they were seated now, midway through dinner.

His attraction to her had grown with each meeting. Yet he couldn't quite define it. He knew it lay somewhere in her angular body, somewhere in those eyes when they looked into his. Her temperament, the confident way in which she talked about her career and what she wanted from life. Also, her lips, though a bit thin, were soft and inviting and definitely contributed to her appeal.

The evening after their first dinner together, he'd taken her to a video arcade. Before he knew it, she had bought her own tokens, selected the machine next to his, and played as though she were a regular. He had stopped his game, fascinated, watching her play. She felt his stare and looked over. She brushed a few stray wisps of hair from her forehead and returned her attention to the game. If she was aware of his continued gaze, she didn't let on.

She was pretty, though not the beauty Mary Ann was. There was an unrestrained, yet controlled, air about her. He sensed it even as she reached for her wine glass. Her forearm was gently shaped, her finger tips femininely tapered, yet her movement for the glass was quick and confident, as though before moving, she had calculated precisely the distance and velocity needed to retrieve the glass. He couldn't help thinking about what she'd be like in bed, whether her aggressiveness accompanied her sexual appetite as well.

As she replaced her wine glass, she noticed his staring. She nodded in the direction of his dish.

"Eat, Silverman; it's good."

He picked up his fork and moved some food around his plate. What the hell was he doing here? He'd spoken to Mary Ann before going out tonight. The ritual telephoning now happened only every two or three days. They were always polite. He always wanted to know all about Jamie. This time he hadn't asked when she was coming home.

She'd been to a lawyer. She didn't say so. But he could feel it. Her mother had convinced her. He knew. He thought of Jamie. Of what life would be like not having his daughter with him.

This time it was Denise who was watching him. She had no difficulty seeing the anguish in his face.

Albert Lacona had stayed inside his Harrisburg home for two days straight. Apparently, he wasn't going to come out until that well-dressed black man went away.

Bob Jacobs sat in his government car across from Lacona's house. He was tired and bored. As Silverman had ordered, he'd been on Lacona for three weeks now, following his every move. He waited for him to leave his house in the morning, followed him to work and home again, sat there at night until his bedroom light went out, then waited an hour longer before returning to the motel.

At first, Lacona had gone about his daily routine without change, watched the out-of-place black man sitting at the other end of the bar at the Pirate's Den with, if not disinterest, slight amusement. He had stayed home every night but one. And on that evening he'd taken his wife and kids to the movies.

But then he'd begun to be visibly annoyed. By the middle of the second week, he'd stopped going out to lunch. Then he'd taken different routes home. And for the last two days, he hadn't come out of the house, hadn't even looked out the window.

Spring had turned too quickly to summer. Jacobs was uncomfortable in the car. He sat there an hour or two longer, watched the local police car circle once again, the policeman looking at him as he passed. The locals probably felt a loyalty to a fellow public servant like Lacona, but no one dared to bother Jacobs. After a short while, he got out of the car and walked down the street to the Arco station to use the men's room.

He left the car where it was so that Lacona could see it and know that Jacobs would be back.

The door of Silverman's office slammed shut. Even Jan jumped as the two elegantly dressed elderly men stormed past her on their way out.

Silverman knew there were few people who dared act as brazenly as they had in a federal prosecutor's office. But he had no doubt that these two were certainly in that select group. He also knew Higdon would not have tolerated their behavior, would have handled them much differently. It bothered him slightly, but he shrugged it off. He told himself, once again, that he wasn't Higdon.

As Jacobs had requested, Silverman had telephoned the president of First Merchants Bank and invited him and his general counsel to his office for a conference. At the meeting, following friendly but patronizing conversation of how interesting the young prosecutor's job must be, he'd told the two distinguished gentlemen that the government had acquired certain information to the effect that First Merchants Bank was still microfilming checks. Both had remained seated stiffly before him, but their faces looked as though someone had just sucked all the air out of the room. Silverman could easily see that Jacobs's information was correct. He waited for their response, then politely asked if the information was true. He was met with a barrage of insults.

Both men worked him over in tandem. They accused him of using big-brother spy tactics, told him that the internal affairs of the bank were none of his business, that he had no legitimate authority to pry.

Silverman waited patiently for their tirade to end. Then, still showing them the same deference he had exhibited at the beginning of the meeting, he showed the lawyer the subpoena he'd prepared, just in case. He very politely told the lawyer that he certainly hoped he wouldn't be forced to haul the president into grand jury and ask him about microfilming under oath, subject to the criminal penalties for perjury. Silverman looked directly at the president as he spoke. If the bank did have the microfilmed copies of Ames's canceled checks, they didn't have to answer right away, he told the lawyer. They should talk it over among themselves. And if they wanted to produce the records informally at Silverman's office, well, that was perfectly okay. They could then disregard the subpoena's requirement for the president to appear before the grand jury.

That was when the president had blown up, said he didn't have to take this harassment, snatched the subpoena from Silverman, and stormed out with his lawyer, slamming the door behind them.

"Come on, man. Do it, baby—it's nice, real nice."

Bob Jacobs's son stared at the small red capsule lying on his frayed bedspread. Then he looked at his friend. His friend had already swallowed his.

"Hey, wow, Dickie. Come on, man. Don't do me alone, man." As he spoke, the friend delicately placed his hands on each side of his own head; then, slowly, his head rolled around as though some machine were revolving his neck and his hands were along for the ride. He moaned from the sensation the capsule caused to shoot through his system. His eyes began to roll upward in their sockets.

Dickie watched his friend, who now was unable to speak, remaining seated on the other chair beside the bed in a trancelike state.

He picked up the pill from the bed, examined it, then quickly popped it into his mouth, swallowing hard.

At first, there was absolutely no reaction, but then, just when he decided the pill was a dud, it hit him.

His first sensation was heat, pleasant internal heat. Then the fire grew. His skin tingled; some energy source was shooting through his body. His room was there; he could sort of see it. But he was no longer in the chair. Only his body was. Oh, the heat, the tingling. He was somewhere, distinctly away, yet there in the room.

He could hear the knocking. It grew louder. He wanted to undo the latch, and he would have if he had been still in his body. Vaguely, he could identify the voice on the other side of the knocking; he could understand the words. He was in eighth grade; he knew a lot. And he would have let her in if he were still in his body. He'd tell her, explain. The knocking echoed in his ears, each knock followed by thousands of crisp rapid-fire snare-drum patters. He'd explain later, he decided.

"Richard," his grandmother screamed, "you open the door this minute. Do you hear me, boy?"

He could hear. But he wanted her to knock again, wanted that machine-gun sound to attack his senses again.

And anyway, he felt so sleepy. He watched his buddy fall from his chair, slamming his head against the bedpost on his way down. He'd be all right; he was just resting. Dickie could understand that.

Jesus. Man, he felt so sleepy.

Grand jury had lasted until six P.M. Silverman had finished with the last of the Lacona witnesses. No new surprises. He walked by Jan's vacant desk and into his office.

Higdon hadn't shown up for that day's session, and he'd enjoyed doing all the questioning alone. But Higdon's absence in grand jury was unusual. He'd been out a lot again, but even during his past absences, he would always be present for that. Silverman thought it might be his concern over his scene with Mrs. Franklin. She was not present either. It was a rare absence from grand jury. It worried him, and he made a mental note to call her tomorrow.

He walked over to read the messages Jan had left on his desk. She had left a cardboard carton on his chair. He opened it, removed two letters, and saw the batches of copied checks inside.

The first letter was a simple cover letter; the president of First Merchants told him the subpoenaed "papers" were being delivered today, thereby avoiding the requirement of his grand jury appearance. The second letter was a copy, the original's having been addressed to the assistant attorney general in charge of the Justice Department's Criminal Division in Washington, D.C.; the chief judge of the federal court in Philadelphia; and Miss Eccleston. It complained bitterly about Silverman, accused him of using "police state tactics," called his treatment of them "harassment." He tossed the letters on his credenza, then picked up one of the batches of copied checks, removed the rubber band, and thumbed through them.

He found the one he was looking for, rewrapped the rubber band, and did the same with a second batch, then a third.

The initials E.R. they had seen in Ames's check spreads that Stoffman's accounting firm had produced stood for someone named Elaine Robertson. Each month there was a personal check made out to her by Ames. Jacobs would have to check it out, but apparently she was merely a mistress, after all. Ames was keeping a woman.

He put the box on the floor by his chair. No sooner was he seated than he saw the pleading. It must have been hand delivered while he was in grand jury. Jan had placed it in the center of his desk with a pink message slip on top: "Blair Smith, deputy assistant attorney general, Criminal Division, Washington, D.C., wants you to call immediately after grand jury re attached." Smith was chief assistant to Terrance Cook, the assistant attorney general who was head of the Criminal Division.

So White had made his move. Silverman began reading, "Motion to Terminate Grand Jury Investigation." He flipped to the certificate of service on the last page; it showed that in addition to him, the attorney general himself, Terrance Cook, Raymond Higdon, and Miss Eccleston had been sent copies. He flipped back to the beginning.

At first, it seemed like a routine motion; the allegations were fairly standard. But paragraph IV was different:

It is further alleged that the grand jury itself has expressed to the prosecutors its desire to conclude the present inquiry. See attached affidavit in support thereof. The prosecutors are embarked on a fishing expedition of the worst kind, apparently even contrary to the wishes of the grand jurors themselves.

Mrs. Franklin. It had to be. Silverman quickly turned to the affidavit. But it wasn't Mrs. Franklin's. Though it had obviously been written by White, the signature was that of the nervous man from the State Roads Commission, the one who had witnessed her tirade, the one whom Higdon had badgered, and, of course, it exaggerated what had really happened.

He skimmed the rest of the motion. In the "Request for Relief" paragraph at the end, White had asked the grand jury judge to interview "the grand juror who rose and placed on the record the grievances of the entire grand jury."

Silverman thumbed through the Department of Justice telephone directory that had lain on his credenza. He dialed the Washington number for Blair Smith. His secretary had apparently gone, too; he picked up the phone himself.

"Hello, Blair Smith?"

"Yes."

"Hi. This is John Silverman, from Philadelphia . . . returning your call."

Silverman politely waited for a greeting. Instead, he was met with the brusque silence of an efficient, self-important Justice Department junior executive. This guy was nothing more than Terrance Cook's lackey, yet officious hostility seeped from the line.

"Mr. Cook asked me to get in touch with you," Smith announced, his boredom with having to do this clear enough in his voice. "Have you seen Richard Franklin White's motion to terminate your grand jury investigation?"

Silverman could sense a certain smug glee in the question, as though Smith would enjoy seeing Silverman defeated. Well, he is just a drone, Silverman thought. No use wasting energy on him. But his blood was starting to boil.

"Yeah. I've seen it."

"Well, Mr. White met with Mr. Cook and me today when he delivered our copy. Looks like you boys have a problem up there."

He had to let me know he was at the meeting, Silverman thought.

"What can I do for you, Mr. Smith?"

"*We've* also received some correspondence from First Merchants Bank of Philadelphia. Shows a copy to you. Seen it?"

"Yeah."

Silverman was about to ask the snooty little son of a bitch how much longer they were going to play twenty questions. He decided against it.

"Mr. Cook thinks it advisable for Raymond Higdon and you to come to Washington and meet with him about your investigation. Your appointment has been scheduled for one week from today at three P.M."

"I'll check with Higdon and get back to you. What about the U.S. attorney; does Cook want her there?"

Silverman was trying to keep this exchange businesslike but could hear the contempt creeping into his voice. *Mr.* Cook, Smith's silent reprimand seemed to be telling him.

"You all can decide that for yourselves. Don't bother to call me unless there's a problem with the date." Abruptly, Smith hung up.

Arrogant bastard, Silverman thought as he ripped a sheet from one of the legal pads stationed at the corner of his credenza. He wrote a note to Higdon and left to place it on his desk so he'd see it first thing in the morning.

He flipped the light switch in Higdon's office. He placed the note on the desk and was about to leave. But something kept him there. It was more than an opportunity to look around alone. This was Higdon's room. It seemed as sealed off as the man himself, yet without him here, it had a certain openness. His customary resistance to an outsider's presence was gone.

Although there were pieces of him present, even the room seemed more relaxed without Higdon in it.

Silverman slowly circled the room. On Higdon's worktable, next to the neatly stacked yellow legal pads, lay one sheet of paper, face down. He picked it up.

It was the copy of Ames's letter to the governor about the Resorts deal. Higdon had asked Jacobs for it, said he'd take the responsibility for investigating its authenticity. Yet obviously it had lain there ever since. Higdon had done nothing. Why?

Silverman replaced the letter on the worktable, face down, exactly as he'd found it.

He moved closer to Higdon's immaculate desk, then stepped behind it. He sat in his chair.

At first, he was uncomfortable, afraid that Higdon, or anyone, would walk in and find him. He was violating forbidden territory.

After a few moments, though, he began to feel more comfortable, even secure in a way. He sat back in Higdon's chair and thought about the case. About himself. About Higdon.

He allowed Higdon's seat to swivel slightly to the side. He was facing Hidgon's closed desk drawers, three in vertical order running down the right side of his desk. By now, the last glow of dusk had been absorbed into night. The room shone from its harsh overhead fluorescent lighting. He resisted the urge to peek, to violate Higdon's precious privacy. But he was alone. Curiosity fought off propriety. He pulled open the first drawer.

Empty. Absolutely barren. He tried the second. The same. Then the third.

Three totally vacant drawers.

What was Higdon? The emptiness. The genius of mind. A frail little man. Was that it? Was there no more? Silverman carefully closed each of the drawers as though they actually were connected to Higdon's torso.

The loneliness that had seeped into the room's pores was now exposed. A childlike loneliness. The chill of desolation crept into Silverman's bones.

Silverman pressed the switch; the lights flickered once before the room returned to darkness. He felt his way through Pat Ramondi's outer office to the dimly lit corridor.

He'd decided. He would pay a visit to Higdon at his apartment. He wasn't sure really why. But the impulse to go, to see him now, unannounced, was too strong to deny.

19

As he climbed the musty narrow stairway, the music, which was loud enough at the bottom, began to blare as he neared the top. He knew nothing about opera except to recognize it. The volume was much too high, the music bombastic, the singer, a soprano, shrieking in some guttural tongue. He thought it was God-awful.

He stood before Higdon's door, the music blasting within. After a moment's hesitation, he knocked. No response. The record was drowning out his presence. He knocked again, louder, almost pounding. The record stopped, instantly killing the soprano's wretched screaming.

Silverman could hear the creaking of footsteps approaching the door. Then nothing. What was Higdon waiting for, Silverman thought, unaware that other than his landlady's rare trips to the top of the stairway, there had been no visitors before. Higdon had to be standing just a foot or two away. So this time Silverman's knock was gentle, a tap. Still no answer from inside.

The silence lasted too long. Silverman turned to leave. But Higdon's voice emerged from the door.

"Yes?"

"Ray?"

"Who is it?"

"It's me, Ray. John."

Again, silence. Silverman half expected Higdon to return to his record player, replace the needle exactly where he'd removed it, and pretend that Silverman wasn't out there, knowing after a while he'd go away. Then he heard the latch turn.

The door slid open an inch or two. Higdon peeked out. Then, as though there was no choice, he opened it farther, but he stood in its path, across the threshhold from Silverman.

"Hi," Silverman said.

Higdon nodded.

Silverman glanced past Higdon, getting a quick glimpse into the room. Unlike his office, the room looked cluttered. He noticed some oversized books piled on a table. He looked back at Higdon, his eyes automatically registering his surprise.

Higdon hadn't shaved for a day or two. But his beard wasn't full. There were little darkened patches of stubble, one on his chin, one or two matted on his otherwise baby-smooth cheeks. He was wearing a faded blue terry-cloth bathrobe, the drawstring unpulled. Underneath, Silverman could see one of Higdon's customary starched white dress shirts. It looked as though it had been worn for a few days; the crispy whiteness had turned to a soiled grayish hue. Higdon wore trousers, but his feet were bare. He looked as surprised as Silverman. "Can I come in?" Silverman asked, trying to act as though nothing was unusual, as though paying a visit to Higdon was fairly routine.

Higdon stood his ground. As Silverman became convinced that Higdon was going to slam the door in his face, he moved aside for Silverman to enter.

Cluttered wasn't the word for it. Silverman had expected a replica of Higdon's office. Instead, he found himself in a musty little apartment—he thought it more like a rented room than an apartment. There were yellowed bullfight posters on the walls, and piled high from the floor near an old Victrola were what appeared to be stacks of opera records. Nothing seemed to be in its place.

Higdon had been eating. In a chipped bowl on the coffee table was lukewarm canned tomato rice soup. The bowl was surrounded by cracker crumbs.

Silverman stood awaiting directions. Higdon told Silverman to have a seat and disappeared into the bathroom. When he returned, Silverman noticed he'd closed the robe's drawstring. Higdon took a chair across from Silverman.

Silverman knew it was up to him to speak. He could see that Higdon was off guard, almost stunned by his visit. Suddenly, he regretted having come there.

"White's filed his motion," Silverman said at last.

If they had been on the phone, Silverman was sure he'd have received a lecture on how information like that did not have to be provided to Higdon when home, that it could await his return to the office. Here, face to face, with Silverman in Higdon's inner sanctum, for some reason, Higdon didn't—or couldn't—react.

Silverman told Higdon about the First Merchants checks and then brought up the subject of Terrance Cook.

"The assistant A.G.'s office called. They've set up a meeting for us in Washington next week to discuss the case."

Higdon seemed to be taking it all in. Still he said nothing. Now Silverman was certain he had to get out of there. He rose to leave.

"Well, I guess I'll be going," he said.

Higdon didn't move. The expression on his face betrayed the discomfort he felt.

In the eternity of the next few seconds, Silverman remained standing, waiting for Higdon to rise and show him out.

Higdon looked from Silverman around the room, as though for the first time he was aware of their surroundings; then he seemed to stare at his own bare feet. After a while, he looked up and said, "Want a Coke, or coffee, or something?" But the gesture came too late.

"No, thanks. I've really got to get home." Finally, Higdon showed him to the door.

It wasn't until Silverman had returned to the street that it occurred to him that Higdon had wanted him to stay. He just didn't know how to do it.

The evening was warm. But Silverman couldn't feel it. He was numb. Instinctively, he knew what he needed. Higdon's isolation, his cloistered life, the corpselike coldness that surrounded him, was like a vacuum, sucking into it the warmth and passion of human emotion. It had created a void for Silverman, one that had to be filled with the intimacy of another's contact. And the void had to be filled now. There was only one person.

He spotted the pay phone at the corner near the schoolyard and walked toward it to call her.

"There are those who would say this is a waste of an expensive wine," Denise Owens said.

She took another sip of the fifteen-year-old Bordeaux that Silverman had brought with him, along with the large white bag containing cheeseburgers and fries. They were seated at the samll table of the breakfast nook in her apartment.

"Nonsense," he said as he polished off his third cheeseburger. He took a sip from the juice glass that contained his wine.

"Certainly can't claim that it enhances the flavor of our main dish," Denise teased.

Silverman held his juice glass toward her in a gesture of salute.

"It enhances the flavor of one's soul," he said.

This was his third glassful. He was getting a little drunk, but he didn't mind.

She looked so pretty to him. When he had stood before her apartment door, awaiting entrance, he wondered how she'd react. She'd seemed quite at ease when he'd called to invite himself over, almost as though she'd expected his call. He wondered how she'd be dressed—if life were a forties movie, she would be wearing a robe.

In fact, she wore jeans and a silklike blouse. As he'd followed her into the apartment, he'd noticed how nicely shaped and firm her little behind was. She'd led him to the table where he unpacked their dinner while she uncorked the wine.

In the middle of the meal, with a little joke about atmosphere, she'd lit a candle and turned off the light.

When Denise saw that Silverman was finished eating, she rose and walked into the kitchen. He noticed the momentary pale glimmer of light from the refrigerator. After a few minutes, Denise returned carrying two small dishes loaded with ice cream and chocolate syrup.

"Think of it as baked Alaska," she said as she set one of the cold dishes before him and returned to her seat.

He couldn't remember tasting anything as good.

After dinner, they remained seated in the candlelight. He watched as she bent forward to light a cigarette from it. The wine's effect was disappearing, yet a nice warm afterglow remained.

At first, Silverman permitted his mind to bathe aimlessly in the soothing liquid of his surroundings. Then he felt as though he should say something, make conversation. Nothing came to him. He had become increasingly comfortable with Denise each time he saw her, though he still didn't feel totally at ease—after all, he hadn't been on a "date" since college. Yet he felt a strong need to be with her. He watched as Denise finished her cigarette. Once again, their eyes met. Now there was no need for talk.

Denise stood and went over to him. She remained standing before him, then placed her hand on his shoulder, bent and gently kissed him on his lips. She took his hand, and he rose to follow her.

The bedroom still contained faint traces of the Shalimar she'd used after he had called. Together they sat on the edge of the bed. She turned to him, her lips moving to his. They kissed, harder this time, her tongue filling his open mouth. The instant excitement of her warmth rushed over him. He felt himself harden. Slowly, he pushed her back onto the bed. He lay closely beside her, their arms around each other, their bodies pressing, their kisses forceful and luxurious. They continued kissing passionately. He fumbled with the buttons of her blouse. Gently, she stopped him and undid them herself. As the blouse slipped from her shoulders, he saw there was no bra, her breasts small, yet firm, her erect nipples a beautiful saddle brown.

Silverman watched her remove the rest of her clothing; then he undressed. He returned to the bed, admiring the feminine curving of her hips, the dark bushy triangle covering her groin. This time it was she who gently pushed him back on her pillow.

She slid on top of him, the warmth of their touching generating heightened excitement. Denise began to moan softly as their bodies rubbed and pressed. Her hand moved down to touch him, and he thought he would explode. He rolled her back, and before moving, he looked down at her. Her eyes were closed. She was waiting; she, too, was ready.

And then it hit him.

Which came first it was hard to say: Mary Ann, the case, Jamie, Higdon. All of it landed against him with a force that literally took his breath away. It was as though he'd been slammed in the stomach. He actually gasped for air.

Denise dreamily opened her eyes, realized something was wrong. She reached for the night-table lamp. As she did, her breast brushed against his arm. She looked into his face, then leaned back against the headboard.

"I think we'd better talk," she said.

He brushed back his hair. "I'm sorry" was all he could say.

He watched helplessly as she lit a cigarette. Her hands were trembling. He felt like dying.

She studied him as he waited for the inevitable reproach he knew he deserved. He was lost. For the first time in his life, he was really lost, control absolutely gone.

"What are you looking for, Silverman?" she finally said, her voice not at all reproachful but gentle. She seemed to understand.

Their nakedness now seemed unnatural. She sensed it and slid under the covers, holding the sheet over her breasts. He didn't move.

"I'm sorry," he said again. Was that all he could say? he

213

thought. He felt like an idiot. His eyes pleaded with her, telling her all she needed to know, more than he knew himself.

"John," she said, "I don't want to take you from your wife. If you can't handle this—on this level. I understand."

"It's not that—" he said, stopping in midsentence. It *was* that. And more. And she could see it.

He sighed and moved to gather up his clothes from the floor.

She touched his arm, and he turned back to her. The sheet had slipped from her breasts. He watched her as she pulled it back up. And she watched him watching her. His erection had returned.

She smiled. "Hey," she said, "so you walk around with a hardon for a few days. It's not the end of the world."

He tried to laugh it off, but the attempt was feeble. She saw that, too, and reached over, kissing him on the cheek.

"Go home, Silverman," she said, a sort of love in her voice.

Silverman fumbled with the key until it found its way into the lock. He was in a hurry; the phone in his apartment was ringing. At four A.M. only one person could be calling. Mary Ann. And it had to be an emergency. It was Jamie. Something horrible was wrong. God was punishing him for what he'd almost done with Denise.

In his rush for the phone in the kitchen, he accidentally kicked over the ceramic umbrella stand in the entranceway. It rolled, then smashed into the wall. He'd left the apartment door open; the noise reverberated through the hollow hallway.

As he touched the receiver, the phone's ring seemed suddenly to die. He grabbed it, anyway.

"Hello!" His voice was urgent. He waited for Mary Ann's hysterical cry.

"Where you been, man?" Jacobs screamed, outrage filling his voice.

In Silverman's excitement, it didn't compute. "What? Who is this?" he demanded; then he recognized the voice. "Bob?"

"When there was no answer at your place, I called Ray," he said. "Ray said you'd been there. But that was hours ago."

Silverman turned on the kitchen light to check his watch. Why was Jacobs calling at four A.M.? He was supposed to be in Harrisburg. On Lacona.

"Where are you?"

"Philly."

"What's wrong?"

"I'm at the hospital. My boy's here. Drug overdose."

214

"Jesus! He okay?"

"I hope so. If he doesn't have brain damage. The other boy, the one that was with him, he's in a coma."

"I'm sorry," Silverman said. And he was. But because of what happened, Lacona had been cut loose. Jacobs interrupted his thoughts.

"Get up there, man."

"What?"

"I've been trying to reach you. Get up there. To Harrisburg. Pick up on Lacona."

"You're crazy. I don't know how to do that," Silverman protested.

"John," Jacobs said, "you've got to. In a way, it's perfect. A change of tactics. Up until now, Lacona's seen a black man. That's what he'll be looking for. He won't spot you. If you do it right."

During the next five minutes, Jacobs gave Silverman directions and instructions. Then the doctor called for him, and he abruptly hung up.

Thirty minutes later, Silverman's car was pointed westbound on the bumpy and potholed Schuylkill Expressway—to the Pennsylvania Turnpike, then Harrisburg.

Silverman found the house without any trouble. He parked across from it, on the far side of the street. But figuring that was too obvious, he pulled out of the space, backed up, and parked three car lengths behind. He could still see the house, and now he felt that he had created "cover" for himself. Jacobs had said he should always be within range but never obvious. He checked his watch: 6:45 A.M. It was now official. Morning was here, and he hadn't slept all night.

The only time he'd felt any fatigue was about an hour before dawn as he traveled westward toward Harrisburg on the turnpike. It was the only time he had thought of Denise and what had happened. But then the heavy cloak of exhaustion seemed to roll away, like the green sloping farmland he was passing, somehow drawn to the large fiery sun rising in his rear-view mirror. The closer he'd gotten to Harrisburg, the more alert his senses became. He began to feel energized.

He studied Lacona's house as though an intimate knowledge of its design was somehow crucial to the success of his surveillance. It looked more or less like all the others on the block, standing obediently, stacked too closely side by side, facing identical narrow, neatly mowed front lawns: white clapboard,

215

small porch, lacy curtains. It was America. But America of the 1930s and 1940s. An antique neighborhood, almost a time capsule. Except for the cars. Most were at least three or four years old, still not the black square sedans that had once stood guard at the curb.

Silverman settled in.

At first, he was acutely aware of everything. A raised window across the street from Lacona's house. A newspaper boy— only it was a girl—flinging papers across the lawn. He even made note of the team emblem on her red baseball cap. Consulting his watch at five-minute intervals, he carefully observed every sight and sound of the awakening neighborhood. Soon people would be leaving for work. Ten minutes later, he realized it was Saturday morning. And twenty minutes later he realized he was sleepy—and bored. No one had ever mentioned surveillance in law school. What the hell was he doing here?

10:45 A.M.

He had to find a bathroom. And he was hungry. It was too hot in the car.

Could he leave? Where could Lacona go? Jacobs said he never left the house. Anyway, it was Saturday.

Well, he had to take a piss. And he needed something to eat. He turned the ignition key and pulled out of the space, passing Lacona's house slowly.

11:55 A.M.

Thanks to the small shopping center he'd located a few blocks away, he felt better. He'd eaten at the drugstore lunch counter, had bought a disposable razor, and shaved in the gas station men's room. Silverman turned back onto Lacona's street, then encountered his first problem. No parking spaces.

He slowly rode the street, passing the house for the second time.

He found a parking space two blocks over. Silverman took it, left the car, and walked back to Lacona's street. This time on foot, he passed the house a third time.

He was less than one house away when, behind him, he heard the high metallic whining of stretched screen-door springs, then the wooden slap of the door snapping shut. Someone had stepped out onto Lacona's front porch.

Silverman froze. He wanted to turn around and look but realized he couldn't without calling attention to himself. He had to move. Instinctively, he dropped to his knee, untied and retied first one shoelace, then the other. He felt silly, as though the whole world were watching him. But looking over his shoulder, he could see the man on the porch hadn't taken notice.

Silverman got his first look at Lacona.

He was as Jacobs had described him—fiftyish, slightly overweight, dark hair, glasses—a bureaucrat.

Lacona stepped from the porch and seemed to be surveying his lawn. As he did, he surveyed the street, then walked back inside. The screen door flapped shut behind him.

2:10 P.M.

Silverman found a parking space on Lacona's street, at the head of the block. The house was three-quarters of the way down but sufficiently in view.

It was hot. People were staying inside their houses. The neighborhood was quiet. Silverman's presence had gone unnoticed, not because he was so good at this but because he wasn't expected. Lacona was used to the black man and the black man's government car. Of course, Jacobs's surveillance had been obvious by design. That's who Lacona had been searching for this morning, probably double checking to make certain his tail had really been called off. Lacona probably now believed he was free, just as they had hoped. Silverman tried to think that through, examine the possibilities, the moves. But it was too hot in the car, and he was drowsy and too soon asleep.

4:15 P.M.

If it hadn't been for the rumbling of the van that passed by his parked car, he probably would have missed him.

Silverman woke with a start. He was bathed in sweat. It must have been 120 degrees in the car. He took off his tie and threw it in the back next to his suit jacket. Almost immediately, he saw him. Just a glimpse as Lacona quickly stepped from the sidewalk into a car.

Silverman sat up and gunned the motor. As soon as Lacona's car left its parking space, he pulled out and began following.

4:45 P.M.

Silverman thought he was getting the hang of this, was pleased with himself and relieved that Lacona had decided, at last, to go out. He'd followed Lacona at a discreet distance, skillfully maneuvering through the Saturday traffic to the edge of downtown, where Lacona had pulled into a self-park garage. Silverman found a space on the street and waited for him to come out.

He watched as Lacona headed up the narrow alleylike street. He was still in full view, so Silverman stayed in the car. When

217

Lacona disappeared through the main entrance, Silverman got out of the car and followed. He was walking toward the Harrisburg bus station.

Just off Third and Chestnut, at the town's urban fringe—a combination train station and Greyhound bus terminal—the grotesque building seemed to sway under the weight of its own dilapidation.

Once through the main entrance, Silverman found himself in the bus portion of the station. In spite of the heat outside, it was tomb cold inside the terminal. Aged yellowish gray paint peeled in large chunks from both the ceiling and walls. On either side of the room was a large ornamental fireplace. The entire building smelled of accumulated grime, poverty, and stale urine. Silverman searched the faces of weary travelers and bus-station regulars for Lacona. At first, he missed him, but then spotted him as he replaced a magazine on the newsstand rack and headed for the glass-enclosed lunch counter at the far end of the terminal. Silverman took a seat at one of the long wooden benches, Lacona in view, and waited.

What a place. Seated a few feet from him was a shopping-bag lady, three brown torn bags at her feet, each crammed full with rags, newspapers, and other assorted refuse. She had a goatlike tuft of gray hair dangling from her chin that she pulled at as she mumbled to herself, angry at God knows what, Silverman thought.

One bench over was a cheap-looking young girl in a waitress uniform. He watched as she sat, her hair dyed blue black, staring at nothing, cracking her chewing gum. She seemed to sense his attention and looked over at him, her eyes both defiant and interested. She smiled openly; he looked away. Lacona was still at the counter, sipping coffee. Silverman rose and walked to the men's room.

There was no door, simply a peeling partition, the sign long since ripped off. In its place, the words "men's room" had been written in black magic marker by an untalented hand. Silverman went inside.

As he entered, he surprised the room's only current occupant. An obese young man in his early twenties, dressed in fat man's dungarees, T-shirt, and black and white high-topped sneakers. He was standing, leaning over one of the sinks, squeezing pimples at the long cloudy mirror. Through the mirror he'd caught Silverman's quick disgust. He was embarrassed, but in his world it emerged as aggression.

"What the fuck you lookin at?" he growled at Silverman.

218

This was no time for a confrontation. Silverman quickly turned and left.

As he returned to the bench, he glanced at the lunch counter. Lacona's seat was empty. He searched the terminal. Gone.

Shit! Two seconds. It couldn't have been more than two seconds. A whole goddam day of this and in two seconds he'd lost him.

Silverman broke into a run for the exit. He stopped abruptly outside, spotting Lacona walking down the narrow street, heading right for Silverman's car.

So Lacona had known all along. He was going to stand by the car and wait for him. Silverman was convinced of it. His heart started pounding. He braced himself for the inevitable confrontation. Then he watched as Lacona walked right past his car, totally indifferent to its presence. Silverman had no time to savor his relief.

Once again, he followed.

Lacona turned the corner and walked the desolate block of Fourth Street, passing small shops, a Salvation Army store front, then, in the middle of the block, disappeared through the entrance of one of the stores.

Silverman stood before the frosted glass door, wondering what to do. It was clear that he couldn't just loiter in front of this place. He reread the sign, "Olympia Adult Books," and the command below it: "You *must* be 21 to enter." But there was really only one way to handle this. He tried to suppress his embarrassment and went in.

The room inside was unusually clean, spotless, in fact, and brightly lit. Act natural, Silverman told himself as he surveyed the place. Act as though this isn't your first time.

The wall space was covered with plywood racks holding magazines and 8-mm. films in boxes with picture fronts. To the right of the entrance, on a raised platform, sat a man surrounded by magazines, newspapers, dildos of assorted sizes and colors, and jars of creams and lotions. The proprietor, Silverman concluded as he studied the man seated up there, quietly reading something. He was youngish, dressed in an open-necked sport shirt. From time to time, he looked up, checking that things were in order. Too young. Probably just the day manager, Silverman thought.

Whoever he was, he noticed Silverman, nodded and smiled an innocent "welcome brother" smile, then lowered his head back into his reading material.

219

Don't look ashamed, Silverman told himself. Act natural.

Silverman was curious. With his pick of the store's pornography, what did the proprietor—or manager—choose to read? He couldn't resist, took a step closer to the platform and peered over it.

This time when the manager looked up at Silverman, he wasn't smiling. He was considering. Considering how much of a weirdo this guy was. And whether it was necessary to throw him out. Or so it seemed to Silverman.

Silverman smiled sheepishly and gingerly retreated from the counter, directing his attention to one of the racks of magazines against the wall, pretending interest in one of the covers.

The manager watched a moment longer, then returned to his reading, which Silverman had managed to see and recognized. The *Daily Racing Form*.

There were one or two other customers in the room, each slowly surveying its glossy offerings. But no Lacona. Then Silverman noticed the drawn curtains at the far end of the room and below the sign "Peep movies 25 cents." He walked closer, studying the assortment of crotch shots on the magazine covers against the wall.

Just before the curtain, against the far wall, he reached a section that momentarily stunned him. More crotch shots. But the photos were of prepubescent children: they were smiling wickedly into the camera, their legs apart, posed for defilement. Repulsed, he turned away.

The manager was watching him again. Silverman saw it, glanced back at the child porn, and realized what the man must be thinking. He wanted to protest, to deny. But he cautioned himself to keep his cool, avoid a disturbance. Quickly, he moved to another section and waited a few seconds, not turning around but trying to feel if the manager was still watching. He couldn't tell. After a few more seconds, he slipped through the curtains.

Silverman found himself at the head of a corridor, five or six rows of booths at either side, a dollar changer at the far end. He barely had time to notice that the door of each booth contained two photographs of sex scenes, the letters "A" or "B" above each, when the booth nearest him opened and Lacona stepped out right in his path.

Silverman fought for an explanation, a cover story. But Lacona ignored him and simply stepped into another booth and closed the door. It took Silverman a second to move; he had to swallow his heart. He realized it would be too risky for

Lacona to see him standing there a second time. He had to get out of the corridor, so he entered the vacant booth next to Lacona's.

It was narrow and dark. Above the door frame, there were twin projectors facing backward, directed at a mirror slanted down toward the door. Silverman could see that the film would be reflected off the mirror and projected down against the screen pasted to the back of the door. He sat on the tiny ledge facing the closed door. To his right, fastened to the wall, were two coin boxes, the letter "A" over one, "B" over the other.

He could hear Lacona next door as he plunked a coin into one of his boxes, then heard the flickering as the film began to roll.

If he could hear Lacona, Lacona could hear him. He reached into his pocket. To his relief, in addition to some other change, he had five quarters. He inserted one into box "B." Almost immediately the film began, simply continuing from where the preceding quarter had ended it. Because of the mass of tangled bodies, it took Silverman a while to realize what he was watching.

On the screen, there were three men. No women. One had just ejaculated in the face of one of the others; the third seemed to be frantically licking everywhere.

What the hell? Silverman thought as he ripped open the door and leaned out to look at the two still frames on the door's outside, advertising what could be seen inside.

There was a man, standing across the corridor, sheepishly smiling at him. He knew what Silverman was watching, and he was waiting for an invitation. Damn! He'd have to pick the one wrong booth, Silverman thought, as he quickly closed the door and pressed his feet against its base for security.

He heard another coin drop on the other side of the wall where Lacona sat. Silverman dropped his next quarter into box "A."

This time the film contained a heterosexual orgy. Clever, Silverman thought; two films, one gay, the other straight, theoretically designed to provide the viewer with privacy of selection. But it must be the only such booth the creep in the hallway had had no uncertainty over which film Silverman had chosen. As the film rolled, he pressed his feet more firmly against the door, listened for Lacona's film, could hear its flickering. He began to pay closer attention to the activity projected onto his tiny screen.

There were three participants: a muscular black man with

a cock the size of a horse's and two pretty white women, one of whom lay on her back, her legs spread open, the other woman's face buried in her crotch. The black man was leaning over the reclining woman's face, his huge penis jammed into her mouth. He was so big she apparently had to use both hands to hold its base as she sucked, drawing it deeper beyond her lips, her hands moving in a slow, rhythmic motion.

By now, Silverman's interest was intense. Surveillance had its moments, after all. But just as the actors seemed distracted by something beyond the camera range, the film snapped off. He quickly inserted another quarter.

The picture resumed from where it had stopped.

Two more people had joined the party. An Oriental woman with beautiful silky waist-length hair and a second black man. Everyone's position changed, all of them now on the huge bed, each connected in some form or another to a partner. One of the women was on her hands and knees, her breasts bouncing like water-ladden balloons, as the black man with the enormous erection, his head thrown back in ecstasy, wildly pumped behind her. Trying to keep pace with the frantic activity, the camera moved from position to position—close-up to close-up. Silverman was caught, absolutely fascinated. And in spite of himself, aroused. When the film halted, he immediately dropped in another quarter, then another, his last.

The film stopped. He considered leaving the booth for a second to go to the dollar changer. Then he realized he'd completely forgotten Lacona. Sitting absolutely still, he listened for the sound of film next door. It was quiet. He waited for another coin to drop. It didn't. Silverman opened his door, took one step out, and looked around the corner. The other booth was open, Lacona gone.

He rushed to the curtains at the beginning of the corridor and peeked out into the magazine room. There were three or four men busily perusing the racks. A tiny masculine woman with a boy's duck-tail haircut, wearing a leather motorcycle jacket, stood near the entrance chatting with the manager on his platform. But no Lacona.

Silverman was panicky. Searching back down the corridor, he saw that several of the booth doors were closed. Was Lacona behind one of them, or had he left? He had to act, to decide.

Realizing he'd have only a minute or two before the manager would be down upon him, he began forcing open the doors. His intrusions brought shouts of protest, each increasing in rage with the company of the others. Behind one door, a man, his pants down around his ankles, masturbating, looked up in morbid shock.

After Silverman hit the last door, he hurried through the curtains into the main part of the store. The manager was already down from his counter, heading toward the disturbance. Silverman passed him, graciously smiling and nodding; the manager looked confused. Silverman kept walking, knowing he had only a second or two left for his escape.

He made it. Outside, he broke into a run—he wanted to put as much distance as possible between himself and the manager, who he hoped hadn't followed him.

Then it hit him again—he'd lost Lacona.

He slowed down at the corner and looked for him. Still nowhere in sight. He ran to the bus terminal.

Inside, he searched the cavernous station area, then ran for the loading pier. He found him.

Lacona was sitting, idly staring straight ahead, in the window seat of one of the Greyhound buses. He checked the masthead for its destination. "Philadelphia."

Silverman walked slowly away until he was certain he was out of Lacona's range, then ran through the station for his car.

Carefully lumbering through the pier's narrow alley, the bus made its way for the street. When it turned the corner, heading out of town, Silverman pulled in safely behind.

20

It was 11:37 P.M. The Philadelphia bus station wasn't much better than the one in Harrisburg. Silverman sat on one of the benches, his car illegally parked outside as he waited for the disembarking passengers to make their way through the terminal.

The trip had been harrowing. In the dark it was hard enough to keep the bus in sight, and the driver made it worse by speeding. Silverman nervously had managed to keep up. Half way in, he had to stop for gas. That had meant really speeding to catch up. Once in Philadelphia, he overtook the bus to get to the station first.

Now, as he sat on the bench, he noticed the crowd from the bus coming through the doors. He spotted Lacona, waited until he left the terminal, then followed.

Lacona's pace was rapid. He covered about twelve blocks, zigzagging his way out of the seedy downtown area surrounding the Greyhound station. Wherever it is he is going, Silverman thought as he struggled to keep him in sight, he sure is in a hurry to get there.

Silverman stood at the corner across the street from the building Lacona had just entered, slightly out of breath. Lacona had gone in through the doors on the right. From what Silverman could make out, the entrance lead directly to a wide carpeted stairway.

The building had three floors; the top one, from where Silverman stood, looked like a remodeled loft. The windows at the top were newer and larger than those on the other two floors. Even from across the street one could hear the thumping of amplified music. Red and blue lights flashed, alternating with each other and the darkness. Silverman played his hunch that the top floor was where Lacona was heading.

Silverman went for the doors.

He stood at the top of the stairs, not because the three-story climb had been so steep but because of the sight facing him.

The place was enormous, the music deafening. The dance floor was directly to his left. Suspended above it were four large amplifiers, rock music blaring from each, enveloping the gyrating dancers in an invisible sheet of sound. To the rear was the crowded bar; on the sides, an assortment of tables and couches. The place was packed; there was barely room to move. Lights flickered as though they had the power to accelerate time.

Despite his bizarre day, Silverman was astonished by this sight. He noticed a few women on the dance floor. But they were dancing with women. The rest of the population was male: dancing with one another, standing with one another, affectionately holding one another. The walls were lined with large black and white framed photographs of posed male torsos, all muscular, hairless, bare-chested, each in skin-tight slacks, suspenders, and bow tie. There were no faces, only ovals with a bowler cavalierly tilted over each. The bar and seating area were separated from the dance floor by a row of thick green cylindrical cactuses, each protruding, pointing erectionlike to the high ceiling.

Silverman held his breath and made his way for the bar.

Despite his apologies, no one seemed to move as he pushed his way through the crowd. He thought he felt someone pat his behind.

He finally found a place at the bar and searched the room. Lacona was sitting on a couch, chatting with a young man.

His companion was in his twenties; his features, too perfect, too kempt, were a gay version of rugged handsomeness. They were touching one another. Silverman could see this wasn't their first meeting. This was a rendezvous, a reuniting of two lovers, separated too long.

So that was it. He and Jacobs, and Higdon had missed all the clues. The anonymous trips to Philadelphia, the expensive clothing, the sex movies, the evening in the barber's apartment. But there he was. And there was the rest of the money. The money they couldn't find was now accounted for, seated next to Lacona on that couch.

The young man standing beside Silverman watched his smile of victory but misinterpreted it as interest.

"Hello, love," he said.

Silverman turned, instantly realizing the problem.

"Hi," Silverman said.

"What's your name?" the young man asked politely.

Silverman told him.

"I'm Jason. Hello, John," he said.

They shook hands. Silverman kept a watch on Lacona.

"Hello."

"May I buy you a drink?" the young man cooed.

Silverman looked at him, his eager, expectant young face. For a split second, his mind focused on "Mom" Sutcliffe's face, and he smiled broadly. What the hell, he thought.

"Sure. Thanks."

The young man signaled for the bartender, a cherubic-looking fellow with golden curls, dressed in a tapered white sailor suit.

Just then, Lacona rose from his seat. Silverman watched as he walked into the men's room.

He had an idea.

Silverman left the bar, ignoring the young man's entreaties to stay, and walked into the men's room.

Lacona was standing at the urinal. Silverman went to the sink. As he washed his hands, he noticed Lacona look over. He was studying Silverman, as if trying to place him. Silverman smiled, a too friendly, inappropriate smile from one man to another. Lacona returned the smile. As he came over to the other sink to wash his hands, he looked up in the mirror. Silverman smiled again; the smile was returned. Lacona hadn't recognized him. He dried his hands and left.

Silverman waited a few moments, giving Lacona a chance to return to the couch, then walked out of the men's room toward him. The two men watched him coming.

He looked down at Lacona. "May I join you?"

Hardly waiting for a response, he sat on the sofa, on the opposite side of·Lacona's friend. Now he ignored Lacona and instead smiled at the younger man. He held out his hand.

"John Silverman," he said, smiling softly. They shook hands.

"David Phillips."

Silverman had given his last name on purpose, knew that Lacona would recognize it, hoped he'd now remember passing him in the peep movie corridor. He figured he'd have just a few more moments before Lacona's shock wore off.

"Do you live here in Philadelphia, David?" he asked, sliding his arm around the sofa's back.

David glanced nervously at Lacona, but missed Lacona's frozen stare.

"Yes."

"Me, too. What do you do?"

"I'm an actor."

"Then you must live in Center City. I bet you live in Center City."

David shyly smiled a no. He was obviously uncomfortable with this man's quick inquisitiveness.

"Where, then?"

"South Philly."

"Really. Where in South Philly? I have friends there."

"Norwood."

Lacona pushed himself from off the sofa and stood, ramrod straight.

"Come on, David. We're leaving." His eyes glared down contemptuously at the prosecutor.

David was bewildered; he looked up at Lacona. In his confusion, he thought that his friendliness had caused Lacona's outburst. "Albert?"

"He's one of the prosecutors, damn him," Lacona said, his gaze still locked on Silverman.

Silverman stopped smiling. "That's the missing piece of the puzzle, Albert, isn't it?" He stood. "Now I know. Now I've got enough, don't I, Albert?"

David was about to express his disgust, but Lacona grabbed his arm and pulled him away, David talking all the while.

Silverman watched as they disappeared down the stairway.

"Hello, Bob. I know it's late. I'm sorry to wake you."

Silverman was outside, calling from a pay phone attached to the wall of a filling station. Yet despite the street noises, when Jacobs spoke, Silverman could hear he hadn't been asleep.

"Where are you?"

For a moment, Silverman ignored the question. "How's your boy?"

"He's okay. Thanks. He'll be okay. He's home now." There was a pause. "The other boy died."

"I'm sorry."

Another pause. "Yeah."

Jacobs repeated his question. "Where are you?"

A truck rolled by, rumbling the pavement near the phone booth. Silverman shouted, "I'm in Philly. I've got it."

"Got what?"

"The missing piece."

"What?"

"I said the missing piece. I know how and where Lacona's money—the money we couldn't find—I know where it's going. I've found it."

"You found it?"

"He's got a lover. His money's going to a lover."

"I knew it. I knew it was a broad."

"Well, that's not it, exactly..."

Despite his fatigue, Silverman slept poorly. He was too excited, was at the office by eight A.M. the next day. The previous night he'd looked in the phone book, just to make sure. He was listed: David Phillips, 127 Norwood Avenue. All they needed to do now was trace the money. It was there; he knew it—the rent, the clothes. They'd subpoena bank records. Now there was a real tax case on Lacona.

There was something else now, too. To prove their case, the prosecution would have to show a jury, prove in open court how—and on whom—Lacona had spent that money. That he had a homosexual lover would come out in court, and Lacona would know that.

Promptly at nine A.M., Russell Haile called. They dispensed with the formalities quickly.

"John, Albert Lacona told me to call you this morning. I don't know what's come over him. He insisted that I call you first thing. He wants to see you, talk about cooperation, about a deal."

"Okay."

Haile had thought Silverman would have expressed some enthusiasm, some surprise.

"John, he's in Philadelphia right now and wants to see you. He told me some of what he's got. I won't tell you until we cut a deal, but it's pretty exciting stuff. But he's scared, too."

"Did he tell you anything? Give you any reason for his change of heart?"

"No. I asked him. He's bent out of shape about something, but I don't know what."

"Russ, I think you ought to know something. Can you and I talk first alone?"

"Of course. Do you know the reason for his turnaround?"

"Yeah, And you should, too... You say he's got some good stuff."

"You'll see. First, let's cut a deal."

* * *

Silverman searched the hotel lobby until he spotted Higdon and Jacobs. The meeting with Lacona was to take place in a hotel room, not in the U.S. attorney's offices or in Russ Haile's. At this stage, secrecy was important. No one was to know Lacona was cooperating.

Silverman had told his colleagues he'd meet them here. He hadn't explained why. He hadn't told them he was having lunch with Stanton Turner first. But he'd wanted Turner to know about Lacona, about the case having been cracked open.

The three of them stepped into the elevator. Jacobs pushed thirty-one, then quickly held back the closing doors as an elderly couple hurried in.

Tourists, thought Silverman as he watched the husband: unfashionably cut white hair clearly once blond, checked sport coat, too loud, too small-townish, buttoned over a protruding belly.

The wife asked Jacobs to push twenty-one, as though that was why he was there; the husband smiled in thanks.

Higdon ignored the others, stood stiffly, facing forward, staring directly ahead, a solitary passenger speeding upward.

Silverman stood to the side of his senior man, watching. The day before, when he'd told him about Lacona, for just a second or two, Higdon had shown clear, unambiguous excitement. Silverman had seen it as it escaped from behind Higdon's eyes, momentarily changing his usual surly expression. Then, just as quickly, he'd gained his control. He'd adjusted his glasses and announced that it would be he who would tell Miss Eccleston. Silverman had said fine.

The doors slid open on twenty-one. Silverman heard the muffled voices of the elderly couple as they walked down the hall to their room. The elevator doors closed. For the first time, he heard the near subliminal Muzak softly drifting from somewhere under the elevator's ceiling.

No one spoke. Thirty-one. They walked from the elevator and studied the black plastic plaques fastened to the corridor wall. Room 3127 was to the left. They walked silently on the thick carpeting; the only sound was the rustling of their clothes.

A few quick knocks brought Russell Haile to the door. The defense lawyer stepped aside to allow them entry into the day room of the two-room suite. Silverman introduced Jacobs. Haile nodded at Higdon, who barely acknowledged him, searching the room instead.

"Where's uhm . . . ?" Higdon asked, not seeing Lacona.

229

"Other room," Haile said, nodding in the direction of the closed connecting door.

Haile's huge Irish frame towered over Higdon. As though he were sensitive to his diminished appearance, Higdon removed himself to the other side of the room, near the windows, and took a seat in one of the chairs gathered around a marble-top bridge table.

Slowly the others joined him. Haile and Silverman had met the previous afternoon. The prosecutor had refused to discuss a deal until Haile had at least given him a rough outline of his client's information. So as not to surrender Lacona's rights, they had played the criminal lawyer's game of the hypothetical conversation.

Speaking about an unnamed "hypothetical" client, Haile had provided some of Lacona's evidence, stressing the strong points and down playing the weak ones, making it all very general. It looked good.

Later in the day, after meeting with Higdon, Silverman telephoned Haile and offered the deal. It had been Higdon's idea.

The deal would most likely turn out to be total immunity for Lacona, but it would look to others—to the jury—like limited immunity only, with prosecution for a lesser offense. It was something to hang over Lacona's head. Cooperating with the government was difficult; he had to know he was still on the hook; if Lacona displeased the prosecutors or lied, they could still send him to prison.

The deal Silverman offered included immunity from prosecution for anything and everything Lacona would tell them. He wouldn't be asked any questions about what he had done with the bribe money he had received. He would tell them how he had gotten the money, and where it had come from. That was all.

Someday, on the witness stand, Lacona would tell the jury about his deal. He'd say that he had no assurance whatsoever that he wouldn't be prosecuted for the crime of tax evasion arising from his not having reported as income the bribe money he'd received and spent on "personal matters."

In actuality, however, Lacona was the first real witness in a big case, and the prosecution almost assuredly would never bring charges against him.

The deal, now termed a plea agreement, had been recorded in letter form. Someday, a trial jury would see it. Its language was composed for their eyes and their ears. It spoke of how

Lacona fully understood "that truthfulness and total candor" from on the witness stand were the essential requirements for his receiving lenient treatment.

Silverman removed the letter from his inside jacket pocket, carefully unfolded it, then placed it on the marble-top table.

"Here's the letter," he told Haile. "We'll need both your signature and your client's."

Haile picked up the letter and started to read. When he was finished, he looked at Silverman, then at Higdon and Jacobs. He nodded.

"Okay. It's fine," he said, pushing it back across the table. "But there are a few remaining problems."

Haile allowed his long legs to stretch out before him; his elbows propped on the chair's arms, he held his hands toward the prosecutors as though he were a priest delivering a benediction.

"My client is very concerned that his...uhm, private... affairs will be brought out in open court. If not by you guys during your examination, then when he's cross-examined by the defense."

"We'll do the best we can, Russ," Silverman answered. "We'll try to keep it out on relevancy grounds when he's on cross. And, of course, we won't touch it during our direct. That's the best he can get. It's the best anyone could get under the circumstances. You know that."

Haile did know that. This "problem" was a throw away, merely prelude to another. Slowly, Haile sat up in his chair.

"There's another thing, guys," Haile said. "I told my client about your tentative interest in trying to get a taped conversation. He's dead set against it. Won't do it. Under any circumstances. It can't be part of the deal."

"Look," Higdon interrupted impatiently, "we'll work these details out later. Get him in here, sign the letter. I want to get started."

"Hey," Haile said, visibly annoyed; he didn't like Higdon, and he wouldn't be intimidated by him. "That guy," he continued, pointing with his thumb behind him toward the door. "He's putting his ass on the line for you. We'll take this one step at a time."

"What are you talking about, Haile? He's not doing a goddam thing for us. He knows we've got him. He's doing it for himself. And you know it."

Silverman watched both men. A confrontation was seconds away. If it happened, the day would be gone. Wasted.

"Russ," Silverman interjected, "you know we're going to do what we can. It's in our interest as well. You have our word we'll take it slow with him. Let's talk about taping later. Look, Lacona's in there, upset, listening to us arguing in here. He'll feel a lot better after he's opened up to us. What do you say? Let's begin."

Haile studied Silverman, then took the letter, rose, and went into the other room.

Silverman took advantage of the opportunity.

"Ray, cool down, man," he said, trying to keep things in control.

Higdon looked at him. He was cool, completely in control, knew exactly what he was doing. Now Silverman clearly saw that. He'd been playing nice guy to Higdon's tough guy, just as Higdon wanted him to. He was setting up the threat, letting Haile know that his client couldn't get away with too much.

Silverman exchanged glances with Jacobs, his appreciation for Higdon's finesse clearly visible.

Haile and Lacona entered the room. The letter had been signed. It was placed on the table.

Lacona stood sheepishly beside his lawyer, obviously frightened. Haile made the introductions. Everyone shook hands. Jacobs offered his chair to Lacona and moved to the easy chair behind the others. Everyone sat.

Silverman watched the captive Lacona sitting quietly beside his lawyer. The "first meeting," which to him signified the strangest part of the prosecutor's role, was about to begin.

At the beginning of the investigation, Silverman's job was to target the offender, then pursue him. At some point, the decision was made whether the target would be a defendant or a witness. If a witness, he'd be pursued more vigorously; His life would be made miserable; cooperation was his only salvation. Then, when the bargain was made, the deal struck, the antagonists would shake hands and sit down together. No longer was the prosecutor an ogre. Instantly, he became the target's best friend and protector. It was he, and only he, who had the power to save him from the bad guys—his former friends, who were soon to be on trial, and their lawyers. In exchange, he had to do only one thing: please his new friend, tell all. He who had been a force pursuing him relentlessly was, in reality, a smiling, compassionate human being who appreciated and empathized with his dilemma and would be there at the helm to guide him through the terrible storm that was to come in the courtroom.

Lacona was about to make new friends.

Russ Haile knew his role in the drama. Though Haile addressed the prosecutors, his remarks were for Lacona.

"Gentlemen, we've signed the letter. My client is ready to be interviewed, but some problems still remain. We will need to explore further the chances of getting a taped conversation. And there is Mr. Lacona's . . . Albert's . . . discomfort with his job. Retaining it and living a charade frankly is not favored by us. We'll discuss that later. Let's proceed."

"Albert," Silverman began with familiarity. "Russ has filled us in, generally. Please start from the beginning and tell us all you can remember, in as much detail as you can recall."

Silverman knew the beginning would be the most difficult.

"Look, before you begin," he added, "I want you to know something. We know how hard this is for you. We've been through this before with others. We understand. Do the best you can first time. Don't worry, we'll go over it many times before you take the witness stand."

Lacona looked to his lawyer for support, sighed, then began his story.

He and Phillip Brooke Lane had been friends for many years. They had met when both were involved as ward healers in municipal elections. Throughout Lane's meteoric rise in politics, Lacona had been behind the scenes, working. And, with the assumption of each new office, his friend had rewarded him.

Sure, they hadn't seen as much of each other, particularly socially, as in the early days, before Lane had become so prominent, but that was merely because the mayor had been too busy with his responsibilities to the people. He stopped at this point. Quietly, he told them that Lane was unaware of his "sexual preferences."

Well, it began about five or six years ago, sometime after the election. The mayor had invited him down to City Hall. They had chatted about old times. Lane seemed happy, satisfied with his new post; he spoke of the loyalty Lacona had shown him throughout the years. The time had come for a major reward: the chairmanship of the State Roads Commission up in Harrisburg soon was to be vacant. But the governor owed the mayor a favor. Lane wanted Lacona to be commissioner. They'd shaken hands heartily; Lacona had been delighted.

Lane had then spoken of his plans to revamp and improve the city's road and highway system. He had explained how federal and state funds would be used. It was going to be a major undertaking of the new administration, and he, Albert Lacona, would have the responsibility of carrying out the plan. Lacona had assured him of his support.

And then, still smiling, Lane had spoken of how there would be many construction companies interested in performing this very lucrative work. He was pleased there was a bidding process in effect so that "politics" would not be involved in the selection of contractors. However, caution had to be exercised in making certain that the "right contractors" would get the job. They had to be well qualified. Careful standards were needed to "control" the performance of this work.

Take this relatively small company, for instance, Regal Construction. They had a fine reputation. The mayor was certain there were others, but here was a fairly small company that had an excellent reputation. He hoped they would be qualified to bid. He knew that a company like Regal could be counted on to perform as expected.

Lacona got the message, loud and clear. He and the mayor had each smiled at the other. Not one explicit word had been said. Lacona had thanked the mayor again and assured him of his loyalty and "cooperation." And that was the beginning.

"How did you know what to do?" Silverman asked.

He then explained how, a month or so after his appointment as commissioner had been approved by the state legislature, he had received an envelope in the mail. Inside was a key and a note. The note read, "Box 11752, Main Post Office."

Inside the box was an envelope that contained three thousand dollars in cash and five Regal Construction Company bid slips, all made out for the same job but each with a different bid figure inside. No instructions. The rest was up to him.

"What'd you do?"

"Are you gentlemen familiar with our bidding system?" Of course they were; that's what they'd been investigating for the past several months. Silverman and Jacobs smiled at Lacona's nervousness.

"The first thing I did was to have a copy of the deputy commissioner's key made. That wasn't hard. He keeps it in the center drawer of his desk. While he was at lunch, I took it and had a copy made. He never knew it was gone. I already had the combination to the safe in which the bid box was kept." He leaned forward, momentarily lost in his explanation. "By the evening before the next morning's bid opening, all of the bids had been submitted.

"I returned to the office around midnight, opened the safe,

and used the two keys to open the box. I removed all the envelopes and opened them. The bid Regal had submitted through the ordinary process was not the lowest, so I removed it, selected one of the five Regal bid slips which was lower than the other contractors' bids, put all of the bids in new official envelopes, and restamped them with the official seal. I put them back in the box and put the box back in the safe."

He leaned back. "The next morning, I stood there with the deputy and others as one of the clerks removed the box and opened the bids. Regal, of course, was low bidder."

He went on to tell them how he had repeated this procedure before each bid opening. On some occasions, he'd found the post office box empty—no money, no bids. He had surmised that Regal didn't want to win every bid; that obviously, would have cast suspicion on them.

"And that's about it. I've followed the same procedure for the past five years."

His story was over. Lacona looked anxiously at the prosecutors, searching for assurances, comfort. Haile patted his arm. He'd done just fine, he said. Now there were questions to answer.

"Did you ever try to find out in whose name the box was rented?" Silverman asked.

"No."

"It's gotta be a phony name," Jacobs said from behind him. "The yearly rental paid in cash or by money order. But we can check it out."

"Did you ever speak to Mayor Lane about all this again?"
"Never."

"How about Regal?" Silverman asked. "When did you learn the identities of your benefactors?"

"I still don't know. At least, not from firsthand knowledge. I've read the papers about Ames and Stavaros . . . I've never even seen Stavaros. I know Mr. Ames; that is, I've met him once or twice at political functions for the mayor. But I couldn't swear that he's an owner of Regal."

There was momentary silence. Silverman and Higdon exchanged glances. It was time for the next step. Silverman turned to Haile.

"Russ, may we talk to you out of the presence of your client?" Then, to Lacona, he added, "This is routine procedure; just lawyer talk."

Lacona looked apprehensive; he looked over at Haile for instructions.

"Yeah, Albert. Go into the other room for a while," Haile told him. "I'll come and get you when we're through."

Lacona did as he was told.

There would now be an assessment. Was he telling the truth? Did he hold back?

Higdon took command.

"There's no corroboration," he said.

Haile felt the challenge. "No corroboration," he repeated. "Nothing to support his story. It's his word against the mayor's. And Lane could always express shock and surprise that Lacona understood him to mean anything sinister by what he said. There's absolutely no proof."

"Russ, did he save any of the unused bid slips?" Silverman asked.

"No. He threw them away." Haile answered quickly. He wanted a reading himself. "But what about his story?" he asked Silverman. "Do you believe him?"

It was Higdon who responded.

"We want to talk alone, Haile. Go join your client."

Haile shrugged and left. When the connecting door had closed, the three men looked at each other. There was no need for the question to be spoken.

"I believe him," Jacobs said. "He might be holding back some, but I believe him. Our targets are certainly smart enough to do it that way."

"Yeah, me, too," said Silverman. "We've got to run down that post office box, trace the ownership and the rental payments. I think he's telling the truth, though he is uncorroborated. That's a problem."

Higdon drummed his fingers on the table, stared at Silverman, then Jacobs.

"Bob, how long would it take to get a phone kit up here?" Higdon's voice sounded urgent.

"About an hour."

Lacona's cooperation was now a secret. How long it would remain that way was anyone's guess. Higdon also believed him. But Lacona was only one piece of the puzzle. And without corroboration, Lacona would be easy game for a good defense lawyer at trial. No, they'd need corroboration. A consent phone tap. A recorded conversation.

"Call for the kit," Higdon told Jacobs. "We'll do it right now. He'll call the mayor, say he can't stand the pressure much longer, needs help, wants to talk to him. He'll ask for a meeting.

We'll send him in there strapped with a body recorder. We'll see if we can't get the mayor to incriminate himself."

Silverman considered the plan. It was the right move. He watched as Higdon walked for the door, knocked once sharply, opened it, and ordered Haile and Lacona back in.

Once everyone was reseated, Higdon spoke to Haile.

"Okay, here's what we're going to do. Lacona is going to place a call to Mayor Lane in a little while, after some equipment arrives. We're going to monitor and record the call, with your client's consent."

Before continuing, Higdon shifted his gaze directly to Lacona and outlined what he should say to the mayor. "Finally, he'll ask for a meeting, and then he'll go to the meeting wearing a body recorder. That way we'll get a second recorded conversation. Only that one will be in person." Lacona, silent, intimidated by Higdon's stare, remained frozen, then looked helplessly at Haile.

"For Christ sakes, Higdon," Haile said accusingly, leaning toward the table, "why couldn't we have discussed this while Albert was in the other room. I told you he has strong feelings against surreptitious eavesdropping, and you—"

Higdon interrupted Haile in midsentence. He, more than anyone else in the room, knew from years of experience at first meetings how to handle this situation.

"Albert," he said, speaking directly to Lacona, "please listen closely to what I'm about to say. We are going to help you. So long as you are completely cooperative and truthful with us, you can count on us to be in your corner. But you must rely on us to make the decisions."

As Higdon leaned toward Lacona, Silverman perceived that his demeanor was forced, unnatural, but was certain Lacona couldn't see it. Higdon was tender; he spoke to Lacona with odd compassion.

"You must understand, Albert, that you *must* cooperate fully. You have no choice. The only choice you had was whether or not to cooperate. You can't have it both ways. If you don't want to stand trial and go to jail for everything we've got on you, you must do what we say . . . Okay?"

By now, Lacona's head was bowed slightly. He sighed away the futility of resistance and nodded okay.

"Bob, make the call."

As Jacobs went to the phone, Silverman watched Higdon, still leaning toward Lacona as if he were consoling a friend who had just lost someone very close.

Even though Silverman hadn't been to Storyville for a while, Charles, the maître d', remembered him, seemed genuinely pleased to see him again.

Unlike Higdon, Silverman wasn't used to being alone. Without a wife around or Jamie to play with, there was a void. He tried thinking about Mary Ann. What would he be doing with her? It didn't work. He couldn't keep her in his mind.

For the better part of most days—and nights—he was satisfied. The case occupied his thoughts completely. But from time to time, even it wasn't there. Tonight he wanted to relax, knew it was necessary but wasn't sure what to do. First, of course, he had tried the racing form, then Pac-Man's Revenge. Neither worked. Though he hated to admit it, it was human company he needed, almost craved. He felt alone, really alone: John Silverman in the solitary company of his uncertain future. And he didn't like it. So it was off to Storyville. It seemed his only choice.

He'd been sitting at a table near the side of the room, well out of sight of the stage and the tables grouped near it, when he saw her coming down the steps. He watched inconspicuously as Charles led Denise Owens and the man who obviously was her date to one of the tables near the front, within the reflective arc of the stage lighting.

Denise took the seat facing in his direction; her date moved his chair to her side, his profile to Silverman.

Silverman hadn't seen her in a while, watched as the waiter came over for their drink order. He found himself looking for imperfections in her date.

The image of their last night together flooded his memory.

She said something to the waiter—her order, he guessed—then looked in his direction. She saw him. Seemed not at all surprised. Smiled and mouthed hello.

He waved, wondering if he should go over. Maybe she'd come to him. But she looked away from him and back to her date, seemed no longer to be aware of Silverman's presence.

A little later, their drinks had been delivered, and the music was in full swing. She was facing the stage, listening, moving slightly with the beat. She seemed to sense his staring, turned in his direction, looked at him as though she, too, were remembering that night, then turned away again.

Silverman took his last sip of beer and left.

* * *

238

Stanton Turner's secretary had buzzed to let him know the gentlemen had arrived and were standing outside of his office. He rose from behind his massive oak desk and walked to the center of his room to greet them as they entered.

He shook hands heartily with each man, then guided them toward their seats.

Turner hadn't arranged for the meeting. Not directly. But it was at his initiative that it had been scheduled.

It was curious how life provided opportunities.

The gentlemen waited expectantly to hear what he had to say.

21

Silverman pressed the rewind button and watched as the tape silently spun to its beginning, the right reel shrinking as the brown plastic ribbon flew on its journey across the machine.

It had been almost a week since the two conversations had been recorded, and he had listened to the tape at least six times since then, trying to picture the mayor, see the expression on his face—his mannerisms—as he spoke to Lacona.

Jacobs had been right about the post office box. The official application on file showed the box had been rented to a William Gregory with an address in central Harrisburg. A phony. Each year's rent for the box had been paid in cash; none of the postal people could provide a description of the payer. One clerk had a vague recollection of a woman's having paid last year, but he wasn't certain.

But the phone conversation had gone well. He leaned forward, pressed the play button, sat at his desk alone, and listened once again to the phone call from the hotel room the day of Albert Lacona's first meeting.

"Mayor's office."

"Mayor Lane, please. Albert Lacona calling."

"Hold please, sir."

"Mayor Lane's secretary."

"Hello, Mrs. Nelson. This is Albert Lacona. How are you today?"

"Hello, Mr. Lacona. Just fine, thank you. Would you like to speak to the mayor?"

"Yes, please."

The sound of the tape slowly winding in the silence as Lacona waited.

"Hello."

"Hello, Mr. Mayor. How are you?"

"Hello, Albert. I'm fine, thank you."

Next came the part they had rehearsed with Lacona. He was nervous, paused too long before beginning.

"Uhm...Mr. Mayor, I'm...uh, in Philadelphia...I've just come from a meeting with my lawyer. I've been under a lot of pressure, you know."

"Yes, Albert?"

"My lawyer wants me to cooperate with the prosecutors and the grand jury. I simply don't know what to do anymore. There's just so much pressure a man can be expected to bear...Mr. Mayor. I need help. May I come and see you? I've got to talk to someone about this."

"Hold on a moment, Albert."

As the tape continued winding, Silverman waited once again for the secretary's voice. That would come next. Each time he listened to this part of the tape, he wondered. Was that the mayor's normal way of handling such situations, or was he just being careful, perhaps even fearful of speaking to Lacona over the phone?

"Hello, Mr. Lacona?"

"Yes?"

"The mayor asked me to set up an appointment for you. He simply cannot see you today. He apologizes for having you make another trip in, but would Friday at eleven be convenient?"

"Yes, yes. Fine. That'll be fine. Thank you."

"We'll see you then. Good-by."

"Good-by."

Silverman pushed the stop button; the machine snapped off.

The light at the end of the tunnel. Silverman could see it. Indictment. The beginning of the end. Or so it had seemed.

And Lacona had given them something to go to Washington with. They had gotten his story and the tape of the phone conversation before their Wednesday meeting. In fact, Higdon had called Terrance Cook and had suggested that the attorney general himself would certainly be interested in what they had.

They had met with Cook and the attorney general, who was, surprisingly, much older looking in person than in photographs. Silverman alternated his gaze between him and the large plaster bust of Oliver Wendell Holmes that stood on a pedestal at the far end of his office. Both seemed saddened at the idea of Philadelphia's mayor having been involved in serious criminal wrongdoing.

Higdon had done most of the speaking, filling the others in. He mentioned the transaction involving the resort complex in the Bahamas, that their pursuit thus far had been unsuccessful but that it might have promise. Silverman wondered if Higdon would mention the letter. He didn't. Lacona had fallen in their laps too quickly for Higdon; the letter was still untouched.

The meeting had ended with encouragement and support. The IRS agents would be put back on the case. White's motion to conclude the investigation would now most certainly be lost. And nothing at all had been said about the letter of complaint from First Merchant's Bank.

Silverman looked at the machine, sitting dormantly on his desk, waiting for the touch of a button to come alive. Jacobs had made the arrangements for the Friday meeting with Lane. After arriving in Philadelphia, Lacona had gone to the hotel room in which they had had their first meeting. An electronics expert had outfitted him with the device. The small microphone was taped to his chest. The battery pack fitted unobtrusively in the small of his back. He waited uncomfortably with Jacobs and the electronics man until it was time to leave for City Hall. Then, before entering City Hall alone at eleven, a block away, out of sight of the entrance, the expert had turned the machine on. Immediately after the meeting, they had another rendezvous so that the tape could be removed and sealed. The prosecutors did that in order to convince the jury that no one had tampered with the tape. Lacona had been well rehearsed.

With perverse fascination, as if each playing would somehow change the words, Silverman pressed the play button again and listened to the rustling, crackling sounds of Lacona's clothing as he entered the mayor's office. He bent towards the machine. The fidelity was bad, and the voices, slightly muffled, sounded far off in the distance.

"Sit down, Albert."

More noises as Lacona fidgeted briefly in his chair.

"Ugh, Mr. Mayor, I'm terribly sorry to come here like this . . . but I'm at my wit's end." His nervousness was apparent. "My lawyer, uhm . . . He says that I've got to look out for myself . . . Russ, that is, uh, my attorney says I should cut my losses. You know, cooperate. Tell the grand jury what I know. Tell them about . . . well, you know. About . . . uh . . . everything."

Silverman tried to picture Lane at his desk staring at Lacona. There were more rustling noises; Lacona was fidgeting too much, and the microphone was rubbing the inside of his shirt. His next sentence was garbled.

Silence again. Then, for the sixth or seventh time, Silverman listened to the mayor interrupt Lacona.

242

"My lawyer wants me to tell them about our . . ."

"Albert, are you recording this conversation for the U.S. attorney's office?"

His look must have been penetrating.

"Albert?"

"Yes. Yes, I am . . . I'm sorry, sir. They told me I had to. I'm so sorry."

"You're wearing the recorder on your body?"

"Yes."

"It's running right now?"

"Yes."

"I think what they've made you do is despicable. Obviously, you've been under too much pressure. You must have taken leave of your senses to permit them to try and involve me in whatever it is you might have done. I don't blame you, Albert. You are obviously not responsible for your actions. You know, in truth, that I have done nothing wrong."

Silverman heard him pick up the phone and tell Mrs. Nelson to come in at once. He listened to the door open.

"Mrs. Nelson, please show Mr. Lacona out. He's leaving."

Silverman rewound the tape.

Not only had the mayor apparently seen through their charade; he had turned the situation to his advantage with a short, self-serving speech. But he had been strangely silent since then, had kept what happened a secret. Silverman wondered why and waited. They all waited.

Lacona hadn't been to his office since that day. His time bomb was ticking. Haile was worried about his client, said Lacona was morose, had talked of suicide.

Higdon, too, had listened to the tape. Silverman watched him closely. Not a speck of emotion. He had looked blankly at him and Jacobs and then had returned to his office. Not surprisingly, he had been out with "the flu" since then.

Silverman and Jacobs had concluded that Lacona could be salvaged as a witness if, but only if, his importance to the case could be down played to the jury. They needed more, and they needed it fast.

There was no time to waste and only one lead to follow. He called Jan into his office, told her to bring her steno pad.

"I want you to send a telegram to each grand juror telling him or her to be here the day after tomorrow at nine A.M. Tell them they're going to be in session.

"Before you call Western Union, get me Cook at Justice."

243

He'd discussed it with Jacobs. The chance he was taking was enormous. Jacobs thought it much too risky.

Silverman had listened politely to his investigator. Jacobs was experienced, his judgment proven. But it was going to be done. Silverman was going to do it, with or without Jacobs's approval. Day after tomorrow at nine A.M.

One-thirty P.M. The grand jury was in session.

The grand jurors had returned to the room, ready for their afternoon's work. Higdon's expression was sullen as he walked up the hall. He passed Silverman, the witness, and her lawyer, ignored them all and entered the grand jury room.

Silverman turned to the lawyer. "Frank," he began, his tone too cordial given the circumstances, "I want to say a few things to Mary before she and I go back into the room. I want your permission to speak to her out here informally—in your presence of course."

"Sure, okay."

Francis Eckert was in his sixties. He looked every bit the successful attorney, but there was something missing. He wore the correct attire: gray pin-striped suit, horn-rimmed glasses. He was tall, stood erect, smiled pleasantly. But somewhere in his eyes there was a kind of blankness. He was a nice guy. Not a bright lawyer. And here, inside a federal courthouse he was a fish out of water. He knew it, and he knew that Silverman knew it.

He had been hired by Donald Ames for the express purpose of shepherding Ames's secretary through the grand jury. His instructions, which he had followed without question, were clear and narrow: help Mary Burke take the Fifth Amendment and then get her out of there as quickly as possible.

But things that he and Ames hadn't anticipated had happened. Mary really needed a lawyer; she had become, in a very real sense, his client. He tried, without success, to anticipate what was to happen next, but he was out of his depth. All he could do was await Silverman's next move.

Silverman turned to Mary. She was almost his height, though lanky, her tightly curled hair artificially darkened by a cheap home rinse. Instinctively, she took one step backward.

"Mary," he said, "you were in there this morning, so you know the preliminaries. After the oath has been administered, we'll begin by advising you of your rights once again. Then we'll go over what happened before lunch . . ."

His voice faded into the distance. She could hear him, but

his words seemed to be in another room, meant for someone else. As she stood there, her memory leaped back to the previous day and replayed for her the nightmare she had been living.

She had brought the subpoena into Ames's office literally within seconds after the deputy U.S. marshall had served it on her. It had been expected, but the marshall had been so official, and now it was real. She had been summoned to the grand jury; she would have to testify. And she was frightened.

Ames had seemed so unconcerned. He leaned back in his chair and clasped his big hands behind his head. "Don't worry bout it, Mary," he had said with that usual grin. "We'll get you a lwayer. You'll go in there at nine A.M. tomorrow morning, take the Fifth, and be back at your desk within an hour. Guaranteed."

That was only yesterday. It seemed so very much longer. Mary thought of how Mr. Ames had tried to make light of the situation, make her feel less anxious. And, as he had promised, she did take the Fifth before the grand jury. She had been in and out of that room so quickly it had indeed been painless. Her only responsibility had been to read the typewritten words on that small piece of paper that Frank had given her that morning:

> Members of the grand jury, upon the advice of my counsel, I decline to answer any questions based upon my rights against self-incrimination under the Fifth Amendment to the United States Constitution.

She remembered thinking that Mr. Ames had been right; it had been easy. She had left the room and had begun walking toward Frank with a relieved smile on her face when Silverman had stepped in front of her and handed her some papers. He had explained that they were going to see the judge and told her to consult her lawyer. She had looked over at Frank, and her heart sank as she saw the helplessness on his face.

They didn't have much time. Silverman directed them to a small alcove down the hall where they could talk. Frank tried to explain to her that the prosecutor had filed some sort of motion ordering her to go before the judge in ten minutes. The judge, he had explained, would force her to testify; she could no longer rely on the Fifth Amendment. Strange how she conjured up an image of the judge, wearing his black robe, pushing her with both hands into the grand jury room as she tried desperately to hold on to the door frame.

She had been so confused. Why hadn't anyone told her this could happen? As she stood there in the alcove, her heart pounding, her thin hands tightly gripping each other, she tried to cope and listen to Frank, but the situation was overwhelming. She had been lulled into a false sense of security and relief. Now she felt betrayed and frightened.

After she and Frank had rejoined Silverman, they had gone immediately to Judge Montarelli's chambers. Everyone there seemed sure that she understood them. They were wrong. It was all happening so fast. The judge had said something about judicially enforced immunity and her obligation to testify truthfully. Something about perjury and something called "false declaration."

Judge Montarelli had seemed pleasant but detached. For a moment, Mary felt almost unable to control her urge to interrupt him, to explain how confused she was, how frightened. She had wanted to explain how she had never married, had lived alone after her mother had died, and so . . . But she sat there, impassive, totally reliant on Frank.

On one or two occasions, the judge had stopped speaking and stared at her. She realized that she was required to make a response and had looked over at Frank for help. He nodded, and she turned to the judge.

"Yes, Your Honor." Her words were almost whispers.

Now, as she stood in the hall ouside the grand jury room waiting for the afternoon session to begin, recollecting how she had faked attentiveness in the judge's chambers, Silverman's voice became clearer. Although she had stood there looking at Silverman as he spoke, she had been trancelike. She wondered if he had noticed. Slowly, his words began to filter into her consciousness.

"Now you know that you no longer have a Fifth Amendment right to rely on. The judge has ordered you to testify. Nothing you say can be used against you in a criminal case, but you have no protection of any kind for perjury."

He paused, looking long and hard at Mary. "Don't lie, Mary," he said sternly. "The only way you can get into trouble with me is if you lie. Lie to me and you'll have more trouble than you've ever dreamed of."

He paused, waiting for Eckert to object to his admonition. As he did, he thought of how quickly prosecutors learned to take advantage of a defense lawyer who didn't know the rules of the game.

On one of the few occasions on which Higdon, as senior prosecutor, had addressed the other assistants, he'd spoken of the phenomenon:

"If the lawyer isn't with it," Higdon had told them, "if he's dumb enough to let you intimidate his client right in front of him, push the client around a little. Don't talk about the government. Personalize it—*you* be the government. Make the witness fear you. Make him think you would enjoy nothing better than to spend some of your time prosecuting him for perjury and sending him to prison. It may not be the politest way of getting someone to tell the truth, but it's effective."

Eckert stood silently beside Mary.

"Let's go," Silverman told her as he stepped toward the closed door to the grand jury room.

He rapped softly; the murmuring voices inside stopped almost immediately. Someone opened the door from within.

The twenty-three grand jurors sat in their seats, deadly silent. Their intensity did not escape Mary. Silverman noticed Mrs. Franklin, still there in the back row. Higdon was in his seat.

"Please sit down." Silverman pointed Mary back into the witness box, then took his own seat.

Mary stepped into the box and sat quietly, fearful that any unnecessary noise would offend those in the room.

"I remind the witness," Silverman announced as he searched through his files until he located and opened the one he wanted, "that she is still under oath from this morning."

Mary dutifully nodded her understanding.

Silverman glanced quickly at Higdon, sitting quietly, still as a cat waiting for prey. But today there would be no interruptions. This was too important. Today, Silverman would take—and maintain—control.

Concentrating his attention on the witness, Silverman advised her of her rights—and her new obligation to testify—and began his examination.

"Now, Miss Burke," he began, clearing his throat, "uhm, I want to, uh, begin this afternoon by asking you some questions about your duties and responsiblities as personal secretary to Donald Ames. First of all, I assume it's accurate to state that you do typing and other standard secretarial functions for him?"

"Yes, I do." She almost whispered.

"You do his personal financial record keeping as well, don't you?"

"Yes, sir."

"Well, uhm, why don't we begin by your describing for the ladies and gentlemen of the grand jury what you do in that regard."

She began a long, nervous, more or less incoherent description of her responsbilities. As she spoke, she instinctively kept her eyes on Silverman. She knew she was the cornered animal and he, the predator. And as she spoke, she wasn't about to look at those twenty-three faces in those rows of chairs. She could actually feel their eyes on her, staring intently. She rambled on, trying as best she could to fill the room with sentences. As she spoke, she kept her long bony fingers tightly clasped in her lap, her thin frame pressed against the chair.

Silverman, his legs crossed, the file in his lap, waited patiently for her to finish. Sensing that there was no longer a need for her to continue, Mary ended almost in midsentence, keeping her eyes cemented to Silverman.

The prosecutor didn't move. He waited a few seconds more before speaking. The silence became pervasive; expectation hung in the air. A grand juror near the rear of the room muffled a cough.

Suppressing his own nervousness, Silverman finally spoke. Without looking at the witness, he began, "Miss Burke, have you ever made penciled notations on any of Mr. Ames's personal financial documents?"

Higdon shifted slowly and deliberately in his seat. Silverman knew immediately that he was showing displeasure. He'd made a mistake.

The question had been too broad, too premature.

Silverman didn't have time to feel annoyed with himself. The thought that Higdon would interject himself into the questioning shot into his mind. He knew he had to act fast if he wanted to keep control of this interrogation. Before either Higdon or Mary could speak, he said, "Strike that question."

Leaning forward in his chair, placing the file back on the table in front of him, he continued. "Let me, uh, let me begin this way. Have you ever prepared accounting sheets for Mr. Ames, listing his personal checks and what they were used as payment for?"

He opened the top file, removed the pale-green sheets of paper, and pushed them toward the stenographer as Mary answered yes to the question.

"Please mark these two documents as grand jury exhibits one and two for today."

As the stenographer picked up a nearby pencil to mark the papers, Mary got her first good look at the green sheets. She felt the hot tingly flush of adrenalin shooting through her body. Uncontrollably, but just barely perceptibly, her body lurched forward in her chair.

My God, it can't be, she thought, I destroyed all those papers. Immediately, trying to wish away what she seemed to be seeing, she thought no, don't panic, they're some other papers, something else. But her hopes evaporated as Silverman walked around the table and gently placed the documents on the small ledge in front of her, allowing her to review them.

She wondered how much they knew. She stared at the documents. The words blurred together on the page. She felt she couldn't lift her head, could sense the prosecutors waiting for her. She knew that the moment she picked her head up, she would be questioned.

She waited, frozen, staring at those green sheets. She had an overwhelming urge to just get up and walk right out of the room without looking at anyone. Then slowly and hesitantly, she looked up at the prosecutors. Her mouth was so dry, she had difficulty swallowing; she wanted some water but didn't ask.

Silence.

"Tell us about grand jury exhibits one and two, Miss Burke." Silverman's voice filled the room, a faint smile curling the corners of this mouth.

"What do you mean? I don't understand the question," came the reply too quickly.

Her next thought, taking only a second or two, flashed on the screen of her mind.

Stoffman, the accountant, had called Mr. Ames after his grand jury appearance.

Ames had hung up and immediately buzzed for her.

He had made it sound so unimportant—so routine.

He had instructed her in that pleasant, informal manner of his to remove from the safe all the check spreads from the file, take them to the paper shredder, and destroy them. She had been confused, had repeated his instructions; did he want her to destroy the current ones for, say, the last three years as well? Yes, all of them. He didn't really provide an explanation, never mentioned the penciled notations she had added as her reminder after the accountant had returned the check spreads each year.

He only made some vague reference to the "E.R." checks he himself wrote each month and his wife's suspicion. But he'd sounded so pleasant and unconcerned.

Mary Burke was a soldier. She had done what her employer had asked her to do. But sitting in that grand jury room with those sheets in front of her, it all coming back to her, she felt weak.

But she had destroyed them all, her mind persisted.

Then, for the first time, she realized what had happened. She had destroyed all the check spreads that had been in the file, but that one year of the audit, the accountants had needed one year's spreads returned, and she had sent them. She remembered now her embarrassment at having forgotten to erase the penciled notes she had put on them. She'd never told Mr. Ames about it. The accountants must have forgotten to return them, and she had forgotten to get them back. They had probably been stuck in a file and had stayed there, like buried treasure, waiting for a subpoena. And there they were in front of her.

She wondered what Silverman was going to ask next.

And then it began. His questions came so quickly. Were there others? Yes. Were they still in existence? No. Had she destroyed them? Yes.

"And you did that on the instructions of Donald Ames, didn't you?"

"Yes."

"And Mr. Ames told you not to worry about it, didn't he?"

"Yes, I suppose so."

"The penciled notations were in your handwriting?"

And so it went. His questions contained all the information, all the facts that she was so afraid to volunteer. All she had to do was answer with a yes or no. She relaxed a little. This had become easier. She felt a strange sense of comfort and reassurance in the quick, rhythmical pace of the questions. Silverman was making it easier for her, she thought.

As she began to relax, she stopped listening intently to the questions. She would get the gist of each question, and when it had ended, she would supply her one- or two-word response. But as the questioning continued, she began to wonder.

If Silverman had all the information, anyway, why was she there? Maybe it had something to do with the grand jurors, she thought, trying to make sense out of it. Maybe it had something to do with the stenographer who was working away furiously at his little machine.

The thought that maybe Silverman didn't know all the answers and was guessing at some of what had happened approached her mind but quickly faded out of focus. By now, she was soothed by the rhythm of the questioning.

But the facts in his questions seemed right. She knew she wasn't being careful enough, wasn't listening intently enough to correct minor inaccuracies. In the lulling comfort of the interrogation, she sensed that he would be satisfied with how things were going. And if he were satisfied, he would let her leave soon. The desire to end this ordeal, to go home and be in surroundings that she could understand and cope with, was overwhelming.

She sensed it before she even perceived it. The rhythm was breaking up. Raymond Higdon, who up to now had been just a motionless figure in the chair next to Silverman's, was coming to life. There was movement. His head picked up, and his eyes found their way to hers.

She thought of Stoffman's telling her about how Higdon had grilled him during his appearance here. How awful he had been. Now it apparently was going to be her turn. But why? What had she done to offend him? All else in the room faded into unimportance. She watched Higdon's movements.

"Wait a minute," Higdon began, his voice heavy with antagonism. "There's something I don't understand."

Mary braced herself.

But before he could continue, Silverman interjected. He placed his hand on Higdon's arm, then half-turned to Mary. "Excuse us a moment, will you please, Miss Burke?"

Silverman leaned forward in his chair, his arms on his knees. Higdon did the same. Their heads were so close they almost touched.

"I want to finish this without interruption," Silverman whispered. "Please hold your questions until I've finished."

Then, in a softer, more appeasing tone, he continued to inform his colleague, "I'm about to finish this line of questions, anyway, and, uh, I'm about to move onto"— he paused, searching from some nondescriptive phrase —"something different."

Silverman was ready for this, prepared. He'd played the scene out in his mind, anticipated Higdon's reactions—and moves. What was about to happen was unavoidable; the confrontation was finally underway.

"Are you telling me I can't clear something up with a couple of questions?" Higdon demanded incredulously.

Higdon was so good, Silverman thought. He'd quickly placed

his younger colleague in the uncomfortable position of appearing unreasonable, of having to respond with something like, "Well, I guess if that's all you want to do, it would be wrong for me to insist that . . ." But this time Silverman was prepared to be unreasonable, to insist on doing it his way.

"Look, I've spent a lot of hours, a lot of late nights, working this case," he said. "There's a lot happening very quickly here. If you want to invest the time—and agony—with us, that's fine. But today you're going to sit there until I've got the facts down; then you can take over."

Higdon glared at him. "I've told you you're not in charge here," Higdon scolded. "You seem to keep forgetting that."

If nothing else, Higdon was predictable.

Just as he had planned when he played this scene in his mind, Silverman became friendly, respectful. He smiled, "Look, Ray, I've almost finished this line, and I've only got one more area to cover. Why don't you let me finish first. Then you can do whatever you like with her."

Higdon shifted gears almost as quickly as Silverman. He turned to Mary Burke and said, "Miss Burke, would you please step out into the hall for a moment?"

Obediently, and with relief for the chance to escape, she quickly stepped down from the box and left the room.

Higdon faced the grand jurors.

"Ladies and gentlemen," he announced with authority, "Mr. Silverman and I need a few more minutes. We will resume in a little while. Please remain in your seats." He turned back to Silverman.

"What other area?" he asked.

This was going to be the worst part of it. "What do you mean?" Silverman asked with forced nonchalance. He felt adrenalin shoot through his body.

Higdon's look of intimidation increased. Silverman waited. He thought of what he intended to do. He'd convinced himself that it was the right move. There was no choice. It was now or never. But what if it didn't work? What if it exploded in his face?

He didn't have time to ponder these last thoughts. Higdon spoke.

"Come on. Don't play games with me, John. What else are you planning to question her about?" Higdon already knew. His chilling look dared Silverman to say it.

"The letter."

Higdon's eyes flashed. "Damn it," he said, pointing his

finger at Silverman. "We agreed that I would send the letter to a documents analyst first. That way, before we went out on a limb in here, we'd know. We agreed to that, John. And now, all by yourself," he added with subtle mockery, "you've made a decision to go ahead. I've sent the letter. We'll wait for the results. You're just not going to do it. Period."

The grand jurors seated closest to the prosecutors' table now noticed that their whispered conversation had become very heated.

Silverman's calm evaporated. As he spoke, he seemed to be forcing each word slowly from his mouth, a faint, sarcastic smile on his lips, his jaw tight.

"What we agreed, Ray, was that you would assume the reponsibility of getting the letter to the lab. That was months ago. And apparently, until a couple of days ago, you haven't done shit. This investigation—and I—will not wait. You want to be here, bust your ass with Jacobs and me? Fine. You want to say home alone with your . . . hobbies? Also fine. But I'm not waiting."

Higdon was stung. He had been moved to a position he could not defend. He looked at Silverman, tried to show his disgust with him for treading into such a personal area, wanted Silverman to believe he had committed a foul, wanted him to back off.

But it was over. They both knew it. Silverman had won.

Instinctively, Higdon moved backward an inch or two, away from Silverman. His glare diminished. He reached to adjust his glasses but for some reason didn't follow through. To Silverman, he seemed younger and smaller, pathetic in a way.

Silverman had committed a foul, had struck for the heart. But he allowed himself no remorse. He'd had a good teacher. Now it was time for appeasement. He'd throw Higdon his bone.

"Ray," he began, leaning farther toward Higdon, "even if we had already gotten the letter back from the documents expert, there's no telling what he'd say. Those guys are bureaucrats. He'd see a letter addressed to the mayor, and sure he'd test it. But chances are he'd write some bullshit report saying the letter may or may not be authentic—and anything else he could think of—so he wouldn't have to incriminate the mayor.

"It isn't going to help us decide what to do in here. And besides, Ray, we don't have the time to wait. Not after what happened to Lacona. We can't let Lane take the initiative. We just don't have any more time. We've got to take a shot at it, try and prove the letter's a phony."

Higdon offered token resistance. "Please listen. There's too much at stake here. If the letter's a phony and she lies about it, she'll go back and tell them we suspect the letter, and we all know how good they are at making up explanations. We don't want the mayor to call another press conference, bring up the letter again, and volunteer why this is all some innocent mistake."

Higdon resumed his crouching position toward Silverman. He surprised John by warmly placing his hand on his arm before he continued speaking.

"Let's not do it today, John," he appealed. "Let's you and me and Jacobs talk about it some more this afternoon. We can always subpoena her back in here next week."

The vision of Higdon's leaning sympathetically toward Albert Lacona in the hotel room shot to Silverman's mind.

"No!" he said, jerking his arm from Higdon's grasp. "Today. It's going to be today."

Without waiting for a response, almost before the last word was out of his mouth, Silverman turned to the stenographer. "Tell the witness to come back in here."

As the door opened and Mary Burke walked apprehensively into the room. Higdon whispered to Silverman, "Jesus, can't we at least talk about it? What the hell's the matter with you?" He caught Mrs. Franklin, leaning forward in her chair, too far back in the room to hear but staring at him nevertheless. He moved back in his chair.

Silverman was already in motion.

"Ladies and gentlemen, could we please come to order? Miss Burke, you're still under oath."

He positioned himself in his chair so that he was facing the witness, his back to Higdon. He felt Higdon's hostile presence nevertheless.

Mary Burke watched, wondered why Higdon wasn't speaking. While waiting outside the room, she had calmed down a bit, and Frank had spoken to her. He was so reassuring. But inside the room again, the fear and anticipation of having to endure Higdon's questioning quickly returned. Now, seated high in the witness box, she could sense that something had happened. Yet the need to listen to Silverman consumed her concentration.

He sounded low-key and friendly. He spoke as if he had some loose ends to tie up, as though there would be just a few more questions and then she would be allowed to leave. By the time he had completed the question, he was slouched in his seat, his back still to Higdon.

"Miss Burke, are you the only secretary in the office who takes dictation from Donald Ames and types his letters, or do some of the other secretaries also do that on occasion?"

"I would say that I type almost all of his letters. The other girls help out with the other things, but I do his typing."

"Approximately how many letters a day does he give you?"

"It varies, Mr. Silverman. I'd say usually about five or six a day." She felt reassured; it did indeed seem as if he were tying up loose ends. She was almost home.

"If I showed you some letters, I guess you could identify them as letters you've typed for him."

He continued to sound matter-of-fact, businesslike, as though he were required to ask these questions of certain witnesses for technical legal reasons.

Maybe he just needs someone to identify some of the letters produced in the subpoenaed Ames International files, she thought. "Yes, I guess so. I'd see my initials at the bottom of the page."

He stood and walked around the table. The smile on his face was friendly. "You're referring to the initials that usually appear at the bottom left side of a business letter. The initials that represent who dictated the letter and who typed it?"

"Yes."

He passed Higdon without looking at him and lifted one of the files that was on the table in front of his empty chair. He removed a thick batch of white letter-sized paper from the file and placed it on the ledge in front of the witness.

"Miss Burke, can you identify some of these letters as some that you've typed for Mr. Ames over the years? You don't have to look at each and every one; just take a general look through the batch."

She began thumbing through the letters. Most were copies of letters that had been retained in the company's files and had been produced to the grand jury. She finished and looked up. "Yes, these are some of the letters I've typed."

"And just so it's clear; they would have been dictated to you by Donald Ames?"

"Yes, that's right."

"Okay, fine." He handed the pile of letters to the stenographer to be marked as an exhibit.

As the letters were being marked, Silverman slowly strolled around the table and sat down again. He was taking stock of the situation. He wanted to continue this charade of winding up his questioning; he wanted to ease her into the letter, not confront her too soon. The timing had to be right.

He thought of Higdon, could feel his presence, still felt the lingering discomfort from the argument they'd had.

And what about the grand jurors? What were they thinking? Could they sense the tension and excitement he felt? He quickly glanced around the room. Some jurors seemed to be paying attention; some didn't. He concluded that they did not anticipate what was to come—that is, what *he hoped* was to come.

Second thoughts nagged at him. What if Higdon were right? he thought. Was he jumping the gun? Should he wait?

But the die was cast. No point in going back over it now, he thought. He knew that if he backed down to Higdon now, he would have no hope of retaining any authority in this case.

"Miss Burke, do you ever take dictation from Mr. Ames on one day but don't get around to typing the letter until the next day?"

"Well, yes, that happens sometimes, especially if he gives me the letter late in the day and I don't have time to type it that day."

"What date do you type on the letter? The date that he gave you the letter or the date on which you typed it?"

"The date on which he gave it to me."

"You mean the date on which he dictated the letter to you?"

"Yes, that's right."

"Well, have you ever typed a date on a letter, that is, a letter dictated to you by Mr. Ames—have you ever typed a date on such a letter other than the date on which you took dictation of the letter?"

"No, I can't remember that ever happening." She didn't want to remember, and besides, he couldn't possibly know. Nobody knew except her, Mr. Ames, and maybe the mayor.

His stomach went hollow. Anxiety rushed to his head, intruding on his thoughts. All he could think was that he'd blown it. Desperately, he forced himself to analyze the situation. Maybe the question had been wrong, so he tried, in those few seconds he had, to review the wording.

Had he been inarticulate? Did he not ask what he'd wanted to ask? He knew he had to ask it again.

As he sat in near total concentration, composing his next question, the door slammed shut. Silverman felt as though he'd actually jumped in the air. He spun around. Higdon's chair was empty. He stared at it. He felt strangely abandoned, alone.

He tried to force his attention back to his problem. He rose from his chair, walked around the table, and stood directly in front of Mary Burke.

"Miss Burke." He looked at her with determination, trying to recapture the force of his earlier admonition to her. "I want you to listen to my next question very carefully and think about your answer before you open your mouth to speak. Do you understand?"

"Yes, sir."

"This is very important. If you answer the question, I want you to do so truthfully. Don't lie. If you want to talk to your lawyer first, that is, before you answer the question, that's fine. You may do so. All you have to do is get up and go outside and take as long as you like before you come back in here. Think over the question carefully. Either answer the question with the truth or don't answer it and go outside and speak to Mr. Eckert. Do you understand that?"

"Yes, sir."

"Are you sure?"

"Yes, sir." She felt a strange sense of relief coming over her.

"Miss Burke, have you ever been asked my Mr. Ames to take dictation and type on that letter a date that was five or six years in the past? Do you understand my question?" He was trying to control his anxiety.

"Yes, I understand the question." Until now, she had been looking directly at him. Her eyes dropped, and her words were barely above a whisper.

"Yes, sir, I've done that."

The grand jurors moved forward in their seats expectantly. "On how many occasions have you done that?"

"Just once."

Without losing a second, he picked up the pack of letters that had been marked as an exhibit and selected the right one with as little fumbling as possible. He quickly placed it in front of her.

"Is that the *once*?"

"Yes."

He tried to swallow his triumphant smile, reached over and picked up the letter.

"For the sake of the record," he began, ceremoniously nodding toward the stenographer, "the letter just identified by the witness is a Xerox copy of a letter written on the stationery of

257

Donald Ames to Mayor Lane. The letter bears a date approximately five years in the past.

"It begins, 'Dear Mr. Mayor, Since speaking with you the other day . . .' and then describes, in so many words, how the mayor is being given the option to buy into Resort Time, Inc. sometime in the future."

He looked up from the letter and turned to Mary, thought he could see relief in her face. The worst was over for her.

"Miss Burke, this letter wasn't typed five years ago, was it?"

"No, it wasn't."

"In fact, it was typed sometime in the last year, wasn't it?"

"Yes, that's right."

"It was typed after this investigation began, wasn't it?"

"Yes." Mr. Ames had given her the letter on the afternoon of Richard Franklin White's call, telling him the motion to quash the subpoenas had been lost but that he had gotten a one-week postponement for production of the records. He had used that time to concoct the letter.

"And there was never any such agreement as that described in the letter. Isn't that correct?"

"Mr. Silverman, I don't know anything about that. All I know is that Mr. Ames told me to type that letter—he gave me instructions, and I followed them. That's all I know."

He believed her. Ames wouldn't confide in her any more than he had to.

"Mr. Silverman, could I go outside and consult with my lawyer?"

Silverman nodded at her. As she got up and walked out, the grand jurors began to murmer. Silverman was too excited to feel satisfaction. His mind raced ahead to what was to come— and to what he would tell Higdon.

The door to Stavaros's office suite was open, the room unoccupied. The phone call had come a few moments before.

Mary's testimony was known.

There was a strange stillness in the room; something was missing. It was too still.

A small object lay on the floor beneath the bird cage. A casual glance would have thought it a child's slipper, perhaps: soft, green colored.

It was, of course, the parakeet. Now simply a tiny carcass, lying on its side, the life crushed from its small body by the angered fist of the man who had stormed from the office.

22

The morning walk from the subway to the courthouse, though short, was pleasant. Silverman stopped to buy coffee and a doughnut from the street vendor near the station entrance, then strolled over to the tiny park across from the courthouse. At this hour, the few benches there were all vacant. Silverman selected one and sat down. He'd eat his breakfast out here.

He had forgotten the week before to take his shirts to the cleaners. Earlier that morning, he was forced to rummage through the apartment for an old one. He found one, on the floor, in the back of Jamie's closet, in an old box full of laundered, but worn, out-of-style shirts from college. It was not until the Paoli local had reached Suburban Station that he finally admitted to himself, however, that the one he had chosen was too tight; it was choking him at the neck. Was he putting on weight? He certainly hadn't had much exercise lately. He'd worry about that, too, when this case was over.

He rested his back against the park bench and carefully balanced his doughnut on top of the styrofoam coffee cup. With his free hand, he quickly undid the top button of his shirt collar, then pulled at his tie.

Earlier, after stepping from the shower and seeing his shirt drawer empty, he had instinctively called out to Mary Ann. Realizing what he had done, he sat alone in the kitchen, undressed, pensive, the only sound the movement of neighbors upstairs.

Mary Ann, his loneliness, his solitary life, intruded once again on his thoughts. Silverman shifted uneasily on the park bench. At home, he had prevented a direct hit at his emotions by frantically searching for a shirt, then quickly dressing and rushing from the apartment, leaving breakfast for later. Now he forced his thoughts to the case and away from her, away from anything besides his work.

Silverman bit into his doughnut, its greasy coating separating almost immediately from the dough. The case was on track, though still far from its destination. Silverman had proved the letter a phony. Mary Burke had come through for him. And while the prosecutors had not yet uncovered any bribe money lining the mayor's pockets, they now at least had something. Donald Ames and the mayor together had participated in a scheme to trick the grand jury into believing that letter was genuine. Both had attempted to obstruct justice, a serious federal crime. Ames, when he had instructed Mary Burke to type the letter, and the mayor when, at his press conference, he had attempted to pawn it off as genuine. And there would be the testimony of Gerald Stoffman, Ames's accountant. He, too, had lied about the letter. Silverman would throw him back in grand jury and confront him with his lie. Silverman considered it a good case, though not an airtight one. Both Ames and Lane would try and explain the letter away. Each would concede that the letter should not have been created. But both would insist, vehemently and with certain logic, that the letter was not evidence of bribery. Done under pressure, it was bad judgment, maybe, but not bribery. And, after all, bribery was what the grand jury investigation was all about. Without it, each would claim, there was nothing. They were innocent.

Silverman took a second bite of his doughnut, deciding it would be his last. He washed the taste away with lukewarm black coffee. It was a good case, respectable, even. But to a law professor, on paper only. It wasn't the case he needed to convince a jury, in a courtroom, at a public trial, to vote guilty. He needed money going to Lane. Dirty money. He needed bribery.

Silverman took a last sip of coffee and rose, crumbling his doughnut in its wrapper, looking for a place to toss it. He spotted a waste bin and walked over to within shooting range. Silverman aimed carefully, then shot. Dead miss. The wrapper and its crumbled contents lay somewhere behind the waste bin, caught in the small bushes. Silverman's first instinct was to leave it. He reconsidered and walked over to pick it up. As he bent over, he heard his shirt rip. He quickly stood, leaving the doughnut in the bushes, and tossed the coffee cup in the bin, stepping quickly away to avoid the splash. He hurried through the park to the courthouse.

On the sidewalk, just before reaching the courthouse, Silverman slowed as he approached a woman and her small child. Hispanic, stocky, looking worn and older than she probably was, the woman held onto the small child's hand as though it were she who was being led. The woman looked toward Silverman, then shyly away. The child stared up at him. She had the same dark, coal-black eyes, pretty hair, pierced ears as her mother. She looked nothing like Jamie. Yet that was all Silverman could think of. He stopped, staring at the child. Obediently, a lifetime's training of respect to the man of the house, the woman froze and held the child for inspection. The little girl stood, innocently watching Silverman looking at her. Jamie, his little Jamie. Silverman tore his gaze from the child, dashed up the courthouse steps, and pulled at the heavy bronzed glass doors.

Once inside the large hollow entrance, waiting for the elevator, he felt the first traces of sweat on his neck and under his shirt; his mind reached out again for the case, unaware that his job, the cause of his drowning, was now his only life preserver.

The elevator doors slid open. Silverman started to tighten his tie, then decided to leave it. He stepped inside, the only passenger on the short, slow trip up. The case was on his mind, but the balance was delicate.

She stuck her head into the doorway of Silverman's office and rapped gently on the door frame.

"Hello . . . you busy?"

Silverman looked up from his desk, quickly laid his *Daily Racing Form* aside as Denise Owens entered the room.

He hadn't seen her since that night when she'd shown up with a date at Storyville. She was easily among the last people he'd expected to pop in on him unannounced. The final few moments of their abortive night in bed together rose in his mind as he stood and stiffly motioned to her to one of the two chairs in front of his desk. As she sat down, he self-consciously walked over and closed his office door, then sat in the second chair.

"So. How've you been?" she asked, noticing his out-of-date shirt, still open at the collar.

Silverman thought she seemed better dressed than usual. There was a radiance about her. Her dark hair seemed a bit longer. Her blouse was silky and clung to her shape; its first few buttons were open. She crossed her legs, waiting for an answer, and he remembered how she had looked, naked, waiting for him. He wished he were somewhere else.

"Fine. I'm fine," he finally said.

She glanced over at the open *Daily Racing Form* lying on his desk.

"Still at it?" she asked, pointing toward the paper.

"Uhm, uhm."

"How's it going?"

"Good. My luck's changing."

Fearful that she'd think he had intended a double entendre with his last remark, he launched into a long explanation of how his paper winnings now almost exceeded his losses. As he rambled on, he was conscious of her scrutiny.

Abruptly, he stopped speaking; he knew he was going on too long. She smiled into the lull. Barely noticeably, both fidgeted in their seats. She, too, now seemed ill at ease.

"I'm doing a feature story on Miss Eccleston," she said. "Just interviewed her."

She rolled her eyes but said nothing further about the U.S. attorney.

Silverman couldn't think of anything else to say.

"Rumors are flying about your investigation," Denise said. "Mayor's scheduled a press conference. Did you hear?"

Silverman hadn't heard. He shrugged.

Silence again. He knew he should fill it with words. But the lull persisted. Then they both spoke at once.

"Listen, Denise, about that night, I . . ."

"About what happened when . . ."

They looked at each other and laughed. Their nervousness suddenly seemed silly. It was Denise who spoke next. She leaned forward and touched John's arm.

"I wanted to see you again. Tell you . . . well, tell you . . . I don't know. Just see you, I guess."

Before Silverman could respond, there was a knock on the door. Without waiting for a response, Bob Jacobs came in to the office carrying an armful of Stavaros's subpoenaed records. He immediately sensed his intrusion.

"Oops, sorry," he said. "Didn't know you were with someone."

Silverman stood to make introductions, but before he had a chance, Jacobs retreated, softly closing the door behind him.

But the interruption had curtailed their meeting. Denise reached for her shoulder bag.

"Gotta go," she said. Before leaving, she turned to him, stepped closer, and said, "I still have a taste for cheap hamburgers and fine wines. If you're, uhm, ever in the neighborhood . . ."

"I'll keep that in mind," he said.

But she could see that he was already thinking of something else.

Jacobs brought a small TV to work. The agents and the prosecutors had planned to watch the mayor's press conference together in the records room, but Higdon got a call from Miss Eccleston, who had also rented a television. The two prosecutors were to watch the press conference with her in her office.

The huge color set was on a table against the wall to the left of her desk. Two chairs had been placed in viewing range. The set was on, the press conference coverage having just begun. From behind her desk, she smiled and motioned for them to be seated.

The Philadelphia skyline was unkind to TV signals, and the picture faded in and out of range. Silverman watched Mayor Lane mount the steps to the rostrum and thought of the last time he'd seen that, wondered if the bartender were watching today, pontificating, telling his customers that he'd known all along that the mayor was going to get "the shit kicked out of him."

The camera quickly panned the reporters, who, as was custom, respectfully stood for him. Soon they would be telling their listeners, viewers, and readers that his indictment was a strong possibility.

The camera returned to the mayor, who waited patiently for the picture to zoom in on him.

No smiles today.

Today was going to be righteous indignation. He began by removing his glasses and saying, with forced profundity, that it was a sad day for the office of the mayor.

When he had last held a press conference to deal with "this problem," he said, he had received the "personal assurance" of the U.S. attorney herself that he had done absolutely nothing wrong and was completely uninvolved in any investigation run by "certain others" in her office. With the broad brush stroke of two words, he had painted a picture of irresponsible, politically motivated junior prosecutors out of control. Out to get him.

That assurance to the contrary notwithstanding, he continued—Silverman quickly glanced at Miss Eccleston, frozen in her seat—he had heard rumor after rumor that her "junior lawyers" were fully intent on indicting him. The image clear:

a weak woman browbeaten into submission by clever, cunning, and vicious opportunists.

There was an explosion of raised hands and shouts for recognition from the gallery of reporters. He ignored them. Today would be a short speech, each word of the prepared text read with precision and not another word said. Not one question answered.

His glasses firmly in place, standing proudly erect, Lane continued reading aloud. Silverman wondered if he himself had written the speech. Perhaps a lawyer had written it. Surely he had one by now.

The mayor struck first with Lacona, went into considerable detail about the taping fiasco, told of Lacona's having broken down and admitted how he had been pressured unrelentingly into becoming an unwitting stooge for "certain elements" in the U.S. attorney's office. Lacona himself had acknowledged the mayor's total uninvolvement. It was on the tape. "Let the prosecutors play that for the body of public opinion," he said. Continuing, he spoke with dripping sympathy for Lacona and his "own problems." Silverman wondered if this was a veiled reference to their witness's homosexuality. Was he reading too much into Lane's remark? How could he know?

Then, more convincingly than Silverman had anticipated, he read his explanation and defense of the back-dated letter. The prosecutors exchanged glances as Lane told how, to save valuable time and energy, a letter had been written to record a clear oral understanding and agreement and had been "dated in accordance with the true effective date of the oral understanding." His businesslike tone and colorless words told everyone listening that this was the way business executives everywhere conducted their ordinary commercial affairs. No further effort was made to reconcile this version with his earlier speech. He would not admit even to a mistake in judgment. He'd save that for later, if needed.

Then, on to the finale.

Lane apologized to "those twenty-three citizens" forced into servitude on the federal grand jury—sounding as if every resident of the city was praying for their deliverance—then made a veiled reference to White's allegations of grand jury abuse.

He did not expect to be indicted, he read, but if indicted, he had no intention of resigning, would fight for his honor and the honor of each and every Philadelphian, the clear inference being that his indictment was theirs as well. He assured his listeners that he would not buckle to the kind of pressure already exerted on "others" but would fight for the complete vindication he so justly deserved. He invoked the good name of his party, his administration, his unblemished record, and lastly, his God.

Ignoring the frantic shouts of the reporters, he left the stage, smiling benevolently, and quickly disappeared through a side door before they could get to him.

It was time for someone to turn off the TV and look at Miss Eccleston. Silverman waited, watching her out of the corner of his eye, frozen. Higdon rose and pushed the off button.

Something had to be said. To Silverman's surprise, it was Higdon who broke the silence.

"Looks like he's scared," he said with raised brow.

She nodded gravely, more in appreciation of the fact that he'd chosen not to belittle her than in agreement.

As he left the office, Silverman thought of her sitting stoically behind that desk, certain that she wouldn't move an inch for as long as possible.

Time had gotten away from him, but Silverman didn't think to look at the digital alarm as he reached toward the night table to pour more whiskey into the bathroom tumbler. He hardly noticed as the two pieces of paper slipped from his knees onto the bed.

He took another hard swallow from the tumbler. He was uncomfortably warm, so he sat up to remove his undershirt. A few beads of sweat trickled into the dark hairs on his chest. As he lay back against the pillow, his body quickly reabsorbed the warmth it had left there.

The half-full tumbler now was perched precariously at the edge of the night table. He took a hard pull and drained it. He reached again for the bottle and poured, but his aim was bad, and some of it spilled.

Earlier that day, when he'd returned to his office after the press conference, he'd caught Jan heading for the door. It was a few minutes before her quitting time, and since he had been up with Miss Eccleston, she'd decided on an early escape. Embarrassed, she asked his permission to leave and quickly gave him his messages. He'd actually had to block the doorway to get her to repeat the message that aroused his interest.

Mr. Turner had called—would be in only until five today.

He'd gone straight to the phone and dialed. He figured Turner had seen Lane's press conference and was calling to congratulate him, probably to invite him to lunch. As the line clicked over and began to ring, he'd decided this time he'd even look forward to Turner's stuffy club.

Mr. Turner hadn't left yet; he'd just caught him.

Silverman reached for the tumbler, hardly noticing the wet ring it had left on the night table. His phone conversation was still only a few hours old. Despite the booze, his mind replayed it, now for the third time.

"John, I'm glad you caught me."

"Yes, sir."

"I felt I wanted to tell you personally, before it became public. It most likely will be in tomorrow's paper."

Silverman was about to take yet another sip, but he felt dizzy, so he returned the tumbler. Now there'd be two rings.

"John. You know my respect for your abilities. You're a fine young man, and I sincerely hope we will always remain as friends."

Silverman let his right leg slip to the floor to steady the bed. It was after the "we will always remain as friends" that he'd known what Turner would tell him.

"I've been retained by Mayor Lane as his defense counsel."

Silverman had been used. Turner's "friendship," his offer of help, counsel, all those luncheons together—all the things he'd told him. That must have been how Lane knew. Lacona had been wired. He wondered how much of what he'd told Turner had contributed to Turner's selling ability to get the case. Turner waited patiently for a reply. Silverman knew that something gallant was expected, something like "Yes, of course, we will remain as friends."

Instead, he hung up on him. He wanted to go home.

He was on his way out when Judge Montarelli's law clerk walked in to deliver a copy of the judge's decision on Richard Franklin White's motion to terminate the grand jury proceedings. White's motion had been denied; the government had won. Silverman could barely take pleasure in the victory.

Silverman grabbed the tumbler off the night table. The dizziness had passed; both legs were now on the bed. He peered into the tumbler. There wasn't much left, so he drained it. He held the tumbler until the burning in his throat passed, then returned it to the table's edge. Now there'd be three rings, each looped through another.

Silverman felt rotten. He couldn't put the call out of his mind. What would Higdon say? How badly had he fucked up the case by trusting Turner?

Silverman picked up the first of the two sheets of paper that had fallen to his side when he'd removed his undershirt.

The first was Judge Montarelli's order. He read it again, then tossed it off the bed. It sailed to the floor, a glider in flight.

He reached for the second piece of paper. It had been lying in his mailbox when he'd gotten home. A letter. Registered mail. Addressed to him, the return address a law firm in Virginia.

He reread it. Mary Ann had retained a lawyer. She wanted a divorce. And custody of Jamie. He knew that he should be upset, but right now he was beyond all feeling.

He watched as it, too, sailed to the floor.

Mary Burke pressed her foot on the pedal of the small wastebasket; the lid snapped up. She held the dangling tea bag over the mouth of the bucket, waiting patiently for it to center itself, then let it drop. She looked at the yellow daisy wall clock above the kitchen sink: 7:26. Right on time. In eighteen years, never late for work.

But things weren't the same there. Mr. Ames was trying to act normal, but his discomfort at being around her seemed to permeate his affability.

Frank said she must continue as if nothing had happened. She had to be there each day, at her desk, secretary to Donald Ames. He had explained that Ames couldn't fire her; if he did, it would come out at trial, make her testimony even more damaging. And she herself felt deep loyalty to the man who had been so comforting, so available to help since Momma had died.

The buzzer sounded. She checked the clock again. Who in the world would be downstairs to see her at this hour?

She walked to the tiny entrance hall, pressed the tarnished button marked "Speak."

"Yes, who is it?" she asked, her voice raised by custom. She waited for him or her to discover the button.

"Miss Burke?" the masculine voice crackled into her hallway.

"Yes. Who is this please?"

"I'm from the U.S. attorney's office, ma'am. Sorry to bother you so early. I have another subpoena here for you. I'm terribly sorry to bother you so early, but I was told not to contact you at work."

She removed her finger from the button and pushed the one

directly below it marked "Entry," held her finger in place, estimating the time it would take for him to open the door, then released it.

Why wouldn't they leave her alone? She couldn't endure much more. And now they wanted her back in that room, back before those rows of staring people. It was unbearable; it was torture.

She stood in the hallway, agonizing, waiting for Mr. Silverman's messenger. The other subpoena had been served at work; she thought of the burly deputy U.S. marshal, remembered his unconcealed pride at displaying his badge in that black leather wallet, at announcing his title.

Strange, this man didn't say he was a marshal. Maybe there was no need to send a marshal now that she had a lawyer. What was taking him so long? He'd make her late for work. Absent-mindedly, she moved closer to the door, impatient to open it. Then she remembered.

She'd asked Frank if they would bother her again, upset her so. He'd take care of it, he'd said, would ask Mr. Silverman to make all contacts directly to him.

Had he forgotten? The outside hall lay silent.

Quickly she turned and went to the phone, found Frank's home number, and dialed.

"Frank, I'm terribly sorry to bother you so early. This is Mary. But there's a man from Mr. Silverman's office on his way up to my apartment to give me another subpoena. Is it all right to let him in? I know how busy you must be; you must have forgotten . . ."

"I told Silverman to send those things to me. I know nothing about it. What did he say his name was?"

"He didn't . . . What's wrong, Frank?" Her hand tightened around the receiver.

"I'll call you right back," he said. "Don't let him in until I call you back."

Silverman got the phone midway into the second ring.

"Hello . . ."

"Sorry to bother you so early, John. This is Frank Eckert. Mary Burke just called and said a man from your office was on his way up to her apartment to serve another subpoena on her. What's it about?"

Despite his headache, Silverman was instantly awake.

"Tell me exactly what she told you," he said.

Frank repeated Mary's message.

"I'll call you right back, Frank." His stomach churning, he hung up and dialed Higdon.

Higdon had obviously been asleep, too. "Yeah, who's this?"

"Ray, this is John." His speech was rapid. "Did you send someone to Mary Burke's apartment?"

"What?" He wasn't sufficiently awake. "Send what? What time is it?"

It would have been easier, and quicker, had he taken the time to explain, but he was too nervous; he pressed again for an answer, raised his voice as if that would make his terse question more understandable.

"Ray, please. Did you?"

"What?"

"Damn it," he half-shouted, lifting himself from the bed. "Listen to me. Did you send an agent to Mary Burke's apartment? To serve a subpoena?"

"No, of course not. What the hell's the matter with you?"

He quickly hung up, reached for the phone book. It wasn't there.

He dialed information. The recorded message began, telling him to try his phone directory first. He waited the eternity of the thirty-second message to click over, then heard the operator's nasal "Directory Information."

"Phone number. Frances Eckert. He's an attorney, but I want his home number." He could hear her punch into the computer.

"Operator, please. I'm in a hurry. This is an emergency." He stood and paced the few steps the phone cord would allow.

She was annoyed. "I'm checking, sir." She punched more keys.

"Operator, forget that number. This is a police emergency. Give me the number . . . Mary Burke. B-U-R-K-E. It's on Locust . . . St. George Apartments."

"Hold, sir . . . 474-1214."

Mary heard the sound of the elevator door opening. Her glance shot to the door of her apartment, her mind measuring the time until the first knock. The phone's ring triggered an uncontrolled, soft, primeval sound. She grabbed for the receiver, just missing it and knocking it to the floor; it dangled on the line. She bent to retrieve it.

"Hello, Frank?"

"No, this is John Silverman. Listen to me, Mary. Do not open your door. Do you understand?"

The first knock. She turned to the door, receiver still at her ear. A few more soft knocks. Too soft.

"Mary, are you there? Are you listening?"

"Mr. Silverman, he's here. He's knocking." She sobbed gently into the phone. She had never felt so terribly alone. She was cold.

"Mary, listen to me. Do not open your door. Please. Just stay where you are. I'll take care of everything. Is your door locked?"

She didn't answer, kept the receiver pressed to her ear, continued sobbing.

"Mary, for God's sake, answer me!"

"Mr. Silverman, I'm scared. Please help me. Please. Somebody help me. Oh, God. I'm going to die."

"Mary, somebody will be there soon. Hang up and stay by the phone. Do not open the door. Okay?"

She quietly placed the receiver on its cradle as if any noise would tell him she was in there.

"Miss Burke?" His voice, friendly, soft, unobtrusive, inquiring if she were there.

A few more knocks. Uncontrollably, she moved toward the door, drawn to it as if it were a magnet. She stood in the hallway, silent.

"Miss Burke?"

"Please. I can't let you in. Come back later . . ." Her sobbing choked her words. "Please go away now." She tried to force friendliness out into the hall.

No more knocking. Only silence. He was standing out there. What was he doing? Her sobs grew louder, the waiting expanding the time to indefinite agony.

At first, she only heard it, couldn't relate the sound to the act. Then her eyes caught the door handle slowly turning. Then it stopped.

She began whispering, begging him to leave, to go away. Her terror grew, control no longer possible. She seemed to be outside her body, watching herself, screaming hysterically, her shrill, fear-infested voice permeating all available air space.

"Please, please, oh, God . . . Please, go away . . ."

23

Gerald Stoffman turned in his desk chair to face the large window behind. The room was bathed in new morning light. A few hours before, in that same chair, he'd prayed for daylight to cleanse his moroseness. But the light of dawn had done nothing, only made him feel more exposed, in danger.

He reached for the paper cup, held it at eye level, inspecting the ring of small hearts that encircled its lip. The bottom was soft from a full night of use. Carefully, he poured another inch of Scotch past the ring. He drank it in one gulp, crumpled the cup, then waited for the burning to slowly subside.

He had managed to convince himself that the investigation was clearing up, going away. Things were returning to normal. He was safe. Ames had been right, after all—nothing had come of it. And then he got the call.

During the first few moments of that last conversation, Stoffman didn't notice the change in Ames's usual easygoing tone, had completely missed its strange dullness. There had been a long silence after they exchanged greetings. Then Ames explained that "a difficulty" had arisen: Mary had testified about the letter. They knew. The accountant could expect to be called back to grand jury. Ames offered him a lawyer.

It wasn't until after the conversation, after he'd hung up and sat there alone in his office, that he'd felt the full weight of what had happened. While on the phone, it was merely another client's problem, something to be discussed, dealt with, and then forgotten at the end of the day.

But the more he thought, the worse it became. His mind fought for some way out. A way for him; Ames no longer mattered. But there was no way. He had lied to them, obstructed justice, and now they had him.

He tried to picture his life in prison. Prison. Would he be raped? God. No way out.

The call from Ames had come almost a week before. At

first, he'd told no one, held it all in. But the horror of it grew inside of him, feeding his anguish.

After Lane's press conference, he'd seen his doctor. He needed something, something to get him through the public embarrassment that lay ahead. And all else that awaited him.

The pills hadn't helped. At first, they had comforted him for short periods. He'd feel warm, almost relaxed, for a while, then drowsy. But that hadn't lasted long enough. He needed higher and higher dosages to sustain the pleasantness. He even tried having a drink or two after he took the pills, but that escape, too, was fleeting. Now, if he didn't take them, he felt even more depressed. Last night, at dinner, he finally told his wife that he had lied, had obstructed justice, and would go to jail.

He stood up and tossed the crumpled cup toward the wastebasket. He missed but made no move to retrieve it. He gazed past the window, not really seeing the city stretched out before him, then turned and studied his office. It was ornate, the mixture of colors overabundant, like his clothes. But to him it was the mirror of his success. He'd made it, had risen to the top, passed all the others. He knew he'd made enemies here at the firm and in the profession, but that hadn't mattered. He was on top.

But now, when they learned, they'd secretly beam with delight. He could hear their soft words of consolation, their eyes barely hiding the pleasure they felt at his misery. And the publicity. It would be in the papers. His parents would learn.

His thoughts were attacking him. With a quick pivot, he turned, as if they'd disappear if his back was to them. He touched the resistant glass of the window, then lifted the latch and pressed his finger tips against the windowpane, helping it swing open on its hinge.

As he stood there, the cool early-morning air fanning his face, he felt momentary relief. Then, without warning, the image of his meeting with Silverman and that other man, the black one, reappeared. Without a consciously firm decision, he lifted his foot through the narrow opening and let it rest on the small outside ledge.

It would be so easy, he thought. Would there be pain? He remembered the trapeze artists he'd seen as a child. He could still see their hands slowly leaving the bar. In his mind, he watched them fall to the net below with the same vividness as when he'd actually seen them years before, sitting next to his mother, squeezing her hand with excitement. What had they felt on the way down? What was it like?

Gradually, he forced his body through the opening.

He looked down at the street, but as he leaned forward, he felt a strange sensation. His legs grew weak, his body tingly. He played at letting go. Not for real. Just in his imagination, just to tease his body. The weakness increased; his grasp tightened.

What would it feel like? Would he feel pain? What would they say afterward? He pictured himself falling; his grasp tightened even more.

Once again, he heard Donald Ames's voice telling him about Mary. He crept onto the ledge. He managed to look down again. He was strangely amused by all of this. It seemed so compelling. All he had to do was exert a minimum of effort. Let go and lean.

But no, he wasn't going to. It was just a game to tease away his problems. Carefully, he turned to re-enter the safety of his office.

He never really decided to do it. He simply let go. His body turned without his willing it to. He heard his foot strike the edge of the ledge. Free. Cold air rushed against his face, half closing his eyelids. A few seconds of timelessness, a kind of silence. Then he heard a scream.

He was still alive. Or was he? It was strangely quiet except for that incessant buzzing noise. And before the blackness, the tremendous, unbearable pressure, then warmth.

The last thing he saw was a hand, blood red and contorted. His.

Silverman waited. Adrenalin had temporarily quelled his hangover. He'd dressed for work but hadn't shaved, had gotten to the courthouse as quickly as possible. Somehow, waiting at his desk would be easier. He'd shave later.

Bob Jacobs and two federal marshals had been dispatched to Mary's apartment. He'd called Higdon before leaving his apartment and had explained. They'd agreed on no police.

Higdon was in, also. Each sat in his own office; each waited. Silverman went for the phone at its first ring.

"Yeah."

"It's me," Jacobs said. "She's okay. . . ."

"I'm going to put you on hold." He called Higdon. "Jacobs is on my line. She's alive. Come on around."

Higdon hung up and hastily walked to the other office. When

he entered, Silverman had already resumed his conversation. Higdon stood in front of the desk, listening.

"Okay. Okay," Silverman said, nodding. "All right, do that. Call again when you get settled."

Higdon watched his younger colleague, body erect and intense, phone pressed against his ear, listening to Jacobs saying he'd take care of everything.

"Now listen, I think it's all right now. But don't be a hero. Bob, if you need anything, you call. Understand?... Okay ... Right. Bye."

He hung up, leaned back and looked over at Higdon. He didn't speak, wanted to allow the relief a moment or two to settle in. Higdon moved one of the chairs a few feet away from the desk and sat down. He, too, needed time. Mary was alive. Their case was still intact.

"Jacobs said she's in shock," Silverman said after a little while. "When they got there, she was alone. The door was locked. Whoever it was that had paid her the visit had gone. They had to get the super to let them in. She wouldn't open the door."

"Where are they now?"

"On the road. He called from a pay phone. They're taking her to a motel in Bucks County; they'll register her under another name."

The phone rang, but Silverman ignored it. Jan would take a message.

Silverman's headache was starting to make its presence felt. What would they do now? Keep Mary hidden until the trial? That could take over a year.

Jan knocked on the door, then hesitantly opened it just enough to get her head and shoulders through. She didn't know what was going on but sensed that interruptions would not be welcome.

"Excuse me," she said. "It's Denise Owens." Quickly, in defense, she added, "I told her you were in conference. She said it was important, to interrupt you."

"Not now. Take a message." Silverman waved her away.

As the door closed, neither spoke, each still contemplating the situation. Finally, Higdon adjusted his glasses, then began. "We don't have many options. The only thing that really comes to mind..."

The intercom buzzer sounded. Silverman glanced over at his phone. The light was still blinking; Denise was still on the line. This time Jan wasn't going to come in; she'd hide behind the safety of the intercom. Impatiently, he picked up the phone, didn't give her a chance to explain.

"Jan, please. I can't talk to her now. Tell her I'll call back when I can."

He was about to hang up as she interjected, "She says to tell you Gerald Stoffman's dead."

He looked over at Higdon and pushed the button. Denise came on the line.

"When? How?"

"Fell from his office window. Less than an hour ago," Denise said.

Fell? Was he pushed? He cupped his palm over the phone's mouthpiece.

"Stoffman's dead," he told Higdon. "Went out a window." He removed his hand from the phone. "Anything else you know?" he asked Denise.

"No, that's all so far. John, we've heard he is . . . was an important witness for you. I'm not asking; it's not for a story. If it's true, I'm sorry."

"Thanks," he said, then hung up.

There was no need to compare conclusions, not after Mary Burke's incident. They'd need to find out more about his death, but for now it seemed to be part of a conspiracy. Someone had ordered the witnesses killed. For Silverman there was no need to select from among the possible suspects. He knew who was responsible. He felt a chill as he remembered Stavoros's nighttime visit to his apartment and Jamie, standing at his legs, looking up at him. What should they do about Albert Lacona? Should he be warned or taken into custody?

Gradually, sounds began to penetrate Silverman's thoughts. He realized Higdon was talking to him. He tried to listen, to concentrate on Higdon's words. He was talking about Stoffman. What to do about Mary. About Albert Lacona.

Even the generally unobservant Higdon noticed something was wrong.

"You all right?" he asked.

Silverman nodded, said he was okay, but he wasn't. All of the events of the past few months swept over him like the rush of a misjudged wave. Stanton Turner, Jamie, Mary Ann, Mary Burke. Now Stoffman. Breathing became difficult. He loosened his tie. Jesus, there was no air in here. Higdon was speaking again, weighing alternatives. Silverman tried hard to listen. But it was so goddam hot in the room. He stared at Higdon, trying to get a fix on what he was saying. But his thoughts raged inside him, out of control. What the fuck was he doing? he thought. To himself? His life? How many more sacrifices would he have to make? He was winning, but he was losing, too. And then, with Higdon droning on in the background, it came to him. This was only a goddam job, he thought. Important, yes. But not by itself, not without a life to surround it. How had he forgotten that. He hadn't always been this way. So desperate to win at any cost. Or had he? He had to take the time to sort this out, now, renew order. He had to get a hold of himself. He sat forward in his chair and interrupted Higdon in midsentence.

"Listen, Ray. I'm going away for a few days."

"You're what?"

"I said I'm going away for a few days."

"Now?"

"Yeah, now."

Higdon stared at Silverman in disbelief, as though this were some kind of sick joke. But he saw that Silverman was dead serious. It was no joke.

Higdon, too, had been affected by the pressure of recent events. He leaned toward the desk.

"I don't know what you're talking about, John. But you're not going anywhere. Not now."

Silverman sprang from his chair. He glared down at Higdon.

"I've got some things to take care of, Ray. Personal things. You know what that means, Ray? *Personal things.*"

Higdon, certain the young prosecutor was having an emotional breakdown of some sort, flinched when Silverman shot up from his seat. The pressure must have been too much for him. Silverman's behavior frightened him, so he said nothing. He didn't answer the question. That only increased Silverman's fury.

He lunged around the desk toward Higdon.

"Personal obligations, Ray," he virtually shouted.

On the other side of the closed door, Jan stopped reading her magazine.

"Personal, Ray. You know, like family. Friends. That sort of stuff."

Higdon didn't move, his frail body fastened in place. He stopped looking at Silverman, stared blankly ahead instead.

"Here, I'll show you," Silverman said as he ripped the letter from his pocket and flung it onto Higdon's lap, where it lay untouched.

Silverman took a step closer. He grabbed the arm of Higdon's chair and jerked it toward him. He leaned over Higdon, each of his hands resting on the arms of the chair.

"Personal obligations, Ray. You see, most people need them. I do. Some of us can't function without them."

It wasn't until Silverman had stormed out that Higdon read the letter. The letter from Mary Ann's divorce lawyer.

He tossed it onto Silverman's desk before returning to his office.

"Mr. Turner will be with you in just a few moments, Mr. Silverman. Won't you please have a seat?"

He thanked the receptionist and took one of the seats of the law firm's eleventh-floor reception area. She offered him coffee, but he declined.

Had it been two days or three? Three, yes, three days since he'd walked out on Ray. That day he'd raced home, thrown some clothes in a bag, and driven directly to Virginia, to his in-laws'.

Jamie was the first to see him. Today, sitting in the reception area, John's eyes filled with tears, just as they had a few days ago when his daughter had run into the vestibule, her arms outstretched, yelling, "My daddy's home!" for all the world to hear. God, how he had missed her. It wasn't until that moment that he had realized how much.

With Jamie in his arms, he had looked up to find Mary Ann's mother. He ignored her cold hello and asked for his wife. She was halfway through telling him she was not home when Mary Ann appeared at the top of the stairs. He thought she looked tired, as though she hadn't been sleeping well.

Reluctantly, Jamie had gone with Mom Mom, but only after John had promised he wouldn't leave without first seeing her.

He and Mary Ann had talked, but nothing had been resolved. There was something different about her. Silverman couldn't figure out exactly what it was. She seemed distant, apart from him. It seemed harder to think of her as "his wife." He tried to convince her that they should keep trying, that he realized he'd neglected her, that he would change. She'd listened, not quite believing him. She'd been through so much, had sent out all those signals that he had never even noticed. It seemed impossible to think that he could change. She told him that she thought she still wanted the divorce, but she agreed to think about it some more. Sitting together at the bottom of the steps, he'd touched her hand. She'd withdrawn it.

He didn't stay the night, had slept at his parents' home in

Silver Spring. The next day, driving back to Philadelphia along the Pennsylvania Turnpike, he pulled in to a Howard Johnson's motel and checked in.

Silverman stayed there, at the foot of the old massive highway, for the next two days—either at the pool, nearly oblivious to the stench and sounds of the constant traffic, to the perpetual motion of America's travelers, or in his room, the air conditioner's fluid hum blocking out most else.

He needed time to think. And ironically, considering his tirade at Higdon, he needed to be alone. He needed to think.

His marriage was very much up in the air. Though the idea of a divorce disturbed him, he had to admit his ambivalence. What if there had been no Jamie? How would he feel about Mary Ann? He was uncertain.

One morning, he spent a lot of time just staring at himself in the bathroom mirror. He, too, looked tired. He rubbed his hand through his uncombed hair and studied his palm. There were a few fallen hairs in it. It upset him. He repeated the act. Again, loose strands lay there. He stayed in bed watching TV all the rest of the morning.

One thing was certain. He'd stay with the investigation. If there was a case to be made, he'd do it. That, of course, had been Turner's advice all along. But now it appeared that the great elder lawyer had had an ulterior motive. A pretty simple one, too. Probably not that unusual for an important lawyer to want another important client.

He was still confused about Turner. How much of Turner had been sincere? How much self-interest?

He didn't know. All he knew was that the first thing he was going to do when he returned to Philadelphia was go see Turner. He would violate the rules of Turner's society. He'd tell him, bluntly and graphically, exactly what he thought of him.

Silverman caught the receptionist's smile, assuring him that Mr. Turner would be only a moment longer.

If nothing else, he'd feel better after he told a startled Turner what a miserable shit he really was. But as he sat there waiting, he wondered what real purpose that would serve. Was that really the smart way to handle the situation?

He noticed the receptionist replace the phone she'd just answered.

"Mr. Turner's secretary says he's finishing up on a long-distance call. He'll be with you shortly."

"Thank you."

Silverman reached for one of the magazines on the coffee table at his knees.

Stanton Turner briskly walked the hall to the reception area. His suit jacket was on and buttoned; his gray hair flopped just slightly with his movement. As he turned the corner, he opened his smile, moved his hand forward to grasp Silverman's.

"Hello, John!" he exclaimed as he turned the corner.

Except for the receptionist, the room was empty.

"They've got somebody in there; they're interviewing a witness," Jan told him. "I think it's pretty important."

He walked to Ray's office.

"Should I go in?" he asked Mrs. Ramondi.

"Let me call in, John."

Must be important, he thought.

"He said to wait outside just a moment."

Jacobs came out and quietly shut the door. He took his arm and walked him back into the hall, his excitement quickening his pace.

"It happened, man. It finally happened."

"What?"

"We've got *the* witness. Like that old man, James Ritchie, we first saw. Only better. Much better. She's in there now." Jacobs couldn't contain his excitement.

"I don't understand. Who is she?"

"She's been out there. Watching us and waiting. Deciding, I think, whether or not to come forward. Now it all fits together. Now we've got a case." He studied the prosecutor. "You feeling better?"

Silverman nodded, waiting for more on the witness.

"She's had some sort of religious experience. We haven't really gotten into it yet. Seems that's what motivated her."

"Who is she? Are you sure she's not just another crazy?"

"Doesn't look that way."

He couldn't remember ever seeing Jacobs this excited.

"She knows things only an insider would know," he continued. "We called you twice yesterday. Ray wanted you here. She came in yesterday. To make an appointment. Said she couldn't stay long."

Jacobs glanced at the door. Higdon was in there with her alone. That wasn't accepted practice; a witness was always interviewed by at least two people. He had to fill John in, but it had to be done quickly. He leaned toward his colleague in a gesture of confidentiality.

"She was his mistress."

"Whose?"

"The mayor's." He waited for Silverman to react.

The prosecutor's skepticism was clear enough. He said nothing, continued his look and waited for more.

Jacobs again glanced in the direction of the door. "Look, we don't have time now. She's been in the company of Lane, Ames, and Stavaros. Other women were there. She mentioned Ames's girl friend from the checks—Elaine Robertson. Mentioned her by name. Only we . . . and they could know her." He searched for another corroborating fact; he had to get back in there. "They'd all be in her apartment . . . for parties."

"Parties?"

"You know. Parties."

The implication was clear enough. Sex parties.

"She doesn't want to talk about that," Jacobs added, considering whether he had the time to explain to Silverman how her reluctance to go into details of sexual activity showed a kind of forbearance, a reliability. No time.

"She's seen Ames and Stavaros hand Lane envelopes. She's sure they were stuffed with cash. Never saw inside. Made a point of telling us that. But the circumstances, the timing; a jury'll believe there was cash in them. And she remembers Stavaros . . . she was in the bedroom . . . she heard him arguing with Lane in the other room. We've still got to fix the time. But she heard him say to Lane, 'You owe me.' If we can prove she heard that around the time he got those betting parlor leases . . . Come on, let's get in there. We can talk later."

Jacobs moved toward the door, but Silverman held his arm.

"Did she ever see cash?"

Jacobs nodded. "Yeah, Lane took care of her in cash. Always cash. Come on, Ray's alone in there."

She looked up as the door opened.

Silverman looked at her quickly, then found Ray.

"You okay?" Higdon asked.

"Uh huh." He looked at her again.

"Miss Levering, this is Assistant U.S. Attorney John Silverman," Higdon said.

"Hello." She held out her hand and smiled.

Silverman stepped closer, held her hand. "Hi." She was beautiful.

They sat in the chairs around the desk. Higdon resumed his interview. Occasionally, he'd preface a question with a reference to something she apparently already had said. Silverman supposed this was being done for his benefit, to allow him to catch up.

He listened, at first watching each as he or she spoke, but then he focused entirely on her. He was seated next to her at such an angle that she couldn't really see him staring. If she did, she didn't let on.

She was young—his age, maybe a little older. But there was nothing unusual in an older man's wanting a young woman. She was telling Higdon about the envelopes. She spoke quietly, said something about "things that happened afterwards," lowering her eyes as she said it. She seemed ashamed of having done "those things" with them. He studied her, watched her profile.

There was something—something familiar about her. He looked over at Higdon, then Jacobs. They were absorbed, trying to get it all. Her story was terrific. But there was something wrong.

She was speaking so quietly, telling the federal government about cash in envelopes going from fat cats to the mayor of Philadelphia, and yet she was so pleasant about it, showed such little emotion.

But that wasn't it. She said something about recognizing a moral obligation to come forward, something about a meaningful experience she had had. The mayor had to be exposed for the wretch he really was. She wanted him punished to the full extent of the law. Silverman was hardly listening, by now desperately trying to figure out what was wrong.

Higdon continued questioning.

She didn't notice Silverman's constant stare. He looked at her pale skin, her frail body. There was something familiar about her. It was as if he had seen her somewhere before. She was just a bit on the thin side but very sexy. Silverman's mind wandered. Her breasts were surprisingly full, considering her slenderness. She probably looked great in a bathing suit. A vague picture of a woman, in a black bikini, lying by a pool, flickered briefly in his mind. It was still too far away. By now, his observation was purely clinical. He was trying to find it somewhere in her face, the color of her hair. The scene flickered again. If he could fix a place, maybe he could bring it in. If he'd seen her, it was only for a moment. He knew that, but where?

She shifted slightly in her chair as she listened to Higdon's question, and Silverman got a slightly fuller view of her face. The picture snapped into focus.

The girl in the black bikini lying on the lounge at Ames's Club Caribe in the Bahamas. He was positive. He remembered noticing that she was sunburned.

Had Ames and Lane and Stavaros been there too? No, that would have been too risky. But she had been there; he was sure he'd seen her that day. He moved back slightly before he spoke, realizing she would turn at the sound of his voice.

"Miss Levering..."

She looked over and smiled, then frowned just slightly at his interruption.

He smiled benignly, showing her he was merely another government lawyer with a routine question. "Have you ever been in the company of Mayor Lane and the other two gentlemen other than in your apartment?"

"Yes. Uhm...at one of the other girls' houses or in a car..." She seemed to be trying to recollect other places.

"How about outside Pennsylvania—vacations, anything like that?"

She answered quickly, taking only a second or two to consider the question. "No, Mr...."

"Silverman." He smiled.

"No." She shifted again, slightly away from him. "I've never done that. Phillip...Mayor Lane was always very conscious of the need for privacy."

"I see. Okay. Thanks."

He nodded at Higdon, indicating he was through, crossed his legs, and smiled at her, then added, as if it were an afterthought. "Oh, uh...one more thing. How about traveling alone. You know, a vacation or something like that—at the mayor's expense?"

Something in her eyes told Silverman she was being extra careful with him. She seemed to be considering his question as a chess player considers all the potential consequences of his opponent's move and his own. She didn't take long to answer, though.

"I've been on vacations, yes. The money came from Phillip."

"Ever at Ames's resort hotel?" He faked a memory lapse. "What's that place called?" he said in the direction of Jacobs.

"Club Caribe."

"Right. Club Caribe. Ever been there?"

She took that extra second or two again. "No. I've never been there." She looked directly into his eyes; her mouth was turned up in a smile, but her eyes betrayed her caution. "I've never been there, Mr. . . ."

"Silverman."

Higdon took over. She turned toward him.

She was lying. Why? He was positive that was the woman he'd seen as he and Mary Ann had strolled through the pool area. Who was she? What the hell was going on?

She shifted again. "Mr. Higdon, I'm so embarrassed by what I've done . . . what I've been a party to. These are despicable men. I'll do anything you want me to, to punish them." She looked across the desk for assurances.

It was out of place; her comment seemed too rehearsed. Why was she soliciting a reaction from them? Silverman watched her impassively, waiting for Higdon.

"Don't worry. With you around, Lane won't be mayor much longer."

Silence. She seemed to be considering her next move. "Excuse me. May I use the ladies' room?"

They all rose with her. Higdon said that Mrs. Ramondi would give her the key. As she closed the door, they sat down again.

Higdon looked at them and nodded.

Jacobs was ecstatic. He shoved back in his chair. "We've got those motherfuckers now. Got 'em right by their balls. She's terrific; she'll burn 'em."

"You all right now?" Higdon calmly asked Silverman.

"Yeah." His mind was still on her, still trying to figure it out. He missed Higdon's frown over his curt reply. Out of the corner of his eye, Silverman saw the tip of her handbag on the carpet beside her chair. She'd gone to the ladies' room without her handbag; women don't do that, thought Silverman.

"Well, we've finally got a case," Jacobs continued. "I don't mind telling you guys now, but before she walked in, I never felt we had enough. I never thought we'd get them. But now that's all changed . . ."

Silverman stared at the handbag. It was wrong. The whole damn thing was wrong. She was the woman in the black bikini. She'd lied to him. What was in the handbag?

"John?" Jacobs noticed him staring at the floor almost glassy-eyed. Silverman didn't answer. In fact, he really didn't hear. Of course. He knew now. A recording device. There was a recording device in there. Immediately, he held his hands up and waved frantically at the others to indicate that no one should speak.

They didn't understand. Jacobs was now convinced that they had a big problem on their hands. John had lost control.

"What are you doing?" Higdon asked. "What's the matter with you?"

Silverman stood, reached over and grabbed Higdon's legal pad, and scribbled a note. He held the pad to show them: "I know her. She's lying. Recording device," it said.

They looked at him, astounded, still not understanding. The pad still in his left hand, he stepped back toward her chair. She'd been gone for a while, might return at any minute. He pointed at the handbag. Didn't they realize that she should have taken it with her to the ladies' room? He bent down beside it. A door slammed somewhere out in the hall. Quickly, he rose and stepped toward his chair. They waited. She didn't return. But she would at any moment.

Silverman wrote on the legal pad, held the one word up. "Talk," it said.

As they spoke of how their case had improved, Silverman walked to the door and listened to make sure she wasn't in the hall, then walked over to where the bag sat on the floor. He bent and gently lifted its large leather flap. Inside, lying on top of a styrofoam cushion was a small cassette tape recorder. The tiny green light at the end was lit; it was running. Higdon rose from his seat and peered in. At last, they understood.

The door handle turned. She was thanking Pat for the key. Silverman quickly let the flap drop and walked over to the window as she re-entered. She took her seat and smiled at the men.

"Miss Levering," Higdon began, his voice calm, matter-of-fact, "we very much appreciate your having come in. We will be in touch with you soon. Thank you."

Everyone stood, smiled at one another as she unobtrusively lifted her handbag, placed its strap on her shoulder, and left.

There was no time. They had only minutes to act. Some of it was clear. It had been a setup, designed to get them to incriminate themselves. The mayor would hear that tape and probably use it. The rest—what exactly had happened—would have to wait; they had to act.

"Who is she?" Higdon asked.

Silverman quickly explained how he'd seen her before.

"She must work for Ames," Jacobs said. "If we lose her now, she'll disappear off the face of the earth."

"Go ahead. There's no time. I'll get a complaint and warrant." Higdon buzzed for Pat to come in so he could dictate the arrest papers. There'd be no problem getting the federal magistrate to sign them; she had attempted to obstruct justice in their very presence. But he would take the papers down to him personally.

Silverman and Jacobs ran down the hall to the fire-exit stairwell, then sped down the windowless staircase to the bottom door. Jacobs peered out into the lobby. She wasn't there. They ran through the lobby onto the steps of the courthouse. Jacobs was the first to spot her; she was crossing the street at the far corner.

They stayed with her, trailing about a block behind. She was heading uptown, just another pedestrian, unaware of their presence.

After about five blocks, she stopped. A dark limousine slowly pulled up to the curb. They could see her toss a small object through the front window. The limousine pulled away.

They looked at each other. The tape.

She stood at the curb and waved for a taxi.

They had missed the limousine's license number, and if they didn't get the cab's, they'd lose her completely. But they were too far away.

She stepped inside and closed the door. "Stay here," Jacobs ordered, and ran toward the taxi as it pulled away.

"Got it. Come on!" he shouted as he came running back.

They hurried to the court house

She was amused by the photograph. It was one of those slick, glossy magazine photos—young couples frolicking in the brilliant blue water of an island beach or lying on the sun-bleached white sand. It had been in the kangaroo pouch of the seat in front of her, an airline publication showing the hedonistic pleasures of far-off places.

She rested her head against the back of her window seat and smiled. It was almost over. The ticket, passport, and suitcase had been in the luggage locker just as he'd said. And the money would be there, sitting in her account, awaiting withdrawal. The first thing she'd buy would be more clothing; she'd packed only the bare essentials.

She flipped a page or two of the magazine; now the young couples were eating, the waiter and chef standing beside them beaming with delight that their guests were so happy—the oversized fish on the silver tray also obviously pleased. Slowly, she placed the magazine on her lap.

For the final time, she ran through her escape, making

certain she had done everything. Donald would have had someone at the airport watching her. She knew that.

She had almost forgotten to dispose of the recorder. He had
instructed her to throw it in the refuse bin of the ladies' room,
but she had done it before boarding—had done everything just
as he had wanted.

She relaxed, looked out the window at the terminal building.
She had boarded at first call, wanting to be away from whoever
was watching her. Now she could hear the low humming noise
as the pilot switched on the electrical system, then the muted
samba music from the plane's public address system. She smiled
to herself; in a few hours, they'd all be in Brazil. And she
would be free.

The humming stopped. The lights flickered quickly; then it
and the music returned. All systems were being checked. It
wouldn't be long now. Passengers were still boarding, most
going through the first-class section to tourist. She watched
them go by, feeling quite secure and a little superior.

Jacobs and Silverman sat impatiently in the speed lane. Now
and then the cars would trickle forward. They had discovered
the cab's destination but still didn't know her real name or
what flight she was on. There had been an accident up ahead.
Silverman knew that with this weather it was only a matter of
time before their government car would overheat.

"We're not going to get there in time," Jacobs said, leaning
forward, trying to see how far ahead the accident was. He sat
back onto the sticky seat. "Shit. Come on."

"You got a suggestion?" Silverman snapped, the emergency
and the heat taking their toll.

They weren't far from the airport. Silverman looked at the
hood, thought he could see the first traces of steam.

She watched a man come on board, smile blandly at the
stewardess, walk a few steps, then turn back to leer at her. He
was obviously a businessman, married, the product of too many
three-martini lunches, and she knew that he would be in the
seat next to hers.

Sure enough. She had no difficulty seeing the delight on
his face as soon as he realized his good fortune. He knew her
type. And he knew that women like her were always available
to men like him.

But he didn't know that now she was different. She had
paid for her freedom. No more Donald Ameses. From now on,

286

her men would be young and beautiful, like those on the beach in the brochure. No more hairy, heavy old men laboring to cover her with their sweaty bodies. From now on, her fingers would feel young muscular shoulders. She would do the selecting. Life had changed.

When he had finished looking her over, he leaned forward and smiled. "Hello. How about a drink after we take off?"

She read the message in his eyes, then smiled her most seductive smile. They are always so sure of themselves, she thought. She let her leg "accidentally" touch his. She looked straight into his eyes.

"Go fuck yourself," she said.

Before returning to the magazine, she lingered just long enough to enjoy the look of astonishment on his face.

The jet engines began their warm-up.

On the road, one of the two police trucks was moving one of the wrecks to the shoulder. The ambulance, its siren screaming, sped away.

She looked out the window and thought about her escape. Ten minutes to take off. Donald had seemed a bit surprised when she had agreed immediately to do it. There hadn't been a moment's hesitation. She knew it was her only way out. A graceful exit, paid for in full. She had known that Donald— and his friends—would pay her handsomely for it. Sure, she'd do it. Money bestowed importance. With her own, she'd get what she wanted out of life. No more compromises. From now on, she would call the shots. *She* would be the important one.

He hadn't really explained in detail how her doing it was going to help them. But he really didn't have to. First of all, she didn't care. Anyway, some of it she was able to figure out for herself. If she could get them to say the kinds of things Donald wanted, the tape would be used against the prosecutors to dirty them up, prevent those in authority from bringing charges against Ames and his friends. She didn't know how well she had done today. But one thing was sure: she'd been prepared. Donald had spent hours rehearsing her, making her go over and over her lines.

The cabin door slammed shut; the no-smoking and seat-belt sign flashed on. Only a few more moments.

The businessman went to the stewardess—to have his seat changed, she assumed. She barely turned when he stood.

Last night, when she had finally satisfied Donald that she

was ready, when she desperately wanted him to leave, he told her he would stay the night. For the last time, she had submitted. This time she had felt absolutely nothing but had begged and groaned, sensing that she should not in any way risk spoiling her escape.

The door opened again. A flight attendant carried some trays on board, and a few more passengers entered. One was a soldier. Must be standby passengers, she thought idly.

It had been easy. They had been so eager to hear her story, though the younger prosecutor seemed a bit strange. But it had gone well. They had all believed her, and Donald and his friends had their tape.

The jets had stopped. Only a minute or two and they would begin taxiing away. The door slammed shut again. She gazed out the window. This would be her last look at Philadelphia.

Another passenger sat in the businessman's seat. She didn't turn. Closing her eyes, she pictured the gleaming white Copacabana beach.

She felt the magazine slipping from her lap, and when she instinctively tried to catch it, felt a hand, a man's hand, grabbing hers. Her first thought was that he was back in his seat for a second try. She turned, to tell him for the last time not to bother her.

"Hi." John Silverman smiled at her. She looked from him to the two men standing in the aisle: Jacobs and a uniformed security guard.

"Looks like we have more to talk about, doesn't it?" Silverman said.

24

It was 4:23 A.M. The illuminated numbers of the digital clock burned into the darkened bedroom. Silverman lay on his side, watching as the radiant numbers nudged time closer to morning.

He had been awake for almost an hour now. He tried every trick he knew to get himself back to sleep, but it was hopeless. He had too much on his mind.

The door to Jamie's room softly creaked as he pushed it open. He entered the room without turning on the light, then went to lie on her empty bed, as if somehow that would bring her closer. Strange how he never felt this way about Mary Ann.

After a while, he got up and felt his way through the darkened hallway to the living room. Although he was completely alone, he left all the lights off, preferring the dark instead. He turned the air conditioner on high and stood before it, waiting to feel the first shot of cool air. Noisy old thing, he thought, as it ground and sputtered its way up to speed. One of these days he'd get a new one. He flopped on the sofa and put his bare legs up on the coffee table. Once again, thoughts of the case filled his mind.

He and Jacobs had taken her from the plane directly back to the courthouse, right to the magistrate. Higdon had been there waiting.

The hearing was short and sweet. There was no question but that she was a "flight risk," so the magistrate had set her bail at one million dollars, high enough to ensure her remaining in custody. Nothing had been placed on the court calendar, so while the hearing had been held in a public courtroom, the press had not attended. They had spent the rest of the day and a good part of the evening interrogating her in their offices.

Silverman had studied her some more in light of the new knowledge that she was Ames's mistress. She didn't seem right for the part, not what he would expect for Ames. She was too young, too frail.

Now that she had been caught, she spoke freely, admitted all. Curiously, she showed no emotion—nothing except what he took to be resignation. She must have been frightened, certainly disappointed, but she allowed nothing to come through.

It was hot in the room. The air conditioner continued sputtering, the grinding noise slowing down. He walked over to it, held his hand up to make certain the escaping air was still cool. It wasn't. He slammed his hand onto the top of the machine, stood there until it picked up speed, then returned to the sofa.

The evidence against Ames—not for bribery—for obstructing justice was piled high. But the woman didn't know anything about the others, had never even seen them. She told them that Ames didn't speak to her about business, and they believed her.

Higdon had seen it almost immediately. During a break in the questioning, when the two prosecutors had gone to the men's room, he'd mentioned it. If she were Ames's mistress, who—or what—was Elaine Robertson, the woman on the canceled checks, the "E.R." on the check spreads?

When the interview had resumed, they had questioned her about other women. She knew of none. But then she paused for a moment, trying to recall something. They had watched her in silence. She remembered, shrugged; it was probably nothing of consequence, she had said, but Ames had once mentioned something about women. They pressed her gently, not wanting to exhibit too much interest.

It had happened after the investigation had been underway for some time. Ames obviously was feeling the pressure, had been drinking heavily, had been "kind of rough" with her. She didn't understand it all, but he was becoming very amused over a thought. He said something about "his women." It might have been "their women"; she was uncertain. Something about women taking care of him, or them. Something about insurance. He might have used the phrase "the best insurance," but his speech was garbled, pretty much incomprehensible. He had repeated whatever he was saying a couple of times, then had dropped it. Now that she thought about it, Donald had acted almost as if he had slipped, had said something he wasn't supposed to say. But he never mentioned it again. She figured he was just drunk and didn't really know what he was saying.

Silverman moved his bare feet off the coffee table. Could

Ames have had two mistresses? But why pay for one by check on a monthly basis and not the other? She told them before the interview had ended that she received money from Ames in cash only, never by check.

His eyes were completely adjusted to the darkness; he looked around, absent-mindedly viewing the silhouetted furniture. Ames would know by now that she hadn't made it to Brazil, would find out soon enough that she had been arrested. He tried to think of the consequences; all he could see was that time was running out.

Elaine Robertson. Damn if it wasn't always the one thing overlooked. But had he overlooked anything? Maybe she was merely an earlier mistress. Jacobs would subpoena her bank records first thing in the morning. That should tell them something. He sighed. He felt exhausted. He really should get some sleep.

Albert Lacona had refused to be placed in protective custody. They had assigned two U.S. marshals to protect him. They were in a car, on the street across from his house. Apparently, Lacona would stay in most days, only occasionally going out for a drive.

What had Donald Ames been saying that night? Had he been just too drunk, or was there some message, some key, in those garbled words?

Silverman leaned over and reached for the phone, got the number from the directory assistance operator, and then, in the darkness, managed to dial. He wouldn't speak to her, just wanted to hear her voice, would hear Elaine Robertson's voice and then hang up. Across town, on the other end of the line, the phone rang. It rang through each of the darkened, completely barren rooms. One phone, lying in the middle of a carpetless living-room floor, ringing for no one to hear, no one to answer.

The vice-president of the United States had spoken longer than he should have. Now, as if he, too, sensed it, he forced his speech to conclusion. With both hands, he held on to the deeply grained wooden speaker's rostrum that had been placed before him on the banquet table promptly after the meal. One by one, he thanked the various mayors seated with him at the head table for their participation and support in the president's Committee to Aid the Nation's Cities.

Mayor Lane, seated third from the end, smiled politely as the vice-president mentioned his name and thanked him. It all seemed cordial enough, but a careful listener would have perceived that the speaker's words were a bit quicker, his smile a bit colder than with the others. Polite applause followed, as it had with the others, but it, too, contained subtle differences in duration and intensity. Everyone there knew that Lane was to be treated with the respect and cordiality due the office, but they were politicians and so perceived quite clearly what was to each and every one of them the unacceptable personal risk of getting too near an overboard shipmate around whom sharks were circling.

The last expression of gratitude completed, the banquet had come to an end. The mayors, their guests, and the Washington regulars stood to begin their final mingling before the evening's conclusion. A few of them spoke to Lane but were careful not to linger. Photographers were there, and pictorial evidence of expressions of friendship were to be avoided. One or two discreetly wished him luck; the rest said nothing about his troubles. Even the press in attendance left him alone. They were, after all, on neutral turf that night. Lane saw them watching carefully from a safe distance and was painfully aware that each would write about how he had handled himself and how the others had handled him.

He stood at the front portico and waited with the other mayors as the line of limousines retrieved their distinguished passengers. He exchanged broad, meaningless politician's smiles, shook hands, and said the same empty words about the necessity of seeing one another soon. Then, when his car arrived, he quickly stepped in as one of the two Philadelphia plainclothes policemen assigned to him held the door.

Once inside, the smile vanished. He sat silently, the policemen in front, and watched as they drove from the White House toward the office buildings on nearby Connecticut Avenue. They slowly passed the offices of many of the city's rich and powerful, but Lane's mind was on something else. The limousine entered Dupont Circle and maneuvered itself into the underground parking garage of the Dupont Plaza Hotel.

With the policemen on either side, he stepped into the elevator and stood quietly as it headed for the fourth floor. One of the policemen was the first out. At the door to the suite, Lane waited as his man quietly knocked.

Before the door opened, he nodded for one to stay in the hall, the other to stand by the elevator. The latch clicked. Donald Ames stood in the opening, then stepped aside to allow the mayor entry. John Stavaros, seated on the sofa, a drink in his hand, watched him come in. He didn't get up. It was clear that the two men had awaited his arrival in near-total silence. All wore the same grim expression. Ames closed the door.

The policeman in the hall instinctively moved from the door so as not to be able to hear.

"My name is Zupnick. Myron Zupnick. I'm from First National Bank. I've . . . uh, I was told to ask for either Mr. Higdon or Mr. Silverman."

The receptionist nodded through the glass window separating her from the waiting area. "Fifth door to the right, end of the hall."

He knew the subpoena dealt with the mayor's case. There had been much speculation at the bank about how the subpoena fit into the investigation. No one knew. Myron Zupnick had never been involved in anything like this before. He was nervous, the elaborate security system he was facing not helping one bit. Slightly built, Myron Zupnick's shoulders were too narrow. He was underweight and short; his thinning hair was darkish but seemingly colorless. Long before reaching his present age of twenty-eight, he had learned to step aside for the other inhabitants of the world. Clearing his throat self-consciously, he asked her to repeat the instructions. She pushed a second button, obviously enraged, he thought. He turned to try to locate the buzzing noise, realized it was the automatic lock release for the door into the prosecutor's wing, ran for it, reaching the handle just as the buzzing stopped. He turned and waited meekly for her to press the button again.

Once inside, he walked down the corridor, counting the doors, trying as best he could to adjust to the grim government surroundings. At his side he carried the valise containing the subpoenaed documents. He was just about to pass the third door when it opened. He stopped. A man, dressed in overalls, wearing handcuffs secured to a chain around his waist, a red bandanna casually tied around his forehead, stepped forward into the corridor, followed closely by a deputy U.S. marshal.

The prisoner stopped and stared defiantly at the young man with the valise. Myron saw he was standing within easy reach; one quick move and he'd be a hostage. Yet he stood, frozen. The marshal poked his captive farther into the hall.

He watched as both men walked away. At the second door, the prisoner turned and winked at him. The marshal grabbed the chain at the small of the prisoner's back and pulled him to the elevator.

Myron hurried to Silverman's office.

"Mr. Silverman is waiting for you. Please go in," Jan said, pointing toward the door.

Silverman shook hands and quickly introduced the young clerk to Higdon and Jacobs, both of whom had joined him for this meeting. Myron looked flustered. He waited to be told what to do. Silverman held his hand out for the bank documents. With a muffled apology and nervous grin, Myron opened the valise and handed him the package.

Silverman spread them out on his desk. For five years' worth of transactions, there sure weren't many. There was a signature card in the name of Elaine Robertson; the signature was flowery, obviously belonging to a woman. The copies of microfilmed bank statements showed little activity. Her canceled checks were not available, thanks to the repeal of the Bank Secrecy Act. In addition to her name, the signature card contained Elaine Robertson's address, which they already knew, her social security number, and other "vital" information. It would be up to Jacobs to check out that information.

They studied each bank statement. There was an obvious pattern. Each and every month for five years, until six months ago, someone would deposit a check into the account. Each check was in the same amount as the checks written to "E.R.," as shown on Donald Ames's check spreads and his "Elaine Robertson" canceled checks. The only withdrawals from the account occurred once every three months. The withdrawal check was always in an amount equal to about two-thirds of the balance of the account at that time.

So Elaine Robertson would get a monthly check from Ames and deposit it in her own checking account. But what was the money used for? Not for rent. Not for groceries. And why did she withdraw money from the account only once every three months? Why always two-thirds of the balance in the account? Who'd she write the check to?

"Coffee, Mr. Zupnick?" Silverman asked.

"Uhm . . . no. Thank you." He drank only tea, but was too timid to ask for some.

"How long you been at the bank?" Silverman asked.

"Be, uh, six years in September. I was a teller till last December. . . . Now I'm branch head teller," he added proudly.

Jacobs walked around to the other chair in front of Silverman's desk and sat down next to the teller. He could see the young man's nervousness and so smiled warmly at him. He wanted to put him at ease.

"Mr. Zupnick..." Jacobs began.

"Myron. It's, uhm, Myron."

"Fine," Jacobs said, smiling. "Listen, Myron. Can you tell us anything about this account?"

"Not much activity for five years, is there?" Myron said, relaxing a bit.

"That's for shitten sure," Jacobs said, still smiling, easing him into conversation.

"Myron," Silverman said, catching the teller's attention. "You see, that's what had us concerned, this pattern of activity." He shrugged. "Do you know anything about this? Are you the right guy for us to talk to, because we really need help with this."

"Well, you see... actually, that's why I was sent here. I think I can help you some. Uhm... I was her teller... uh, I mean she would usually come to my counter. I handled most of those transactions." He sat back. He was warming to this. These prosecutors needed him. "I saw those records, noticed them on Mr. Peterson's desk. You know, after they were copied. Mr. Peterson's the manager," he added, shifting forward slightly. Myron reminded Silverman of a weasel. "Anyway," Myron said, "I told him I had handled a lot of that"—he pointed at the papers on the desk—"so he sent me."

Actually, Myron remembered Elaine Robertson quite well. She was the most attractive woman he had ever seen. Tall, dark hair, beautiful eyes. She was flawlessly beautiful. When she had stood before him at the counter, he had tried not to stare, but her eyes were so inviting, especially when she smiled. She had become a major subject of his daydreams, dreams in which he was transformed into a virile, desirable man and she, of course, found him irresistible.

"What can you tell us about these withdrawals?"

"Sir?" He turned toward Jacobs, shaking himself out of his reverie. "Oh, the withdrawals, yes, uhm... Well, she'd, uh, she'd make those deposits..." He leaned toward the desk and pointed at the statements. "You know, once every month, and then on occasion, she'd present her check, made payable to the bank, and would request a manager's check. We call them manager's checks.... They're, you know, like cashier's checks. It's a bank check signed by two bank officers and made payable to whoever the customer directs."

"Do you remember the checks? Who the payee was?"

"Yes. I do. It was always the same. She'd always ask that the manager's check be made payable to Klaus Froemer."

Anticipating their next question, he added, "I have no idea who he is."

Jacobs turned to his colleagues. "Simple and effective," he said. "Anyone seeing her check would learn nothing but that she had paid the money to the bank. And anyone looking at the bank's check would not know that the funds represented by the check had come out of her account."

"And, of course, the bank doesn't microfilm anyone's checks anymore, anyway," Silverman added. Then, realizing it at the same time as the others, he added, "Except for their own . . . Everyone keeps their own canceled checks. At least for a time." He looked over at the teller. "Myron, surely the bank has retained their own canceled checks. The manager's checks."

"No. That is, we don't keep the checks. We microfilm them, as we do other records. You know, for storage and space reasons." He reached into his valise. "I've brought copies with me. But Mr. Peterson said I shouldn't volunteer the information; I should produce them only if you ask. And then I'm supposed to insist on a subpoena."

Higdon walked over. "You'll have a subpoena when you leave here. Give me the records."

Myron thought that he would have preferred handing them to Silverman or the other man, but dutifully he removed them from the valise and handed them over to Higdon. The three men looked at them together.

The back of each check bore the endorsement of Klaus Froemer; below that were several bank stamps, the first one just below the signature showing where the check had been deposited for collection.

"Credit Suisse," Myron said, repeating the bank name on the checks. "You probably know this . . . but uhm, it's a large commercial bank in Zurich. . . . Zurich, Switzerland. All the checks were deposited there. I never knew that. I never knew what she did with the checks until I saw those copies.

"Looks kind of suspicious, doesn't it?" Myron said, tilting his head. He was beginning to enjoy being a part of the team.

Jacobs and Silverman exchanged quick smiles.

"Tell us about Miss Robertson," Higdon said. "What does she look like? What did she talk to you about when she stood at your counter waiting for those checks?"

"She's pretty. Very pretty." He described her, told Higdon

how she was always very pleasant, smiled a lot but never really talked much, just the usual small talk.

"Let me see that signature card," Higdon asked Jacobs. He studied it, then looked up at the teller. "It says here she works as a secretary at—" he read from the card—"Amtex Corporation. She ever talk to you about that . . . about her job, her boss, anything like that?"

"No, sir . . . But I'll bet it involves some kind of foreign trade business or something like that."

"Why do you say that?"

"Well, she's European, you know. That is, she speaks with an accent. I'm not sure. It sounded German."

"Or Swiss," Jacobs added.

Myron smiled at him. "I guess."

Higdon looked at the card again. "She lists a social security number and gives her citizenship as U.S.A."

"Maybe she's naturalized," Myron said, enjoying his new role as federal investigator more than ever.

Silverman leaned forward, his elbows resting on the green blotter that covered his desk.

"Well, Myron, try to think. Can you remember any conversations you had with her? About anything, really. Her job, your job. Any questions she might have asked. Anything."

He was embarrassed to tell them again that despite the way she treated him in his fantasies, this beautiful woman never really gave him anything more than a pleasant smile or perhaps a "good morning." There was only that one time that he'd spoken to her, but you could hardly call it a conversation. Not that he hadn't tried.

"Well, I only remember one time that I . . . uh, we spoke . . . you know about something other than the manager's checks . . . I mean, her asking me for a manager's check. That was the time she came in after the robbery."

Myron looked at them; he didn't know why, but judging from their appearances, he apparently had said something that interested them. He told them the story.

Two or three years before, Elaine Robertson had been in the bank, standing at his counter, waiting for her manager's check. The young man standing in the front of the line at the next counter had given the teller a note telling her he had a gun, not to sound the alarm, and to give him all her cash.

Myron had left his station to get the necessary two officers' signatures on the check. He returned and gave her the check, and she left the bank, never realizing that the other teller was being robbed. Neither did he, for that matter.

"Well, the robber didn't know that the teller had pressed the silent alarm, had given him bait bills and a dye pack. He got to the door when the dye pack exploded and the red dye hidden between the bills covered his clothes. The police stormed in, and it was all over. I believe the robber never went to trial; he pleaded guilty and got a reduced sentence.

"The next time I saw Miss Robertson, I told her what had happened, what she had missed."

He had hoped it would have come out more fully, hoped he could have elicited more than the raising of her eyebrows. And then he was embarrassed at even having told them it was a conversation. But they seemed disinterested in what she might have said. He looked at them, his confusion apparent.

"Did the other teller activate the surveillance camera?" Higdon asked.

"Yes."

"What was the name of the robber? Do you remember?"

"No, is it important?"

"Yes."

"May I call my office?"

Silverman pushed the phone toward him.

"Ronnie Baker," he said after the call.

Now Higdon took the phone. He called Mrs. Ramondi.

"Please find out which assistant handled the Ronnie Baker case," he instructed her. "It's a closed file. Bank Robbery." He waited, staring at Myron. "Thank you." He hung up and walked out of the office.

Myrons said nothing. They all waited for Higdon's return. After a few minutes, he came back with the file. He opened a folder marked "Evidence" and extracted the photographs. He spread them on the desk so that Zupnick could see them.

Four black and white photographs of the bank's counter taken by the two surveillance cameras that were mounted high on the wall behind the tellers. Myron was only in the last picture, which was taken after he returned with the signatures. All four photos showed the back of the other teller. In front of her counter stood a young black man. Obviously, the robber. And at the head of the other line, to his right, stood a dark-haired, tall, rather attractive woman.

He pointed. "There she is. I guess you had her picture all along."

Higdon took a pencil from the desk, selected the best shot

of Elaine Robertson, and carefully drew a circle around her head and shoulders.

Albert Lacona stepped from the front porch of his house onto the cement pathway leading to the sidewalk. The rain hadn't cooled things off much. Still, he had to get out for a while. Before all of this, when he still had his job, there were plenty of ways in which he could escape. Even then he could only stand to be around his wife for short periods. Now he couldn't tolerate it at all. Perhaps she had sensed something all along. They hadn't slept together for so long. But she hadn't known about David. He was sure of that.

Today he finally told her. She became so quiet, so pensive. She seemed to be trying hard to understand. But she had accepted it as if it were the final confirmation she had been waiting for.

He walked around to the driver's side of his car, looked down the street, easily spotting the two U.S. marshals in the parked automobile.

He wanted so badly to see David, yet knew that they probably would never be together again. It seemed as if that damned investigation would never end.

Once inside the car, he rolled down the window and waited before inserting the key into the ignition. Pumping the accelerator, he inserted the key and turned his wrist. The motor churned a few times, then stopped; damned wet weather always made it hard to start. He tried again, allowing the car to moan a few times before the motor turned over. As he pressed down on the accelerator, the car roared, spewing exhaust fumes into the humid air. He released the hand brake and pulled away. The marshals gave him lead time, then followed.

Both cars passed the young-looking man on the far side of the street walking toward Mrs. Frederico's house. They hardly noticed him. Average looking, unremarkable, he walked slowly by, the package he carried as unobtrusive as he. He didn't seem to notice the two passing cars, mounted the steps to the porch, then used the key she had given him to open the old glass-centered door.

Such a nice, quiet man, Mrs. Frederico had told the other two boarders. He said he had been in the army, had come to Harrisburg to settle down, find work. He'd been there almost a week now.

He passed his landlady on the stairs, smiled politely, and said good afternoon. He had such a quiet, pleasant voice.

Mary Burke would have recognized that voice.

"Okay. Thanks.... No, no need to send me anything yet. I'll get back to you."

Bob Jacobs put the phone down. He'd make the rest of the calls later, but there was no longer really any need to. Except for the address, the information on Elaine Robertson's signature card, all of it, was phony.

He'd checked the social security number; its real owner had died several years before. The State Department had no record of an Elaine Robertson as a naturalized citizen. The only name that even came close was a seventy-three-year-old woman who lived in Nebraska. Amtex Corporation didn't exist, its address a parking lot.

All they had was a name, address, and a photograph. There was a stake out on her Rittenhouse Square apartment. No one fitting her description came in or out.

A blowup of her face had been made from the bank pictures. The other agents had copies; maybe they'd turn something up.

There was really nothing to do. It was as if the woman in the photo had simply disappeared from the face of the earth.

He picked up the phone and dialed the next number.

Silverman looked up from his *Daily Racing Form* to find Higdon standing in front of him.

"Join you?" Higdon asked.

Silverman shrugged, folded the paper, and moved aside so that Higdon could sit on the bench beside him.

Today Silverman had brought his *Daily Racing Form* to the small park behind Congress Hall. It was the tourist season, and the building itself was too crowded.

Strange that Higdon should come looking for him. He studied Higdon's sullen face, thought for a moment that he was here to bring up the topic of their relationship, to discuss what had happened to them. There was a time when he would have welcomed it. Now he didn't much care.

He was about to reopen his paper when Higdon spoke. He didn't look at Silverman, stared straight ahead instead.

"Terrance Cook at Justice called," Higdon said.

"What'd he want?" Silverman asked.

Higdon sighed.

"Said he wants the grand jury to indict Ames now for obstruction of justice. Wants us to drop the mayor for now. Go after him later."

"What'd you tell him?"

Higdon stood and slowly began walking back to the court-house.

"I told him I wanted to discuss it with you first," he said over his shoulder.

Special Agent Thomas had just about given up. He had shown the photograph to almost every shopkeeper in the Rittenhouse Square area. No one seemed to know her; not a single person in any of the shops near her apartment had recognized her picture. It was hot, and he was tired—and bored. He almost skipped the bank on the corner.

Now he stood at the branch manager's desk, waiting for Jacobs to pick up the phone. The teller who had recognized her stood beside him, still holding the photograph.

"Hello, Bob," he said when Jacobs had finally come to the phone. "Have I got a surprise for you."

The application for a search warrant had been given to the magistrate's clerk. His secretary told them they could wait for him in his chambers. He was on the bench but wouldn't be long.

Silverman, Higdon, Jacobs, and Special Agent Thomas sat in the chairs in front of the empty desk. Higdon held the bank's signature card Thomas had brought them.

"You know, I almost left," Thomas said. "The manager checked his customer records and told me there was nothing on Elaine Robertson. Then I showed him the picture, and he didn't recognize her." He smiled at them, obviously proud to have found out what he had actually stumbled on.

"A teller came over to see the manager to get him to authorize something or other. He looked over at the picture I was holding and said . . . I mean he just smiled and said it. 'That's Rose Edwards,' he said. I said no, her name was Elaine Robertson. He said if it was, then they were twins because he'd waited on her for years and her name was Edwards. So the manager got out Rose Edward's signature card, and I couldn't believe it."

Higdon looked at the card. It was in the name of Edwards, all right, but everything else—social security number, date of birth, place of employment, and apartment address—was exactly the same as on the other bank's signature card for Elaine Robertson.

After Thomas had called, Jacobs had gone to the bank with

a subpoena. They had been very cooperative; the records would be ready in two days. The teller had remembered her quite well, and he had remembered more. The same pattern had occurred; each month she would deposit a check; about every third month she'd write a check on her account and request a bank manager's check. The manager had permitted Jacobs to see the bank's canceled checks, although he wouldn't allow them to be removed from the bank until all of the other records were ready for delivery.

The same pattern existed. The checks were made payable to Klaus Froemer, deposited in Credit Suisse. And this time they had a bonus. The teller had remembered who had written the monthly checks she had deposited. He had recognized the name, had read it in the papers. John Stavaros.

Silverman stood and paced the floor, forgetting for a moment that they were in a judge's chambers. "We've got the missing link. We've got it now. That money—the money from both accounts, that's the mayor's.

"The Ames checks, the peculiar amounts from the check spreads. Now Stavaros giving this woman checks, all of it going to the same account in Switzerland. We've got it. We've got them paying off Lane. We've got their source."

"We don't have it yet," Higdon said. "We don't have her. Without her, whoever she is, we don't have it."

"That's right," added Jacobs. "We've got to find her."

Silverman continued pacing. He wasn't really listening to them, was too absorbed in the discovery. "You know," he said more to himself than to them, "when you think about it, put it together, I'll bet you that those Ames checks represent Mayor Lane's share of his financial interest in the resort deal. That's his share. We're going to prove that he was in that deal—in it secretly all along."

He sat in his chair, looked at Higdon, then at Jacobs. "And Albert Lacona is going to testify that the mayor made it clear that Regal Construction should be the low bidder on those road-construction contracts. We're going to prove the benefit and we're going to prove the payoff."

"You know," Jacobs said, "we might be able to tie Lane into the awarding of those off-track betting parlors to Stavaros's company. Maybe there's a percentage relationship between that money and the tenancies."

"You mean maybe Lane's a part owner of that deal as well?" Silverman said.

"Yeah."

The door opened, and the magistrate entered, still wearing his robes. They rose and waited for him to be seated.

Silverman presented the case. Special Agent Thomas swore to the matters contained in the affidavit he had prepared in support of the search warrant. Silverman told the magistrate what they had discovered, leaving very little out. It was important for them to search that apartment, important to find something to lead them to her. The warrant had to be signed.

It didn't take long. The magistrate listened, obviously fascinated by their discoveries.

"The court will sign the warrant," he said, "and direct that it be executed immediately."

"Here he goes again," the marshal said to his partner, tapping his shoulder and waking him. They both watched Albert Lacona walk from his house to his car. Today they were parked on the opposite side of the street, about four car lengths from his.

Lacona stopped, turned toward them, obviously considering whether or not to go over. He stood a few seconds, then slowly began walking. When he got to their car, he didn't say anything at first, just stood there.

"Good afternoon, Mr. Lacona," said the one on the passenger side, a little too cheerfully.

But Lacona was in no mood for friendliness. "Look, I'm sick of you watching me. I want you to get out of here," he said. "I'm not an animal in a cage, and I'm sick of being treated like one."

"I'm sorry, sir. We're just following orders."

"Goddam it, you're not here at night! I see you drive off. Is that how the government is going to protect me, on the day shift? Call your superiors; call Silverman or Higdon. I don't want you around anymore. Is that clear? You better do it. I don't care what my lawyer says. I'm going to sue you for invasion of privacy if you don't leave me alone. Stop following me. Is that clear?"

"Nice fellow," the marshal in the passenger's seat said as Lacona turned and walked over to his car.

"Yeah, a prince. I suppose we'd better call in."

"Okay."

He bent to retrieve the microphone below the dashboard, still watching Lacona as he opened his car door and got in. He had just put his hands on the microphone and was about to sit back when he saw the small colored wire hanging from the bottom of Lacona's car.

"Jesus, stop him!" he shouted to his partner. "The car's wired!"

As one marshal opened the door, the other pressed hard on the horn.

Lacona paid no attention. The car wouldn't start again. He turned the key and pushed on the accelerator; the motor groaned. He pressed the pedal to the floor, forced the key as far to the right as possible. There was a click, and instinctively he removed his foot from the pedal. Too late.

His ears buzzed from the noise, the hot blast of the explosion pinning him to the seat. Then his head flew back, the windshield crumbled. He fought for breath, but there was no air. Blood spurted across his face.

That nice young boarder had left. Mrs. Frederico was cleaning his room for the new tenant when she heard the noise. She rushed to the window, then screamed.

The men who had helped them execute the warrant had gone. The door to the apartment was open, the frame split where the latch had been. Silverman had never participated in a search before, but he and Higdon and Jacobs had come along. No one could be found to provide a master key, so at Higdon's instruction, the door had been forced open.

The three of them were seated on the floor of the empty living room, not far from the telephone. They had walked through each of the empty rooms without an exchanged word. Spread before them on the barren floor were the search warrant, the bank papers, and a copy of her photograph.

His back against the wall, Silverman sat watching Higdon. His jacket was off, and for the first time Silverman could remember, the top button of his shirt was unfastened and his tie was down.

"Okay if I come in and fix the lock?" the old man asked.

They all turned at the sound of his voice. His face was lined and cracked with age. Except for the loss of youth, he looked much as he had the day years before when he'd stepped off the boat in his new country. He wore coveralls, the tool tray in his right hand.

"Yeah, go ahead," Silverman said as the old man put his tray down beside the door frame and began working.

No one spoke for a while. They watched him trying to repair the door.

"Well, what now?" Silverman finally said. "What the hell do we do now?"

No one answered.

"Where the hell are we going to find her? Without her, all we can prove is that she's their mistress." Silverman picked up the photo, then tossed it back on the pile.

"We've still got the documents," Jacobs said almost apologetically.

"Not enough. Without testimony, without the right explanation, it's not enough." He shook his head. "We've simply got to find her . . . Maybe she's an actress. Maybe the accent's a phony. We could check the theatrical union."

"Or maybe we'll just indict Ames," Higdon said irritably. "Maybe that's what we'll have to be satisfied with."

"Maybe that's what *you'll* be satisfied with," Silverman snapped. He could barely control his anger.

Higdon glared at him.

"Wait a minute. Wait a minute. Hold it," Jacobs interjected. "Let's calm down and think about this."

Jacobs watched them, glaring at each other, his first reaction to leave them alone. But then it occurred to him—they were sitting on the floor of an apartment in an Ames building. Ames International had bought the entire building over ten years before.

"Wait a second," he said, as much for his own benefit as theirs. "The apartment was in a phony name—and empty— but it's in an Ames Building. An Ames apartment."

The prosecutors looked at him. He was right.

Jacobs nodded. "Yeah, maybe there's another apartment." They looked over at the man working on the door.

"Hey, buddy," Jacobs called.

He looked at them sitting on the floor. It was obvious that he hadn't been paying any attention to them.

"Can you come over here for a minute?" Jacobs asked.

He wiped his hands on his coveralls and walked over.

Jacobs picked up the photo and stood as the old man walked over.

"You employed by Ames International?"

"Yeah," he said, staring at the photo in Jacobs's hand.

"How long?"

He shrugged. "'Bout twenty years."

"Carpenter?"

"Carpenter, maintenance man."

"You ever been in any of the other apartment buildings?"

"Sure," he said, still looking at the photo.

Jacobs handed him the picture. "Nice-looking woman, huh?"

"Yeah." He smiled.

"Ever seen her before?"

"Sure."

Jacobs's glance shot to Silverman, then Higdon.

"Where?"

"Building C."

"Where's that?"

"Two buildings down."

"Which apartment?"

"Don't know. Seen her come out a couple times. Handsome woman." He handed the photo back to Jacobs, waiting obediently to see if he could go back to work. Jacobs nodded, and the old man wiped his hands on his coveralls again and returned to the door as if nothing important had happened.

They quickly picked up their papers and headed for Building C.

The doorman recognized her photograph, told them which apartment. No one responded to their knocking. They stood in the hall, listening for sounds of activity inside the apartment, the fear of another set of empty rooms as yet unspoken.

The elevator door slid open. They turned to see her step into the hall. She was tall and beautiful, her hair dark, her eyes even prettier than in the photo. When she saw them standing in front of her door, she stopped for a moment, then slowly continued walking toward them. She seemed strangely unperturbed at the sight of three strange men at her door.

No one spoke. Jacobs reached in his pocket and removed his badge. But it really wasn't necessary. She knew who they were. She turned toward the door, inserted her key, and opened it.

"Come in, please," she said.

25

Eighteen months had passed since the Thursday morning the grand jurors were led into Judge Montarelli's courtroom.

After they had been seated in the first three rows of benches behind the railing, the court clerk had asked them in the formal, archaic language that, for some unknown reason, was still used to address jurors if they had anything to bring to the court's attention.

Higdon and Silverman had stood as the foreman ceremoniously handed the indictment to the clerk. It had been no secret that the mayor had been indicted; the press had packed themselves into the spectator's gallery behind the jurors.

Silverman had waited for the judge's acknowledgment that he could speak and then calmly and quietly summarized the charges—fraud, tax evasion, bribery—reading the names of the three defendants last.

The reporters had then made a rather disruptive mass exit for the pay phones at the end of the hall.

For the next day or two, the grand jurors had become sought-after celebrities. A few had allowed their pictures to be taken for the evening news, but none agreed to be interviewed. Judge Montarelli had given them a strong warning about the continuing need for secrecy before dismissing them.

Silverman had worried about Mrs. Franklin, fearful that she easily could be coaxed by a reporter into "going public." She had shown up at the defendants' arraignment on the day they formally entered not guilty pleas to the charges, had sat quietly—and inconspicuously—in the last row of the courtroom, then had gone home.

As expected, it had taken a long time for the case to come to trial. Mayor Lane had chosen not to resign his office. With tears in his eyes, his lawyer Stanton Turner on one side, his wife on the other, he stood before the press and the cameras and told everyone who was listening that he would fight to the end for the acquittal and total vindication he so richly deserved.

Mario Pincus, an aging but quite successful and aggressive criminal defense lawyer, had joined the defense team as Stavaros's counsel. Pincus had at one time been investigated for allegedly having mob affiliations, but nothing had come of it.

Every conceivable pretrial motion had been filed, attacking much of the prosecution's case. The hearings had consumed weeks of court time. In the end, all of the major defense motions but one had been denied. The judge had granted the defense request for a change of venue because of the massive pretrial publicity given the case. He had ordered the trial moved from Philadelphia to Pittsburgh.

March that year was bitter. The air retained the full chill of winter, but it was barely noticed by the lawyers. They had been in trial for over two months, spending virtually every waking hour either in court or in their hotel rooms preparing for the next day's session.

The government's case hadn't gone as well as the prosecutors had expected. There had been serious disagreements between Silverman and Higdon over the order of proof and what parts of the case should be highlighted for the jury. Their relationship was again as strained as ever.

The basic elements of the charges contained in the indictment had been proved. Albert Lacona had survived the explosion. The doctors had said that his not having closed the car door when he started the motor had saved his life; he had literally been blown out of the car. His legs—or what had been left of them—had been amputated; he had been severely burned. The judge had permitted defense cross-examination about his homosexual lover but had forbidden the prosecutors from eliciting any testimony whatsoever about the attempt made on his life. The reporters covering the trial all agreed that Lacona had been an unappealing, more or less unconvincing witness.

Mary Burke had been as nervous on the stand as she had ever been. On two occasions, the judge had to recess the trial to allow her time to compose herself. She told the truth about the letter, but on cross-examination, she tried to help her former employer in any way she could, apparently still unconvinced that Donald Ames would have taken any part in a plot to harm her.

Silverman and Higdon knew they couldn't use any of the evidence they had against Ames for obstructing justice; his case would have been severed for trial from the others because of prejudice, and they needed him there at the defense table next to Lane and Stavaros.

The prosecution's final witness had been Swiss-born Noel Reichman. She had received full immunity from prosecution in return for providing the testimony needed to explain the real purpose behind the phony names she had used, the bank accounts, the various checks—and the money. Silverman had handled her direct examination.

Ames and Stavaros had met with her, she had testified, and had given her instructions as to how she should accomplish the task of getting the money out of the country. They had paid her generously, listing her as their employee in other companies of theirs and issuing checks that had been deposited in yet another bank account.

She was an airline stewardess and so traveled frequently to Europe. The checks had always been placed in a locked box at the post office in Zurich; she would never see them after that.

Silverman had asked her about meetings and conversations with the defendants. She had never met Mayor Lane, had never even seen him before entering the courtroom that day. But she could recall conversations with the other two men. Over defense objection, she was permitted to testify that she understood from things Ames and Stavaros had said to her that the money represented by the checks was destined for Lane, that it had been deposited in a secret numbered account, and that it was payoff money, the total amount for the mayor just short of a half a million dollars.

Her cross-examination had lasted two full days. Each defense lawyer had taken his turn at her. Her deal with the prosecution was the subject of heavy interrogation. White focused his examination on her "alleged discussions" with the defendants. She had been unable to provide any corroboration or precision as to when they had occurred; she admitted she couldn't remember their exact words. In the end, still insisting that she had not fabricated the conversations, she admitted that neither man had actually said anything about the mayor or payoffs. Jacobs thought White had made her look like a liar.

Klaus Froemer—if there was such a man—had never been found. The prosecutors had tried to explain away his nonappearance.

The defense case had lasted almost as long as the prosecution's. Mayor Lane was portrayed as nothing more than an old and good friend of Ames's; he insisted that he and Stavaros

309

were unacquainted. As for Resort Time, Inc., he stuck to his story of never having received "a tangible benefit" from the venture, insisting with subtle incoherence that the interest he had received really was something of a future right to ownership.

Stanton Turner had called two expert accountants to the stand to dispute the testimony Jacobs had given for the prosecution that the money represented Lane's percentage interest—his bribe—in the resort deal and the off-track betting parlor rentals. Both accountants had stated that Jacobs's testimony was nothing but an unproved theory, "figure juggling," a point of view without real proof.

And then, before concluding the mayor's case, Turner let the jury hear the tape of the conversation between Lacona and Lane. When the tape had finished, he had stood before the prosecution table and announced to the jury that the recording had been arranged by the same men who had sponsored Lacona as a credible witness. He rested his case.

It had been a bad moment for Higdon and Silverman, forced to sit there quietly as Turner scored points at their expense.

Both Ames and Stavaros took the stand. Noel Reichman, they said, had been their common mistress. The bank accounts, the false address, the fictitious names all had been designed to keep her in the generous and elaborate style rich men provided their women and to minimize the risk of their wives and children learning of their immoral behavior. Each had said that he now was terribly embarrassed to have to admit publicly to having kept a mistress. But that was far preferable to being accused unjustly of having bribed Lane. Each hinted that Ms. Reichman herself was salting that money away in Switzerland for her own old age. The general consensus was that the prosecution's cross-examination had been only moderately effective.

Richard Franklin White's final argument had been spellbinding. The crowded courtroom had remained respectfully silent throughout his four-hour speech to the jury. At one point, Silverman thought he saw one of the jurors nodding in agreement as White was telling them not to convict his client for having made the foolish mistake of back dating a letter to verify an oral understanding and save a dear friend, who held the important and sensitive position of mayor of a great city, from unnecessary embarrassment.

But now it was over. The case had come to a close. Three days before, the judge had instructed the jurors and sent them to their room to deliberate on a verdict. Everyone except the defendants had spent their days waiting in the courtroom and adjoining halls for the jury to come to its decision.

Some of the lawyers would chat with one another from time to time, yet all scrupulously avoided any prediction of the outcome. Silverman stayed away from Turner throughout the trial and was sure that no one had noticed his distance.

He was standing by himself at the end of the hall when the bailiff came out and announced that the jury had just sent a note to the judge: they had a verdict.

When the defendants arrived, everyone returned to the courtroom. The tension was quite evident; there was a strained silence, the crowded gallery seated as still as those at the trial tables.

While waiting for the judge, Silverman turned in his chair to survey the spectators' gallery. Donald Ames's wife sat quietly next to the mayor's. Denise Owens was seated in the front row with the other reporters. Their eyes met; she smiled.

In the last row, he again noticed the older woman who'd been there since the trial began. Though he'd only seen her face for a moment, the day of her husband's death, he finally recognized her. She was Mrs. James Ritchie.

Silverman heard the entrance doors swing open, and he turned to see Mary Ann enter the courtroom. She spotted him immediately and nodded.

"All rise."

Everyone stood as the judge came to the bench. He took his seat, waited patiently while everyone sat down again, then turned to the bailiff.

"Bring in the jury," he commanded.

The bailiff went through a side door and returned after a few moments, leading the jurors into the courtroom.

Silverman looked over at the defense table. He and White exchanged glances; White winked at him. He watched the mayor seated erect, scrutinizing each entering juror.

"Ladies and gentlemen of the jury," the bailiff announced. "Have you reached a verdict?"

Silence followed, none of them wanting to be the first to speak. Then, more or less in unison, they all mumbled that they had.

Silverman watched them, then once again glanced at the mayor. He had leaned forward now, his elbows resting on the table, a faint, nervous smile on his lips. Next to Lane, at the end of the table, just across the aisle from Silverman, sat Stanton

Turner. He must have felt Silverman's stare; he turned and looked at him.

"Members of the jury, who shall speak for you?" the bailiff asked.

Another silence. Then one or two of them said that their foreman would.

"Mr. Foreman, please rise," the judge commanded.

The foreman, a fifty-two-year-old bricklayer, slowly stood.

Silverman and Turner were locked in each other's gaze. There were only seconds more to go. Turner began what was probably to be a smile but dropped it. Silverman looked away.

"Mr. Foreman," the bailiff said stiffly, "how say you to count one of the indictment? Is the defendant, Phillip Brooke Lane, guilty or not guilty of the charge for which he stands accused?"

All eyes were on the foreman. The courtroom was still. He didn't answer immediately, looked slowly around as if he'd never been there before.

"How say you, Mr. Foreman?" the judge repeated.

He looked down at the sheet of paper he was holding.

"We find the defendant guilty."

26

     Silverman darted into the subway car just as the doors were closing, and looked around for a seat as the train began to move. He'd spent too much time at Mike's News-stand—dallying over the last movements in the routine that had been his life for the past few years. This was his last working day as a federal prosecutor and his last day commuting from Wynnewood Station.

     Silverman unfolded his *Daily Racing Form* as the train pulled away from the platform and into the darkened tunnel. He hadn't seen her for a while. Until three weeks ago, he'd been in trial in Pittsburgh, and he hadn't seen her in the subway for the last two weeks. Maybe she'd been on vacation. Maybe she'd been ill. But she was there now, across the narrow aisle, looking just as he remembered her, her eyes burning into his and his *Daily Racing Form*. Silverman looked over and smiled at the Subway Lady. As was their custom, the smile only increased her rage. Without a spoken word, her look telegraphed her message: how could you, a nice young boy, continue to squander your hard-earned money at the race track? What of your family? How will you feed them after such folly?

     Silverman buried his head in the first race.

     His handicapping system was working a bit better. Earlier this week, one of his "long shot" selections had actually come in. Unfortunately, he was still $25,000 in the hole. But he was getting closer, his system absolutely on the verge of perfection.

     The Subway Lady couldn't keep her eyes from him. He looked up again and smiled, then continued scribbling his calculations.

     Soon he'd be living near Jamie. The marriage was over. His gesture of understanding had come too late. Mary Ann intended to go through with the divorce. He tried to understand her feelings, but at first he felt hurt and resentful. All he could see was his world falling apart when he needed the stability of home and family most. Gradually, however, he had come to understand, and after all, he thought, maybe it was for the best. He could never give her the kind of life she wanted. He didn't want it for himself. He was sure of that now. But at least he'd have Jamie—that was what was really important. And Mary Ann would let him see her as often as he wanted. There would be no problem with that.

The previous day, the judge had sentenced Mayor Lane and his codefendants. Each had received a three-year term of imprisonment. But the judge had suspended all but six months of their jail terms. Six months in jail; less, actually, with time off for good behavior. Silverman thought of the bartender's prediction: "They'll all get convicted and go to some country-club prison for rich people and sit, real polite like, on their asses for six months." He'd seen it from the beginning. What else had the bartender said? It was always the little man who suffered. He'd been right about that, too. To Silverman, Albert Lacona was the investigation's one real victim. His life had been ruined beyond repair. Silverman had been sickened at the sight of Lacona, ashen, seated in the witness box at trial, his face and hands skin grafted, his eyes dull, broken both spiritually and physically. And, ironically, Anne Eccleston was going to be the case's one major benefactor.

Somehow, the administration in Washington had concluded that the U.S. attorney herself, more than anyone else, was the person most responsible for the successful prosecution of a Philadelphia mayor. She had been offered an important high-level position in Washington with the Justice Department. But Miss Eccleston had declined. And why? She had been convinced to run for mayor. "Mayor Anne Eccleston." Silverman was glad he was leaving town.

The train momentarily slowed to a crawl in the darkened tunnel. The lights flickered, remained off for a few seconds, then flashed on again as the train quickly picked up speed on its last lap to Silverman's station.

The day before, the term of this grand jury had expired. The jurors had been summoned in by the prosecutors, thanked perfunctorily for their services, and then sent home. And Mrs. Franklin had finally "gone public." With the information from her spiral notebook, she had attempted to get the press to tell her story of "grand jury abuse." But she had waited too long; no one seemed interested. A tiny article had appeared in the "What's News" column of the Inquirer's local Sunday magazine section. That was it. No further activity. Silverman could see that the press thought she was simply a kook, much as he once thought about the late James Richie. A new grand jury would be empaneled. The next day Higdon would work with it. Jacobs would remain available as needed.

Silverman thought of Jacobs. He would miss him. The two of them had gone together to Storyville the night before. They had vowed to stay in touch, but they knew they wouldn't. It was just the way things went. And today was Silverman's day to say good-by to Higdon.

Raymond Higdon. The consummate prosecutor. He, of course, would stay in the office, would remain an assistant U.S. attorney. No more, no less. That was his job. Silverman now knew that inside that frail body, behind those dark-rimmed glasses, there existed two Raymond Higdons. The first was the ace prosecutor. The hunter, his skills among the sharpest around. That Higdon was to be professionally respected. But the second Higdon was lonely, the computer chip for interpersonal relations somehow destroyed long ago. He was a shell, hard on the exterior but empty inside. That Higdon was to be pitied.

What had been accomplished? And at what cost? Silverman had done it. He would take with him from Philadelphia the knowledge that more than anyone else, he had made the case. He had earned his spurs, had become a prosecutor. A lawyer. He realized, however, how very close he had come to ruining his life in the process. That he could have allowed his job to become dominant over all else, had risked all because of his inability to maintain perspective, and had come so goddam close to the edge still frightened him. Whatever the future held in store for him, he couldn't let things happen like that again. He *wouldn't* let things happen like that again.

Silverman felt the train slow down, grinding its way into his station stop. He refolded the *Daily Racing Form* and placed it in his briefcase for later use at lunch time. As he snapped open its hinges, he looked over at the Subway Lady. Her glare was as intense as ever. Today was the day. He could see it in her face. She would speak to him today. Before she had a chance, he smiled at her and spoke.

"It's only a game," he said, as he left the train.

ABOUT THE AUTHOR

Ron Liebman was on the prosecuting team responsible for the convictions of former Vice-President Spiro T. Agnew and Maryland Governor Marvin Mandel. He is currently a partner in a law firm in Washington, D.C., where he lives with his wife and two daughters.